GOING TO JERUSALEM

by Willie Snow Ethridge

AUTHOR OF "IT'S GREEK TO ME,"
"THIS LITTLE PIG STAYED HOME," etc.

GOING TO JERUSALEM

New York. THE VANGUARD PRESS, INC.

ACKNOWLEDGMENTS

For permission to quote, acknowledgment is due to Harper and Bros. and to
Dodd, Mead & Co., Inc., as follows:

From *Trial and Error,* by Chaim Weizmann, published by Harper & Bros.
From *In the Steps of the Master,* by H. V. Morton. Copyright, 1934, by
Dodd, Mead & Co., Inc.

Manufactured in the United States of America by
H. Wolff, New York, N. Y.

Contents

8　　　　　　　　　　　　　　CONTENTS

GOING TO JERUSALEM

1 . I take off—and on

I WAS no more prepared for Jerusalem than I will be for heaven.

And that goes, too, for Israel and Palestine and the other countries of the Middle East, where I have recently spent several months with the roommate, who was the United States representative on the United Nations Palestine Conciliation Commission (P.C.C.).

My mind about that area of the world was virgin soil. My ignorance amazed even me; the longer I live, the more positive I become that I didn't learn anything in school except that one doesn't march to the "Star Spangled Banner." Of course, this is a pleasant piece of information to have, but not at all practical. I haven't been called upon to march in years.

As for Israel, I was aware that it was the new National Home for the Jews, and I was pleased about it. I had rejoiced when the announcement came that the Jews in Palestine had formed the independent State of Israel, and on that rainy Sunday night in May, 1948, when its creation was celebrated in Madison Square Garden, the Shug (the absurd nickname of the oldest offspring) and I lay flat on our stomachs for hours before a television set in the Smith Davises' apartment in New York, drinking in every move and every word. Frequently, we, like the people we saw in Madison Square Garden, were in tears, and again and again we turned to each other and whispered: "Isn't it wonderful? Isn't it marvelous?"

I didn't know much about Zionism, but it seemed so right that the Jews who had been so horribly persecuted by Hitler now had a home of their own and there was a place that they would know they were wanted.

The Arabs never crossed my mind. I had never seen an Arab except in the movies, and then he was always dashing by so swiftly on some fine steed with a sheet flying behind him that I never got a real good look at him. But what other way was there to see him? All Arabs wore sheets and lived on horseback.

So with this thimbleful of knowledge, I started across the seas. The roommate was already in Jerusalem; he always gets everywhere ahead of me. He had left home hurriedly, giving me no assurances of joining him because conditions were so unholy in the Holy Land; but after six weeks he cabled that the tension had eased and he thought it safe for me to come.

As usual, I had to pay my own way. Uncle Sam, who gives money freely to practically everybody in the whole wide world, is stingy as he can be with me. I don't understand it, especially when I'm so generous with him. It's a little streak in him which I must say I don't admire. As I had sold my only lot, on which I had hoped some day to be buried, to get enough money to go to Greece in 1947, this time I had no lot to sell. Fortunately, though, I had some money from the book I had written about that trip, so I hauled (hauled is scarcely the word, it wasn't that heavy) every cent of it from the bank and put it down on a one-way ticket. I figured the roommate could pay my way home if he wanted me back. I was taking a long chance.

My ticket read to Athens, Greece. From there I could catch a ride on a U.N. plane that shuttles between the Middle East and Greece to buy supplies and to attend, I suspect, to other official matters. When I boarded it, I was informed that the

roommate and the other members of the Palestine Conciliation Commission had left Jerusalem temporarily for a
conference with Arab leaders in Beirut, Lebanon, and it was
there I was to join him. I am ashamed to admit it, but I was
vague as mist about Lebanon. I remembered there was something in the Bible about the cedars of Lebanon, but just
where was Lebanon on the map? I wished I hadn't laughed
quite so hard about the postmaster back in Kentucky who had
asked me one day when I was mailing a letter to the roommate: "Is Jerusalem in Palestine or is Palestine in Jerusalem?"

The U.N. plane was an old C-47, curved by its exposed
ribs like the body of some prehistoric animal. It had been
used in the Burma theater to haul goods across the Hump.
Where the U.N. had acquired it I'll never know—perhaps
from a junk yard in New Jersey. Small, half-loose pieces of
cloth flapped from the wings in the wind.

I took a hard, uncomfortable seat, one of a row running
lengthwise of the plane. Such seats are called bucket seats,
which I had heard of for years, but happily had never had
the misfortune of sitting on. Why they're called bucket seats
is a mystery. They aren't topless like buckets, nor round like
buckets, nor do they have handles.

The other side of the plane was stacked with boxes of
groceries for the U.N. personnel in Haifa, which is now Israel's leading harbor. The fact that the boxes were crammed
with such articles as cans of tobacco, bars of chocolate, bottles of vitamins, Aunt Jemima pancake flour, sacks of sugar,
and all kinds of canned goods gave me my first hint that food
might be high and somewhat limited in the Jews' new homeland.

I was mulling over the best way to acquire one of those
boxes when the copilot, a very handsome young man, ap-

peared and invited me into the nose of the ship to sit with
the pilot, also a very handsome young man.

We were flying southeast across the Mediterranean, straight
as a ruled line. The sea was gray and smooth, only slightly
roughened here and there, like a rug swept against the nap.
Innumerable islands, humped in the middle and with turtle-
shaped appendages, lay sunning on the surface of the water,
their hide-colored shells brightened with traces of green, as if
they had dived to the ocean's bed and brought up shreds of
moss.

We flew close to the water, beneath a heavy sky, for we had
to land at the Isle of Rhodes, where there are no flying instruments to bring in a plane through clouds and rain.

"We always must make a visual landing at Rhodes," the
pilot said.

"But it's dangerous, isn't it, to fly so low?" I asked. "We
could hit a mountain."

He grinned. "But there are no mountains from here on into
Rhodes." He showed me the map. The sea now was all bright
blue; not an island on it.

"But suppose a submarine comes up for air suddenly," I
persisted. "How about the periscope? Wouldn't we hit that?"

His brown eyes twinkled responsively, but he did not deign
to answer.

Before landing at the airport, we flew over the city of
Rhodes, and the pilot pointed out the towering hotel, resembling a half-dozen at Atlantic City, where Dr. Ralph Bunche,
the U.N. mediator, and his Armistice Commission were sitting with the Arabs and Jews, trying to reach armistice bound-
ary settlements.

At the Rhodes airport we picked up a member of the U.S.
committee of the P.C.C., Frazer Wilkins. The roommate had
sent him to confer with Dr. Bunche and had asked him to

keep an eye out for me on his return trip. He greeted me as if we were old friends. He is a good-looking man in his early forties, with fair hair and, I suspect, fair skin, though it is tanned to wrapping-paper brown by his years in the Middle East, and bright blue eyes that study you intently as if you were a brand new specimen that he must catalogue. He has been with the State Department for about fifteen years, and has been stationed in such exciting places as Bagdad and Tangier. He was a bachelor during the P.C.C. stint, but has married since.

As soon as we began to talk, he discovered my ignorance of Middle East geography and said, "Here, I'll draw you a map of Palestine as it was before partition and of the seven countries of the Arab League."

"Seven," I blurted, having thought, when I thought at all, that all the Arabs were in a vast place called Arabia.

"Yes, seven," said Frazer sternly. (Young men of the State Department always say all things sternly.)

He dug a sheet of paper out of his pocket and drew off the Arab countries before the creation of Israel. Along the Mediterranean coast, beginning at the north, were Lebanon, Palestine, and Egypt; then to the east of them, Syria, Transjordan (now calling itself simply Jordan), and Iraq; and to the south, occupying practically the whole peninsula between the Red Sea and the Persian Gulf, Saudi Arabia, ruled over by that picturesque figure, Ibn Saud, and the little country of Yemen. The map on page 17 shows what they looked like.

The map clarified matters considerably, but I could see there were facts here of which I had never dreamed, and how I do dislike facts. They clutter up the mind and get in the way when I'm writing. Instead of being able to write whatever my fancy dictates, I have to write what the facts show, and facts somehow always show things in the most sobering manner. Did you ever notice there are no fun facts?

But I refused to hear more from Frazer for the time being. I excused myself and went forward again to sit with the pilot. He had just glimpsed Haifa, a faint white smear on the horizon.

"Are we going to hit it on the nose?" I questioned.

"Not exactly. We can't go straight into Haifa; we have to fly up to the little town of Acre and follow the corridor into Haifa. The Jews won't let us fly over any of their cities or air fields."

"The Arabs are just as particular," put in the copilot.

We reached the coast and flew south over bright green land. I was excited; it was my first glimpse of Israel, and it looked amazingly prosperous and beautiful. Haifa, like a sitting person, rests its body on the curving beach of the blue Bay of Acre, but leans its back against the steep slopes of Mt. Carmel. All the buildings and houses seen from the airport are a clean white, but the trees that billow up around them are, even in winter, a lush green. The bay is strewn with ships, for Haifa is the port that receives all the Israeli immigrants.

We unloaded the boxes of food and took off again, flying north this time, and still following the shore. In almost the wink of an eye we were crossing the Israel–Lebanon border. Here in Lebanon the land, too, was green close to the sea, but almost immediately it rushed up into the mountains, divided like children's houses of blocks into many squares and steps.

"That couldn't be terracing, could it?" I asked the pilot.

"Yes, it's terracing."

"All the way up those mountainsides?"

"Yes."

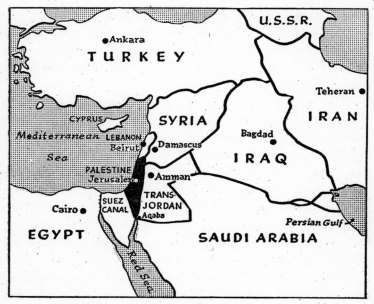

Palestine and the surrounding Arab States

"Who did it?" I thought maybe they had been built like the pyramids in Egypt by some king with millions of slaves.

"The Arab peasants," the pilot answered in the most nonchalant way.

"You mean they got off their horses long enough to build those hundreds of miles of rocky walls we see down there?"

He cut his eyes around at me and grinned. He seemed to think I was joking. "Yeah, they got off their horses," he said, his chuckles still tumbling out.

I didn't say anything but continued to stare out of the little window at the open drawers of terracing, filled with some sort of planting that was not yet in leaf.

"There is Tyre," announced the pilot.

Yes, I could see it jutting up into the Mediterranean like a capital Y.

A few minutes later he pointed out Sidon. "It's mentioned in the Bible, you know," he said.

"Certainly, Sidon and Gomorrah," I replied, very pleased with myself.

"No, ma'am, that's Sodom and Gomorrah."

"Oh."

Sidon, too, sat out in the sea, its ancient gray walls splashed with small white waves. Near by, a narrow river dyed the water around its spewing mouth to a tired green. It seemed sad that, after all the terracing, sand continued to wash away.

Then we were over a small forest of trees on the outskirts of Beirut, and soon we were settling down fast on a wide spread of brick-red sand. The runway was frighteningly short and dashed abruptly into the Mediterranean. I shut my eyes and held my breath, waiting for the plunge, but right on the beach's edge we stopped. Knees shaking, I stumbled out of the plane into the arms of the roommate.

2. Beirut's wonders—and ours, especially Bussy

THE TEEMING CITY of Beirut and the picturesque land of the Lebanon were my introduction to the Arab world and the Middle East. They were a flattering introduction and in many ways misleading, for Beirut is much more cosmopolitan and modern than other cities of that area and the Lebanon has the second highest standard of living of any Arab country. Palestine comes first.

The St. George Hotel, at which the P.C.C. and the representatives of the Arab nations were staying, was an imposing structure rising on a spit of land that jutted out into the clear, leaf-green waters of the Bay of St. George. The roommate's room, which I of course shared, was on a front corner with a balcony on two sides, one hanging over the water, the other over the street. I could sit there and eat oranges, which abound in the Lebanon, and throw the peels into the sea and watch them bob like miniature canoes between the blue and purple and salmon-colored fishing boats anchored there. As in Greece, the Mediterranean here kicks up only baby-clothes ruffles and so makes a very narrow beach.

The bay is arc shaped, and the Lebanese Mountains rise almost without hesitation from the shore's edge to the faraway sky. The high peaks were banded in snow and shone with a buffed radiance in the clear, clear air. To gaze across the green water and then up the weathered gray slopes to the bright, irregular rim of snow was an exciting experience.

But I had little time for looking at the sea and mountains;

goods are displayed in the middle of the alleys, flat on the cobblestones, and in shoe-box-sized shops called "suks."

Each alley specializes in certain articles. In one alley all the suks sell shoes, or at least they display shoes. With so many of the population barefoot, I doubt if they sell very many. They hang the shoes in great bunches, as if they were bananas, from the door jambs, the ceiling, the overhanging roofs. In another alley are piece goods, with the bolts stacked like lumber outside the doors; in another, jewelry; in still another, leather goods. . . .

But it is in the street of the fresh vegetables that I lose my mind. They are jungle-thick with all the grasses known to man or beast. Piled up loosely, they form small mountain ranges on the cobblestones. Lettuce, mint, water cress, endive, parsley, mustard greens, and innumerable other greens, the names of which I never learned. Old women in black sit cross-legged behind the mounds, and as they wait for customers, they munch away, like rabbits, at the assorted leaves.

The cabbages are as big around as tricycle wheels. Later, when I told the roommate about them, he said, "Thank God, I don't have to eat them." There are radishes galore, the long and the round; onions, asparagus, potatoes, cauliflower, peas. I stare at all these luscious things, stunned. I can't understand where they come from. I've never heard or seen pictures of Arabs gardening, but they must be the best truck growers since Adam.

But in addition to getting the feel of the Middle East, I became acquainted during those first days with the members of the U.S. delegation and of the other two delegations, the French and the Turkish, who made up the personnel of the P.C.C., and of the Arab leaders who were attending the Beirut conference. The task of the P.C.C. was to bring the Arabs and the Israelis together to discuss and to agree, if pos-

sible, on the terms of a permanent peace. As a preliminary
step, the P.C.C. had invited the seven nations of the Arab
League to send delegates to Beirut so they could canvass with
them the plans for a meeting with the representatives of Israel and decide on a basis of negotiations. All the nations, except the little one of Yemen, had complied, so the St. George
swarmed with delegates. Some were dressed in *kaffiyehs* and
loose, flowing robes, but the majority of them wore Western
clothes, except for the red tarbooshes on their heads. For me
it was a most confusing time. I never passed through the
lobby without the roommate introducing me to someone with
a name absolutely foreign to my ear and tongue.

The bar of the hotel was the only spot not overrun by
Arabs. The Mohammedan religion prohibits drinking, and
though, as I learned to my amazement, there are many Arabs
who are not Mohammedans but Christians, the majority of
the delegates were orthodox and teetotalers. Only once did
I see two *kaffiyeh*-draped heads nodding above the bar, and
they caused such a sensation that everyone kept pointing them
out and whispering, "Look, that's a sight you probably will
never see again," especially after the headcloth of one slipped
down over his right eye, making him look as tipsy as a top.

But, of course, I couldn't stay in the bar to escape tying my
tongue in knots with Arab names; I could only hover under
the wings of the members of the American delegation. Their
names, thank goodness, were easy to remember. Besides the
roommate and Frazer, there were John Halderman, a long-
faced, loosely hung together individual who is an attorney
with the State Department; William, better known as Bill,
Sands, a distinguished-looking, sophisticated, career diplomat who is first secretary to the American legation in Beirut,
but was loaned to the U.S. delegation because he knows the
Arabs and speaks the language fluently; Allan Fletcher, an ex-

ceedingly good-looking, fair, and engaging youth, whose role was decoding and coding secret messages; two young men, Bob Yount and Joe Reeves, who took turns driving the delegation's car and doing other special assignments; and the roommate's secretary, Kenneth Bussy, called Bussy by almost everybody.

Now, Bussy was and is a very special character. He was twenty-five but looked much younger; had a quick, radiant smile that was full of good humor and very white teeth; and had a cocky head of thick, curly, brown hair. He was sent out by the State Department as a personal secretary, but he had never done that type of work before and wasn't suited to it. In Beirut where he had no regular working hours because the roommate was so constantly in conferences, he was frequently A.W.O.L. One evening at six o'clock, after the roommate had torn his sparse hair all day because he could not find him, Bussy stuck his grinning face into our door and asked blithely: "Mr. Ethridge, is there anything I can do for you today?" I draw the curtain quickly on the roommate's answer, but it had no effect, for another afternoon at four o'clock, he showed up for the first time that day and announced: "This is just a token appearance, you understand."

He said anything that popped into his mind, and many absurd things, better left unsaid, did. One day at lunch I started to help myself to some ripe olives, a weakness of mine; but they are a weakness of Bussy's too, and he snapped: "Keep your cotton-picking fingers off those olives."

Besides ripe olives, I have a weakness for the moon, and I was shocked to see that in Lebanon the new moon didn't come up tilted a bit sideways, as it does in Kentucky, but, most peculiarly, flat like a canoe on its curved back. I mentioned this phenomenon to Bussy. "Gosh," he said, "you're the funniest woman I ever knew; the idea of a woman your age noticing the moon."

And as time went on, I learned he had no sense whatsoever about conventions. He would come into the roommate's and my bedroom almost any time of day or night, and for an amazing variety of reasons. Sometimes he wanted me to sew a button on his shirt, and when I agreed, he would strip off the shirt from his back and hand it to me. Once, when I was in bed, he burst into the room and, after a few preliminary remarks, asked: "You don't mind if I use the telephone, do you?" and, without waiting for an answer, stretched himself on the roommate's twin bed and called a long-distance number.

As he talked, I mused over what I should say to the house officer, if there was a house officer and if he chanced to come in. Should I say simply, "Believe it or not, officer, he dropped in to use the telephone"?

After several such occurrences, I must say it jolted me when he announced one day, "I learned my manners when I was very young at a military school."

Yet he had real charm. He entered a room with that aura that shouts, "Here I am! I know you're delighted to see me." And everybody was. Like a child, he expected love—and got it.

But besides getting to know Bussy and the others involved in the peace effort, there were many people living in Beirut who opened their hearts and houses to all of us visitors. Beirut is an amazingly social place. Being the capital of Lebanon, many countries have legations there, and during our stay practically all the legations had parties. Our American minister and his wife, Mr. and Mrs. Lowell Pinkerton, not only had one party, but half a dozen for various groups, and they kindly invited the roommate and me to several of them. They were friendly and gay affairs, for the Pinkertons are friendly and gay. Mr. Pinkerton is one of those responsive people who make you feel much more attractive than you really are, and Mrs. Pinkerton is a gentlewoman.

Then there was the British minister, Mr. Houston-Boswell, who looked exactly like Edward VII—the same kind of mustache, the same hair, parted in the middle, and the same prominent nose and ruddy complexion. The roommate had known him in 1945 in Bulgaria, so he and his wife were especially good to us. Usually they sent us written invitations, but one morning I answered the telephone to hear Mr. Houston-Boswell's hearty voice booming: "And I suppose, my dear young lady, you've had your ba-ath."

I hadn't, and the question threw me into confusion. Somehow it seemed so awful to confess to this proper-sounding Britisher that I hadn't had my ba-ath. "Well-er, no, sir," I stuttered, "not exactly, but I er-er, I'm going to have it any moment now."

"Good girl," he exclaimed, and, evidently reassured, invited me to lunch.

Unfortunately I couldn't accept, for I had another engagement.

"That's too bad," he said, "but, no matter, I will give you a rain check."

"Thank you so much," I murmured.

"I can give you a rain check with perfect confidence," he chatted on. "Did you ever see anything like this beastly rain this year? You will be interested to know we've already had forty inches instead of the normal thirty-one. It's a deuced lot of rain, you know—almost four feet."

Then there were the French and Turkish ministers, who gave enormous receptions with tea tables a room long loaded down with pastries. The Arabs are a sweet-toothed race and they have innumerable shops stuffed with cakes and cookies

as imaginative as fairy-book illustrations; when people have
afternoon parties, they move the complete stocks, or so it
seems, into their dining rooms.

Then there was the youthful president of the American
College of Beirut, Dr. Stephen B. Penrose, and Mrs. Penrose, who invited us to have coffee one Sunday evening with
Harold Hoskins, chairman of his board of trustees, who was
on a brief tour of inspection.

Dr. Penrose in the fall of 1948 succeeded that veteran
educator, Dr. Bayard Dodge. Dr. Penrose had taught at Beirut
in 1928–31, so returning there was like coming home. But
also it was like the beginning of a great adventure. To be the
president of the American College of Beirut is to be the head
of a very amazing and challenging institution.

Spreading on the flat top of a foothill of Mt. Sannin, a
thousand or so feet directly above the bay, it not only looks
more romantic and beautiful than any college I have ever
seen, but it does more to enlighten its section of the world
than any college that I know anything about.

Its forty buildings are fashioned of limestone rock, the color
of heavy cream, and they rise gracefully from grounds bright
with flowering Judas, yellow mimosa, and innumerable dark
green pines in which wisteria runs riot shooting off its purple
bombs. Above the buildings are the snow-capped peaks; below, the far-stretching, two-toned sea.

Out of the doors of these buildings, as commencement
speakers say, have passed 15,000 graduates and former students. Many of these graduates are now practicing medicine
in the wide Arab world, for the medical school is Beirut's
biggest professional school, but a large number of others have
gone into public life and have become leaders in Arab countries. There were more alumni of this Beirut institution serving as delegates to the San Francisco Conference than from

any other college or university in the world. Nineteen of its graduates were there, and today there are twenty or more serving in various capacities in the United Nations.

But all the graduates are not Arabs. In the present student body of 2,600, there are forty different nationalities and eighteen religions. There are even fifty-four Jews living and studying side by side with the Arabs, but they are not Palestinian or Israeli Jews.

So Dr. Penrose has an exciting and full-time job. To find a free Sunday night for a coffee party was a rare accomplishment.

And then there were other people who gave other parties. I regretted leaving my best black suit at home. I had come to the Middle East to work and to learn; I had not taken into account the social proclivities of people, and particularly of Americans and Arabs, no matter how adverse the conditions.

3. Ruins, but not of stone and plaster

A FEW DAYS after reaching Beirut I was invited on a trip into the interior of Lebanon with Miss Charlotte Johnson, a Red Cross worker, and several other Americans. Miss Johnson explained that she was going on an inspection trip of two camps for Palestinian refugees, but she would end up at the famous ruins of Baalbek.

We started off early in the morning in a station wagon and crept through the downtown section of Beirut. The streets were anthills of humans; they scrambled along in the middle of the streets and refused to get out of the way until the nose of the station wagon sniffed at their rags. "Hit us and see if we care," they seemed to be saying.

But besides the problem of the pedestrians, there were the cars that bore down upon us, swooped across our bumper, side-swiped our fenders, bumped our rear. They were long and sleek and new, mostly of American make, driven by rich Lebanese and in shocking contrast to the dirty, patched peasants.

Before we were out of the city limits, we began to pull steadily into the mountains. On a long climb we got behind a streetcar piled like a moving van with the household goods of some wretched citizen. At one corner an octogenarian stepped off, undid three crates of oranges that were tied to the back of the car, and hoisted them to his own back.

It was a warm, sunny day and peaches were in bloom. Against the walls of the sturdy houses, fashioned of white stone blocks, they had a fragile, dewy-eyed look.

And then, almost before we knew it, we were in the snow of the higher peaks and were pulling our coats closely about us. Men were chopping the snow into rectangular pieces to store them for the summer. Small tunnels to hold them had been dug into the hillsides.

At one narrow point of the road, where the snow towered higher than our station wagon, we met a string of the blackest goats I had ever seen. Of course, the glaring white background could have had something to do with it. They were burrowing beneath the white drifts, hoping to find some sort of growing thing.

"Goats are a problem in this part of the world," commented Miss Johnson. "They eat everything. Why, not even trees can grow."

As abruptly as we had climbed up the range, we began to drop down. It is really very narrow, this Lebanon range. I was surprised, especially when I learned that it rises in places to almost ten thousand feet. And it is fairly short, too. It runs only about ninety miles, due north and south, and never more than a mile back from the coast.

On the far side from the sea, it steps down in rough, jolting strides until it reaches a long, flat, fertile plain. It is the alluvial plain of Bk'aa. Like a gigantic river of reddish-brown water it spreads between banks of low, gentle hills, where little villages of square white houses and flat roofs look incredibly neat beneath the pointed ruler of a minaret.

Every inch of the plain is under cultivation, though it is too early on our visit to be green. Whole families are working in small patches. The men are plowing with oxen and crude wooden plows, as other men must have plowed these same fields in Christ's time; and the women and children are stooped close to the ground, their hands burrowing in the rich dirt.

"They are planting potatoes . . . or something," the Arab driver of the station wagon comments. "You know potatoes?"

"Yes, I know potatoes."

There are acres and acres of vineyards, with the vines growing in an unusual fashion—flat upon the earth; and there are acres and acres of cherry, apple, and apricot orchards.

A string of camels, with blue beads about their heads to keep off the evil eye, and bells tinkling at their throats, scallops the edge of the highway. They are the first I have seen on this trip and I hang out the window to get a close look at them. A small donkey leads them, furnishing all the brain work, and three men trudge by their sides.

"Are those men Arabs?" I ask Miss Johnson.

"Oh, no, they are Bedouins," she answers. "We differentiate between the Bedouins and Arabs, though I suppose, generally speaking, they are Arabs. The Bedouins are nomads who live as a rule in the desert, and are committed to roaming about because they have flocks and herds that must find grazing places. They live mostly in Saudi Arabia, Syria, and Iraq. In the Lebanon and Palestine where the land is suitable for cultivation, there are no Bedouins to mention. The peasants of those countries have lived literally for centuries on the same pieces of land, working their fields and vineyards and orchards. Haven't you heard how angry the Arabs got with Mrs. Roosevelt because she called them nomads?"

"No," I say.

"Oh, they got furious, simply furious. Someone, who didn't agree with Mrs. Roosevelt's position on the partition of Palestine, asked her: 'What about the Arabs who live there?' or words to that effect, and Mrs. Roosevelt answered in a column that she wrote for the *Ladies' Home Journal.* 'They [the Arabs] have not developed their country and are a nomadic people who will lose very little territory.' She said more, of course, but that gives you the idea."

I lie low. I can see that this is no time to admit that dear Mrs. Roosevelt and I had thought very much alike.

"Out of the 910,000 Palestine refugees now being fed by U.N., there are only 60,000 Bedouins," Miss Johnson continues. "That means, you see, that 850,000 of the refugees were settled people with homes, farms, groves, businesses, law practices. . . ."

"What do you mean, 910,000 refugees?" I break in rudely, for I haven't the slightest notion what she is talking about.

She stares at me for a moment in shocked silence; then explains that that is the number of Arabs now on relief, as a result of the Arab-Israeli war, and the figure is not hers, but the official one of Mr. Stanton Griffis, director of the United Nations Relief for Palestine Refugees.

"Where have they refugeed from?" I persist.

Another shocked look, but I'm getting used to them. "They

are refugees from the area of Palestine now occupied by the Jews."

"You mean these Arabs were forced to leave their homes, lands, businesses?"

She shrugs her shoulders. "What do you think? They left."

Curious as to the whereabouts of these refugees now, I learn that Mr. Griffis estimates that 300,000 of them are in Lebanon, Syria, and Transjordan, and 610,000 in what is left of Palestine and in the Gaza strip.

I mull the figures over as we drive on the edge of the lush plain. The land reminds me of the delta country of Mississippi, except that this is more cleanly cultivated and there are no houses, nor barns, nor fences; all of it is left for planting. There are only flat rocks here and there that mark the divisions of property.

"The Arabs have marked their lands like that for over a thousand years," Miss Johnson remarks. Then, looking over the wide, flat sweep, she says with a sigh: "Just think what tractors would do here if the peasants only had the money to buy them."

Storks stand in the fields, migrating from Egypt to Holland and other European countries; a circle of men, women, children, and two oxen sprawl together on the ground, having lunch, and everywhere, as far as my eye can see, yokes of black oxen are pulling those wooden plows.

At last a group of weather-stained, yellow stucco barracks, surrounded by a high wall, looms on our right. This is Camp Wavell. It once housed British soldiers but now shelters 3,000 Arab refugees. On the wide, bare spaces before the ugly buildings are scattered men and children in pieced-together robes and threadbare shirts and pants and dresses.

We stop at the office building, and the director of the camp leads us to a huge garage where he with seven teachers, who are refugee inmates of the camp, have recently started a school for 300 children. The American Junior Red Cross has supplied the pencils, copy books, drawing paper and crayons, and the Palestine refugee committee has furnished the tables and chairs.

As we enter a bare, drafty section of the garage, about half a hundred young boys jump to their feet. Their dark-complected faces beam with welcome; their sharp, black eyes meet ours inquisitively. They, too, are in rags from the tops of their heads, which are covered in a variety of styles—one has on a straw hat—to the soles of their feet. Two are wearing bathrobes, and several have on sweaters more full of holes than yarn.

They sit down, and I see above their heads on the wall behind them a large printed sign:

LOOK AFTER SPARES
THEY HAVE A LONG WAY TO COME

The admonition refers to the spare parts for the mechanized equipment of the British army which used this garage during the second World War. How ironic that it should hang now above these Arab waifs!

There are seven classes in the one garage. The teacher in the next section is yelling so loudly that I don't see how the other six make themselves heard, but somehow they manage to give lessons in Arabic, English, history, geography, religion, and writing.

There are no girls in the classes, though there are about 200 in the camp between the ages of six and twelve. But there are not enough teachers to go around, so, it being an Arab world, the boys get whatever education there is to be had.

Coming out of the garage, we are besieged by screaming

men. I am terrified; my only thought is that they have learned who I am and have decided to mob me. Just why me, I'm not sure; but since I have been in Lebanon I have become conscious of the Arab animosity toward the United States, the Arabs holding us and England largely responsible for their plight, and I wouldn't be surprised at their taking out their misery on any one of us. Coward that I am, I shrink close to Miss Johnson and the director of the camp; in time, I learn that it is not I, but the baker, who is the object of their wrath. It seems he has the Red Cross contract to bake for 6,000 refugees and he is making a miserable botch of it. He is supposed to supply each refugee daily with three small, flat, round loaves of bread, each weighing 450 grams, but he cheats.

Their voices rise to shrieks and their fists knock in our faces as they denounce him. He delivers the bread wet so it will weigh the required amount. One young man pushes forward with one of the beret-sized loaves and shoves it beneath Miss Johnson's nose. He tears off a piece to show the sogginess of the dough.

Not only is the bread wet, it has no salt in it, and it is delivered late. Sometimes the baker does not come until one o'clock in the day and they are starved, starved, starved! Miss Johnson tries to argue with them that they should save a loaf from one day to the next so that they will have some for breakfast, but they howl they cannot save it; it is not enough. They point to their flat stomachs, their bony fingers and arms.

While they are still protesting, Miss Johnson shoves through them and heads back across the former parade ground to the office building. Walking briskly, she explains the food situation to me. The money to buy it is furnished by the United Nations, which in turn gets it from its members, the United States having appropriated sixteen million dollars so far; but the distribution is in the hands of three organizations: the League of Red Cross Societies, the International Committee of the Red Cross, and the Quakers. The money is barely enough to buy the necessities; Miss Johnson uses the old Bible word, "pulses." It amounts to two dollars per person a month. The basic ration is flour; to this are added small quantities of beans, sugar, rice, lentils, oil, and dates.

Two remnants of men catch up with us and urge Miss Johnson to visit the underground caves where refugees are living, but she says, "No, I have seen plenty of refugees in caves and my time is short." The barracks are bad enough. They are as cold as refrigerators and as packed as sheep barns. Miss Johnson says there are people from thirty-one villages near Haifa in one barracks.

I go into a large room, partly partitioned by strips of quilts and blankets, which holds fifty people; in another, there are forty. I talk with one woman who has seven young children, some of them babies, and has been in the camp for seven months. The children swing on her full skirts as she talks and dart quick, shy glances at me from their dark eyes. Another woman has two little boys, born deaf. Her face is as strong and rugged as an arrowhead, but the little boys' faces are round and soft and shining with friendliness. I feel my throat contracting queerly and hurry toward the door.

In the office building there is a clinic, and Miss Johnson introduces me to a doctor and two nurses. The doctor says there is a great deal of illness because the camp is so damp and cold and there is no heat. To make matters more serious, many of the refugees come from the area around Tiberias in northern Palestine, where it is very warm. They are ill with malaria, dysentery, but particularly bronchitis.

We leave Camp Wavell and travel a mile or two to Camp Gourand, which squats in the very shadow of the ruins of

Baalbek. Here we are taken in charge by a young Arab with a disturbingly gentle face, made even more gentle by the folds of the spotless white *kaffiyeh* about his head and slim, stooped shoulders. He is Muneb Fa'wr (he hands us his calling card). He is the unofficial leader of the camp because he was the school principal in one of the villages from which many of the refugees came. A dapper young Frenchman with the Red Cross is the paid director.

"I am from Galilee and I long to go back there," Muneb Fa'wr tells me in English. "I had my house, I had my olive trees, and I had my teaching. I want to go back whether it is governed by Jews or by Arabs. I will be very happy to leave this bad thing." He looks about the filthy, jammed, muddy camp, and his large, light-brown eyes are full of pain. "I left my everything. It is not easy. I did not read in the history something like this. I didn't expect to be pushed out of my country."

"Had you lived in Galilee long?" I ask.

He frowns in puzzlement. He doesn't understand my Southern brand of English.

"I mean, had your family lived there long? I mean your mother and father, your grandmother and grandfather. . . . Say, a hundred years."

"Of course." His voice explodes. "A thousand years! From the beginning of Islam! From the beginning of time! Always!"

We talk as we walk along a dirt street of the camp, flanked and followed by dozens of men, children, and babies. "Notice this building," he says, pointing to a two-storied, dilapidated, yellow stucco structure. "Seven hundred people living there. Notice this building . . ." and he gestures toward another, just as miserable. "One thousand living there."

Altogether, 3,080 refugees live in Camp Gourand. There

are 710 women, 650 men, and the other 1,720 are children under fifteen.

"Too much widows here without husbands," comments Muneb Fa'wr sadly. "Their men were killed fighting."

There are forty villages represented, but the majority come from three in Galilee.

The muddy road is blocked. A woman sits on the ground, her bare feet pulled partly beneath her, grinding wheat between two round stones. She had bought the wheat with money she had brought from Palestine. Her thin hand grasps a wooden stake stuck into the top stone and drags it around and around. Her dress was once cerise but is now a soured-watermelon gray-pink, and it is topped by a coat too old and patched to own a color. There are unexpected freckles on her nose, and the hair that escapes from the brown-black scarf on her head is auburn. Miss Johnson says she is no doubt a descendant of the Crusaders who invaded this part of the world in the twelfth and thirteenth centuries.

When she finishes grinding the wheat she will make bread, Muneb Fa'wr explains, but it is unnecessary, for along the street, on small raised places above the mud, are women already making bread. It is an amazing business. They take the meal, mix it with a little sour milk, called leban, roll it out with their bare hands to the size and thinness of a large dinner plate, flop this about on their bare arms until it is as large and transparent as a lady's straw hat, and then toss it onto a pillow for final shaping. Now it is ready for the stove, which is nothing more than a black tin bowl turned upside down over a few stones and a small flame. Almost as fast as the bread is spread over this contraption it is done.

The fires for these midget stoves are made from a weed so thorny that not even the goats will eat it but leave it for the camels and the refugees.

"Each day girls walk seven kilometers to gather this," remarks a ruddy, round-faced boy at my elbow. "It is very difficult doing."

I can easily believe him.

He then tells me about his home in Galilee, which was bigger, he says, "than the cinema." Then adds proudly, "We had a sewing machine, a piano, a radio, everything. My father was a farmer and raised tobacco, wheat, and lentils. My brother was a policeman and he made forty Palestinian pounds a month."

The boy tells me his name is Rizq Kaddura and he shows me a small snapshot of himself in full Arab regalia.

As the Arab leader and I move on, Rizq and the other fifty odd "camp followers" move with us. We form a sad, bedraggled parade. We go into the abandoned cinema and find it stacked with people and bundles of thorns. One woman crouches in a corner with three children whose big eyes are painted with black kohl oil to keep off disease. Another woman, barefoot, with long pantaloons reaching to her ankles, cooks lentils over an open fire in the midst of the bales of weeds. Thick smoke worms toward the ceiling.

"Yes, it is dangerous to cook in this place," Muneb Fa'wr says when he sees me staring at the fire, "but what can we do? They must cook somewhere and they have no stoves. They left everything behind in Galilee."

His eyes stare mournfully at me. "We were the last part of Galilee to be taken. When the Jews attacked us, we got the women and children out and then we fought back until we couldn't fight more. We had only guns in our hands against tanks and planes.

"We began walking and we walked for seven days till Tyre, and we remain there. More than 7,000 of us were in Tyre, all from Galilee. But then the winter is about and we

can't live without tents, so the Lebanon government opened
this camp for us and we come here."

Rizq, who has not left my side for a moment, pokes me
gently with his elbow. "Will you come meet my mother, my
sister?" he asks eagerly.

"Your family is here?"

"Of course. We sleep in a stable with eight other families.
Will you have coffee with us?"

He asks it with such youthful warmth and charm I cannot resist him. We leave the others and hurry along the
muddy road and enter the low, narrow door of a stucco stable.
Pieces of cloth hang on lines like washing, separating it into
stalls, and a few pieces of matting partially cover the dirt
floor. Women and children are everywhere, and the noise is
terrific. I wonder how anyone ever gets any sleep at night.

"My mother," Rizq says with grown-up poise as a slender
woman with a long-suffering face comes up to us and holds
out her hand. And then he murmurs, "My sister," and there
is such a tone of pride in his voice I turn quickly to see a
beautiful young girl with skin the creamy color of a peeled
banana and dog-brown eyes.

"She will have coffee," Rizq says to his mother, but when I
see that she must make a fire of thorns between a few stones,
I beg to be excused. "The Red Cross inspectors are waiting
for me," I say—and truthfully.

Rizq and all the other inmates of the camp accompany me
to the station wagon.

"Good-by, my sister," Rizq says, shaking my hand. "You
have seen our sadness, our life. Thank you for your visit."

We pile into the station wagon to go at last to the Baalbek
ruins, but Muneb Fa'wr will not say farewell; he insists that
we go to a near-by village to see his family. He has found a
small, empty house and has secured special permission to move

his wife and children there. With the summer coming on, he is afraid of a serious epidemic in the camp. The village is a good many miles away, but he walks the distance morning, noon, and night.

"The walk is all right," he says. "Especially in the morning, it is very good."

He leads us into a boxlike affair of two rooms where there are several families living and he points out a small lad and exclaims in a voice that simply struts: "That's my boy!"

Then he begs us to sit down, but Miss Johnson and the other Americans hesitate. I see them eyeing doubtfully the thin pads on the floor, close against the walls.

"Just five minutes, please," he pleads.

Ignoring the disapproving look on Miss Johnson's face, I sit. Life is too short to go through it worrying about germs.

Then Muneb Fa'wr sits, too, but on his crossed legs upon the floor. He reaches out and grabs a laughing, crawling baby and plops him into his lap. He wears neither diaper nor pants. He gurgles, "Ba-ba," and Muneb Fa'wr doubles over with laughter.

When he recovers, I say, "Your baby is beautiful."

"Yes," he admits without a moment's hesitation.

"Has he teeth yet?"

"Yes, two from both sides."

A young woman appears on wooden platform shoes, but steps out of them as she comes through the door to bring us tiny cups of black coffee. She has on everything: long, blue pantaloons with red polka dots, and over them an orange dress, and over it a brown sweater, and, around her head, a black scarf.

"Is this your wife?" Miss Johnson asks Muneb Fa'wr.

"Yes," he answers, and then evidently remembering that we are Americans and are accustomed to meeting wives, he introduces us. But as soon as she passes the tray of coffee cups, she glides from the room.

A few minutes later we, too, glide, but not as gracefully as she. (There is something very lovely about an Arab woman's walk.) We must hurry if we are to view the ruins and reach Beirut by night. To be frank, I have lost interest in the Baalbek ruins; I will go with Miss Johnson and the others, of course, but I have seen too many human ruins this day to care about those of stone and plaster.

4. Mr. Frangie's English confuses him—and me

THERE WAS NO TIME to inquire into the why's and wherefore's of the Arab refugees for the next few days. George McGhee, who was then an assistant to the Secretary of State, but is now Assistant Secretary of State, which doesn't sound very different, but most definitely is, arrived for a flying visit and was a fine excuse for more dinners. Usually with a half-dozen sheets of yellow scratch-paper in his hand on which he was writing down notes or reading out notes to the roommate and Frazer, he, with my enthusiastic cooperation, ate innumerable snails cooked in butter, garlic, and parsley.

But the high point of his visit was a dinner given, so the invitation read, by the Foreign Minister of the Lebanon, H. E. Hamid Bey Frangie and his wife, at a large downtown club. The hour was at 8:30, which is the usual dinner hour in the Lebanon, though some are at 9 o'clock. I was very grateful for the years of training in late dining that I had endured in Louisville at the River Valley Club.

H. E. Hamid Bey Frangie met us at the door of the wide hall and uncertainly we moved on, peering about for Mrs.

Frangie. Everywhere there were strange women—and men, too, for that matter—but it was the women who concerned us. The roommate, since becoming a special representative of the State Department, is very conscious of his manners.

"There, I think that is Mrs. Frangie," he said, indicating a distinguished-looking elderly woman near the door who was shaking hands with another couple.

Quickly we moved forward and held out our hands. "It is so nice of you to have us," we said.

She looked a bit taken aback, but she smiled and shook our hands. Evidently she does not speak English, we decided.

We moved on only to see immediately another woman who definitely *is* Mrs. Frangie. How we knew, I'm uncertain; it was just instinct with us. Again we held out our hands and repeated, "It is so nice of you to have us."

And again we were met by a startled look, a smile—and silence.

We didn't understand it until we sat down to dinner and learned that Mrs. Frangie was not present, but ill at home. (The wives of Arab political figures in the Lebanon seemed always be ill at home. I was invited one day with the Commission to lunch at the home of the President of the Lebanon, but was informed a little later I was not expected because the wife of the President was indisposed.)

But before we sat down to Mr. Frangie's dinner much happened. The French delegation, headed by M. Boisanger, arrived, and, as is their custom, each member bowed over my hand and kissed it. I loved it, so a few minutes later, when I was introduced to General William Riley, the very handsome assistant to Dr. Bunche on the Armistice Commission, I said: "I do wish you American men would learn to kiss the ladies' hands."

And he promptly, without batting his brilliant blue eyes, answered: "Go to hell!"

This would have discouraged any other woman, I am sure, but having lived so long with the roommate, who is passionately fond of that injunction, I took it in my stride and made my way toward our American minister, Mr. Pinkerton, whose rather devilish face I spied across the room, and repeated my wish.

Down went the head of Mr. Pinkerton, and I felt my knuckles brushed by his bristly mustache.

Ah, I thought to myself, that's the difference between a general of the Marines and a diplomat.

At dinner I sat, though sagged is the better word, between Mr. Frangie and His Excellency Yussef Yassin, the representative of King Ibn Saud of Saudi Arabia. I was thrilled. His Excellency Yussef Yassin was my dream—and Hollywood's—of any Arab "sheik," pronounced, as you, perhaps, know, but I didn't, "shake." Around his handsome, swarthy face, beginning at the brows, was a short, soot-black beard, resembling an inch-wide piece of heavy braid. He wore a white silk *kaffiyeh,* bound to his head with black silk ropes, and a long, thin, black robe which hung open to reveal a pajama-like suit of some soft, gray material.

In spite of our limited knowledge of each other's language, he and Mr. Frangie and I had a very pleasant time talking about horses in Arabia and Kentucky.

"And you are from the part of Ken-tuck-ee where the green grass grows?" Mr. Frangie asked at one point.

"Not green grass," I said, "bluegrass."

"Ah . . . blue grass." Mr. Frangie's face was full of wonder and he spoke in excited Arabic to His Excellency Yussef Yassin.

Then they both looked at me queerly, critically.

"Blue grass?" Yussef Yassin repeated.

"Yes."

He shook his noble head. "What causes it blue?" he inquired.

I was at a loss. I shook my not-so-noble head.

"You yourself seen it blue?" he persisted.

"Well, not exactly," I confessed, "but they tell me in Kentucky that is because I have never got up early enough in the morning."

His large, soft brown eyes twinkled.

Platter after platter of food went about the table. The first was a masterpiece of cold sliced lobster stacked upon the bright red shells and surrounded by shrimps as big as horseshoes. The second was sliced chicken in jelly; the third, a great loaf of pâté de foie gras; the fourth—oh, stars, I don't remember. After the third course I was in a daze.

Near the end of the dinner, the guests began pulling carnations from the large bowls down the center of the tables and pinning them on their neighbors and themselves. H. E. Yussef Yassin, after a valiant struggle—not with me, you understand, but with a bow at the neckline of my black crepe dress—succeeded in pulling one through the loose threads that held the bow, and I pulled one through the frog of his "pajama." The carnation on me wasn't shocking, but on him it was as out of place as a corsage on a priest's robe. He grinned at it sheepishly several times, and finally, when I wasn't looking, slipped it out.

The last course was the inevitable platter of fruit.

"The plums are American," Mr. Frangie remarked proudly.

I looked for the plums. I saw apples and oranges and tangerines and bananas, but no plums.

"Plums?" I questioned.

"Ah, I should say apples. My English confuses me."

"Think nothing of it," I urged him. "My English frequently confuses me."

"We grow the apples here, but we buy the seed in America.
Here in the Lebanon we can grow anything. Ab-so-lute-ly
anything."

After such a dinner it was easy to believe him.

5. Past imperfect

THE ARAB REFUGEES continued on my mind. I suppose if
I had been better prepared for them, they wouldn't have
shocked me quite so badly, but for some reason the words
"Palestinian refugees" had always rolled off of me; I had never
understood they were Arabs who had lost the homes and
lands they had occupied for over a thousand years. I was in-
dignant for them and wanted to talk about them all of the
time, but the roommate and the other members of the American delegation tried to "shush" me.

"Don't let yourself get emotional," advised the roommate.
"Try to maintain an even balance. The Arabs aren't lily
white and neither are the Jews. It's a confused, complex
situation, as you will find out."

How right he was! Except that he had understated it. I
had once thought Greece and the Balkans were Greek To
Me, but they began to seem as simple as a first-grade reader
compared to Israel and Palestine. I learned the background
of the struggle during a good many hours of asking questions,
listening to the conversations of the members of the Commission, and reading books.

The Arabs have been living continuously in Palestine for
fourteen hundred years. The Jews have been living every-

where except Palestine since the dispersal in 135 A.D., when they were driven out by the Roman Emperor Hadrian; yet many of them have regarded it through the centuries as their homeland. It was mentioned in the prayers of the Orthodox, and a yearning to return there was deep in their hearts.

Nevertheless, the Jews made no effort to re-establish themselves there until near the close of the last century. In 1882, following the pogroms in Russia, some students started a movement back to Palestine, and in about a year's time there were six rural settlements with a population of about 200 families. The real beginning of the drive for a Jewish National Home, however, was the publication in 1896 by Theodor Herzl of a small volume entitled *Der Judenstat*.

The exciting pages of that little book and the first Zionist Congress at Basle in 1897 made the Zionist movement into a political reality. A few years later, in 1901, the Zionists founded in London a most significant institution, the Jewish National Fund. Its purpose was to collect money by voluntary contributions from all corners of the world for the purchase of land from the Arabs in Palestine.

But the location for the Homeland came very close to being changed when, in 1903, England offered the Jews a charter for Uganda, a large plateau on the upper Nile. The offer was tentatively accepted at the Zionist Congress, but the original back-to-Palestine group opposed it violently, and when the experts sent by the Zionist organization to study the suitability of the land for colonization gave a discouraging report, the pro-Palestinians won.

Dr. Herzl died in 1904, but the movement he had engendered continued under other leaders, chief among them, the present president of Israel, Dr. Chaim Weizmann.

Now, while the Zionists were working to lay the foundations for their National Home in Palestine, the Arabs who occupied it, and their Arab neighbors, were under Turkish rule. Though they resented their Turkish rulers and secretly plotted against them, their first real hope of liberation came with World War I when the Turks entered the war on the German side. Then the Arabs wrote to a representative of the British government, offering to throw their weight on the side of England and the Allies on the one condition that the Arab nations should be given their independence when the war was won, and England agreed. The agreement is officially set out in the Husain-McMahon correspondence.

But, ignoring this agreement with the Arabs, which was kept very hush-hush, England promptly worked out a plan with France and Russia for the division of the Turkish Empire, including the Arab countries, among the three of them. This plan, the Sykes-Picot Agreement, is too detailed to go into here, and it really doesn't concern us except as it relates to Palestine. That Arab country, instead of being declared independent and free, was to be put under an English mandate.

Before this happened, though, on Nov. 2, 1917, the most important document in the history of Zionism was issued in London—the historic Balfour Declaration. Why it was signed could easily fill a book—in fact, the arguments have filled many; but the important thing is that it was signed and with the informal approval of President Wilson and the French.

The Balfour Declaration stated that:

"His Majesty's Government views with favour the establishment in Palestine of a national home for the Jewish people, and will use their best endeavours to facilitate the achievement of this object, it being clearly understood that nothing shall be done which may prejudice the civil and religious rights of existing, non-Jewish communities in Palestine or the rights and political status enjoyed by Jews in any other country."

Understandably, the Declaration threw the Arab world into a panic. How could England be offering Palestine as a National Home to the Jews just two years after the McMahon pledges of Arab independence? Thirty months later, when England's mandate over Palestine was announced, the panic exploded into bloody riots, which continued at intervals through the early twenties.

But with the falling off of Jewish immigration into Palestine in the late twenties and early thirties, the Arabs felt more secure and the tension lessened. Jewish immigration slowed down to a mere trickle, and by 1927, the climax of three years of economic depression in Palestine, Jewish emigration actually exceeded immigration.

Then came Hitler. Quickly, the picture changed. Though the German Jews who began to emigrate from Germany preferred the United States and England, many of them because of immigration restrictions and other causes did go to Palestine. And as their numbers mounted, the tensions again mounted, and the 1936–37 riots were extremely violent.

The riots led to the appointment of the Peel Commission to re-examine the whole Arab-Jewish problem. The report of this Commission culminated eventually in the British White Paper of 1939. This limited Jewish immigration to a total of 75,000 during the next five years, after which there was to be no Jewish immigration without Arab consent.

World War II, coming on the heels of the White Paper, submerged for a time the dilemma of the Jews, but in the autumn of 1945, after the tortures of the gas chambers and the miseries of the D.P. centers had been widely publicized, President Truman urged the British to raise the immigration ban into Palestine and to admit 100,000 Jews as quickly as possible.

This interference of President Truman with Great Britain's conduct of her Palestine mandate was—and still is—deeply resented by the British and the Arabs. Again and again in Lebanon I heard both British officials and Arabs say that if only President Truman had not entered the picture England could have settled the Palestine enigma peacefully. They claim that in the conferences of Arabs and Jews that were under way in London at the very hour of Mr. Truman's message, England had the problem whipped, but his championship put new heart into the Zionists and made them intransigent.

But be that as it may, Great Britain rejected Mr. Truman's plea "because of conditions in Palestine" and suggested instead a new inquiry to be conducted by an Anglo-American committee. It was the tenth such inquiry up to that time. (The Palestine Conciliation Commission was the thirty-sixth or thirty-seventh; both the Jews and Arabs have lost count, but they make no bones of their weariness and boredom with them.)

In April, 1946, after innumerable conferences and arguments on three continents (all committees or commissions have innumerable conferences and arguments on at least two continents, but, of course, three are preferable) the Anglo-American committee adopted a unanimous report recommending that 100,000 Jews be admitted into Palestine, as President Truman had suggested, and that a trusteeship under the United Nations be set up to supervise the country until the time when the Arabs and Jews would beat their swords into plowshares.

The committee emphatically rejected a partition of Palestine, which had been suggested, but insisted that a solution must be arrived at by which "Jew shall not dominate Arab and Arab shall not dominate Jew."

England decided to throw in the sponge. The British had found their mandate too costly in money and lives. The Arabs and Jews were constantly at one another's throats, and the British efforts to keep the peace inevitably cost British lives. Foreign Minister Bevin announced in the House of Commons in February, 1947, that his government was referring the whole Palestine problem to the United Nations.

The next month the United Nations decided to send forth another committee—the U.N. Special Committee on Palestine, familiarly tagged U.N.S.C.O.P. It was instructed to gather information on all subjects from all sides pertaining to the situation. The testimony of the Jewish leaders of Palestine alone fills a book of 559 pages in fine print. (I have read all of it and could include large sections of it right here if I weren't writing a book of my own.)

Finally, the majority report of U.N.S.C.O.P. recommended to the General Assembly that Palestine be partitioned into an Arab area and a Jewish area. The idea was agreeable to the General Assembly, but the drawing of the partition lines was a difficult, painful task. At this time there were 600,000 Jews in Palestine and 1,110,000 Arabs, and the Jews owned six per cent of the land and the Arabs ninety-four per cent. Finally, though, the lines were drawn and the General Assembly formally adopted the partition plan November 29th, 1947. For the final draft—at least final for the time being—see page 53.

Great Britain immediately declared she would have nothing to do with partition. She would end her mandate over Palestine by May 15th, 1948, and would withdraw all of her soldiers and civil personnel not later than August.

In Palestine the Arabs, too, refused to have any part of the scheme. They declared they would never accept partition of their country. Never! Never! New riots raged. Soon a war between the Arabs and Jews not only seemed probable, but inevitable. An outside army would be necessary to implement the partition and to keep the peace. But where was this army to be recruited? The British insisted they were leaving on schedule no matter what happened, and the U.N. had no international force. Was a United States army to be sent to fight in Palestine?

Was the world situation stable enough to allow a war to spark and spread in the Middle East? Was the United States too hasty in backing partition? Was . . . oh, there were many frantic questions. Some diplomats and authors, and even laymen, hint that the Arabs' oil played its part, but when I asked the roommate, he said, "Absolutely not," and of course I accept his word.

Whatever the questions and answers, the United States, on March 19th, 1948, reversed its position on partition. As a government we were no longer in favor of it.

"The Palestine Commission, the mandatory power, the Jewish Agency and the Arab Higher Committee have indicated that the partition plan cannot be implemented by peaceful means under present conditions," declared our U.N. representative, Senator Austin, in announcing our about-face.

A temporary trusteeship for Palestine under the Trusteeship Council of the U.N. was the policy of the United States now, and a special session of the General Assembly was called to consider it. But the Jews of Palestine didn't wait for the creation of the trusteeship. On May 14th, the eve of the official date for the ending of the British mandate, they declared the formation of an independent State of Israel.

The same day, the same hour, President Truman recognized the new state. In a statement to the press, he said: "This Gov-

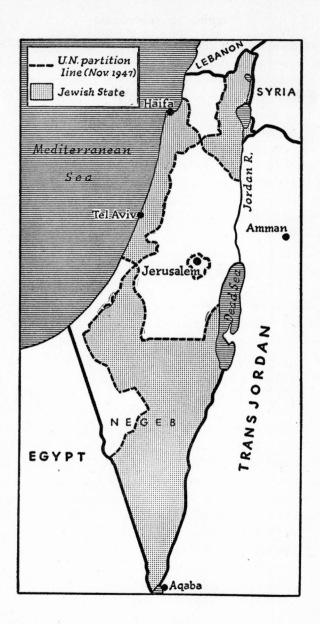

ernment has been informed that a Jewish State has been proclaimed in Palestine, and recognition has been requested by the Provisional Government itself. The United States recognizes the Provisional Government as the *de facto* authority of the new State of Israel."

It would have been fine for the Jews and the Arabs and for you and me if that had been the end of the Israel–Palestine story. But, no, the Arabs and Jews who had been fighting sporadically for months, not to mention years, began now with the end of the British mandate to fight in earnest. Horrified, the world heard the dispatches of war. The Arabs were besieging Jerusalem; they held the road from Tel Aviv to Jerusalem, and the inhabitants in the Jewish-held part of the city were suffering from lack of food and water, especially water. Rumors were rampant. The most persistent was that the Arabs would push the Jews into the sea.

The United Nations went into action to get an armistice, and on June 11th, less than a month after the war began, the Arab and Israel authorities issued cease-fire orders and accepted a four weeks' truce.

No truce, I am sure, has ever resulted in such a war of ill feeling as this one. The Arabs claim it lost Palestine for them. They were winning, they argue, when the U.N. cease-fire order came. Naturally, I'm not enough of a war strategist to know. Both sides do agree, though, that at the beginning of the truce the Arab arms were superior to the Israelis'; but at the end of the truce this situation was reversed.

The truce resolution, you see, called upon all governments "to refrain from introducing arms or fighting personnel into Palestine, Egypt, Iraq, Lebanon, Saudi Arabia, Syria, Transjordan and Yemen." It worked effectively as far as the Arab countries were concerned, but Israel brought in ship and airplane loads of war equipment, supposedly from Russia by way of Czechoslovakia.

When the Arabs refused to prolong the truce and started fighting again, the Israelis were ready for them. There was no longer danger, if there had ever been any, of their being pushed into the sea. The second U.N. truce on July 18th found the Israeli lines in Palestine as shown on the map on page 57.

Throughout these difficult weeks, the U.N. mediator, Count Folke Bernadotte, with a staff of American and French assistants, was striving to prolong the truces. In line with the General Assembly's instruction "to promote a peaceful adjustment of the future situation in Palestine," he released on July 4th, 1948, a new set of proposals for the partition of Palestine. These differed from the original plans of November, 1947, in several instances: a portion of Galilee was to be given to Israel in exchange for the Negeb; Haifa was declared a free port, and Lydda a free airport; Israel was to become a member of a dual state joined in a union with Transjordan, and the immigration laws of Israel were to be subjected to review by this dual state.

Two months later, Count Bernadotte was assassinated in Jerusalem by some members of an Israeli terrorist gang. Dr. Ralph Bunche, his American assistant, became acting mediator.

The General Assembly now conceived a new plan. (Nobody can say it hasn't tried.) On December 11th, 1948, it decided that the U.N. had no business trying to fix the specific boundaries between Israel and Palestine; these lines should be drawn by Israel and the Arab nations which had been fighting the war. But they had to have a neutral body to bring them together and to serve in the role of referee. And so the Palestine Conciliation Commission was born. And so

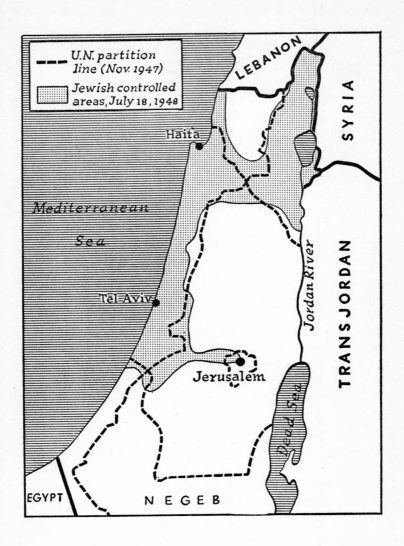

I got to the Middle East in what might be the ninth inning of the Israel–Palestine struggle—or might be just another inning in a struggle that has no ending.

6. 'Twas my fortune—not my face

THE ROOMMATE had told me that all Arabs are not lily white. Well, now I have found it out for myself. I have been involved with a character who has shaken my faith in all races.

It began on a Saturday morning when Bussy and I set out for the bazaars to shop for a narrow leather belt. We started on foot, but after puffing up a few sky-tilting blocks we decided to catch a streetcar. We couldn't make the first car that stopped; not even a mouse could have squeezed on. Though the second was not much better, we put our heads down and rooted through the underbrush of humanity to the interior. Immediately, while I swooned, two Arabs, just like Southern gentlemen, stood up and offered their seats to an Arab woman and me.

Facing me were two women heavily veiled in black, and one of them held a baby—at least I figured it was a baby from the outlines—close to her breast and completely covered, and perhaps smothered, by the many folds of her clothes.

After a short ride, Bussy said it was time for us to get off and we plowed through to the rear platform, but the streetcar refused to stop. Block after block we continued to ride. Men and boys hopped off and on while the car was moving, but on account of my old bones I was afraid to try it. Finally, though, when I was beginning to think we were headed for Damascus, the motorman slowed down almost to a halt and I sprang off without cracking any bones.

As usual, the narrow streets are squirming with people and yakity-ing with noises. We go only a few paces when a man's voice shouts something in Arabic, but as a man's voice is always shouting something I pay no attention to it. Then, suddenly, I find myself standing alone in the street, a hair-breadth removed from the end of a great pole with an iron umbrella attached to it, the kind the Beirut police-men stand under in the middle of the intersections to direct traffic. I am doomed to be run through, I see in a flash. But, no, there is Bussy. He rises from the cobblestones where he and all the other pedestrians have fallen prostrate and lunges upon me like a football guard. When I come to, the pole and umbrella are out of sight—around a corner, I suppose.

We head for the street of the leather suks, but I am held up by the entrancing picture made by thousands of white candles. Like stalactites (or are they stalagmites?) they hang from the ceilings and doorways of many suks. They are as long as broomhandles and elaborately decorated with gar-lands and rosettes of wax and silver spangles.

"If you buy one of those candles, I swear I won't carry it for you," Bussy warns me.

I am terribly tempted, as he rightly suspected, but I realize I should have a cathedral for a candle like one of these.

While we are still admiring the candles, the villain of this piece appears. Having all the outward characteristics of a nice young man, he turns up suddenly at Bussy's elbow and asks pleasantly, "Remember me?"

Bussy, having had a hard night the night before, peers at him in some confusion and says, "I remember your face, of course, but I'm afraid I don't remember your name."

"You know, in Damascus . . ."

"Of course," answers Bussy, smiling. "Of course, I remem-ber you, but your name?"

The young man then mentions the name of a friend of Bussy's in Damascus, and Bussy smiles even more genially. "Of course, of course, but your name?"

"Just call me Vic."

Bussy introduces me, and, pleased at having made an Arab friend, we continue our shopping expedition.

"What is it you would like?" Vic asks me.

"I'm looking for a narrow, black leather belt."

"Good," he says. "Follow me."

We follow him and find a belt.

"What else?" he asks.

Bussy wants to pick up a pair of shoes that a friend has asked him to get. They have been made by hand from a picture in an ad in *Esquire*. The cobbler proudly shows us the shoes and the picture. The shoes are a perfect copy.

"How much?" asks Bussy.

"Twelve dollars and a half."

Instantly I, too, decide to have some shoes made, but it seems they can't be made by the same cobbler. He makes men's shoes only.

"I will take you to the man who makes my mother's shoes," Vic offers.

Naturally, I have never had shoes made to order before and I am unprepared for the procedure, but I like it. I always like attention. The cobbler draws a picture of my foot; he feels my corns, my flat arches, my bunions, my ingrown toenails.

"I want the shoes very soft," I say. Vic interprets.

"Ah-ah," says the shoe man, grinning. "Soft . . . ah, soft . . . soft as a baby's sweater."

He has an enchanting grin, for his teeth are even and white as skinned almonds in his swarthy face, and above his upper lip is a dapper mustache, curling up at the corners.

When I have chosen a pattern, I ask: "How much?"

"Twenty-five pounds."

In American money this is seven and a half dollars, which seems fair enough for shoes as soft as a baby's sweater.

Strolling through the bazaars once more, Bussy gives Vic some American dollars to change into Lebanese money.

"Wait for me right here," Vic says, "and I will be quickly back."

As we wait, an old Arab with his head draped in a *kaffiyeh* comes along, tinkling together with the fingers of one hand two small tin cups while with the other he carries a basket loaded with samovars of coffee.

"Shall we have some?" asks Bussy.

"Fine." I feel we are on the largest midway of the largest state fair in the world and that drinking coffee will be the next best thing to eating hot dogs.

But just as we are about to give our order, Vic dashes up and with a horrifying oath—at least to me, though perhaps to him, an Arab, it is not horrifying at all—stops us. "You have coffee here in the street?" he asks incredulously.

"Why not?" I ask.

"——, it not done, that is all. I am shocked! Shocked!"

For a few minutes Bussy and I think he is going to have a breakdown, but he recovers and eventually asks us to come at three o'clock and have coffee at his aunt's house.

Bussy and I are charmed.

"All right," Vic says. "I send a taxi to your hotel for you at three o'clock. Correct?"

"Correct."

We part with a gift of violets, handshakes, and many assurances to meet again at three o'clock.

Twenty minutes later as I walk in the door of my hotel room, the telephone rings. It is Vic. "What do you do now?" he asks.

I do nothing now, but I'm sensitive about ever admitting I do nothing, so I answer: "I'm getting ready to write a letter."

"Oh."

Then there is a long silence while I wait for Vic to say why he is calling, and, finally, he does say: "Well, don't forget I send taxi at three o'clock."

Bussy and Joe Reeves and I have lunch together while all the higher-ups of the Commission are away at a stag luncheon at the home of one of the Lebanese dignitaries. In the middle of the meal I am paged. Again it is Vic. "Are you ready to come now?" he asks.

"Well, not quite. What time is it?"

"Now the time you ask . . . It is two-thirty. I send taxi in ten minutes. All right?"

It is not all right, but unaccustomed as I am to an impetuous Arab, I say yes, it is all right. He tells me the number of the taxi, which I don't listen to carefully enough, and hangs up.

Bussy and I invite Joe to come with us for coffee with the aunt, and we go out of the hotel to find a row of taxis backed up to the curb across the street. All the drivers begin shouting and gesturing to us. I have, of course, forgotten the number of Vic's taxi, but I believe it has a six and seven in it. We see such a license and move forward.

"Telephoni," cries the driver. "Telephoni."

"Yes, telephoni," we say and climb in. A few blocks from the hotel the driver draws up to the curb and Vic joins us. He has a paper bag of something in his hand.

"I am sorry I didn't have time to dress for coffee with your aunt," I apologize, for I'm still wearing the red flannel dress I had on in the morning.

"Yes, that is too bad," he answers bluntly; then, after a

moment's consideration, he adds: "So we will not go for coffee this afternoon with my aunt, but another time. This afternoon I will take you to a very lovely place on the sea for
coffee. You like that? I want you should be happy."

We ride rather idly for several miles until we come to a
wide, flat place on the Mediterranean where the new airport for Beirut is being built. We sit in the car and watch the
tractors drag at the uneven, red earth.

"It is very lovely, is it not?" asks Vic, beaming at me.

I have seen lovelier things, but I say, yes, it is lovely.

At last we move on, riding along the blue, blue water.

"You want coffee?" Vic asks as if no mention of coffee had
ever been made.

"Yes, yes," Bussy and Joe and I chorus.

"Good. We stop at a place I know and have coffee."

"Good."

"I have brought some oranges from my aunt's garden. We
will have oranges with our coffee."

"Wonderful."

We stop at a crude little pavilion that perches on a rocky
promontory overhanging the sea. Beneath us are huge brown
rocks, and the tide, which is stronger than usual, shakes its
lacy curtains of spray continuously against them. We lean
over the flimsy wooden rail of the tavern to watch it.

Vic orders a pipe called in Arabic, I believe, a narghile, but
in English, a hubble-bubble. It is extremely popular in the
Arab world, but so unwieldy to take about. You could never
take it in your coat pocket or even in your suitcase. It begins with a small gray piece of charcoal atop a wad of tobacco, which sits on one end of a section of pipe that runs
into a large bottle of water. Fortunately for all, this bottle
rests upon the floor at the smoker's feet and is connected to

the smoker by a long, flexible hollow cord tipped with an amber stem.

Having never had one draw on a cigarette, much less a pipe, I am very leery of this contraption, but my desire to understand the customs and the people of the country in which I am a guest overcomes my reluctance and I agree to take a puff or two. Gingerly, I put the stem into my mouth and suck my breath in, but nothing happens.

"Suck harder," advise Bussy and Joe and Vic.

I suck harder and bubbles plop in the bottle of water and a faint taste of smoke warms my mouth.

"Suck some more!"

And while I suck, a photographer (one is always just around the corner in the Lebanon) pops up and takes my picture. I look frighteningly like a monkey, my lips pursed out over the stem, my cheeks drawn in, my little eyes sharp with purpose.

After we smoke we have thick, sweet coffee in small cups and the oranges from Vic's aunt's orchard. The sun is warm upon our backs; the sea is a rinsing-water blue, and afar off, across the bay, the mountains soar into a world of snow and sky.

"Are you happy?" Vic asks me.

"Very happy," I answer.

"I bring you here just so you become happy."

I am very touched. I only wish the roommate could hear him.

When it is time to return to the hotel, Vic calls Bussy, and then Joe, to one side, but I pay no attention. We climb into the taxi which has been waiting and come shortly in sight of the St. George.

Suddenly Vic, gesturing toward the driver, asks Bussy: "What shall we pay this man?"

"What?" cries Bussy.

"I ask what shall we pay this man?"

"You'd better ask him," Bussy says shortly.

Vic does and announces that the sum is fifteen pounds —about four and a half dollars; then adds nonchalantly, "I'm so sorry, but I'm caught a bit short of money. Can you two boys pay?"

Scowling, Bussy and Joe make up the sum between them; but they smile as they tell Vic good-by and assure him that they will come with me for lunch on Tuesday at the aunt's house.

"I will call in my aunt's car for you," promises Vic. "This taxi business is expensive."

Going into the hotel, I try to excuse Vic's behavior about the taxi fare. "I suppose the coffee and pictures took all his money," I suggest.

"Hell," says Bussy, "I gave him the money for the coffee and pictures."

"The hell you did," Joe exclaims. "I gave him the money for the coffee and pictures."

They grin at each other sheepishly. They had both paid for the coffee and pictures.

"Well, it was a nice party Vic's aunt had," Bussy comments. "It just cost me nine dollars."

At seven o'clock on Monday morning the telephone rings. Yes, it is Vic.

"How are you this morning?" he asks pleasantly, as if the hour were nine or ten o'clock.

"Fine, thank you."

"And how is your husband?"

"He is fine, too."

"That is very good . . . Now, when can you go to the shoe shop to fit your shoes?"

This question comes as a surprise, for I had no idea that I had to fit them. "Do I have to fit them?"

"Certainly. You must go this morning. Can you go at eight-thirty?"

"Well-er, not very well. That's a bit early, don't you think? How about ten o'clock?"

"Yes. I shall send taxi."

"Never mind," I say quickly. "I will manage."

"As you say, but where shall I meet you?"

"How about under the clock on the main square?"

"As you say."

Feeling faintly—ah, so faintly—like a Vassar girl meeting a Yale man under the clock at the Biltmore, I start out, but at the last second I have a funny feeling that I should not go alone. I cast about for someone who is not busy and I find Bob Yount.

At ten o'clock we are waiting under the clock, and at one minute past ten Vic with another Arab shows up. We move along the narrow, jammed streets, Vic walking ahead with me, the new Arab with Bob. As we turn the corner into the alley of the shoe suks Vic says: "Tell your friend, Bob, to wait here at the corner with my friend. We will be back in a little while."

"But why?" I ask.

"The street is so crowded." He shrugs his shoulders. "There is no need for your friend to go."

"I'm sorry," I say, "but if it is not too crowded for me, it is not too crowded for my friend."

His face darkens for a coin-flipping moment and his black eyes stop smiling. "As you say," he says quietly.

The shoe man is surprised to see me. There is to be no fitting; no fitting at all.

"I don't understand it," I say to Vic. "I don't understand

it." But as fantastic as it is, I do understand instantly. And Vic knows I understand. Abruptly, without a word about Tuesday lunch with his aunt or even good-by, he dives into the stream of people, followed by his friend.

7. Days of chopped duck, Crusaders' castles, terraced slopes

HELD IN BEIRUT by the continuing conferences of the Commission and the Arabs, I tried to see as much of the Lebanon as possible.

One bright Sunday morning, Frazer, Bill Sands, Joe Reeves, the roommate, and I set out to visit the ancient town of Byblos (now called Jebeil) from which the Bible supposedly derives its name. History has it that the Egyptians first imported from here papyrus on which the Scriptures were originally transcribed, and so they were named for the town; but just how the word "Byblos" became the word "Bible" I will leave to the language professors. (I don't want to be greedy and act as if I know everything.)

Going through Beirut to head north along the coast, our ears rang with the clanging of the church bells. We could have been driving through almost any town in the United States on a Sunday morning, which seemed incongruous with so many pole-slim minarets holding up the deep blue canvas of the sky; yet the fact remains that in the Lebanon there are as many Christian Arabs as there are Moslems.

Out in the country, though, the peasants who were visible were not on their way to church, but were in the banana groves, setting out new trees. There is only a narrow strip of flat land between the Mediterranean and the first rocky outcroppings of the Lebanese range, but near Beirut this strip is jungle-lush with banana groves and many varieties of vegetables. I didn't see one square foot uncultivated.

The road, heavy with traffic, twisted between this cultivated strip and the bulging foundations of the mountains. I felt as if I were driving between two worlds—a tropical one and an arctic one, though, of course, I've never seen an arctic one. I'm not at all sure whether yellow broom could sprout from the rocky crevices as they did on these mountainsides, or whether brilliant anemones could gather on the jutting shelves, but what I'm trying to say is that the scenery on the right hand was a world apart from the scenery on the left.

Reaching Jebeil, we parked the car and walked through a shadowy bazaar street with its shutters painted blue and the sky partly blocked out by pieces of roof. There was no hint here that long, long ago Byblos had been a thriving Phoenecian port. The Arab guide, who attached himself to us, gave the date as 2,400 years before Christ.

"It's the oldest city in the world," he insisted.

And Frazer, already weary of old walls, muttered, "Could be."

The graveyard of these ancients is a junk yard of crumbling columns and huge stone slabs on a sunny slope facing the sea.

But near it is the ruin that had brought us to Jebeil. It is the gigantic Crusaders' castle built about 3,000 years after the Phoenicians and after two or three other civilizations had come and gone. The guide and Bill Sands rattled these civilizations off as casually as Broadway seasons, but I never got them straight.

I agreed with Frazer when he remarked with considerable bitterness: "There is nothing so trying as ruins, especially when they are six layers deep."

The castle, though, I liked. It stood on a high promontory, with the Mediterranean at its feet, and it had everything that a castle of crusading knights should have: moats, draw-bridges, banquet halls, guardrooms, and a secret passage to the sea.

On our return trip we stopped on a flat cliff that hung over the water and, bathing in the warm blaze of the spring sun, had lunch. The St. George Hotel had put it up for us in brown paper bags—a bag for each of us—and, in spite of the roommate's unhappy remarks about what he termed "chopped duck" because the pieces looked as if they had been hacked with an axe, it was delicious. Besides the duck, everybody had a small loaf of crisp bread, unchopped, slices of rare roast beef, a hard-boiled egg, and bananas and oranges.

Sprawling there, sometimes watching the green sea with its flounces of eyelet embroidery, and sometimes the narrow roadway with its desultory stream of colorful people, I was very glad to be alive and in the Lebanon.

The food and sun had almost lulled us to sleep when the roommate aroused us to look at an Arab gentleman walking down the highway with a handkerchief spread over his head beneath his red tarboosh.

"He must be trying to wean himself from the *kaffiyeh*," the roommate commented.

It wasn't very funny, but, being the only remark made for about an hour, we enjoyed it hugely.

Another day I drove due south to the Crusaders' castle of Beaufort on the very border of the Lebanon and Palestine. As all the members of the Commission were hard at work, I went with a delightful Englishman, Major Chichester. He pronounced his name like a sneeze, in the rushed-together British manner—Chist-r. With a good number of other English officers, he was in a school near Beirut to learn Arabic.

He came for me in a huge, twenty-year-old Rolls-Royce. The front seat was only a few inches from the floor, which thrust my knees in front of my face, practically blocking my view.

Again the road lay along the water, this time running south, and again I sighed over the heavenly colors. Near the shore, this morning, the water was a soft, spruce green and swirling with snowy flurries of waves, but a hundred feet out it turned to the deep blue of new bluejeans. The line between the colors was as straight as a book edge. A green ship with white masts was making for the harbor.

"I never before saw a green ship," said the Major. "It's a real duck-egg green, what?"

His speech was so British, I could scarcely understand him. A few minutes later, passing some half-finished, or half-torn-down houses—I couldn't tell which—he said sadly: "The Arabs never finish anything. They take little pecks day after day, week after week, and they never get through."

The country that day was as beautiful as any I have ever seen. True, there was not much real country, only a band about a mile wide between the sea and the quick, up-springing mountains. But this band was as gay as an Indian beaded belt; there was the silver sheen of olive groves and the yellow green of banana, lemon, and orange trees, threaded through and about with patches of scarlet poppies; red, purple, and pink anemones; gold-shaded daisies; and tiny, orchid-colored cyclamen.

Riding through the acres of olives, the Major said: "I hate to think of picking all those olives; they're such silly little things," and he sighed deeply as if they were really his responsibility.

Besides the groves of olives and fruit, and the flowers, there are many small plots of vegetables—lettuce, beans, and

peas. Children stand by the side of the road, holding out
heads of lettuce and strings of fresh-caught fish.

The circus parade of color stops fairly abruptly when it
comes up against the stony slopes of the mountains, but more
sturdy stock climbs on and on. Frequently the mountains are
terraced to the unbelievable height of 3,000 feet. Like the
steps to our Capitol in Washington, they move up gradually,
tidily, and at regular spaces. And they're done with rocks,
not mirrors. Millions and billions and trillions of rocks. The
Arabs must have been building on them since the beginning
of time.

Many vineyards grow on these steps, but here in the South,
back from the coast, figs predominate; now in the early spring,
the fig trees are so bare they have a whitewashed look.

We nose up into these terraced slopes beyond Sidon and
Tyre. The country is as open as the sky and in the far distance we see a village neatly arranged on the benches of the
hills, like a group of football fans who have arrived early.
The white baton of a minaret is lifted above them. And far
off to one side, on the curved rim of the land, we see a woman
with a pitcher on one shoulder, and her arm raised in a lovely
arc to steady it.

As we climb, the road gets narrower and steeper and more
full of boulders, and my ears begin to hurt. The castle of
Beaufort is now directly ahead and above us, filling practically one whole side of the sky. The Crusaders built it, I
keep telling myself, but it looks like a composite illustration
of all the castles of all the fairy books ever written. It is not
a part of the earth, but of the world of clouds.

When the Major and I abandon the Rolls Royce and walk
part way around the castle we come upon a view that makes
my knees buckle, and I sink ignominiously to the ground.

"It's too much for you?" questions the Arab guide who has joined us.

"Yes, much too much."

The ground drops straight down from the castle's foundation for some thousands of feet to the Litany River. (My notes say 3,000 feet, but I was excited and may have increased it a little.) The river is directly beneath us—a gray-green shoelace curving around the insteps of the spreading crags. I can hear, in the sound box of the gorge, the rushing of the water and the clear, sweet tinkle of bells swinging at the throats of goats which look no bigger than bars of chocolate.

Suddenly I see an eagle, no less, wheeling below me. The Major sees him, too, and exclaims: "Ah, he is really going jolly quickly. I'd very much like to fly like that, I must say."

We take out our paper bags of lunch and gnaw away at our chopped duck and loaves of bread (the St. George never varies its picnic lunch menu). The Arab guide and two young boys watch us with solemn eyes, but refuse to share even our bananas when we offer them.

We eat and look. The flat, green land at our feet, beyond the gorge, is Palestine—or, rather, Israel. There is a road winding through it from the Lebanese border, but it is quite empty. There is no traffic these days between the Lebanon— nor any other Arab country for that matter—and Israel. Afar off, there is a town of white walls and flat red roofs, except for one round blue dome that tops, no doubt, a former mosque.

It looks peaceful. There are no hints of the ferment that seethes there.

8. I get told about Tel Aviv

THE BEIRUT CONFERENCE over at last, the Commission packed its bags to return to Jerusalem. Nothing was settled except that the Arabs would meet with the Israelis somewhere, sometime, to discuss terms for peace. There was no hurry, though. The Arabs don't believe in hurrying.

Dr. Ralph Bunche, on a visit about this time to Beirut from the Isle of Rhodes, where he had finally got the Israelis and the Arabs of Egypt, the Lebanon, and Transjordan to sign armistices, warned us that it would require more patience than we had ever dreamed of to get a peace.

"Both sides take forever to do anything," he declared. "The Arabs because they don't know what they want, nor how to go about it, and the Jews because they do know what they want and just sit tight." He shook his distinguished head and sighed.

This was at a dinner party a night or two before he left for the United States. He was looking forward to getting home and returning some day to his original job of teaching school. The teaching profession, he argued, had it all over the role of diplomat, especially when the role of diplomat called for mediating an armistice between Israelis and Arabs, which took twelve, fourteen, and frequently sixteen hours a day—and night.

"Give me school teaching any time," he said. "Where else can you find such hours?" His skin, which is as light as many a white man's, has a glow, an animation, about it as if his blood were mixed with sunshine. "Did you ever see a school professor with ulcers?"

Nobody had, but Mr. Pinkerton, who was sitting across the table from Dr. Bunche, still preferred his job of diplomat. Eyes twinkling, he demanded: "Well, so what? You teach school and you live to be eighty instead of seventy. But what will you do with those last ten years?"

Instantly Dr. Bunche answered: "All I can."

And that finished that argument.

A day or so later his visit ended, and a few days later we left for Israel–Palestine.

Our first stop was Tel Aviv, that most publicized of Israel's cities, built, if you remember, from a wide empty space on the sand dunes of the Mediterranean to a bustling metropolis of approximately 250,000 inhabitants. As Mr. W. Turnowsky says dramatically in his *Pocket Guide to Palestine:*

"It all started when a society of Jaffa Jews took the daring step of leaving the boundaries of that ancient town and decided to build a garden-suburb on the northern outskirts of Jaffa.

"A handful of sixty tiny villas—that was the beginning of Tel Aviv, the first all-Jewish town in the world since the downfall of the Jewish State nineteen centuries ago. . . .

"That was in 1919—less than forty years ago. Those pioneers did certainly not even dream . . . that they were putting the cornerstone to Palestine's largest town."

The Commission stopped in Tel Aviv to have a meeting and lunch with David Ben-Gurion, Israel's Premier and Defense Minister, and I stopped, of course, because they did, but I wasn't invited to lunch. Instead, our U.S. Ambassador, Mr. James G. McDonald, wearing with an air of superb jauntiness a navy blue beret on his thick, white locks, took me to the embassy to spend the day with Mrs. McDonald, his daughter Barbara, and himself. They live in a fine residential area of Ramat-Gan, a town of about 13,000 people on the outskirts of Tel Aviv.

Driving there, Mr. McDonald, who is so enthusiastic about Israel that the Arabs speak of him bitterly as Rabbi McDonald, pointed out a large chocolate factory and a fruit-processing plant which takes all the surplus oranges and turns them into juices, marmalades, and preserves. Also, Ramat-Gan manufactures textiles and leather and light metal articles, and does considerable diamond cutting. Indeed, as the Ambassador said, it is a very busy industrial center, with fifty factories, one hundred work shops, and four thousand workers.

The residential section is spread over low hills and looks very similar to residential sections in the United States, except the houses are more modern and the roofs are mostly flat. Flowers and shrubs edge formal gardens, and wisteria vines in full bloom curve over walls and doorways.

Mrs. McDonald is a rather frail, gentle-voiced woman, and the daughter, Barbara, a tall, slim blonde with blue eyes that peer seriously at you from behind heavy glasses. Mrs. McDonald had been in Tel Aviv only a few months but Barbara had come over with Mr. McDonald and was well acclimated. She listened with a rapt and approving face while her father talked to me of the achievements of the young state and of the remarkable personality of its leader, "B.G.," as he affectionately calls Ben-Gurion. (I gather that the president, fast-aging Dr. Weizmann, is regarded more or less as a figurehead.)

But I didn't spend my whole day with Mr. McDonald and Barbara being "briefed" on Israel; I went sight-seeing for several hours in Tel Aviv and Jaffa with Mrs. McDonald and the McDonald's chauffeur. I mention the chauffeur particularly because he, as a citizen of Israel, took the tour into his own hands and did not allow a "peep" out of Mrs. McDonald. Well, I take that back—he did allow her one peep.

Tel Aviv is a flat, crowded, noisy city, and, though no doubt it is a terrific building accomplishment, it is no more attractive than the downtown area of any big industrial town. The streets, except for one or two exceptions, are narrow and jammed with traffic; the buildings are starkly and monotonously modern; and the people are tense, grim-faced, and purposeful.

Khaki uniforms are everywhere. I feel I'm back in Louisville on a Saturday afternoon of the war years, when Fort Knox opened its gates and the town was flooded. Every man from sixteen to thirty-six and every young woman seems to be in khaki. They swagger through the crowds on the sidewalks and along the curbs in the streets. It is of no consequence to them that the Arabs claim the U.N. truces, and not the Jews, defeated them; these soldiers of Israel are positive they are the victors. They have given the lie to the old cliché that Jews could not fight. They did fight and with great bravery. And now on the streets of Tel Aviv they strut like heroes.

At the corners, long lines of people laden with brief cases, shopping bags, bundles, and babies wait for busses.

"It doesn't seem as if there are enough busses," I comment idly.

"We have plenty of busses," the chauffeur declares firmly and loudly from the front seat, "but they are being used for the army."

We move from Tel Aviv into the former Arab city of Jaffa, riding along King George Avenue, which still clings, in spite of systematic bombing, to vestiges of grandeur. The debris now is several stories high, but it was a broad, palm-dotted street, lined with many blocks of substantial office buildings, shops, hotels, movie houses, restaurants, schools, hospitals, hotels, mosques.

"This used to be all Arab," says the chauffeur. "Now the Arabs are finished. It is all ours. Just two months it has been Jews, but you would think it has been Jews for years. It used to be dirty, but now it is nice and clean."

I had read about Jaffa (you see I had done my home work conscientiously) in *The Palestine Guide*, edited by G. Olaf Matson and published in 1946, two years before the creation of Israel, and had learned that "from time immemorial Jaffa has been the principal and natural port for Central Palestine," and the roommate had told me 72,000 Arabs had lived there, but only 3,000 remained.

I look at the large buildings facing the avenue. "The Israelis will be able to put a great many immigrants in these buildings," I suggest.

"Oh, yes," the driver agrees. "At least twenty or thirty thousand."

We come to a barbed-wire barricade across the street, guarded by a half-dozen Israeli soldiers.

"Some Arabs didn't leave," the driver explains, "and they are kept in this section of Jaffa behind barbed wire."

"You mean they're prisoners?"

"Well, not exactly, but for their own protection they must stay in one place. It wouldn't be smart for them to go about anywhere."

"But how do they make a living?"

The big shoulders above the wheel shrug.

A guard removes the barricade and we drive inside. Many Arab men shuffle along the sidewalks and sit at tables in front of small cafés. They look old and ragged and tired.

"The Arabs sit all the time," the chauffeur says in disgust.

Having crossed the Arab section and reached the barricade

on the far side, we retrace our way, then turn off King George Avenue and head down a steep hill to the vast gray wharves along the water front. There are acres of them and they are stacked with thousands of crates of oranges, ready for shipping.

"Are these wharves still Arab?"

"Oh, no, they're now Jewish."

My eyes wide, I stare at the walls of fruit. "I never knew there were so many oranges in the whole world," I say.

"Yes, there are a great many of them." And it is Mrs. McDonald speaking in her soft, cultured voice. "The Jews, you know, have done wonderful things in this country with oranges. I suppose their oranges are the best in the world."

"But the Arabs grew oranges hundreds of years before the Jews," I argue.

"Maybe," the chauffeur puts in, "but we Jews have taught the Arabs how to grow them better."

I don't doubt this at all, but I do believe in giving the Arab his due, so I get out *The Palestine Guide* and refresh myself on these lines:

"The soil behind the hill on which the old city (Jaffa) was built is fertile and bountifully provided with fresh water enviting [sic] the enterprise of agriculture which nature repays richly in this region.

"The excellent gardens and orchards of modern Jaffa are world-renowned, and from the old records it is evident that they have always been luxuriant and famous. The ancient town occupied the crest and slopes of the hill; the modern city flanks the main hill to the N. and S., while to the eastward stretches the great zone of orange groves and gardens which are the principal source of Jaffa's wealth. In spring the fragrant orange blossoms lade the balmy atmosphere with intoxicating sweetness."

I want to read the paragraphs to Mrs. McDonald, for I don't believe she knows these facts, but the driver might overhear me and I am completely awed by him. For one frightening moment, I even wonder what he would say if I were to point out that when the sixty Jewish pioneers moved out of Jaffa to start Tel Aviv right next door on the "barren sand dunes," they were as clever as the pioneers of Miami or Palm Beach in selecting a spot with a hinterland of rich, well-watered soil.

We leave the wharves and drive back into the business section of Jaffa, passing the handsome Jaffa post office, more shops, and several large automobile salesrooms and garages.

"Were these Arab?" I ask once more.

"Yes."

"Now Israeli?"

"Yes, yes. Don't worry—all occupied by Jews."

Then back into Tel Aviv, and along Rothschild Avenue, with a lovely park down its center and on both sides several good-looking buildings. One is a movie house.

"It is nice, isn't it?" the driver asks me. "We have about ten like it."

It is showing *The Best Years of Our Lives*.

Then along a wide drive on the ocean front, and my opinion of Tel Aviv shoots up. Nothing, to my way of thinking, adds so much to a city as an ocean (I pine for one all the time in Prospect), and when one sweeps in with taffeta noises right at the front door I'm lost in admiration.

And here I see my first relaxed Israelis. The small cafés opening to the sea are well filled with people.

Subdued as I am by the chauffeur, I can't resist taking a wee poke at him. "Look," I say, "a lot of people are sitting and talking in Tel Aviv, too."

"Yes," he answers promptly. "They make business in café."
I give up, and see what is left to be seen of Tel Aviv from
a deep well of silence.

9. Behind jeeps we entered Jerusalem

WITH A JEEP bulging with Israeli soldiers armed with Sten
guns ahead of us, and another jeep, bulging likewise, behind
us, the members of the Commission and I set out in a half-
dozen cars and station wagons in the middle of the afternoon
for Jerusalem. From the standards on our running boards
fluttered the blue and white flags of the United Nations. I
thought we looked like a parade, but no one turned to look
at us. Evidently the Israelis in their tempestuous existence
had already seen enough parades.

Shortly we were in the country, a rich, deep-green country
marching with columns of orange trees, slightly stooped with
their packs of bright fruit, yet nevertheless jaunty with
twigs of blossoms tucked in their glossy, leafy helmets. The
sight and heavenly smell of them made us hungry and thirsty
and we were wondering how to halt the parade and negotiate
a trade when the lead jeep whirled about and ordered everybody to stop.

The top sergeant explained his jeep was out of gas and he
must detour to some near-by place to secure some. Gas is a
very scarce commodity in this part of the world and filling
stations are few and far between. We were to stay quietly
put just where we were until he returned.

"Bring us some oranges, please," called the roommate to
him.

Waving his arm, he swooped off in swirls of dust.

We were in a town of unmistakable Arab characteristics: a candle-slim minaret above a mosque, and flat-roofed, almost square stucco houses squatting shoulder to shoulder close to the ground.

On our left, across the village road, was wide, lush land sweeping to far-away slopes of gently rising hills. A village of white houses nested at the foot of them. In the foreground, near the village road, the field was crimson with poppies, but beyond it was green, green, GREEN!

"You're looking at a part of the rich Plain of Sharon," the roommate explained, "and those are the Judean hills off there in the distance."

The Judean hills—how beautiful they sound.

"And the town?" I ask.

"That is Lydda."

"From here it looks Arab."

"It is Arab, or rather it was Arab. The Jews hold it now. During the fighting between truces they took it and all that land in front of you."

Alexis Ladas, a Greek in the U.N. secretariat, strolls up and pokes his handsome head inside the car. "You know the name of this village, don't you?" he asks me.

I'm touched. Everybody knows I'm ignorant and is trying to educate me.

"It is Ramleh and it was a very prosperous, crowded Arab village," he says. "It had a population of 9,000 Arabs, but there is not an Arab now. Not one. The Jews have moved Bulgarian refugees into the houses."

I wonder if the Arabs are among those I have seen at Camp Wavell and Camp Gourand. "Where are the Arabs now?" I ask Alexis.

"Oh, they're refugees themselves now, living somewhere in tents, no doubt."

I notice green bushes growing out of the roof of the mosque.

In more swirls of dust, the sergeant roars up. He tosses us five oranges, swoops the jeep about, and sprints to the front of the line.

Eating the oranges, which are the juiciest and sweetest I have ever tasted, and dripping them all over ourselves and the car, we move out of the village and into the country beyond.

"The Arabs are very worried about their orange groves," the roommate tells me. "Since they left the country there has been no one to look after them. In the long, dry summer they have to be irrigated, but last summer there was no one to irrigate them. If they have to go another summer without irrigation they will all die."

"Why don't the Jews irrigate them?"

"They are still technically Arab orange groves, though the Arabs have fled the country."

For miles the land continues flat and green, but it is not under cultivation this spring. It, too, was owned by Arabs who have fled, and the government of Israel has not got around to settling new immigrants upon it. The cream villages of sun-baked mud lie lifeless in the low afternoon sun.

Abruptly there are hills and we begin to climb—and climb. For about forty-five minutes we climb continuously up and around the bony, white shoulders of innumerable hills. I am shocked. Nothing I have studied in Sunday School all the days of my Georgia youth has prepared me for this wild, rugged country about Jerusalem.

Along the steep sides of the road lay the wrecks of armored cars, tanks, jeeps, and trucks. Twisted and rusted and raped of all their usable parts, they testify to the valor of the Jews who tried unsuccessfully for so many weeks to take this road from the Arabs and join the section of Jerusalem which they held to Tel Aviv and the coastal plain.

As we climb, the sun goes down behind us, dragging with it the respectable gray-blue veils of the day to reveal long, twisting alleys of violent color.

"Over there in those hills is Deir Yasin," Frazer comments.

The name spoken out loud sends shudders along my spine, as in other days the names of Jewish villages, the inhabitants of which had been massacred by Arabs, sickened me. It was at Deir Yasin that members of the Irgun and Stern gangs (Jewish terrorist groups) massacred on the night of April 7th, 1948, 254 Arab men, women, and children, and threw their bodies into a well. Or, to be absolutely exact, 253 men, women, and children. For when the officials of the Red Cross three days later dragged the bodies from the well, they found a small child still warm and faintly breathing.

The story of the events of that April night is not pleasant reading. The bellies of pregnant women were gashed open, the privates of men were mutilated, a baby was placed on his mother's knee and then both baby and mother were shot, a girl nineteen was raped four times. . . .

On the third day of these atrocities, the underground army of the Jews—the Haganah—marched quietly in and took over from the terrorists. The Haganah flag went up and officials of the Red Cross were permitted to enter.

But by then, of course, all the Arabs who were able to escape had fled, and so had all the Arabs of the many neighboring villages, fearing, naturally, a similar fate. And now their villages, stacked like square canisters on the shelves of the precipitous slopes, look quite empty, quite dead.

We see them across the terraced valleys on both sides of the highway, and we are as silent as mourners rolling through a vast cemetery.

Soon the sunset sobered too, leaving only the clear, tense, tense blue of a Palestinian evening sky. And then one bright star slipped out, and then another, and another, and another.

"From the top of the next hill you can see Jerusalem," Joe Reeves says, and sure enough as we breast another rise I see the tarnished gold lights of the city scattered rather haphazardly against a spread of darkness.

"A few more hills and we'll be there."

"A few more hills?" I ask incredulously. It seems to me we've been going up bare, barren, desolate hills for hours, though the whole trip from Tel Aviv is only about thirty-five miles.

"Jerusalem, as you know, is three thousand feet above sea level," says the roommate.

No, I didn't know, but I'm moved by the roommate's tactfulness.

"And, of course, it rarely gets hot in Jerusalem. Cold, yes, cold as blue blazes, but in summer the temperature rarely goes much above seventy degrees, and in the evenings it is always too cold to sit outside."

If shocks could give me malaria fever I would be down with it at this moment. How come, I wonder, there are no pictures of Jesus and the disciples in overcoats?

We drive down the main street of the new part of Jerusalem, a rather wide street lined with many modern buildings, and come to the King David Hotel. It is an imposing structure of cream-colored stone blocks, sitting a good many feet back from the sidewalk. Slim trees and green lawns give it a resortish air. It is owned by the Egyptian Hotels, Ltd., an Egyptian and British concern, I believe.

Across the street from it, soaring into the deep blue sky, is the Y.M.C.A. It is very beautiful and I stand on the sidewalk and gape at it for many minutes. It is built in three sections, the middle being this tall, square, graceful tower that goes up I don't know how many feet. *The Palestine*

Guide, that you would think might be of some help at a time like this, simply says, "massive tower rising to a majestic height," as if anybody couldn't look at it and tell that. Then there are low right and left wings, and all of it built of a soft shade of clean white stone. The building was a gift—and here *The Palestine Guide* lets me down again. It says, "the gift of Mr. Jarvis of New York." But what Mr. Jarvis? Or is there only one Mr. Jarvis in New York?

The roommate's voice barking, "I don't suppose you want any of these coats," brings me back to the immediate problem of getting my share of the luggage out of the car and into the hotel.

The big main doors are bolted, to my surprise, but no one else is taken aback. The other members of the Commission have stayed at the King David before, of course, and they know that the doors have been bolted since the beginning of the fighting between the Arabs and Jews.

We creep through a small side door, which is much more easily guarded, and come into a lobby about the size of a town square. It is absolutely empty except for the clerk behind the desk and three or four members of the Israeli army who are constantly on duty here. The hotel is closed to the public; only people connected with the U.N. are admitted. (By the time this is published, things, I am sure, will have changed and everybody who can afford the King David will be welcome.)

After registering, the roommate and I clatter across spacious white marble floors and begin ascending spacious white marble steps.

"The elevator will be fixed by next week," volunteers the bellboy.

"You've been saying that for six weeks now," retorts the roommate, grinning.

Our apartment is on the third floor and at the rear of the hotel, and its many windows open toward the Old City of Jerusalem; but when the roommate tries to point it out to me, I can see nothing except black walls and towers bulking against the deep blue sky sparked with stars. Not one light shines anywhere.

"As you know," says the roommate, "Old Jerusalem is still Arab and it is cut off completely from this new section which is in the hands of the Jews. Unfortunately for the Arabs, the electric light plant, though owned by the British and protected from bombing by the flags of three nations, is located in New Jerusalem, and the Jews refuse to allow the Arabs to have current. Since May 18th, 1948, the Arabs have had only lamps and candles."

"But what about Frigidaires and electric stoves and water pumps?"

"They can use none of them."

"But how about radios and electrically run furnaces and sweepers . . ."

"No, none of them."

Exhausted, I go to bed, but am waked almost immediately, or so it seems to me, by the roommate, who wants to show me the sun rise over the walls of the Old City. I stagger forth shocked that the sun should know no better than to rise at such an uncivilized hour so near the cradle of civilization.

About a mile away, across a shallow valley, on a long, rocky ridge, run pale yellow, house-high, crenelated walls, exclaimed over by minarets and steeples and domes and towers. The sun itself is not yet visible, but the sky is flushed and tremulous at its imminent approach and infuses all the ancient rocks and cement of the Old City with its excitement.

"Right there in front of us is Jaffa Gate, leading into the

Old City," explains the roommate. "It is closed now and has been closed since the beginning of the trouble.

"To the right there is Mount Zion and there, in the background, climbing above the Old City, is the Mount of Olives." The roommate is as busy gesturing as a guide on a sight-seeing bus. "If you look beyond the Mount of Olives —down that valley to the right—you can see the Dead Sea. See it? That small smear of gray-blue—afar off there—between the mountains. And beyond the Dead Sea, if you look hard, you can make out the hills of Moab."

The roommate rolls off the names of these Biblical places with relish. I am reminded that he once, when very young, had something of a reputation as a Bible scholar. On one occasion he was even awarded a white ribbon by the Baptist Young People's Union for reciting the books of the Bible faster than any other B.Y.P.U.-er. Or was it by the Methodist Epworth League? I can never keep the roommate's Baptist and Methodist eras straight in my mind. I believe he belonged originally to the Methodist Church but switched to the Baptist when that more prosperous denomination acquired a pipe organ. (The Methodists had only an organ pumped by hand—frequently the roommate's hand.) But it could easily have been vice versa. Anyway, the knowledge of the Bible that he stored up in those years now gave his voice a smug tone of intimacy.

"Mount Zion, right there outside the city walls, to our right, was the scene, remember, of the Last Supper," he continues.

This I do remember and I want to go immediately to the Old City and begin exploring, but the roommate reminds me that a state of war still exists between Israel and Arab Palestine and that I must have a U.N. pass to cross the lines, and even with a pass I must give at least twenty-four hours' notice to both the Israeli and Arab authorities of my intentions to cross.

"How do I get a pass?" I ask impatiently.

"Keep your shirt on," he answers. "It takes time."

It seems that there is scarcely a more frustrating dilemma known in the present-day world than to be caught in Israeli territory when you want to be in Arab territory or to be in Arab territory when you want to be in Israel. Though no man's land between the new and old cities of Jerusalem is scarcely an eighth of a mile wide, unofficial people, including newspapermen, have had to fly to the Isle of Cyprus off the coast of Turkey to get from one to the other. And people who couldn't afford to make that long trip to a neutral area have lingered for months on one side or the other and then died of old age and rickets.

It is only because I'm connected to the U.N. by marriage that I have a ghost of a chance of getting a pass.

"If you're lucky," says the roommate, "you may be issued a pass in two weeks. I said, maybe."

10. That man with the black patch

THE FIRST AFTERNOON we were in Jerusalem, the roommate, Frazer, and I were invited to tea at the home of Ruth Dayan and of her husband, Colonel Moshe Dayan, who was at that time the governor of Israeli Jerusalem. From the first sip of tea, I liked them both immensely; and as time went by and I saw them more and more, I liked them even better.

Ruth is of Russian descent, but she was born in Palestine and spent all of her thirty-odd years growing up with, and sharing the problems of, the Jewish National Home. She was in an agricultural school, studying to be a dairymaid, when she met Moshe, fell head over heels in love with him and, without waiting to get a diploma or a certificate or whatever it is one gets when one graduates as a dairymaid, married him.

"Arabs danced at our wedding," she confided to me. "That, of course, was when the Arabs and we were very friendly with one another."

Even now she is less bitter about the Arabs than most Jews whom I met, and more reasonable about all Arab–Jewish relations. She has a well-balanced mind, a ready tongue, and a happy disposition. Her eyes are lively and green; her hair, deep auburn and so curly it's unruly; and her face, narrow, slim-cheeked, and sharply pointed.

Her distinguished husband is, at the age of thirty-three, one of Israel's heroes and top diplomats. On that tea-party afternoon, he had just recently returned from the Isle of Rhodes, where he had represented Israel at the armistice talks with Transjordan.

He wears a black patch over an empty socket; this could be terrifying if the remaining eye, a soft brown, weren't so full of warmth and, frequently, of humor. Ruth told me, but not at the party, the bare outline of his military exploits that led to the loss of the eye. It is a story typical of Palestine—a story of the struggle of the Jews against the British during the mandate and then of the struggle beside the British during World War II; and, always, the Arabs looming in the background.

"Until 1936 Moshe was a farmer," Ruth said, "but then the Arab riots began and lasted, as you know, until 1939, and Moshe became a sergeant major in a sort of special police outfit under the British. But at the same time he was training secretly with the Haganah—our own army. The British didn't believe in the Haganah and forbade them to train, but, nevertheless, they trained all the time. Sometimes they were caught, and when they were they were put in jail. One day when they were caught, Moshe was training with them and he was locked up with the rest.

"I remember it was the eve of New Year's and he was supposed to come home for the holidays. We are very sentimental about holidays and I was terribly excited over his coming home. I baked a cake and roasted a chicken, and then I dressed myself up in my best clothes and took the baby—we had just one baby then—and walked up the road to meet him.

"I waited and waited, but he didn't come. Finally, I got to saying to myself, 'I'll wait until three more cars pass and if he doesn't come by then I'll go home.' You know how you do. And then three more cars would go by and he hadn't come and I'd say, 'Well, just three more,' and then, 'Just three more.' I made many promises, but at last I did go back."

She was silent for a long time, no doubt living over that interminable night, but when she started again her voice was matter-of-fact.

"Moshe in those days had a very fine dog, a boxer, and as he was passing through our village on the way to prison, he threw the dog out with a note tied to his collar. I was outside next day, playing with the baby, when the dog showed up. The note said he and forty-two others had been taken prisoners, but not to worry; the British had nothing against them. Moshe didn't even have any arms on him. In a proper court he could have said he wasn't with the group that was training —but it wasn't a proper court. It was . . . but, wait, that comes later.

"As soon as I got the note I went rushing to find someone to help us. I thought I'd go crazy. I went about finding my English friends, but they were so afraid. . . ." Her voice was metallic with disgust.

"The trial was a long, beastly affair. They brought Moshe and the others in chains into the court, a military court. The British soldiers were crying, 'Don't give them a trial. Put them up against the wall and we'll shoot them.'

"I remember it was the time of *Gone with the Wind* and I said one day to Moshe, hoping to make him laugh: 'If you get ten years, I'll give you *Gone with the Wind* to read.' I never dreamed, of course, that he'd get ten years. But he did; all of them did. Ten years of hard labor in the fortress of Acre. A very horrible place, dungeons and moats and God knows what. They were found guilty, like criminals. When the sentence was pronounced you could hear a pin drop."

You could have heard a pin drop in the room, too, when she finished this statement. For several seconds she said nothing, then, shrugging her shoulders slightly, she added: "I didn't get to give him *Gone with the Wind* after all. When he passed me he was already chained to the other boys."

"Oh," I managed to murmur.

"They were all very nice boys," she went on. "They were young and just married. I had to go out and tell their wives."

"Weren't they in court?"

"No, only I was allowed inside. I had English friends who did use their influence that much. The women were standing at the gate when I told them. They grew hysterical. They wanted to tell their men good-by, but they were taken out in closed vans. They could see only their hands waving out of a small window."

There was another silence that seemed long, but, perhaps, was only a few seconds, and then Ruth said: "I felt I must get Moshe out. I simply must. I decided to go directly to see General Barker at the British headquarters at the King David, but he wouldn't see me. Said I could write a letter, so I wrote a long, tragic letter. The sentence was reduced to five years.

"During the first few months it was awful, awful. The head of the Acre fortress was a very cruel man. The first time I saw Moshe he was in coarse, drab brown and his head was shaved; the place teemed with lice. There were a hundred prisoners behind barbed wire, and we visitors stood six feet away, shouting at them.

"I used all the influence I knew to get him out. I stopped at nothing. And one day he and all the others were transferred to an agricultural farm and seeing him became quite simple. I used to go to the farm to buy rabbits. Every day three of us wives would go—we took turns—and we spent the day near them in the fields. We bribed the British guards to keep watch for the officials. It is very easy to bribe British guards."

Again that loathing of the British hardened her voice.

"Then suddenly one bright morning I got a message to bring Moshe's civilian clothes. I had no idea what the message meant; but when I reached the farm I was told I could take Moshe home."

She stopped. Her manner indicated there was nothing that could be added to that remark.

"But his eye," I said hesitantly. "You haven't told me how he lost his eye."

"That was later, when he was fighting beside the British," she answered calmly.

"Which war? I'm confused."

She grinned. She has a quick, wonderful grin.

"The second World War."

"Of course. I should have known."

"During the war, the British asked him to go with a special sabotage unit into Syria, behind the lines of the Vichy French, and capture a fortress which was full of Vichy troops. He went, of course, threw a bomb into the fortress and captured it."

She made it sound very simple.

"Then he went up on the roof of the fortress. He wanted to see if the British troops, who had been promised him, were on the way. He put his field glass up to his eyes to look around, and he got a bullet through the field glass."

"Oh, Lord!" was all I could say.

"He was wounded very seriously. One whole round lens was embedded in his head, part of his nose was shot off, and three of his fingers were smashed."

"Oh, Lord!"

"And there he was, behind the lines of the enemy—and no British reinforcements anywhere in sight." She was quiet for a moment, contemplating, no doubt, the ghastliness of it. "They had no ambulance, no cars—they had had to creep, you know, through the lines—so they slung a military rug between two horses which they captured, put Moshe on it, and started back toward the British lines.

"For thirteen hours he traveled that way before they found an ambulance. You can imagine his suffering. Finally, the pain was so great that he begged them to stop and take the glass from his eye.

"While this was happening, I was on the Syrian border; I had gone that far with him and had seen him off. For twenty hours I waited to hear from him. Then I got a message to come to the hospital in Haifa. It took me a whole day to get there. The doctors were waiting for me to sign the paper giving permission to remove what was left of his eye." Her voice sank to a whisper. . . . "He was quite unrecognizable.

"All night I walked the street in front of the hospital in

case he needed me. And all night the Vichy French were bombarding Haifa. They made an awful noise."

So, that is the story of the black patch that sets him so distinctly apart from other men in Israel; but it is, of course, not half the story of his life. As you see, it doesn't even bring him up to the Jewish-Arab war in which, in spite of having only one eye, he took a leading part.

11. "And the walls came tumbling down"

THOUGH THE NEW SECTION of Jerusalem held by the Israelis is an up-to-date looking city of fine office buildings and shops, beautiful suburbs, and wide streets, there is little to interest a visitor (the places of Biblical and historical importance are, naturally, in Old Jerusalem); the shops are fairly adequate, but because of the terrific inflation in Israel, the prices are out of sight; the few movie houses show mostly old pictures and Westerns and, so far as I could learn, there is no music or theater. Tel Aviv has its own opera company and symphony, but neither came to Jerusalem while we were there.

As for night life, it is practically nonexistent. The members of the P.C.C. found only one night club, The Eden, and it is only a bar and dining room on the first floor of a rather small hotel. A woman runs it. The food is not exceptional. Like the King David, it serves mostly baked chicken and canned peas and carrots; but there is a man who plays the piano, and when the desire to dance becomes an obsession, tables and chairs are pushed back to clear a space a little bigger than a double bed. The young Israelis sometimes rock the walls with the folk steps of the Hora, but more often they sit about, heads close together, talking earnestly. And no matter what they are doing, the place has to close on the stroke of midnight.

The majority of the inhabitants of New Jerusalem dress in Western clothes and look like people in any other part of the world; only the Orthodox Jews add color. With their lean, pale faces framed in two tight curls and their slim, almost emaciated bodies buttoned up in form-fitting black coats that reach to their ankles, they glide in and out of the work-a-day crowds. Atop their heads, which I understand are shaved except for the two front curls, are frequently large-brimmed hats of some sort of long fur.

Even the young boys, fourteen and fifteen years old, are required to dress in this fashion. They don't like it, so I was told by a young Israeli newspaper reporter, who took me on my first sight-seeing tour of Jerusalem, but there is little they can do about it, except to run away from home, and then they can't run far. No Israeli is permitted to emigrate now. Of the hundred thousand Jews in Jerusalem, only about three thousand are Orthodox, and the number is similarly small in the rest of the country. Nevertheless, they form a hard, irredentist core that many people predict will cause serious conflict in the years to come among the preponderantly non-religious Israelis.

Having seen the crowded, beehive quarter in which the Orthodox Jews live, and having visited the shops, The Eden, the magnificent post office, Barclays Bank, and the other public buildings of New Jerusalem, I was ready and waiting for the special pass that arrived one Saturday morning, allowing me to cross the Israeli and Arab lines into Palestine. Fortunately for me, the Jerusalem committee of the P.C.C. was traveling that day to Jericho, and they had agreed that if the pass came in time I could go with them.

The Jerusalem committee was composed of one man from each of the three countries forming the P.C.C., and its special task was to draw up a plan for the internationalization of Jerusalem and the Holy Places near by. As you know, Old Jerusalem and the surrounding territory are packed with spots that are sacred to Christians, Jews, and Arabs. Indeed, many of the spots are sacred to all three; it is absolutely impossible to say to whom they are most sacred.

For the last thousand years or more these places have been in the hands of the Arabs, and during these years, except for short intervals, they have been accessible to all faiths and races. But with the bitterness between the Jews and Arabs so great, and the future of the land that cradles these places in doubt, the U.N. General Assembly took steps on December 11th, 1948, to safeguard them for the people of all creeds. The steps consisted of resolutions, which I will not give *in toto,* for they are quite detailed; but I will quote the sections pertaining to the main job of internationalization. The U.N.

"Resolves that in view of its association with three world religions, the Jerusalem area, including the present municipality of Jerusalem, plus surrounding villages and towns, most eastern of which shall be Abu Dis; most southern Bethlehem; most western, 'Ein Karim (including also the built-up area of Motsa) and most northern, Shufat, should be accorded special and separate treatment from the rest of Palestine and should be placed under effective United Nations control. . . ."

and

"Instructs the Conciliation Commission to present to fourth regular session of General Assembly detailed proposals for a permanent international regime for Jerusalem area which will provide for maximum local autonomy for distinctive groups consistent with the special international status of the Jerusalem area."

It isn't simple, you see, especially as the State of Israel sees no reason for the new section of Jerusalem to be internationalized, though large sections of it were built by Arabs, and the Arabs see no justice in their section being internationalized and the Israeli part left to Israel when they, the Arabs, have always protected the Holy Places and allowed free access to them.

The members of the Jerusalem committee grow haggard by night trying to reach a happy solution, and they exhaust themselves by day interviewing the innumerable heads of the three religions in both Israel and Palestine. The trip to Jericho was to visit some dignitaries of the Moslem faith.

Nine o'clock was the hour set to pass over into Palestine. (It sounds as if I'm dying, doesn't it, and passing over the bar to the "land that is fairer than day"?) If we missed the nine o'clock crossing there would not be another one until twelve o'clock. The barriers were lifted only four times a day, and then just long enough to clear the waiting cars.

I came down to breakfast at eight o'clock and found great excitement in the lobby and dining room. Workmen were removing the sandbags that had been stacked for almost a year in front of the first-floor windows and doors to protect them from Arab bombs and shells. I caught the fever of excitement and drew my weekly napkin from the large white paper envelope in which it was folded between meals and whacked at the top of my soft-boiled egg with an extra flourish. The egg, by the way, was either the smallest or the runner-up to the smallest egg ever laid. Whether it is because the Israeli hens are undernourished or that they are just dainty that way, they lay eggs no bigger than peach culls. When the quota for breakfast is only one, as it was at the King David, and there is no bacon or sausage, it leads to bad feeling toward all barnyard fowls.

Exactly at nine we of the Jerusalem committee reached Mandelbaum Gate, which is really not a gate at all, but two barricades—one Israeli and one Arab. They are shouting-distance apart. The narrow strip of land between is heaped with broken cement, tangles of barbed wire, and fallen stones, and the houses in the neighborhood gape with shattered walls, crushed roofs, and tumbling steps.

A half-dozen members of the Israeli army, natty in khaki, white belts, and spats, man the Jewish barrier. A stocky, grim-faced sergeant saunters over, takes our passes one by one, studies them, and then, peering into the car, calls out our names. As we answer he checks us off a list which he holds in his hand. Finally, satisfied, he signals to the guards to raise the telegraph-size pole that bars the way.

Now we are in no man's land, and Bob Yount drives carefully in the worn path so the car will not hit a mine that might be hidden in the debris.

A hundred or so feet beyond is the Arabs' check point. The bright red-and-white checkered *kaffiyehs* of the Arab Legion guards look absurdly gay at this early hour and in the midst of so much rubble.

"There is Miss Haliby," cries Bob, and I look out and see a woman, of all sexes, among the Arab guards. She, too, has on the checkered *kaffiyeh,* with the Arab Legion insignia on the black camel cords above her forehead, and a khaki uniform.

Coming briskly toward our car, she smiles warmly, her teeth gleaming as white as Country Gentleman corn in her dark face. "How are you, Mr. Yount?" she asks in a voice that is deep and musical, and holds out her hand.

"And you, Mr. Halderman?" to our U.S. member on the Jerusalem committee.

"And you, Mr. Eralp?" to the Turkish member.

I am introduced, and she turns toward me as if she has been waiting my coming for weeks. Her eyes, which are unusually large and a deep brown, are cordial with welcome.

"And how is Mr. Ethridge?" she asks. "And Mr. Wilkins?"

Barely glancing at my pass, she waves us on. I am reminded of my dear Greek friend, Eleni Angelopoulos. Miss Haliby has that same friendliness, that same glow, that same quick energy. But she has no Greek blood. Her father was a Palestinian Arab, her mother, a Russian. She has been active in military affairs since the British mandate when she had the terrific title of Postwar Administrative Assistant in the Financial Secretary's Office of the Palestine Government. It was enough to kill any ordinary woman—the title, I mean; what her duties were I wouldn't dare say.

Since the end of the mandate she has been the external liaison officer for the Arab Legion, a tremendous honor in that ever-so-exclusive male world. She has the rank of captain, and is entitled to wear the full uniform of the Legion, but she rarely bothers with these privileges. She is much too busy at her job for vanities. Her friends say she has only two outfits—the khaki suit with a few pullover sweaters and a dressy silk frock.

Though she looks to be in her late thirties, she has never married. She has not even been in love, her friends declare. "There is no nonsense about Miss Haliby," one of them assured me. "She just wouldn't believe a man who said, 'Darling, I love you.'"

As we are pulling away from the Arab barricade, a red-faced, green-capped Belgian, wearing around his arm the blue and white band of the U.N., dashes up. "Excuse me, please, but someone here has an appointment with the King."

We look at each other inquiringly, and shake our heads.

The Belgian dashes to the next car. It seems it is Mr. Hussein Yalcin, the head of the Turkish delegation, who has the appointment with the King—King Abdullah of Transjordan. Somewhere back along their checkered careers in this very checkered world, Mr. Yalcin and King Abdullah served together in the Turkish Parliament, and today Mr. Yalcin is going to pay a call on his old friend. He gets into a car for Amman, the capital of Transjordan, and is whisked away.

After this royal interruption, we proceed to a hostel known as the American Colony, where transients such as we gather to discuss plans, have lunch, tea, dinner, and, at times, even sleep. Here we pick up a huge and handsome Arab, Mousa Husseini. Someone whispers to me that he is a cousin of the Mufti, but I, never having heard the word "mufti" outside of clothing circles, am not impressed. (Later, I learn that the Mufti was the top ranking Arab in Palestine until he went to Germany during World War II to throw his weight on the side of Hitler. Now he is in Egypt, an exile from his own country.)

Mousa Husseini, I very much fear, was a Nazi, too. I know he spent many years abroad and he holds a doctorate from, I believe, a German university, and has a German wife. Now, though, he is back in Jerusalem, taking an active part in the Arab cause. On the trip to Jericho he is our official host, and a very delightful one. His eyes are black and twinkling; his cheeks round and red as a Christmas ball; his mustache, small and dashing; and his hair, black, thick, and curly.

Out in the barren, hilly, rocky country between Jerusalem and Jericho, Dr. Husseini says: "The story goes that the Lord sent some angels out with bags of rocks to scatter over the whole world, but their bags broke over Palestine and all the stones were spilled here."

It is easy to believe. We plunge up and down the skeleton carcass of the once plump earth, but always more down than up. A sign by the side of the road announces, SEA LEVEL, but still we go down, down. Jericho is four thousand feet below Jerusalem, which is quite a drop in only twenty-one miles.

We swoop around a sharp elbow of land and see the Jordan plain below us—a wide, white platter of land, empty except for the eggplant blue of the Dead Sea on the far right and the parsley green clump of banana and orange trees around the city of Jericho in the foreground.

Between, on the flat stretches of sun-hot sand, crawl faint black lines of women outlandishly hatted in bales of brush. Like overladen ants, they are winding their way to a huge encampment of black tents so close to the base of the hill which we are descending that I failed to see them at first. In their fashion, the tents shelter twenty thousand Palestinian refugees.

Our road runs close beside the camp. Hundreds of children are practicing some sort of sport under the direction of a white-uniformed young man.

"Tomorrow the Y.M.C.A. is having a feast day for the refugees," Dr. Husseini explains, "and the children are learning games for the occasion."

A litle farther on in the valley are the tents of fifty thousand more Arab refugees. Small rectangles of blackish brown, they stretch like vast junk heaps on the white, treeless land.

At Jericho's leading hotel, a crude, cream stucco affair, the Jerusalem committee disappears to confer with the local Moslem leaders and I decide to retire to the Ladies' Room. I approach the desk and say to the manager in a very refined way, "Can you tell me where I may wash my hands?"

He speaks little English and doesn't understand my brand at all.

"Wash—my—hands," I yell very slowly and loudly.

"Ah-h-h!" The light dawns. "Cer-tainly, madam. Follow me."

He leads me to his own room where there is a wash basin and a towel and a bar of soap, and, heaven help me, I have to wash my hands. When I finish, he pours cologne over them and I smell terrifically.

Then he takes me up on the flat roof of the hotel and points out the sights of Jericho. There to the left of us in the gold-white distance is the River Jordan; and there behind us towers the Mount of Temptation where the Devil offered Jesus the world spread at His feet. Now He would experience no temptation, for the valley is covered with the rags of tents of the Arabs.

Along the road in front of the hotel roll in a long green parade the armored cars of the Iraqi army. They are withdrawing from the Tulkarem triangle, which they held for Palestine until King Abdullah relinquished it in the armistice terms between Transjordan and Israel.

A woman who speaks no English pops out of a small penthouse on the roof and holds out to me a pan of butter. I don't know whether I'm supposed to dip a finger into it and have a taste or to draw a design upon it. I look inquiringly at the hotel manager. "She just want you to see it," he says. This is helpful, I must say. I have seen it, but she continues to hold it in front of me. I smile, I nod my head, I clap my hands. But still she holds it out, but not with a giving gesture, and spouts Arabic, fountains and fountains of it.

When I'm measuring the distance from the roof to the ground, she turns and goes into the house, but before the manager and I can make the stairs she is back with a basket of strange fruit. I take one and bite into it. It is sweet and tangy and has three huge seeds at the core. I smack my lips loudly; I am sure lip smacking is a universal language. The woman smiles happily, and the manager and I dart for the stairs.

In the lobby Dr. Husseini is waiting to introduce me to his wife and their dog, Billy. The wife is a very pretty blonde with hair as pale as an old satin wedding gown, blue eyes, and tiny white teeth. The dog is a wooly, white fox terrier.

We walk about the town, which is miserably crowded and dusty and hot and stinking with thousands of refugees, armored cars, trucks, camels, sheep, and the merchants of Jericho carrying on their businesses in the street. We practically fall over a barbershop. The barber is shaving a customer, with the hot sun shining into his upturned face. Flat baskets of greens, almonds, bananas, and oranges form bright pools along the ground. We step around them, endangering our lives before the wheels of the continuously rolling Iraqi army. Women, with the lower half of their faces tattooed in purple and thinly veiled, glide by, balancing mattresses of thorns on their erect heads. The heavy embroidery on their silk blouses is close and fine, like petit point. The long skirts of some are looped up in front through their pink and cerise and red cummerbunds to give their bare feet more freedom.

Bob Yount, who has joined us, stares unhappily at their full skirts and comments: "Life is many folds."

Mrs. Husseini's light laughter tinkles out and she says: "The Arab peasant woman's idea is not to show her figure."

"I'll say," says Bob.

The crush in the street is too great. We duck into the cool, green shade of a small park where, without plan, grow bananas, date palms, pomegranates, and olive trees; but even here the refugees intrude. A half-dozen, with political pull, no doubt, have pitched their tents in the outer rows of trees. Pots, pans, and rubbish clutter around them, and in front of one is a prayer mat with an old, ragged figure kneeling upon it.

Back at the hotel I have lunch with the committee and the Moslem dignitaries, but I draw a veil upon it, for I sat between two turbaned Arabs who spoke no English, and in spite of the quality and excellence of the meal it was painful. I find talk as necessary to the enjoyment of food as taste buds.

After lunch we get into our cars and head across the sand to the Dead Sea. Though I know not one living thing can survive in it, there is nothing dead about its looks, for little waves are snapping their silver-ringed fingers over every inch of it. On the far shore, the mountains of Moab rise in soft, violet-shaded, snowlike drifts.

I want to taste the water. I scoop up a palmful and lap at it. My mouth is turned inside out, my tongue is corroded. It is beyond the taste of salt; it is beyond the taste of anything I have ever tasted before.

Getting back into the cars, we head north over the white wasteland toward the River Jordan to see the place where John baptized Jesus. We pass the twisted wreckage of the once prosperous Palestine Potash Works, a concession operated by a Jewish company. As it was in Arab territory, the Jews mined it during the war and blew it to smithereens.

An Arab guard, watching over the debris, stops us and urges us to turn back. There is no longer a road this way to the Jordan, he says; the river has been out of its banks and washed it completely away.

"Ma-lish," says Dr. Husseini and shrugs his big shoulders. (Ma-lish is the Arab word for "never mind," "it is not important," "don't worry," and the Arabs, I assure you, would be tongue-tied without it.)

We drive on. To the right are hints of an abandoned or-

chard and garden. "Yes," says Dr. Husseini, "in spite of the
heavy salt content of the land, the Jews managed to cultivate
a few banana trees and vegetables here. At terrific expense,
they brought water from the mountains and washed the soil
until it was fit for growing. They did it simply to prove it
could be done; it was not economically sound."

The land gets rougher. The salt flats are cut by ditches,
troughs, gulches. We bump in and out of them, and my old
teeth rock in my head. The heat, too, is terrific; the sun stabs
into the sand, striking off trillions of silvery saline particles
that sear the eyeballs.

"This place where John baptized Jesus better be good,"
says Bob, the iconoclast, shifting the gears into high.

Another Arab Legion guard waves us down. A fringe of
black silk balls edges his *kaffiyeh*. We can never get through,
he says. The way from here on is deep in mud from the recent overflow.

"*Ma-lish*," repeats Dr. Husseini.

Going ahead, we begin almost immediately to plow
through mud. Shortly we come to a huge truck, bogged down
to its axles. The load of loose salt it was hauling is piled like
a small mountain in the mud beside the wheels. We try to go
around it and are stuck, too. We get out and slide about,
gathering thorn branches to put into the ruts.

Finally, unstuck, we head for higher ground and are soon
bumping over enormous, round boulders that push up
through the sand like the tops of gigantic mushrooms.

"Now, this is what I call a first-class road," Bob comments,
but no sooner are the words out of his mouth than the land
rolls into a deep ravine, and we, of course, roll with it. We are
lurching along a dry river bottom with only rocks, the size
of wheelbarrows, to stop us.

"Have you ever been over anything like this before?" Dr. Husseini asks Bob in tones of pleased excitement.

"Well, not in a car," drawls Bob. "But I rode over something like it once on a horse."

One bank of the ravine subsiding for a moment, we lunge up it to comparatively flat ground and see the stucco walls of many monasteries in front of us.

"We are very close now to the baptismal spot," Dr. Husseini explains, "and the Abyssinians, Syrians, Greek Orthodox, and Roman Catholics have monasteries here."

"How do they get their Sunday papers?" asks Bob.

No one answers him and he persists: "It would be a bit awkward, wouldn't it, if they decided to go to a movie some evening?"

The Jordan is still out of its banks and it is as ugly and as reddish brown with mud as the Ocmulgee in Georgia when it is on a rampage. I feel let down. It is no stream for baptizing.

Billy, the fox terrier, escapes from the car and rushes for the water. In an instant he is being carried downstream by the swiftness of the current.

"Save him!" everyone cries. "Save him!"

Bob, who is teetering upon a rock in shallow water, adjusting his camera to take a picture, kneels and catches Billy by the scruff of his neck. As he deposits him upon dry land, we laugh with relief.

"Now, just where is the spot where John . . ."

"Look," screams Mrs. Husseini. "Look at Billy. He is drowning again."

It is true. He is back in the river and being swept swiftly away from shore.

"Save him!" we cry again. "Save him!"

And again Bob balances on the edge of his rock, grabs Billy by a few long hairs, and throws him upon the shore.

"Now where . . ."

"It was right . . ." begins Dr. Husseini, and then breaks off to exclaim, "Hell, that fool dog is in the water again. He will drown this time sure enough. He is very tired."

But the rest of us cry, "Save him!" and Bob does. This time he doesn't toss him upon the land. He marches to the car and shuts him in the trunk.

The place of the baptism is not impressive; but the fact that the story of a gentle man baptized on this lonely spot in a day of no newspapers, no Associated Press wires, no publicity agents, no telephones, no movies, no radio, no television could spread to the farthermost parts of the earth is to me terrifically impressive.

We drive back to Jericho and on to the site of the Old City, where "the walls came tumbling down," and we would have gone on to the top of the Mount of Temptation, but we remember just in time that we must start for Jerusalem immediately if we are to make the five o'clock crossing. And make it we must, for it is the last crossing of the day and if we are not there when the barriers are lifted we will have to stay the night in Arab Jerusalem, where we have no rooms and no clothes.

We make it by a hairbreadth and find waiting for us there red-headed, florid-faced Colonel "Red" Shelby of General Riley's U.N. staff. There has been some trouble at the barrier lately; he is standing by to facilitate our crossing. With him is a delightful-looking character, whom I recognize at once as a photographer. He has all the earmarks: a beret, a small, pointed black beard, and a sport shirt open at the neck. Yes, Bob tells me, he is an official photographer for U.N. When I hear his name is Wagg, my day is complete.

12. Mark, Luke, and John agree it was an ass

ON PALM SUNDAY AFTERNOON, Frazer, Bob, Joe Reeves, and I take our stand within the old walls of Jerusalem near St. Stephen's Gate to watch the procession that commemorates Jesus' ride into the city almost two thousand years ago. Though it is my first visit to the Old City, there is no time for sight-seeing; almost as soon as we pass through the lovely old Gothic arch of the gate, where a sign proclaiming, "Money Changer," catches our eye, we hear the approach of the marchers.

A Franciscan monk by the name of Brother Francis joins us. He is an American and is a friend of a friend of Joe's. His eyes are a twinkly brown, his cheeks are fat and carnation pink, and from his chin wags a reddish-brown beard. He suggests that we stand on a balcony overlooking the narrow street through which the procession will pass, but Frazer says he cannot take good pictures from a balcony and he is much more interested in taking pictures than seeing the procession. So we back up against the wall of a monastery, abreast of the street.

Dozens of policemen are about, the silver spikes atop their khaki helmets catching the sun and tossing it back into our eyes. Bells begin to ring—bells of all the Catholic churches and monasteries and nunneries of Old Jerusalem. Dozens and dozens of bells. The air shakes with the up-and-down rhythm of their ringing.

"Here they come," says Brother Francis, and the next minute we are flattened against the wall by tides of fervent marchers, crying "Hosanna, Hosanna," and waving palm branches. There are brown-whiskered, black-whiskered, blond-whiskered, red-whiskered, pink-whiskered, auburn-whiskered, curly-whiskered, kinky-whiskered, straight-whiskered monks and priests. They are wearing robes of brown, black, beige, and white, and they have sandals on their feet.

"I never saw white-robed priests before," I whisper to Brother Francis.

"They are missionaries from Africa who have come here to convert the Mohammedans to Christianity."

"Oh."

"A great many Mohammedans have become Christian, you know."

"Yes, I know."

Indeed, from the parade it looks as if all the Arabs of Jerusalem have become Christians. "How many Christians are there in Jerusalem?" I ask Brother Francis.

"Ten thousand. That is, Roman Catholics. These in the parade are all Roman Catholics. It's quite a gang when they all get in the Church of the Holy Sepulcher."

"Or in a parade."

They flow by steadily. Nuns with white bonnets the size of sails, exquisitely pleated; schoolgirls in white with blue crusaders' crosses; clipped-haired boys in black coats and khaki shorts; Arab Legionnaires in their "table-cloth" *kaffiyehs* and sharply pressed uniforms; Boy Scouts, looking like no Boy Scouts I have ever seen before because white *kaffiiyehs* adorn their heads and float about their young faces and khaki shoulders.

"Damn," mutters Frazer. "I've already had two palms stuck in my eye."

A gorgeous figure with a pillow-paunch in shimmering orchid-colored satin looms in the arch of the Gate. He is

Bishop Gelot, murmurs Brother Francis, but Bob dubs him "the purple wheel." This word, "wheel," is Bob's favorite for all V.I.P.'s (Very Important Persons.)

"He is an Arab—a native Palestinian," says Brother Francis, "and quite a guy."

I am beginning to suspect Brother Francis comes from Brooklyn.

Frazer dashes into the middle of the street to take the bishop's picture; he must have that full, flowing white mustache, that bejeweled cross, that gay robe; but he has competition. A monk has hopped out of his place in the procession to take the bishop's picture, too. But who will take the monk's picture? He is more colorful than the "purple wheel." His hair beneath the tiny skullcap and his goatee are soot black and crisply curly; his robe is a rich brown and falls in heavy folds to his sandaled feet, and about his ample waist are ropes of white silk and black beads. He is a figure out of the Middle Ages, except for the incongruous brown leather straps over his shoulder from which dangle an empty camera case and a light-meter.

More children, their faces glistening with sweat, their voices hoarse from chanting. They are from the schools and orphanages, Brother Francis says. There are so many, many orphans in Palestine.

"Kids, kids," he mutters. "Listen to 'em. They've yelled themselves out."

And we've worn ourselves out. It is growing late and we must move quickly to make the five o'clock crossing into New Jerusalem.

As soon as we're in the car, Bussy begins turning the pages of his Bible. He has just bought this Bible in Bethlehem. We had driven there before going to the Old City to view the procession. Bethlehem is only five miles from Jerusalem as the crow flies, but then, of course, we are not crows and had to cover a much longer route. But still we had plenty of time to see the spot where Jesus is supposed to have been born (it is a grotto, gloomy and cold, and now several feet beneath the massive Church of the Nativity, and not one thing like the stable, sweet with straw, as I had always pictured it) and more time to visit the shops.

Bethlehem, as you can imagine, was a thriving tourist center before the War and like most tourist centers sells innumerable souvenirs: Bibles bound in olive wood; crucifixes, lockets, beads, crosses, matchboxes, icons, rosaries, and all other conceivable small objects out of mother-of-pearl; cigarette boxes; ash trays; Jerusalem pottery; and short, intricately embroidered velvet coats.

The shop owners, or their sons, or cousins, or uncles, or grandfathers, or brothers stood in the streets and urged us to enter their emporiums.

"Come right in," they pleaded. "We do not want to sell you anything; we just want to give you something. A little remembrance of your trip to Bethlehem. That is all, my lady, my gentlemen."

The remembrance was a pressed wild flower of Palestine pasted upon a small card. I gathered enough of them to play a game of Canasta.

And I drank at least a dozen cups of black coffee. Everywhere we must have coffee. Clerks bustled about in every shop passing small brass trays laden with small cups.

Bussy, who was broke—he's always broke—decided he must have an olive-wood-bound Bible. He had found a beautiful one for practically nothing, he reported to us. Would Frazer lend him the money? Would Joe? Bob? I? He was not particular; he must have the money.

For such a cause we could not refuse him and, grinning,

he departed to return a few minutes later with a Bible bound in a very light shade of olive wood, a short velvet coat, and several ash trays.

Now, riding back to the Israeli side of Jerusalem, Bussy thumbs happily through it until he comes to Mark's account of Jesus riding into the city. After a moment's study, he reads it aloud to us:

"And they brought the colt to Jesus, and cast their garments on him; and he sat upon him.

"And many spread their garments in the way: and others cut down branches off the trees, and strawed them in the way.

"And they that went before, and they that followed, cried, saying, Hosanna; Blessed is he that cometh in the name of the Lord:

"Blessed be the kingdom of our father David, that cometh in the name of the Lord: Hosanna in the highest.

"And Jesus entered into Jerusalem, and into the temple."

Then Bussy turns the pages to Luke's account, and then to John's. He reads them through, every word, and then looks up, a dazed expression on his youthful face. "What do you know?" he demands. "They all three agree He rode into Jerusalem on the colt of an ass."

Poor, dear Bussy. He's already been in Palestine and Israel too long. He has lost all faith in three people's being able to agree on anything.

13. "And to each according to his needs"

BEFORE GOING TO PALESTINE, the only Hebrew word I knew was *kibbutz*, the name for a collective settlement where there is complete pooling of labor and sharing of rewards; where, actually, the principle "from each according to his ability and to each according to his needs" is put into everyday practice.

The *kibbutz* is a commune on the very highest plane. There is no private property and no exchange of money, except once a year when a few dollars are given out to cover the expenses of a two-week vacation in the materialistic, outside world. Frequently, this amounts to only thirty dollars, which certainly can't be stretched very far in view of the inflated currency, but the sum can be more in a *kibbutz* with an unusually high standard of living.

The first *kibbutz* was established in Palestine in 1909 by a group of Russian Jews, and by now there must be around 200. I know there were 150, according to official figures, in 1947, and since then, especially during the past year, many others have been started. A *kibbutz* offers the quickest and least expensive way of absorbing a large number of immigrants.

Naturally, I was anxious to visit not just one *kibbutz* but several (the plural is *kibbutzim,* though I was always saying *kibbutzes*) and, happily for me, Ruth Dayan offered to take me on a tour of Galilee and the Plain of Esdraelon, where they are as thick as towns in New Jersey.

We started out at dawn on a Monday morning, for Colonel Dayan had a business engagement at Tel Aviv at an early hour and we were going to ride with him that far. We rode practically in silence, for none of us was quite awake and I hadn't even had a cup of coffee.

I was enough alive, though, to notice below the hills of Jerusalem the wild flowers that had flared into bloom since I had traveled that way last. Like the wide windows of florist shops, the flat land was massed with forget-me-nots, cornflowers, hyacinths, purple lupines, poppies, and in the background huge clumps of yellow dill.

I erupted frequently with "oh's" and "ah's" and "look's," but got little response from Colonel Dayan.

"Moshe thinks there are too many flowers," Ruth explained, smiling. "He thinks the land should be under cultivation; it should be growing wheat, potatoes, oats."

"We just need a little time," Moshe said.

I nod. The land, I realize, is some that belonged to the Arabs, and now that the Arabs are in exile there is no one to cultivate it. Moshe's dream, of course, is to settle Jews upon it and to make it bloom more intensively than ever before with food for Israel.

I recognize the charming little town of Ramleh, where we had stopped on our way to Jerusalem. The bunch of grass growing from a crack in the minaret is much longer.

"Moshe was in charge of the commandos that took this town and Lydda from the Arabs and opened up the way to the Negeb," Ruth comments calmly.

"Were many killed?" I ask.

"Oh, no, there were very few casualties."

We come into Tel Aviv, and, though it is not yet nine o'clock, the stores are open and the streets are full of people.

"Everybody is awake and ready to sell you anything," says Ruth dryly.

We have breakfast at the Kaethe Dan hotel on the beach, and the sea is unusually rough and the waves vault almost in the window. The dining room is well filled and everyone is talking Hebrew with amazing animation for such an early hour.

Everyone except Ruth, that is. She talks to me in her excellent English about the Jewish–Arab war, which I begin to understand is *the* War, as the Civil War is *the* War in the South. She says that five thousand Jews were killed.

"It is a whole generation," she says, "and that's a very tragic loss for a building nation."

After breakfast we stroll along the wide cement promenade on the ocean front, named Sir Herbert Samuel Quay after the first British High Commissioner to Palestine.

"When my parents came to Palestine from Russia forty years ago," Ruth reminisces, "there was only one street and one school in Tel Aviv."

It begins to rain and we dash for the unpretentious white stucco buildings that house Israeli's Parliament. They were originally a hotel and a movie theater, but were quickly converted into a home for Israel's government when it so suddenly became an independent state.

The Parliament chamber is austere, with dead-white walls unrelieved except for twelve colored seals representing the months of the year. There are one hundred and twenty members, all Israelis, except for three Arabs from Nazareth. The Arabs wear earphones, and a man sits in a glass cage toward the back of the raised rostrum and translates the Hebrew into Arabic. Both languages are such mouthfuls that my heart aches for him.

Fortunately for me, Parliament is in session, but unfortunately, the members are debating the same question that was being debated across the Ohio River in Indiana when I left home—compensation for war veterans. I could have stayed at home and read the *Courier Journal* and known all the arguments.

There are many vacant seats in the well of the chamber where the members sit, but the galleries are full of excited spectators. They lean forward tensely, listening to every word of the debate.

David Ben-Gurion comes in and causes a commotion in the galleries. Everybody, including Ruth and me (Colonel Dayan has left us long ago), stands up and peers down at him intently. Seemingly unconscious of the interest he arouses, he walks heavily to his seat in the middle of the well, where there are twelve chairs reserved for the ministers.

He, like so many of the present-day leaders of Israel, was born in Russia and came to Palestine during the latter part of the last century, in what is generally called the "second wave." His face has strong, Slavic features, but is softened by a halo of thin, wild white hair.

Uninterested for the time being in veterans' compensation, Ruth and I adjourn to the restaurant on the first floor. It reeks of garlic. Ruth shows me Peter Bergson, one of the leaders of the terrorists, whose name was mentioned in connection with the assassination of Count Bernadotte. He looks pompous, cocky; his small, sandy mustache flares with arrogance. He is standing in the middle of the restaurant, haranguing a small group encircling him.

"He belongs to the Herut Party—Herut meaning Liberty," Ruth tells me. "They're fascists and they're always making a nuisance of themselves. They're in opposition to everything.

"Most of them never really fought for Israel, but they pretend they know military matters better than anybody else." Ruth speaks vehemently. "They stayed mostly in America. They never suffered, never lived in a *kibbutz.* They have always been somewhere else and now they come to Israel."

Bergson's group disperses and moves to the long buffet at the far end of the room. "Look, he always tries to make an impression. He always waves conspicuously to everyone." Ruth's green eyes flash with fire.

"You know he has now changed his name back to Hillel Cook?"

"No, I didn't know."

"Yes, everybody here is changing his name." Her anger over Bergson—that is, Cook—is forgotten. "People are taking Hebrew names, though of course Cook is not a Hebrew name; that was Bergson's original name. Now that we are a nation—a Hebrew nation—it is fitting that we take Hebrew names. For instance, Ettinghausen is now Eytan and Shertok is now Sharret."

I have a brain storm. Why not get out a *Who Was Who in Israel?* Maybe I could make a fortune.

"Changing one's name to Hebrew is not just a fad," Ruth goes on. "The government insists on it, especially when a person is representing Israel abroad. Naturally, we don't want to be represented by someone with a Russian name or a Polish name or a Czech name when we are a Hebrew nation."

"I suppose not," I say a bit doubtfully, thinking of the "foreign" names of some of the people who represent us abroad.

"Luckily, the name of Dayan has always been Hebrew, so we won't have to change it."

I'm relieved to hear it. I have an awful time getting one name and one face together and if now, in the beginning of the trip, I were forced to learn a new name for Dayan I don't believe my mind would stand up under it.

We leave Tel Aviv early in the afternoon and head north, riding through the rich coastal plain that stretches from Tel Aviv to Haifa. Fields of grain, groves of oranges and lemons, and patches of eucalyptus trees roll away from both sides of the highway.

Just before we get to Haifa we turn inland and follow a winding road through a narrow valley of rocks and wild flowers. Poppies! Poppies! Poppies! The ground runs with them. Here and there, though, high on the hillsides are villages, their walls soft cream stucco, their roofs red tile. Vineyards, pruned close, staircase the slopes.

"These villages have been Jewish for forty years," Ruth says. "All this land in the King's Valley belongs to the Jews."

Maybe, but the wild flowers and rocks think it is still theirs; they flaunt themselves even in the vineyards. Marguerites, tulips, iris, dill, and millions and trillions of poppies. Never have I seen a land more bright.

But there is nothing bright about the sky. It hangs low over Mt. Carmel on our left and glowers at us. At any moment we will be deluged.

One village is walled in and Ruth explains that when the Jews first settled in this valley they were afraid of the Arabs who surrounded them, so they walled themselves in and kept guards constantly on watch.

The narrow rockiness of the King's Valley empties suddenly, like a stream, into a huge, tossing lake of green fields, broken only by many small brown islands of *kibbutzim* and villages. It is the fabulous Plain of Esdraelon.

"It is a very rich plain," Ruth says with pride, "and every inch of it not occupied by a house is under cultivation. Do you know, the name Jezreel, which is the ancient name of Esdraelon, means 'God sows'?"

Our road skirts about it for a while, then turns sharply and dips into it. There is a large village on the encircling hills near the entrance, serving as a suburb for Haifa, which is only ten miles away. The people who live here are mostly from Yugoslavia, and they work in the factories and oil refineries of the city. The hills are thickly wooded with oaks, and only small plots are cleared for gardens.

Farther into the valley, Ruth points out a settlement of "Orthodox Jews." I gather such a settlement is a rarity.

"They are so Orthodox," she relates, "that they refused to

use the milk from the cows on the Sabbath. They had to milk them, you understand, to prevent the cows being uncomfortable, but they milked onto the ground. But now they have found some invention that does the milking for them and they milk into pails." She laughs delightedly. "It was just more than they could endure to waste all that milk."

We sail on like a ship through the waves of wheat and rye and barley and come in sight of several trim-looking villages, and Ruth tells me they had been German. "They were Nazis, and when the war came they sent their sons to fight in Germany. So we finished with them."

I steal a glance at her. Her face is unperturbed. She could be saying, "It looks as if it might rain."

"The villages are now ours," she declares, "and they are very nice."

Ruth and Moshe's village of Nahalal is on our route, but we circle around it, for we have no time to stop this afternoon. We are trying to reach, before dark, the *kibbutz* of Ashdot, farther north in Galilee.

I spy land lying fallow and am amazed.

"That was an Arab strip running like a finger down into our land," Ruth explains in nauseated tones, as if it were a finger down the throat. But when she adds, "but the Arabs have now run away," the tones sing.

We near the hills on the west and they are covered by a young forest named for Mr. Balfour, of the Balfour Declaration. It is a modest recognition, I muse to myself, for the man who did so much for the Jewish Homeland; but a little farther on I discover there is a village named for him, too—Balfouria. It is a large village, and looks prosperous.

Beyond the Balfour Forest, the hills are bare, gray rock. Soon we begin to climb into them. It is almost dark and Ruth asks the driver: "Why don't you turn on your lights?"

"I have tried to turn them on," he answers, "but there is something wrong—they won't turn on."

We are in the hills of lower Galilee and they appear completely deserted. Why don't car lights ever go out in populated areas? We creep around curves; we stumble down hills. The world is a crepe-de-Chine black through which the road shows faintly gray. We watch it with all six eyes.

"We can't go on like this," Ruth announces. "When we come to a village, I'll find a phone and call for help."

"What kind of help?" I ask.

"I don't know." She couldn't sound vaguer. "Maybe I can ask someone to come for us."

For a long time we feel our way. Once we almost run down a cat; once a donkey with a man on his back. Finally we reach a village and Ruth leans out the window to find a house into which a telephone line runs.

"Stop," she orders suddenly. "I think this house has a phone."

The driver leans forward to turn the engine off—and swoosh! there are lights. He has accidentally turned something he has never turned before.

Rejoicing, we drive on and pass two *kibbutzim,* so Ruth says (I can't see a thing). They are Degania A and Degania B, two of the oldest and wealthiest *kibbutzim* in all Israel.

"They had the toughest sort of time during the War," Ruth tells me, and I know of course by now she is speaking of the Jewish—Arab war. "They are on the River Jordan, which marks, you know, the Palestine—Syria border, and they suffered terribly. All the *kibbutzim* in the Jordan valley suffered terribly. Degania B was almost completely demolished. The Arabs had tanks up in the hills on the other side of the Jordan and they could see exactly where to place their shots.

"The women and children were evacuated after two days,

but the men wouldn't leave. At night the women returned and did all the cooking for the next day, and the washing, and poured cement for trenches, and picked the tomatoes that were ripe in the fields. They couldn't let them just rot. They picked them at night and sent them to town.

"When Degania was practically razed, the Iraqi army came across the border with tanks. They were at the very gates of Degania when Moshe arrived. It was a most critical situation. We had only one anti-tank gun with four shells and a few Molotoff cocktails."

"Molotoff cocktails?" I question.

"You know, bottles hand-packed with very high explosives. Moshe sees the tanks and he takes action in a few seconds. He orders his men to hold the Molotoff cocktails until the tanks are right upon them and then throw them—throw them when they know they can't miss.

"The Iraqis in the lead tanks thought Degania was already in their hands and they stood up in the cockpits to call out greetings to the men in Degania, and it was then our soldiers let them have the Molotoff cocktails.

"And the Molotoff cocktails and the four shots stopped the Arab tanks. Five were left right at the gate. And when the Iraqi infantry saw the tanks were stopped, they were frightened and ran." Her voice is triumphant.

"It was all a matter of tricks that Degania was saved, but I knew it would be saved. Moshe was born there, and I knew for sentimental reasons he would never let it go."

I feel it is midnight when we reach Ashdot and park beside a mammoth barn in a sea of mud, but it can't be very late, for everyone is at supper. We slither through the mud until we reach a cement walk and then we follow it until we come to a building about the size of an airplane hangar. We walk in unannounced and find about a thousand people of all sizes and ages eating with boundless enthusiasm. Somehow we reach a table where a tall, striking-looking woman greets us warmly. To my surprise, she is Ruth's aunt and is one of the founders of Ashdot. I sit down at a wooden table, bare of mats or cloth, and eat; but for the first time since I've been weaned I'm not conscious of what I eat. The people, the bright unshaded lights, the smells, the comings and goings daze me. But there is plenty to eat. I remember seeing soup being ladled out of a huge tin container on wheels, and there are all sorts of cheeses and sliced onions and. . . . I'm vague, I tell you. The plates and knives and forks are tin, and there are no napkins, but no one seems to mind. It is like a huge summer camp, and roughing it is taken in stride.

After supper we stroll along the narrow cement walk to Ruth's aunt's room. We pass cottage after cottage and hear men and women and children talking and laughing. The air is damp and wedding-sweet with the perfume of orange blossoms.

The aunt has one room, about the size of an ordinary entrance hall, with one door and one window. There are two narrow bunks on each side of the room and three straight chairs. Ruth, her aunt, the aunt's son and three young nieces, who have appeared from somewhere while I was in the daze, and I distribute ourselves the best we can. The aunt sits erectly on a straight chair and I am again impressed by her looks. She has an open, weather-roughened face with wide cheekbones and a high forehead. Her eyes are a cheerful brown, and her hair sweeps in deep waves from her brow to a short "duck-tail bob."

As I had seen pictures of this "duck-tail bob" in *Harper's Bazaar* just before leaving the States, I comment on her up-to-the-minute haircut.

She laughs, delighted. "I've been wearing my hair like this since I was seventeen. I'm so happy to hear the styles in America have caught up with me."

Her clothes are utilitarian, yet she wears them with an air of distinction: a red, gray, and black plaid shirt, open at the neck, a pair of faded blue slacks, brown socks, and flat-heeled walking shoes. They, of course, do not belong to her. Like the clothes of everyone else in Ashdot, her clothes belong to the *kibbutz*.

Her story is the story of Israel. It could be told as the personal experience of hundreds, even of thousands, of the first Jewish immigrants to Palestine. She came twenty-nine years ago from Bessarabia in Russia. She was twenty years old and she came alone. People on the boat asked her what she was coming to Palestine to do and she answered, "to build roads." And she did build roads, "knocking big stones into little stones," and she lived in tents by the sides of the roads. And one day she met a man building roads, too, and she fell in love with him and married him.

Then they went to Jerusalem to build houses, and while they were there they met some young people who wanted to start a *kibbutz*, except it wasn't called a *kibbutz* then. They worked, they planned, and they dreamed, and after thirteen years in transit they came to the Jordan valley and began the building of Ashdot. There were one hundred and twenty of them when they moved in. Now there are thirteen hundred—and some of these are grandchildren of the pioneers.

I look at the aunt's son—a wide-shouldered, dark-haired young man. Is he married? Does he have children? No, he is single and is here at Ashdot on a holiday. He is in the navy.

"I didn't know Israel had a navy," I say.

"You can't talk about us that way," he answers.

The aunt also has a daughter and she is in the army, but when she is released she will, no doubt, return to Ashdot.

"She likes it here?" I ask.

"Of course."

And the aunt, after all her years, likes it, too. She glows as she talks about the life. At first she worked in the fields—in the vineyards, in the wheat fields, in the banana groves.

"I was a good agriculturist, too," she boasts, "until I lost my strength."

Everybody in the *kibbutz* works nine hours a day. For the able-bodied, there are no exceptions. They have some choice about the kind of work they do. Like navy men, they can request certain posts, but they don't always get them. Now the aunt is in the sewing house, helping to make the clothes. All the women's clothes and all the men's clothes, even to their suits, are made at Ashdot, and are handed out as they are needed. No one has money to buy clothes. Indeed, no one has money for anything—a fact I know very well, but find difficult to comprehend. There are innumerable times when I have no money, either—but *never* to have money!

"And how about that man on the road whom you married?" I ask the aunt.

She smiles. "I still have him, but he is now secretary for the outside affairs of the *kibbutz* and stays in Tel Aviv during the week and comes home only for the week ends."

"Does he sleep in this room?" I ask.

"Oh yes, this is our room. Each married couple has its own room."

But there is little family life. A baby is taken from his parents as soon as he is born and put in an infants' home, and from then on until he is grown he sees the parents only when it is convenient for them, usually an hour or two in the early evening.

The hour is late and we are very weary. The aunt offers to show us to our room. We go out into the wet night and walk by cottage after cottage as if we were at a large tourist camp in the States. Date palms and banana trees grow in the plots before the cottages, and the harsh rustle of their leaves sounds like the sweep of the surf.

"Here we are," the aunt says brightly, turning toward a house that looks like every other house.

"How about a bathroom?" Ruth asks.

"Oh," says the aunt. "Do you want to go to the bathroom?" She peers at me through the dark.

"Well, I think it would be a good idea, don't you?"

"Then we will have to go back the way we came." Her voice is unhappy. "There is no toilet near here, but there is a spigot on the porch where you can wash."

We retrace our steps, many, many steps, past the house where the aunt lives, and come to a community toilet and shower. We take our turn in a long line.

"How about in the middle of the night or in the early morning?" I venture timidly.

Neither Ruth nor the aunt answers; they merely shake their heads.

Back at our room, the aunt is full of apologies because no one has told her we were coming and the cots are not made up and the sheets, which she gets out of a drawer, are rough-dried; but I'm not disturbed. I'm so tired I could sleep on the floor and enjoy it.

The wall between our room and the adjoining one is paper-thin and I suffer some embarrassment when a man and woman enter it and, laughing and talking loudly, go to bed. I am sure they don't realize there are guests next door. Debating whether to beat on the floor with a shoe or to clear my throat loudly, I fall asleep.

And it is well I slept as soon as I did, for the whole of Ashdot is up at five-thirty the next morning and on its feet. It is a wet, cold morning, and I crawl out shivering and get into my clothes. My coat around me, I go out to the porch to find the spigot and throw a drop of water into my eyes—and there in front of me in the fields are dozens and dozens of men and women bending over grapevines to tie them to supports. How can they do it with the ground and vines so sopping wet? Won't it give them chilblains, pneumonia, rheumatism, arthritis? And have they already had breakfast?

Ruth says no when I put this last question to her; they have only had coffee. They will work for two hours and then come in to breakfast.

We, too, must work before breakfast. We join the aunt and do a tour. Though the grounds are not neat, there are flowers before every door, behind every house, and in the park areas along the cement walk: snapdragons, gladioli, lilies, pansies, nasturtiums, roses. . . . In spite of the "unusual" spell of cold weather, they are in full bloom.

"We send roses to London from here," the aunt remarks. "And to think when we came here there was not a flower, not a tree. We planted all these olives, date palms, oranges, and bananas."

We visit the spotless hospital of twenty-five beds and the house for the nine- and ten-year-old children, both boys and girls. There are twenty-five in this house, and most of them are on the front porch around the spigot, getting cleaned up for the day. One is vigorously brushing his teeth; another is brushing her black, curly hair. One young fellow, small for his age, with a head fuzzy with tight blond curls, is on his knees, mopping the floor of a room that opens on the porch.

We move on to the high school, which is not open at this early hour, but from the outside looks substantial and modern. Three boys are cutting the grass with scythes. It is so wet, the grass sticks to the blades, but doggedly they wipe it off and go ahead.

The kindergarten home is erupting with shouts, songs, yells. "Who wants my drawing?" one tiny blonde screams, holding up a sheet of paper with some colored lines on it. "Who wants my drawing . . . who wants my drawing . . . who wants my drawing?" she chants. Others yell, too, as they play about a table heaped with blocks and beads.

"We have lots of kindergartens," the aunt tells me, "for we have lots of children. For a while, during the first years of the *kibbutz,* we controlled births—children were too expensive; but now there is no control and the place teems with them."

The children sleep six to a room, and they are looked after by members of the *kibbutz* who are trained in kindergarten work. "Our girls are sent away to take nursery courses," the aunt explains, "and many of them become experts."

At the age of fourteen, all the boys and girls are given the opportunity to leave the *kibbutz* to study in agricultural colleges or other government institutions. It is during these years that they usually meet the people they marry.

"It is seldom the boys marry girls from their own *kibbutz,*" comments the aunt. "They know one another too well."

It is time for breakfast, thank goodness. The vast airdrome of a dining room is a veritable bedlam. Innumerable waiters are pushing two-storied teacarts; innumerable men are building tables and benches for a banquet; innumerable women and young people are walking about, providing themselves with food, and innumerable birds are flying through the rafters and darting down at the food on the tables. The bread must be kept covered all the time to prevent the birds from consuming all of it. The tables are heaped with cheeses, herring, onions, sweet cream that is so thick it won't pour, and a cake called halvah, made of sesame seeds, sugar, and cream. Also, there are eggs for the ordering.

The aunt turns me over to a man with a bulging forehead who offers to explain to me the business side of Ashdot. I catch his name as Jacob Shouse, but I don't always catch names correctly. He says he is the Ashdot gardener.

"The head gardener?" I ask.

"The head and feet," he answers with a grin.

Ashdot, like all *kibbutzim*, is run by a committee of men and women elected yearly by the members of the settlement from their own membership. There are twenty-one on the Ashdot committee. Three members carry on the *kibbutz* business on the outside. All marketing is done through the Palestine Co-operative Marketing Society. Ashdot is both an agricultural and industrial settlement—about sixty per cent of its income is from agriculture and forty per cent from industry, but it is difficult to separate them, for much of the industrial income stems from agricultural products. Ashdot has:

A dairy of 300 cows	15 acres of olives
A chicken farm of 10,000 chickens	100 acres of vegetables
150 acres of bananas	200 acres of fodder
100 acres of table grapes	250 acres of cereals
50 acres of citrus fruit, mostly grapefruit	5 acres of roses

"We have good dairy stuff," Mr. Shouse says enthusiastically. "We deliver milk daily to Haifa, Tel Aviv, and Jerusalem. It is loaded very early in the morning and in a few hours has reached its consumers' market. We have worlds of cheese, heavy cream, and butter, but only the children in the *kibbutz* get butter; the rest of us eat oleomargarine.

"We can fruit juices, fruit concentrates, olives—tons of olives, all green—cauliflower. . . ."

I take time out to shudder. Can't think of anything worse than canned cauliflower.

"Sauerkraut, jellies, jams. We make fifty different kinds."

"My goodness, you almost out-Heinz Heinz with his fifty-seven varieties."

Mr. Shouse is not amused, but goes right ahead: "Green pickles, small cucumber pickles, big cucumber pickles. . . ."

"I adore cucumber pickles," I put in quickly, but he doesn't care about this, either.

"We raise grapes, but just table grapes; we don't put them up. The most wonderful grapes you ever tasted come from the Jordan valley. All our fruits and vegetables are superior to any grown in the country. In fact, I wouldn't hesitate to say they are superior to any in the world, due to the heat and rich soil. We have three hundred days of full sunshine. That makes a difference in the quality of the fruit."

Of course, those three hundred days of sunshine mean the land has to be thoroughly irrigated. "There are at least five miles of concrete aqueducts," Mr. Shouse declares proudly. "The main aqueducts run for two miles from the Yarmuk River, which is a branch of the Jordan."

"Do you make money?" I ask Mr. Shouse, for I have heard continuously since coming to the Middle East that the Jews are making the land produce as it has never produced before, but that it is costing them millions. One American business executive told me that every rose costs $150 to produce and that the budget of Israel is out of all proportion to its population.

But Mr. Shouse says Ashdot makes money. Its gross income is about a million and a quarter dollars a year.

"But how much of that is profit?" I persist.

"That's hard to say," he answers cautiously, "but I'd say about ten per cent. Sometimes it is a little more and sometimes a little less. It all depends on the Almighty."

The land for Ashdot was provided by the Jewish National Fund, which retains the title; the buildings and equipment were supplied by the Palestine Foundation Fund (Keren Hayesod) which loaned the money to the settlers at a very low rate of interest. Part of this loan, a so-called "initial subsistence," was written off; but seventy-five to eighty per cent was supposed to be repaid by the settlers in installments. All kibbutzim are financed in this fashion.

"How much did the original settlers borrow to start Ashdot?" I ask Mr. Shouse.

"Not too much."

I try again. "Well, how much does Ashdot now owe the Palestine Foundation Fund?"

"Oh, between half a million and six hundred thousand dollars."

"Is the debt being reduced regularly?"

He shrugs his shoulders expressively. "We keep paying back and we keep borrowing more for new construction. We try to pay back about five per cent of the loan annually, but paying off the loan is not the important thing. We put most of our income into new structures, for we are under obligation to absorb more immigrants all the time. The basic approach to the question of profits is how many immigrants you can absorb, not how much you can reduce your loan. In the fourteen years Ashdot has been in existence, we have absorbed over one thousand immigrants."

I can see my viewpoint has been all wrong. I stop asking

questions, but Mr. Shouse needs no questions. As we say in Kentucky, he has the bit in his mouth. "Our chief expenses in the *kibbutz* are food and clothes and education. We figure it costs a thousand dollars per person, or three thousand per family per year."

"That's a high standard of living," I comment, thinking of the average income of our farmers in the deep South.

"Yes. Ashdot and Afikim have the highest standard of living of any *kibbutz* in Israel."

Having finished breakfast, we do more sight-seeing. On the way we pass two young girls, giggling, their cheeks red, their black eyes sparkling. Mr. Shouse pats one of them affectionately on the head.

"Those are refugee children, brought from the hell of Europe," Mr. Shouse tells me when we are out of hearing. "They knew not what it meant to smile; now they enjoy life. After one year you can't tell a refugee child from one born in the camp. There is a terrific transformation.

"We have groups of children coming continuously from Europe. At one time we had one hundred from Bulgaria, Yugoslavia, and where-not. Another time, one hundred and twenty. The groups stay here usually between two and three years, and most of their time is devoted to study and to becoming men. They are just an expense. When they are eighteen, they become independent. They form their own groups and leave here to make new camps."

We have reached the sewing house, and, as we walk into one of the rooms where a half-dozen women are bent over machines, Mr. Shouse points to a woman in the corner and announces proudly: "That's my lady." She looks up for a moment and flashes us a bright smile.

They are making men's pants out of khaki cloth, and shirts

out of a bright blue material, and sheets and pillowcases. One woman is sewing on buttons with a button machine and it draws me like a magnet. What I couldn't do with a button machine!

"How many garments do you make annually for each person?" I ask Mr. Shouse.

"As many as he needs," he answers briefly.

Going to the barn to see the modern electric milking machines and hillocks of orange peels ground up for cows' food, Mr. Shouse calls gaily to a young boy, an old man, a soldier in uniform.

"I believe you like it here," I say to him.

"If I didn't I wouldn't be here." His tone is matter-of-fact. "I have been here from the beginning and I now have grandchildren here. My daughter married and brought her husband back here and now they have two children. The work is hard, but life is more enjoyable here than in any other place in the world. Nobody has to worry about what job he will have tomorrow, where he will get food to eat, and how he will entertain himself. Everybody here is doing his share to make life secure and pleasant for himself and for everybody else."

I decide it is time for Ruth and me to leave. Any speech after this will be an anticlimax.

14. The good muck

WE RETURN to Ruth's village of Nahalal by a different route so that I may see more of the country. For some time we circle along the Sea of Galilee, except that Ruth persists in calling it the Lake of Galilee. Be it lake or sea, it is violin-shaped and a deep blue, and bordered by palms and eucalyptus trees.

I remember Jesus feeding the multitude with five loaves of bread and three fishes and walking on the water and quieting the raging storm. I wish I had Bussy's olive-wood-bound Bible—or the roommate.

On our left we pass a resort famous for its sulfur springs. It looks deserted now, for this is not the season, but Ruth says many of the "pioneers" of Israel, suffering from rheumatism, come here for the baths.

"The older generation worked such long hours in the mud that a great many of them have rheumatism," she says.

"I can imagine," I answer, remembering the men and women in the wet vineyards at Ashdot.

We come to the city of Tiberias, an amazing and fascinating place of huge old walls and a citadel with four towers, dating back to the Crusaders, and many buildings fashioned of layers of shining black basalt and stone. Abruptly, in the center of the downtown area, we turn our backs on the Sea of Galilee and begin to do loops like an airplane to gain height. Tiberias, it seems, is 682 feet below sea level and we are low-gearing not just to sea level but into the hills. Many modern-style apartment houses and pensions and hotels rear their plain, flat walls and bold windows on the steep slopes.

Before the Arab-Jewish war, back in 1946, Tiberias was a city of 11,700 inhabitants, almost equally divided between Arabs and Jews, but now there are no Arabs left. The feeling and the fighting in this area were extremely bitter.

At the highest reach of the road I turn and peer down at the blue silk brocade gown of the Sea of Galilee, with strands of silver slipping to the surface where the light strikes it. Fields of daisies or mimosa or acacia bed it in bright yellow, and beyond them are the green pillows of gentle mountains, and beyond them, high and solitary, the headboard of Mt. Hermon, slip-covered in snow.

A few miles from Tiberias, an Arab village, with the small, square houses painted blue like children's blocks, lies toppled and deserted. A few miles farther on, another Arab village. Its cream walls are pock-marked with shell holes; its olive orchards and rich fields wild with weeds.

"This village was awful, terrible," Ruth declares with spirit. "It fought fiercely. All the villages along here fought fiercely; they have fought us fiercely since the riots of '36. The fighting was so bad this road was closed."

All about I see deserted Arab villages. They hang like empty pictureframes, a bit crookedly against the blue-green of the hills. The fields were fertile and had been cultivated. The gray rock walls of the terraces were painstakingly done; the olive trees cleanly pruned.

"All this is now our land," Ruth says—and is silent.

She has every reason to be pleased. It is extraordinarily beautiful land. I, who horrified the roommate one Christmas by asking for a load of fertilizer, hang out the car window, eyeing it hungrily. Acres of pomegranates, miles of olives, cows grazing in unfenced pastures.

We begin again to climb. Nazareth is quite close.

"Why are cities in this part of the world on the top of such rocky hills?" I ask.

"For security purposes, of course."

"It seems so foolish."

Ruth stares at me with a look of incredulity. "Anybody would know that you had never fought a war."

"Thank goodness."

"Yes, you'd better say thank goodness."

A road block halts us on the outskirts of Nazareth, and Israeli soldiers ask for our identification cards. Nazareth was

and is Arab in population and, at the very beginning of the
Jewish–Arab hostilities, they announced they would remain
neutral and take no part whatsoever in the War. So there
was no fighting there; but now the Jews occupy it and the
Arabs live under what amounts to military law. No one is
allowed to enter or leave without the permission of the Jewish authorities.

"A friend of Moshe's and mine, a young man from a *kibbutz*, has been sent here as military commander," Ruth tells
me.

"Are these barriers to keep the Arabs who did leave from
coming back?" I ask.

Ruth shrugs. "If they left the country, they left."

Though Nazareth is Arab, it is not Moslem. *The Palestine
Guide* says,"considerably more than half" of the fifteen thousand people are Christian, but Ruth declares that all the Arabs
who are there now are Christian. "There is not a Moslem
left," she says with satisfaction.

Nazareth looks larger than a city of fifteen thousand. Many
large buildings, a soft buff color, fill the slopes and valleys.
Since it was the boyhood home of Jesus, practically all Christian faiths have churches or monasteries or nunneries here.
Their long walls are brightened by the deep green ovals of
cypress, pine, and fir.

We slow up at the Spring of Our Lady Mary to watch
Arab women wash their greens and fill their red-brown pottery pitchers with water. They could be a picture on a Sunday School card, their skirts long and gracefully draped, their
heads covered in flowing veils. It is definitely no costume
for washing greens, but mighty colorful.

I wonder if Mary carried water on her head from this
fountain, too, or did Joseph feel she was too precious? Knowing men, I doubt it. I am fairly sure she glided along this

very road, balancing her pitcher, along with the rest of her sisters.

Today Arab women are not only carrying water but stones. We pass several of them, swaying by on their small, bare feet as gracefully as movie queens entering a drawing room, and on their heads huge baskets heaped with stones. There are lines of camels, too. Evidently a road is being built near by.

The stores carry fresh signs in Hebrew above the old Arabic signs, and on one garage there is a newly painted star of David.

A few miles outside of Nazareth, I look down on my left into the Plain of Esdraelon through which we had ridden on our way to Ashdot. The islands of settlements and co-operative villages are small from this height; they could be clusters of topazes on the green satin bottom of a giant jewelry box. Ruth points out Nahalal.

Nahalal is not a *kibbutz*; it belongs to the second type of agricultural communities that are peculiar to Israel. It is a smallholders' settlement; in Hebrew, a *Moshav ovdim*. Each family is settled on a piece of land, the same size for every family, but it is not privately owned. Like the land of a *kibbutz*, it is owned by the Jewish National Fund, which leases it for a forty-nine-year period to the settler. The settler pays a ground rent of two per cent a year on the value of the land, the rent being "upped" at long intervals when reappraisals are made.

The size of the individual holdings varies from settlement to settlement, depending upon the fertility of the land and the amount of water available for irrigation. But no family can have more land than its own members can work. There is no hired help. That is one of the fundamental rules. In Nahalal, each family is allotted twenty-five acres.

Nahalal is built in the form of a circle. The fields fan out from the houses like the spaces between the spokes of a wheel. In the middle, at the very hub, are the public buildings—the post office, the co-operative store, the machine shop, the school, the auditorium. Around them are the houses for the people who don't farm—the teachers, the clerks, the mechanics. Then comes the big circle of the houses of the settlers who tend the land. There are only seventy-five families, but about a thousand inhabitants.

We drop rapidly down into the valley from the mountain ridge. It is raining steadily and has been, off and on, for days. I can't remember when I saw the sun last. We head directly for Nahalal and in an amazingly short time we reach a wide ring of eucalyptus trees that completely circles the fields of Nahalal. Each family, Ruth explains, has an acre of eucalyptus for building purposes.

An unpaved road, deep in the blackest mud that I have ever seen, cuts the village exactly in half. We will be stuck, I am sure; no car can get through mud that comes up to the hub caps. Ruth cannot understand mud like this in April. She feels we've been double-crossed. "We expect mud like this all winter; but here it is April!" she mourns, all but wringing her hands.

"You have no boots, have you?" she asks me.

I shake my head.

"I will see what I can do. Nobody can get around in Nahalal without boots. In the rainy season it is just not done."

The car slithers into the business section and Ruth wades into the only store. She returns with a pair of boots that would have swallowed Goliath.

"These are the smallest they have," she says. "You'll have to put them on."

I struggle, but they are so high I can't get myself stretched out in a sufficiently straight line to get into them. Especially on the back seat of a car. I need to be hoisted by ropes and lowered into them.

"Why don't you put them on the ground," suggests Ruth, "and step into them?"

"From the hood?"

She laughs gaily.

We do prop them in the mud and I do manage to step into them from the seat. They come up well above my knees and I can't move. How can anyone move without bending the knee? Ruth and I lean against the car and laugh until our tears run with the rain down our faces.

"How about trying to slide along?" Ruth suggests finally.

"And take all the precious earth of Nahalal with me?"

I push like a plow through the mud and it banks up around me higher and higher. I hold up my clothes to keep them from dragging in it.

Ruth's daughter, who has been visiting her grandmother in Nahalal, pops up suddenly before us. She has alert brown eyes, pink cheeks, and is a very gay figure in a bright red sweater, pea-green jacket, and gray skirt.

"This is Yula," Ruth introduces her. "Her real name, though, is Yael, for the one, you remember, who put the stake in Sisera's head."

No, I don't remember at all. I have never heard of her, but, sunk in the mud as I am, I'm in no mood to argue. Why, at any minute, I might be completely submerged, a fate much worse than a stake through the head.

I drag along a few hundred feet (that's the distance I'm traversing, not the number of my feet; they're still two, but they drag like a thousand) and arrive at a tiny cottage nesting in a grove of fruit trees. This is the house of Nahalal's unofficial hostess, Mrs. Nadia Yehuda. I gather you're not welcomed to Nahalal unless you've been welcomed by Mrs. Yehuda. She is a small, elderly woman, quick moving, friendly, exciting.

After a valiant struggle I get out of my boots and go into the front room and sit at a square table. An electric refrigerator purrs against one wall. Behind this wall is the kitchen, and frequently, during our conversation, Mrs. Yehuda darts into that room to watch the cake she is baking.

She apologizes for the way she is dressed, in her work clothes and apron. "I look like two cents waiting for change, as you say in the United States."

But she really doesn't care how she looks, she cares only about Israel and the task that lies ahead. She is one of the "pioneers." With her two children, she came to Palestine from Russia twenty years ago, which, in her opinion, was not soon enough.

"I was afraid I came too late," she speaks with an accent. "I thought the pioneering was already done, the real pioneering. I didn't expect life to be easy, though. I never dreamed to have a home like this." She darts her small eyes about the room—refrigerator, electricity. "I expected to have a box —and live in a box. And I did live for fourteen years in tents and leaky shacks. I had three orange crates for a bed, two for a table, and one for a chair. And I had a wonderful wardrobe made from a half-dozen crates." She laughs delightedly.

"We came originally to this section—all the crowd was two hundred souls—but we did not build homes for fourteen years, and then we did not build them at one time, but one by one. Each family borrowed from six to eight hundred pounds from the Palestine Foundation Fund, depending on the size of the family, as the land was ready. That took time. This spot on which Nahalal is built was a marsh, you know."

I did not know, but having seen the mud, I can imagine.

"There were just little patches of land," she rushes on. "Not a blade of grass—all thorn and thistle. When I heard a bird chirp, I cried. The bird was chirping, I was crying. When I planted little trees, I said, 'Why am I doing this? Will I live to eat the fruit? Will I live to see the shade?'

"To drain the marsh, men stood up to their breasts in water." She spreads her hand on her own breast. "They laid pipes to carry off the water. The Arabs said the water is death, but we never lost a person from water. We were fortified by people who had knowledge."

She breaks off and hurries to the kitchen for coffee. It is thick and black and just what my damp bones crave. She also brings little cakes packed with raisins. She says she has raised and dried the raisins herself.

"I must admit we worked hard," she continues, as if there had been no interruption. "We've put a lot into Palestine, but we've got much more out of it. Everybody here knows what they're working for. Someone else can't build your country for you; you must build it for yourself. Build it with your own hands."

She puts down her coffee cup and spreads out her hands and stares at them intently. "I deplore so much machinery," she says abruptly. "We now lose connection with the earth. I feel deprived of something."

"I like working in the ground, too," I say, but she ignores me.

"I'm going to be sixty-five years old very soon and I can do work from six in the morning until six in the evening. I rest a bit in the middle of the day. I have no help whatever—that's the rule, you know. I am all the family, so I do all the work."

Mrs. Yehuda's two children are now in the United States, one a teacher at the University of Chicago, and the other, a painter. Her husband is a member of Parliament and spends most of his time in Tel Aviv. Just recently she gave up her farm of twenty-five acres and moved into this cottage, with only a small plot for fruit trees, vegetables, and flowers.

"I'm a retired farmer now." She jerks back her sweater and pushes out her chest in a mock gesture of boasting. "Instead of three hundred fruit trees, I have only fifty, and instead of fields of wheat I have only garden vegetables and flowers. I grow all the apples and peaches I can eat, and I dry great trays of them for cake. I grow magnificent olives and put them up myself. My, they're good."

My mouth is watering.

"I buy practically nothing but salt and sugar and a few cereals. This land will grow most vegetables all year round. Only tomatoes and cauliflower are seasonal. We get three crops of potatoes a year."

"Do you grow spinach?"

"Whatever you can call by name. And onions. Whew! Such onions!"

She hops up again to look at the cake, and when she returns she keeps right on talking about Israel. "As I was saying, it isn't the easiest life that is the best. In the long run, we find the hardest way is the best way. To be of service, to have a purpose, that is the best. Refugees are our great task now. We must give them an injection to make them know they are still needed—that there is a place for them. It is like giving them life. Do you know, an average of a thousand immigrants arrive daily in Israel?"

"It's amazing," I say.

"It's more than amazing." Her voice rings. "It's colossal! It's unbelievable! To make a homogeneous group of them—it is a terrific task. But I welcome it! I welcome it! I have all I love in the United States—two children and two grandchildren, but I could not find peace anywhere except here."

Getting on a chair to step down into my seven-league boots, I think of the Arabs. What chance could they possibly have had against such fervent dedication to an ideal? Dear, happy-go-lucky people, they were whipped long before they knew.

The mud has dried and stands out around my boots like a halo about a saint's head. I can't lift them.

"Stand still," orders Ruth, "and I'll tread on you."

It sounds ominous, but I stand meekly and Ruth walks around me, stepping on the mud, and I lift my feet up and leave my haloes on Mrs. Yehuda's stoop. She won't mind. After all, they are the good earth of Nahalal.

But I collect just as much on the short journey to the co-operative store and have to be treaded on again before I can go inside. It isn't worth the effort, really, for the store is practically empty. Two small heads of cabbage, a few dried-up potatoes, and a handful of onions look lonely in a bin.

"Why should the store carry vegetables?" Ruth says. "We raise what we have to have."

The shelves are almost as bare: some cans of salmon, sardines, herring, a few bottles of beer. On the hardware side, there are sprayers, rolls of wire, and a refrigerator.

Money is almost an unknown quantity in this store. The settlers of Nahalal buy everything on credit and they get this credit from the produce which they bring to the co-operative market.

Though I don't understand about money or credit, scarcely ever having enough of either to bother my head about, Ruth insists on my going into the books of the co-operative. (This is what happens to you when you act too interested in things.) So we drag ourselves, boots and all, up some stairs into a large accounting department and meet a bookkeeper who shows me account books, stubs, statements, and heaven knows what. I feel like an internal revenue agent and despise myself.

"The bookkeeping is very complicated," he says.

"Ah, you're telling me!" I quip brightly.

There is a separate account book for each settler and a separate book for each commodity. When a farmer brings in a commodity he is given credit for the amount he brings, and when that commodity is sold he gets his share of the profits in proportion to the amount. For instance, the profit from milk is not divided equally among all the settlers, but just among those who brought milk. This is true, too, of vegetables, fruit, chickens, sheep, cheese—everything. Milk is Nahalal's most profitable commodity, with eggs second.

"The farmer is given credit in his book just as you are in a bankbook when you deposit money in the bank." He eyes me keenly to see if I'm following him.

I am, but at a distance.

"And the farmer can purchase commodities that he needs against this credit."

"Suppose his purchases exceed his credits?" I ask.

"That is all right just so long as he doesn't exceed them by too great a margin. Under normal circumstances, a person can overdraw by three or four hundred pounds [between $1000 and $1300]."

"I overdrew once nine hundred pounds," puts in Ruth, and I warm to her. I can see we are sisters under the covers of a bankbook.

"Of course, there is interest to be paid on the amount overdrawn," says the bookkeeper.

"Of course," I answer, but I'm bitterly disappointed. I had thought Israel arranged things better.

"The interest is three and a half per cent," he goes on relentlessly. "It . . ."

But I refuse to hear more. I hadn't come to Israel to hear about interest. I can hear about that in Kentucky.

It is time to eat, thank goodness, and Ruth and I are invited to lunch at the home of the chairman of the village council. It is next door to the house Ruth and Moshe had lived in before Moshe became military governor of Israeli Jerusalem. Now, by special arrangement, the house is occupied and the land worked by a family of Polish immigrants. The Dayans hope to go back to it when Moshe is no longer on active military duty.

The village chairman, Joseph Dronii, greets us warmly. He looks like a man of distinction. His cheekbones are high and sharp; his small eyes, gray and deep-set beneath heavy brows; his pepper-and-salt mustache, short and evenly trimmed; and his head, bald except for a wide fringe draped from ear to ear.

He, too, had come from Russia. During the first World War he was an officer in a "very special company of Russian cavalry." It was quite an honor and most unusual, he relates, for a Jew to be an officer in the Russian army; but, nevertheless, in 1919 when the war was over, he and his wife came to Palestine.

Mrs. Dronii is heavy-set. She doesn't sit with us at the table, but prepares the lunch in the kitchen, smiling at us frequently through the open doors. Neither she nor Mr. Dronii knows English. They speak Hebrew or Russian (both Greek to me) and Ruth translates. A daughter-in-law appears long enough to be introduced, but hurries off to some household or farm chore. There is a daughter, too, but she is now, queer as it sounds, teaching in Germany.

"The daughter was to have been married during the Jew-

ish–Arab troubles," Ruth tells me, as Mr. Dronii, uncompre-
hending, sits quietly by, tapping on the table with long,
brown fingers. "Great preparations had been made. For days
we had been baking bread, cakes, and biscuits for the feast
we were to have on the evening of the wedding, which was
to be held under the trees, and we had already started cooking the chickens—about thirty of them."

She stops for a moment and looks from Mr. Dronii to Mrs.
Dronii at the kitchen stove. Mrs. Dronii is dishing up something and paying no attention to us.

"The daughter's fiancé was working in a *kibbutz*," Ruth
continues. "He worked in the daytime and patrolled at night.
One morning, the *kibbutz* heard the Arabs were going to attack and so, when the boys took the cows out to pasture, a
patrol went along to guard them." Her voice is flat. . . .
"They were ambushed in a valley near Nazareth. The *kibbutz* heard the firing and others went out to help them . . .
All of them were killed."

My small murmurs of distress attract Mr. Dronii's attention. He peers at me curiously, but Ruth doesn't offer him
any explanation. She is too intent on the tragedy. "The
Arabs went to the British and told them there were ten bodies
in the valley," she says. "This was during the British mandate; the British didn't leave, you know, until May 15th,
1948. Half of our dead were killed while the British were
still here." Her lean jaws harden. "We were very pleased
when they left."

"I know. I've heard."

She shrugs her shoulders, and then with a sigh goes on:
"Moshe came home and told me he knew the sweetheart was
dead. Not officially, but he knew. He wanted me to tell the
family, but I couldn't. I simply couldn't. It was too much,
with the cakes already baked."

Mrs. Dronii brings in lunch. First, there is a relish of chopped egg, beets, and horse-radish; next, soup with matzoth; and then, baked chicken and boiled potatoes. It tastes good, and, in spite of the lump in my throat, I eat everything.

After lunch, Mr. Dronii shows me pictures of the marsh that was Nahalal and of the tents in which he and the other "pioneers" lived. He is most interesting and I am enjoying myself thoroughly when, suddenly, without a word of warning, Mrs. Dronii plops what she calls a spaghetti-cutting machine on the table in front of me and asks that I explain the workings of it to her. Me!

An aunt or a cousin or a sister in the United States had sent it to her, but so far it was no good to her because she couldn't figure out how to work it. And now I had been sent like an angel from heaven.

I have never been able to understand even a can opener, but I study this spaghetti contraption. There is nothing else I can do. It has grooves like a washboard and curling knives like a meat grinder And. . . . Stars, I don't know. It's unfathomable. Slowly I shake my head.

Through Ruth, she questions me. "But you do come from the United States?"

"Yes."

"Then you know about this." She smiles. "This came from the United States. From New York in the United States."

"Yes, I know, but a lot of things come from New York in the United States that I don't understand."

She's puzzled—and unhappy.

"Yes, but doesn't everyone in the United States have a spaghetti-cutting machine like this?"

"I really don't believe so. In fact, I never saw or heard of a spaghetti-cutting machine before."

It's now her turn to shake her head. She's terribly disappointed in me, I can see.

"Maybe, if you study it a little bit more. . . . Yes? . . . Everyone in the United States knows machines, do they not? I'm sure if you . . ."

I'm saved from slashing my throat by a knock on the door. One knock. It is the postman. There is the official paper of the Israeli government and a letter from the United States for the daughter-in-law.

The daughter-in-law is summoned and she quickly grabs the newspaper. "I want to see who have changed their names this week," she says.

There is a whole column of people who have changed their names to Hebrew and she reads aloud those of the people she knows to her mother and father and Ruth. They are excited over the changes. They agree that they sound much better in Hebrew.

Then the letter from the United States is opened. Unconscious of an approaching personal catastrophe, I sit casually munching on a piece of matzo.

Abruptly, there is a cry—a joyous, ecstatic cry. "Oh-h-h," shrieks the daughter-in-law. "My aunt in the United States has sent me a pressure cooker. It should be here any minute."

A pressure cooker! I snatch up my boots and without stopping to put them on, plunge into the mud. A spaghetti-cutting machine is child's play, I'm sure, to a pressure cooker. May the good Lord let me be miles away before it arrives. Israel is not big enough for both of us.

15. I hungered while they wandered

THE sky is a crepe-myrtle pink in the west as I drive to the *kibbutz* of Ginegar on Passover eve. Behind me are Nahalal and Ruth and Moshe Dayan, who has shrugged off the heavy and harassing duties of governor of Jerusalem to join his mother and sister and Ruth and the children for the celebration. I had secretly hoped to spend it with them, but Ruth decided it would be more interesting for me in Ginegar.

So, still wearing the Wellington boots, I roll through the green, green fields of the Plain of Esdraelon. Ginegar is not far from Nahalal, but it is off the plain, on the slope of one of the encircling mountains.

The driver of the car is a young man, and I begin to talk to him—of course, about Israel. In case that statement is a bit confusing, I hasten to say I would have talked just the same if the driver had been a young woman. I draw no lines on sex. He had lived in a *kibbutz,* he tells me, for thirteen years and had liked the life very much.

"But my mother, she kept speaking for us to move to Tel Aviv," he explains in his interesting English. "She doesn't like *kibbutz*. She wants the money to buy what she wants. She not like what they give."

I feel a kinship to Mother, but dare not mention it. Instead I admire the mountains that roll out against the pink sky as evenly as a bolt of gray-blue velvet on a store counter.

"Life much better in *kibbutz*," the driver goes on. "In Tel Aviv I must look for work, must look for bread. In *kibbutz* I had to look for nothing. Well or sick, there is food."

That is something, I admit. Quite something.

Ginegar is a rather disorderly conglomeration of buildings strung along the instep of a mountain. We draw up in front of a large, barrack-like affair, and I wade out into mud almost as wide and deep and black as Nahalal's and begin inquiring for Miriam Greenwald. Ruth gave me her name with the bare explanation that she is from the United States and is expecting me.

When I find her, she is in her room with her husband and a dozen other people. They are sitting on the two narrow beds, the two chairs, and the floor. A young man moves off one of the beds so that I can squeeze in and, without more ado, I am part of the party.

They are mostly young people—in their twenties, I judge —and though they come from many countries, they seem closely and happily knit. They ask about my trip, the work of the Commission, the part of the United States in which I live. Miriam Greenwald is the only American, and before coming to Palestine two years ago her part of the country was Minnesota. She is a small blonde with high coloring, bright blue eyes, and a sharp, prominent nose.

"When I first came I thought I couldn't get used to it," she confesses. "Especially the first day when I went out into the fields with fifteen boys and worked nine hours in the hot sun."

And she isn't quite used to it yet, as she told me, not during the party, but later. She still clings to her United States passport and her pretty clothes. Instead of giving them up when she entered the *kibbutz* and sharing the simple clothes of the other members of the commune, she hid them under her bed and there they still remain. They are a bone of contention between her and her young husband, whom she met and married after coming to Ginegar.

Why she fell in love with him is easy to see. He, too, is blond, with curly hair the color of the new moon, and gay blue eyes, and an open, fine face. He is twenty-seven and has been at Ginegar since he was seventeen, having come from Czechoslovakia shortly before World War II.

It was fortunate for him that Zionism caught his imagination and drew him to Palestine when it did, for Hitler sent his mother and father to a concentration camp where they died in the gas chambers; and his sister, who escaped to Italy, died of typhus; and the sister's husband, a prominent doctor in Prague, was killed by German soldiers. He has no family now, except Miriam, and though he grieves particularly for the sister, whom he feels he could have saved if he had reached Italy in time, he has not lost his sense of humor.

The conversation at the party veers from Kentucky and Minnesota to all America, and in a burst of national pride Miriam cries, "We Americans are such nice people," at which her husband quips, "You've been reading too much about yourselves."

After the laughter, Miriam says, "The Jewish youth in Palestine are very much like American youth. They are full of that same daredevil spirit, confidence, know-how. It is because they are born free. They are born as free as Yankees."

I'm deeply moved. In fact, I want to cry, but Mr. Greenwald won't allow it. He suggests I need a drink.

"What kind of drink?" I ask.

"Banana brandy."

"I never heard of it."

He goes to a small cupboard and pours out a tiny glass of a thick oily mixture.

"Aren't all of you going to have some?" I ask.

"We've already had some."

I take a sip. It is very sweet and reeks of bananas.

"Did you make this in your bathtub?" I question, smiling, but there is no response. No one except Miriam has ever heard of our prohibition days when we (the editorial we, I assure you) made gin in our bathtubs.

When I explain it, there is a general shaking of heads and one young girl says: "No, we don't make this in our bathtub. We don't have a bathtub."

This is greeted with appreciative shouts. It is, in spite of my best efforts, the hit of the party.

Soon after, we make our way through the deep dark and the thick mud to a recently completed, corrugated-iron garage where the Passover banquet is to be held. It was planned for out of doors as no dining room on the place could hold all the members of the *kibbutz* and their kith and kin who have come to spend the holiday with them, but since the weather is rainy it has been moved into this mammoth shed. Places for a thousand are laid on bare tables that extend the length of the building. Tin cans, wrapped in white tissue paper, hold Shasta daisies, poppies, and snapdragons, and the high, wide walls are garlanded with palm leaves, tied at the intersections of their stems with bunches of red and yellow field flowers. The effect is charming.

The Greenwalds and I make our way toward the center of the building and sit before bowls and saucers of food. The bowl is crowded with a large piece of baked chicken, cheese, potato salad, and sliced onions, and the side saucer holds cold fish, which, Miriam explains, has a symbolic meaning. At intervals of three or four feet down the middle of the tables are stacks of matzoth.

"Better have a piece of matzo," Miriam suggests. "It will be hours before we eat."

I laugh gaily, thinking she's joking, of course; but, heaven

help me, she isn't joking at all. It *is* hours before we eat . . .
well, at least an hour.

First, there is the reading of the Seder. Being a Baptist,
I don't understand anything about the Seder, especially since
it is read in Hebrew and the only word I recognize during
the entire reading is "Hallelujah."

A rabbi, with the only beard in the gathering, a luxuriant
one covering his chest, begins the reading, and then others
—men, women, and children—take their turns, some reading
a few lines, and others, pages.

I sit demurely for quite a while, listening to the musical
cadence of the strange words, and then I whisper to Miriam,
"What are they reading about?"

"About Moses delivering the children of Israel out of
Egypt."

"Oh."

I continue to listen. A very small boy, not as old as my
ten-year-old, Mr. Big, reads. I am amazed that a child so
young can read Hebrew. It always amazes me when a child
speaks a foreign language, even when it is his own. I begin
to think about Mr. Big. I wonder if he is reading English
yet. Mr. Big goes to a so-called progressive school, and though
he plays an excellent game of gin rummy, he can't read or
write anything to speak of. The principal says not to worry;
it will come to him in time. In time for what, I wonder. In
time to read and sign his will?

The Seder goes on—and on. Again I whisper to Miriam:
"What are they reading about now?"

"They are still reading about Moses delivering the children
of Israel out of Egypt."

"Oh."

I settle back. It has begun to rain again. The drops hitting
the tin roof sound like a barnyard of chickens pecking. The

windows have no panes, and the doors, huge enough for tractors and binders and trucks of hay to roll through, are wide
open. The rain blows in and the garage is full of dampness
and wind and cold.

A man, new to the Hebrew language, reads and makes
mistakes which the audience loves. It rocks with laughter.
Another reads—and another.

I lean over to Miriam: "What are they reading about
now?"

"They're still reading about Moses delivering the children
of Israel out of Egypt."

"It certainly took him a long time."

"Yeah. Forty years."

Everything goes black, but I cling to the edge of the table
and steady myself. . . . And finally, there is singing—joyous,
hilarious, lusty singing.

"This is a feast of freedom," Miriam tells me beneath the
music. "The Passover is not a religious observance with us,
for we are no longer religious; but it is a celebration like the
Fourth of July in the States. Tonight, we rejoice not only because of the deliverance of the Jews from Egypt, but from
Europe and all the world. The Seder no longer ends with
Moses; it comes on down to the present time. You know, it
was almost one year ago today, on May 15th, that Israel became a state. That is why everyone is so happy."

Men go up and down, pouring red wine. One, wearing a
butcher-type apron, has the bearing of a distinguished patriarch.

"What is he doing with that apron on?" I ask.

"He is waiting on tables tonight."

"But he looks like a man of considerable importance."

"He is. He is head of all the field crops of northern Palestine [she means Israel, I'm sure], but this is his *kibbutz.*

He was one of the fifteen original founders of Ginegar twenty-six years ago, so on holidays he comes back and does his share of the work. You will see several elderly men waiting on tables tonight. They all have important positions with the government, but when they return to the *kibbutz* they do their turns at the most menial jobs."

More wine is passed. The singing rises lustily to the rain-thumped roof. Suddenly everybody is singing: "La-la-la . . . la-la-la-la" and I am delighted. I had no idea "la" was Hebrew. Excitedly I join in. "La-la-la . . . la-la-la-la." What fun it is to sing in the language of the country. "La-la-la . . . la-la-la-la."

"The man at the piano was once a famous concert pianist in Berlin," Miriam shouts.

"La-la-la!" I shout back.

At last we get down to eating, but before I have well begun, men come by with giant buckets of hot soup and one pours a brimming cup into my bowl. What a stew—chicken, potato salad, cheese, matzo, onions all floating in the soup. But why not? It would have got mixed sooner or later.

Supper over, the tables are taken down and whisked away as if by a cyclone, and the benches are moved back against the walls. There is to be a program of dancing. The Greenwalds and I sit with a pretty French girl who has recently come to Israel and does not yet know Hebrew.

Miriam spies a visitor smoking a cigarette and becomes very excited. "Look!" she cries to her husband. "Look! there is a man over there smoking a Philip Morris."

"Who isss thisss Philip Morris?" the French girl asks.

"Who is Philip Morris?" Miriam repeats, shocked to her foundations. "Why he's an American cigarette."

"Don't you have American cigarettes?" I ask.

"Not unless someone gives them to us. We have no money

to buy them, but we receive a regular ration of cigarettes manufactured in Israel."

The theme of the dance program is the harvesting of the wheat crop, which is cut at this spring season, and dozens of young girls in bright yellow frocks touched with green whirl about madly until scythed down by a swarm of straw-hatted boys.

The applause is terrific, so terrific indeed that the wheat springs to life again and the harvesters spring again to scything. Then more applause. And more wheat. And more scything. It looks serious. This thing could go on all night.

But, no, the audience itself wants to dance. All one thousand members of it. They form a ring as big as the main tent of Barnum and Bailey circus and they begin to sing and to stamp and to go around in a circle. It is a form of the Hora and is terrific. Two steps forward, one short step back; two steps forward, one short step back. Over and over and over. For one hour, two hours, three hours.

Dancers fall out gasping, new dancers jump in, chanting, the circle never wavering, never slowing down, never stopping.

"What is it they're singing?" I cry.

"It's a prayer for energy," Mr. Greenwald answers, and I'm relieved to hear it.

A little later, I comment, "Everyone looks so happy," and Mr. Greenwald replies, "They look happy because they have no money in their pockets. Having absolutely no money is the greatest step I know to happiness and equality."

I've heard this before, of course, but I still can't take it in. "No money at all?" I repeat weakly.

"Here at Ginegar we get eight pounds a year [about $25] to go on leave, and we can use it any way we please. Some kibbutzim give the money for vacations only; but here, if we

prefer to skip the leave and use the eight pounds for choco-
lates or cigarettes or presents, we can."

Finally the circle balks. Full-grown men and women stagger to the benches, but those not so full grown grab partners
and churn about in a kind of polka. A young girl, hair flying,
holds a partner by one hand and a mouth organ to her lips
with the other. The wailing of the mouth organ is the only
music; but it is enough. If there were a fiddle and drum they
would tear the garage from its cement foundations.

"This can go on until morning," says Mr. Greenwald.
"How about turning in?"

I'm against it, but what can I do?

Passing the kitchen, we see a half-dozen white-haired men
washing and wiping stacks of dishes. They are talking and
laughing as if it were fun.

We stop in the dining room to study the "work sheet" for
the next day. It being the Passover, no one will work unless
assigned to an absolutely necessary job. "Damn it," Miriam
mutters. She is scheduled for the nursery. It makes her furious; she will have to get up at five o'clock and leave her husband sleeping.

He grins at her teasingly. "You can bring me breakfast in
bed," he says.

Others are listed for the barn, kitchen, and dining room.

We collect my bag from the Greenwalds' room and struggle up the ankle of the mountain to the room which has been
assigned me. The mud is so soft and deep that we slip back
faster than we go forward, especially Mr. Greenwald with
the bag, until we catch hands and form a line like Alpine
climbers.

My bed is narrow, my mattress is thin, and there are no
comforts of home, but I sleep soundly until the birds wake
me with their raucous chatter. I dress, get into my boots, col-

lect my washrag, soap, towel, tooth paste and toothbrush, and go forth to find a place to do my morning ablutions. A good many feet from my door, I see a spigot, standing waist high out of the mud. This is it, I decide unhappily. Naturally, I'd like to have something a little more private, a little more refined, but who am I to cavil over a few inconveniences? Obviously not a builder of a national homeland.

I approach the spigot gingerly, and, standing in mud up to my calves, turn on the faucet. This will make more mud, I realize, for there is no basin, no cement trough; but a girl— I mean a woman—must wash. I will clean my teeth first, but what am I to do with the soap and the washrag and the towel while I flourish the brush? I look around for a bench, a chair, a tree, a rock. There is nothing. Absolutely nothing. Only mud. I start to put the soap and rag and towel in the mud; but I cannot. But where shall I put them? I could put the rag down my bosom and the towel around my shoulders, but what about the soap?

There is nothing to do, really, but plow back to the house and leave the rag and soap and towel on the porch while I clean my teeth; then return to the house, deposit the tooth-brush and tooth paste and gather up the rag, soap and towel and return to the spigot. It sounds complicated—and it is. The arrival of three young women, who eye me wide-eyed during all this shuffling to and fro, doesn't help any, either. Nor does the rain that falls gently, but oh, so persistently.

Mud is the only soft thing about life in a *kibbutz*. Miriam tells me so, as she and her husband, who didn't get to eat in bed after all, and I are having breakfast in the regular dining room, but it isn't necessary. I am already convinced, and my hat is off in awe and admiration to those who can take it. We are having a wide variety of things for breakfast: sliced raw cabbage, olives, herring, cheese, eggs, onions, and are talking about a wide variety of subjects.

Mr. Greenwald is doing most of the talking, and his fine, blond head and his slim-fingered hands move in vigorous gestures to emphasize his words. The words don't come easily, for he is speaking in English and he has some trouble with the pronunciation.

"The idea in the beginning of this kind of *kibbutz* was for it to be on a small scale with very intimate relations—really friendly, close relations, but time showed us it was impossible to hold that close circle. It meant that we must keep the membership down to one hundred people, and that was impractical. We must build up the farm, make it greater and greater, and to do that we must have more people. So, the place grew and grew. But the idea of intimate life is still the ideal."

"And the life, I'd say, is still pretty intimate," puts in Miriam. "Everybody knows everything about everybody. There is no such thing as privacy. Don't think it's an easy life."

"No," agrees Mr. Greenwald, "it isn't easy."

"I don't mean the work." Miriam leans forward excitedly to get in her words ahead of Mr. Greenwald. "I mean the relationships. Can you imagine five hundred people living together day and night and everybody trying to please everybody else?"

"A lot of self-control is needed," Mr. Greenwald says, "for people to know what they can wish and what they should not wish. There are some people who are very selfish. . . ."

"Like me and my clothes," Miriam interjects with a toss of her head.

The color of Mr. Greenwald's cheeks deepens, but he ignores the interruption. "And it is very hard for those people to subject their wishes to the good of all. None of us are ingles. . . ."

"Ingles?" I repeat, puzzled.

"You know ingles . . . ingles in heaven."

"Angels," I exclaim.

"I love his English," Miriam says lightly, making a face at him.

"I wish you'd find other things to love beside my English," he retorts and gets up to go to the kitchen for a second cup of coffee.

"He's more co-operative than anybody I know," Miriam tells me hurriedly. "He wants everything equal—absolutely equal. He yells at me about my clothes and I can't part with them." She shoots her bright blue eyes toward the kitchen to see if he is returning; then, not seeing him, rushes ahead: "It's amazing when you know about his upbringing. He was from a very wealthy family. He had a nurse who carried his books to school for him until he was fourteen. Then he turned on possessions, completely turned . . ."

As he looms into sight she breaks off and becomes engrossed in cracking her soft-boiled eggs.

Across the table from us a man is making a most ambitious sandwich with matzoth, sliced hard-boiled eggs, cheese, onions, which he slices himself, and olives. I'm enchanted, and wish Dagwood could see him.

I try to get my mind back to Mr. Greenwald, who is now telling me about the administration of Ginegar. I hear him say something about one hundred and seventy-two members, and that does it.

"Just one hundred and seventy-two members? I thought there were five hundred people living here?"

"There are, but they are not all members. Some people are here to train; they come as groups to learn how to live together and how to farm before they settle in their own *kibbutz,* and then there are a lot of people here who have not yet been elected to membership. To be a member of the *kibbutz*, you must be a candidate for a year or more, and if during that time you are a good worker and have good relationships then you are admitted to membership. To have good relationships is really more important than to be a good worker."

"You, of course, are a member," I say.

"Yes."

"And you?" I turn toward Miriam.

"No."

There is an awkward silence for a fraction of a minute; then Mr. Greenwald goes on: "The *kibbutz* belongs to the members—they decide on everything. There is a head committee—the committee of secretariat—and then subcommittees; a work committee in charge of distribution of man power; an education committee for schools; a health committee; a building committee; a personal relations committee—this is a very important committee.

"The small committees try to settle all the problems that come before them, but if they can't settle them, then they are brought for settlement before the members. There is a closed meeting once a week of the members. Those problems that have already been settled are just announced—all must be mentioned; but those that are not settled are then worked out. There is also a meeting once a week of everybody, all those who want to come, members and nonmembers."

"I think I understand it," I say.

"I don't believe it," Mr. Greenwald answers flatly—just like a man. "When you get back to the United States you'll realize you don't know anything."

It's a ghastly thought, but I shrug it off. I know I know enough not to join a *kibbutz* at my age.

16. "The Spirit"

From Ginegar I returned to Nahalal to join the Dayans.
Ruth had said she wanted to take me to a *kibbutz* of American immigrants so I could see how they stood up to the hard-
ships of a new country, but when I met her and Moshe they
told me they did not have enough "petrol" for the trip. Looking chagrined, Moshe confessed that he had left his work
card, entitling him to a certain amount of gasoline a month,
in Jerusalem and he could not get any without it. He had
driven to the supply point for the Nahalal area and put up
an argument, but in spite of being a hero and the governor
of Israeli Jerusalem, he had been turned down flatly.

I must be satisfied with a trip to Timourim, a new *kibbutz*
close by, which was, according to Ruth, in the "rough stage."
And I'd say it was in the "rough stage"; it was about in the
roughest stage you can imagine.

It was on top of a mountain, overlooking the Plain of Esdraelon and all the other villages in that part of the country.
Halfway up we had to get out of the car and walk, for the
unpaved road was too steep and too deep in mud. It was difficult. To lift my own weight up, and up, and up, from
boulder to boulder, was bad enough; but I again had on those
giant boots; and again it was raining, and this time sideways.

The mountaintop was as flat as a tennis court, and not
much bigger, and muddy except where big, gray boulders
heaved above the ground. There was no grass, no trees, no
shrubs. It looked as raw as raw liver.

There were four unpainted barracks of sixteen rooms each; a low building, also unpainted, housing the dining room, kitchen, and pantry; and a few one-room structures of cement foundation blocks and canvas walls.

The floor in the dining room was several inches deep in mud, and the wooden tables were bare and spotted with grease, but there was the sniffing smell of onions and garlic and other good things in the damp air. A group of boys and girls were cooking what they called a potpourri on a wood-burning stove in the adjoining kitchen. It was their main meal for the day.

"What's in it?" I asked, peering into the big, black pot. "Everything."

Ruth and I began to talk to a rugged-faced individual from South Africa. I wanted to know why they chose this inaccessible, rocky, God-forsaken, jumping-off place for a *kibbutz*. It wasn't what they wanted, he answered, but there was a long list of groups waiting for land and it was either this or the Negeb. Then, too, the mountaintop is a very strategic position from a military viewpoint. And in addition to the mountaintop, they have close to three thousand dunums of land in the valley.

"Beautiful land," the South African says enthusiastically.

To cultivate it will mean a two-and-a-quarter mile walk down the mountain in the mornings and a two-and-a-quarter mile walk up in the evenings, but "what is a walk?" he asks. Aplenty, I want to say, but I restrain myself. After all, I'm not going to cultivate the land.

This South African with fifty-five other fellow countrymen began the trek to this journey's end a good many years ago in their native country. They were interested in coming to Palestine and living in a *kibbutz*, so they went to a farm in South Africa to learn about agriculture and the communal type of living. Having learned all they could there, they came in small groups to Palestine and "expanded."

After moving about almost as much as the children of Israel under Moses, fourteen of the original group finally joined up with immigrants from Bulgaria, Rumania, and other countries to form the *kibbutz* of Timourim. Seventy strong, they arrived on their mountain peak on June 21st, 1948. There were six married couples, eighteen girls, and forty bachelors.

"There was nothing here?" I ask.

"Nothing."

"It must have been depressing," I say, looking out of the rain-smeared window at the mud and rocks.

"Oh, no!" he cries. "Not if you have the spirit."

"I suppose not," I admit, but doubtfully.

"Of course, at first it wasn't very pleasant. We slept out in the open and it was terribly cold for six or seven weeks. We are very high up here, you know."

"Yes, I know."

"We had no water, except for cooking, and we had to go to Nahalal to wash. . . . And a funny thing, we have no water now, either. Our pump broke down just before the Passover holidays and we haven't been able to get it fixed."

Being a countrywoman I am full of sympathy. I have had pumps break down many times just before holidays and I wonder for the hundredth time how do pumps know holidays.

I hear music from the kitchen that sounds familiar. The half-dozen or more cooks are singing in Hebrew a hymn I've heard many times. Can it possibly be, "O Come, All Ye Faithful"?

It can be and is.

"I always thought it was a Baptist hymn," I say.

"Perhaps it is," says the South African, smiling, "but we make it kosher."

When the last note dies down we return to the problem of building a *kibbutz* from scratch. I want to know what they did first.

"Well, we first built trenches and air-raid shelters—the War was on, you know. Then we built a lean-to for the cows. We had started a small dairy at Einsava, where some of us were before we came here, and we had four cows and two calves. Then we built coops for the chickens. We had started a poultry section, too, at Einsava and we had one hundred and fifty chickens. Next, we put up the barracks. They are prefabricated and we put up all the walls at one time."

"Where are they prefabricated?"

"Here in Israel. We import the lumber, and a plywood factory here prefabricates them; but the roofs are tile, and they took a good many weeks."

"I can imagine." My mouth is wide open with amazement and admiration. "How did you know how to build? Are you carpenters?"

"There were two of us who had done some building before, and the Jewish Agency sent two or three carpenters who helped us for a few days."

He begins to smile and says, pleased: "You know we have here one bachelor of science, two university students, one qualified electrician, and several shopkeepers."

"But they don't know how to build—and farm."

"They learn," he answers simply.

At present, most of the income for the *kibbutz* comes from outside work. The Jewish Agency is paying them by the tree to plant a forest on the mountainside. This help will stop as soon as they begin working full time on their land. After ten months, they have a few hundred dunums in hay and are selling from sixty to seventy liters of milk and two hundred eggs a day to the co-operative.

Ruth and I start the slippery journey down the mountain, but are called back to visit a girl from Pennsylvania. She is pregnant and hasn't got up today, the South African explains, but he is sure she will be delighted to see someone from the States. She and her husband live in one of those one-room affairs—half cement blocks and half canvas—just below the rim of the mountain.

After knocking and being invited in, we step through the door to find the Pennsylvanian and her husband lying in a double bed, reading, while the rain and wind sweep in through a wide, open space between the blocks and canvas.

"We are taking advantage of the holiday to stay in bed," the girl says, smiling. "It is so wonderful not to have to get up."

"But aren't you afraid you'll drown?" I ask.

She laughs gaily and says, "It is nothing."

And that, no doubt, is what the South African means by "the spirit."

17. The governor is a citizen

"How is your luck?" Moshe Dayan asks me.

"Well, I wouldn't advise you to rest on it," I answer.

He and Ruth and their two children and I are beginning our trip back to Jerusalem via Tel Aviv and we have too little gas and too few tires. The rear tire is leaking and there is no spare. The Colonel is very doubtful about our reaching Jerusalem.

"If you hold the tire up," he says to me, "I'll try to make the gas last."

I keep my fingers crossed, but the tire sinks lower and lower. At every town that boasts a military barracks, we stop, hoping to get a new tire, and if not a new tire, at least, air. We do get air, but no tire. And no gas.

After the third or fourth unsuccessful try, Moshe reappears with a bewildered look on his broad face. "What do you know?" he asks, "That man in there knew my name. He said to me, 'Why, Colonel Dayan, you've had two new tires within the last six months.'" Moshe shakes his head in puzzlement. "How do you suppose he knew that?"

His surprise is endearing. He, with a black patch over one eye and a colonel's insignia on his shoulders, is, no doubt, one of the best-known figures in Israel, yet he does not seem to suspect it.

We limp into Tel Aviv and go to that dining room of the Kaethe Dan Hotel, overhanging the sea, for a quick snack. Moshe orders a roast-beef sandwich and when it arrives on matzoth, he is outdone. He is not Orthodox and he dislikes matzoth violently; and, like any man who is served the food he does not like, he complains. But there is no hope for him. For the eight days of the Passover celebration there is no other bread in Israel; the bakeries are not allowed to bake anything but matzoth.

"But why matzoth?" I ask, having wanted to ask it for days.

"When Moses left Egypt he left in such a rush he left without yeast, and matzoth are bread without yeast—unleavened bread, you know," Ruth explains.

Moshe holds the big sandwich with both hands and bites into it. The matzoth crumble in a hundred pieces down his khaki blouse. Ruth and the children and I laugh, but Moshe is not amused.

"The next time you cross the lines into Arab Jerusalem will you bring me back a loaf of bread?" he asks me.

"Maybe, if I'm allowed to cross the lines." I say it teasingly, for permission to cross the Israeli lines in Jerusalem is in Moshe's hands, and the last time I tried to cross I was refused. I had wanted to go to the Jerusalem airport, which is on the Arab side, to meet Jean and Ace Miller, whom I had visited in Athens in 1947, but, not knowing they were arriving until the night before, I was able to give only a twelve-hour notice instead of the required twenty-four.

Still, optimistic by nature, I had hoped to make the crossing. I got up bright and early and came down to breakfast. A moment after I was seated an Israeli corporal appeared at my side, touched his hand to his cap, and said, "I beg to report: A, Colonel and Mrs. Miller have been cleared; B, you do not have permission to cross the lines."

And with that he touched his cap again, clicked his heels and departed.

I was furious. "Who do they think I am—a spy?" I asked the roommate. "What do they think I'm going to do—smuggle ammunition to the Arabs?" The roommate tried to quiet me. The corporal was just following orders.

When I was beginning to simmer down, General Riley, who had spent the night in Jerusalem on his way from Tel Aviv to Damascus, where he was struggling to get an armistice signed between Israel and Syria, came over to our table to say good morning.

"How're you feeling?" he asked me.

"I'm mad. I've just been refused permission by the Israelis to cross the lines. All I wanted to do was to meet two old friends at the airport, but no, I can't go. I'm a bad girl."

"Keep your shirt on," said the General. "I'll fix it up."

And off he strode as only a general of the U.S. Marines

can stride and I folded my napkin in its paper envelope, gathered up my gloves, pocketbook, notebook, and pencil. It was nearing nine o'clock and that was the hour of the crossing.

In about five minutes, the General opened the door slightly, poked in his face, which was very red, and barked: "There is a war going on," and slammed the door shut again.

And that was that. I didn't cross the lines.

But when I refer teasingly to the incident now, Moshe does not respond. His brown eye remains somber, his Slavic face, impassive. Instantly I realize that if I fail to live up to all the rules on my next crossing request, I will be turned down just as promptly as before.

The sandwich disposed of, Moshe goes once again to see about a tire and gas, the children play on an open terrace, and Ruth and I sit and talk. Or rather Ruth talks. There is the rusting hulk of a ship just offshore, festering with angry waves, and Ruth tells me its story.

It is the *Altalena,* which the Irgun brought filled with guns and ammunition to the coast of Israel, a little above Tel Aviv, shortly after Israel had declared itself an independent state.

"The government ordered the ship turned over to them," Ruth relates. "Naturally, the government couldn't have just anyone bringing in arms. They told the terrorists they must hand it over, but the terrorists refused and began to unload it. Then the government sent Moshe to stop them. There was fighting, stiff fighting. Most of the crew abandoned the ship and escaped, but some stayed on and brought the ship down here to Tel Aviv and it grounded."

Ruth grows excited telling about it and her words tumble out, faster and faster. "There was shooting back and forth . . . and shouting. The lunatic leader had a loudspeaker and he kept shouting that the ship was full of explosives and would blow up the whole of Tel Aviv. Everybody was scared to death. . . . Confusion . . . noise . . . but nothing happened. The ship caught on fire . . . not many casualties . . . maybe eight."

When Moshe returns we don't ask him what luck he has had; we don't want to embarrass him; but evidently there is no new tire, for we proceed carefully and slowly toward Jerusalem.

Along the side of the road a large, new water main is being laid from Tel Aviv to Jerusalem. During the War, when the Israeli part of Jerusalem was blockaded by the Arabs from the rest of Israel, the water line to the city was cut and the residents had to depend on the few wells that were in the city.

"We don't expect ever to let that happen again," Ruth declares, eying the freshly upturned earth. "Why, for weeks, we had only one liter of water per person."

I have no idea what a liter is, but I can tell it is nothing to wash in.

"The council requisitioned all the wells and sent the water through the town in a lorry. The women stood in queues in the streets for hours to get just four cupfuls."

Her face with its high cheekbones and flat planes fills with sadness. "It took great bravery to go through the streets to supply the water. Many drivers were killed."

We leave the plain and begin to climb the hills before Jerusalem. They don't look as white and bare now as on my first trip this way. Spring has pushed its way into them, stuffing wild flowers between the rocks and spraying the acacia bushes with yellow dust.

Moshe stops the car and we run up and down the steep

banks gathering armfuls of everything—even, I regret to say, wild onion tops. Or are they garlic? I know King Solomon never smelled like one of these. Nor any lily.

18. The rock of three faiths

It is Good Friday of the Roman Catholic church, and though none of the American delegation, except Joe Reeves, is a Catholic, Frazer, Bob Yount, Joe, and I cross over into Old Jerusalem to follow the procession of the Stations of the Cross. These are among the holiest of the Holy Places and they fill the thinking and talking of the Jerusalem committee of the Commission during practically all of their waking hours; but today we are not trying to solve anything, we simply go to sight-see.

The walled Old City, except for its churches, magnificent mosques, and tiptoeing minarets, is a mass of crooked, decrepit, shoulder-to-shoulder shops sprawling over hills, smelly with age, squalid with centuries, and yet teeming, swarming, bursting with living. Innumerable slits of streets, cobbled and frequently roofed over, poke through the mass, breaking into steps when the going gets too steep.

There is no riding through the streets; it is all you can do to walk. This Good Friday they are packed as tightly as cans of dog food. There are donkeys hauling stones; men carrying long poles on their shoulders seesawing with bunches of bananas; women holding thin, gaudily printed veils across their mouths and noses; women stringing gold coins through their black hair and hanging one or two at the tips of their noses; women balancing, on their heads, boxes of milk bottles, rolls of rugs, trays of green almonds; and little girls begging . . . little girls begging . . . little girls begging. . . .

The shops are brimming over with vegetables, breads, cakes, and lambs. Coming out of Israel, where, in spite of the lushness of the fields and the substantial meals of the *kibbutzim*, I am always conscious of the scarcity of green foods, the variety in these bins in Old Jerusalem amazes me. The white mounds of cauliflower, the red stacks of tomatoes, the emerald ricks of spinach, beans, lettuce, kale, greens; the purple bins of eggplant.

The cheese suks, too, stretch at their seams. The proprietors stand in the street and scrub with brushes dipped in dingy water, but, I trust, no soap, small white cheeses, resembling our Philadelphia cream cheese, and stack them, dripping, on narrow shelves.

On an oilstove before his door, a chef is creating a concoction of rice and nuts and meat that makes my mouth water, and I suggest stopping and having a helping.

"I had a friend who ate that once and he was in bed for a month," Frazer says quietly.

A baker shoves, with a long-handled, hoelike implement, loaves of bread into century-old ovens. The aroma of the baking bread saturates the narrow street. Cobblers sew slippers, butchers show heads of sheep, donkey drivers shout, "Oyah! Oyah! Oyah!"

We are late for the first Station of the Cross, and the second, and the third, and the fourth, and the fifth. There is nothing to do, we decide, but take a short cut to the Church of the Holy Sepulcher, built over the spot where Christ is supposed to have been buried, and see the procession arrive and enter the church. For the next fifteen or twenty minutes, we tear around corners, slip over cobbles as rounded and slick as turned-over bowls, and streak up steps which are cobbled, too, and seem never to stop. I'm panting like a freight engine. Joe takes one hand and Bob the other and, between them, they half-pull and half-swing me along.

We make it. Standing in the courtyard of the Holy Sepulcher, we see twenty or thirty young men marching toward us carrying a huge cross of light-colored wood, no doubt olive. They stop in the courtyard and hitch the cross a bit higher to please a photographer who is taking pictures. A small boy in a black coat and khaki shorts is weeping. I wonder if it is for the Man of Galilee, or has he stubbed his toe?

General Riley appears before the church door, his ruddy Irish blond head towering above a dainty, dark-complected figure with a goatee, dressed in a form-fitting black coat and a wide-brimmed, little-crowned derby hat that looks like a miniature houseboat on the Ohio. They pose for pictures, the General and the Catholic Father grinning good-naturedly into space.

Our old friend of Palm Sunday, Brother Francis, joins us and, staring at General Riley, murmurs, "What a guy . . . what a guy!"

He offers to show us a church which stands near the Holy Sepulcher, but it is locked and no one answers his ring. "Probably everyone is meditating like myself," he says and gives me a wink which I have no idea what to do with. A wink confuses me at any time, but from a monk. . . .

We go to lunch at the American Colony. A dapper young Arab approaches Frazer at the end of lunch and invites us to go with him to visit the famous Dome of the Rock. His name is Nassib Bulos, and he is the liaison officer between the Palestine Arabs and the Commission. He speaks English with an Oxford accent, is slim and beautifully groomed in tailor-made Western clothes, has curly black hair and dark eyes that glow in a friendly fashion behind glasses.

Frazer is skeptical about our accepting the invitation. This

is the Moslem's Sabbath, he points out, and there will be
many people at prayers. He thinks it is dangerous for me, a
woman, to go into a mosque at such a sacred time.

Nassib Bulos assures him I will be perfectly safe; he
wouldn't have asked me otherwise. Frazer gives in, but before the hour of the visit, he gets a fever and makes the three
o'clock crossing back to Israeli Jerusalem. I am touched; if I
am to be mobbed he doesn't, evidently, want to see it.

The Dome of the Rock, sometimes called the Mosque of
Omar, is a magnificent eight-sided building, crowned with a
dome of lovely proportions. It stands in an open paved space
as large as four city blocks, and blots out with its off-white
walls a considerable portion of the blue sky.

Minarets, slim as lighthouses, but much more beautiful,
are on the four corners of the square, and, as we enter it, mu-
ezzin (the men who summon the Moslems to prayer) are
standing on the little balconies that circle the minarets near
their tapering tops and singing out the call that begins: "In
the name of Allah, the Merciful, the Compassionate . . ."

I wish I knew all of it, but Nassib Bulos tells me no more
and there is no other Arab near by to ask.

We do not go immediately into the Dome of the Rock, but
enter a building on the side of the square and climb stairs
to the apartment of an official who serves us coffee and sweet
cakes. Awkwardly we stand about, waiting for somebody or
something. (It doesn't seem polite to ask.) I stand at the
window and look into the square at the long-robed Arabs
hurrying toward the mosque. Nassib Bulos joins me.

"You are a Moslem," I say.

"No, I'm not."

Though I don't say so, I'm disappointed. I can't get accustomed to Arabs' not being Moslems.

"I suppose you're Catholic?" I persist.

He smiles. "No. I'm a member of the Church of England
—an Episcopalian."

It's too much. Whoever heard of an Arab Episcopalian?

"I remember rather vividly my introduction to Christianity," he goes on pleasantly. "A sweet-faced missionary
taught me to sing:

> I am h-a-p-p-y,
> I am h-a-p-p-y,
> I know I am,
> I'm sure I am,
> I'm h-a-p-p-y."

As he sings, I'm convulsed. He, with such an air of importance, sounds too ridiculous chanting this jingle.

The somebody for whom we've been waiting arrives and
announces that we can now visit the Dome of the Rock. After
all of Frazer's concern, the prayers are finished and the
mosque practically empty.

It is stupendous and overpowering. So much has happened
on this spot. The lines of the old carol, though they are not
really applicable, keep singing through my mind:

> The hopes and fears of all the years
> Are met in thee tonight.

For this place of the Dome of the Rock is sacred to three religious groups—Jewish, Christian, and Moslem. And though
only the Moslems worship here now, the dim, cool interior,
touched with tinted dust where the sun spears through high,
stained-glass windows, is aquiver with memories, even with
ghosts. It is the place that best typifies for me the complex-
ity of the Jerusalem problem.

The mosque is built around a huge, naked rock that sprawls
for fifty-eight feet over the bare, dusty ground. In a building

so exquisite, the rock is shocking, almost indecent, for it looks just like a common, everyday run-of-the-mine boulder.

Yet, what a history it has! H. V. Morton, in his book, *In the Steps of the Master* writes:

"This is the rock that formed part of the threshing-floor of Araunah the Jebusite. You remember, perhaps, how David, tempted by Satan, forced on Israel a thing that nomad people hate more than anything: a census. And how David's heart smote him after he had numbered the people, and how he admitted his sorrow to the Lord and confessed that he had 'done very foolishly.' The Lord, however, in order to punish him visited a great pestilence upon his people:

'And when the angel stretched out his hand upon Jerusalem to destroy it, the Lord repented him of the evil, and said to the angel that destroyed the people, It is enough: stay now thine hand. And the angel of the Lord was by the threshingplace of Araunah the Jebusite.'

"So David, in token of thankfulness that the plague should have been stayed, decided to build an altar to the Lord on the rock where the angel had stood . . . and he climbed the uninhabited mountain that frowned above his town to the spot where the Jebusite used to thresh his wheat; and there he bought the threshing-floor for fifty shekels of silver."

This was a thousand years before Christ, but from that moment, as Mr. Morton says: "Mount Moriah was destined to bear the Temple that was fated to form the character of the Jews, that was to bind them together in remote lands even after it had become dust and ashes."

For, when Solomon ascended his father's throne in 966 B.C., he began the task of building a temple around the rock. It took him seven and a half years, and yet it was not a big temple; it was only a hundred feet long by about thirty feet wide. But as Israel grew the Temple grew and became more beautiful, until, in 586 B.C., Nebuchadnezzar burned it to the ground. It was rebuilt fifty years later, but it was not nearly so fine as Solomon's Temple, and the Ark of the Covenant with the cherubim was no longer there.

Herod the Great, the father of Herod Antipas under whom Christ was crucified, decided to restore the Temple to its original magnificence. He started the reconstruction in 20 B.C. and it continued through his lifetime and through the entire reign of Herod Antipas. Jesus must have seen it being built every time he came into Jerusalem. Once he referred to it, according to the Gospel of St. John. It was finally completed, thirty-four years after the crucifixion, and just eight years later it, too, was burned.

Then along came the Moslems. To them the Rock was sacred because they believed Mohammed ascended from it to heaven on the back of his winged steed, el-Baruk; and embedded in the Rock are the "fingerprints" of the angel Gabriel, who had to press with all his might upon the Rock to keep it from ascending to heaven with Mohammed. In 637 they cleared the debris that had collected on it and built a small, temporary house of worship. Then, in 691, the Ommiad Caliph, Abd-el-Malik, built the present mosque.

And though the Rock looks just as a rock should, its setting is beautiful, very beautiful. A row of columns, meeting in semicircular arches, fences it in; and above the arches is a wide band of Byzantine mosaics on a field of gold; and still higher, above the deep band, are sixteen stained-glass windows; and above the stained-glass windows, the heart of the dome, ninety-eight feet above the Rock, decorated in stucco figures that are gilded and painted in soft, rare colors. I stand, gazing up, until my neck gets a crick in it, and my jaws feel locked.

Beyond this inner circle of columns, supporting the dome,

there is another circle of columns and beyond these columns the outside wall, which is embellished with more mosaics and a heavenly spread of blue material written over in gold with inscriptions from the Koran.

On one side of the Rock some stairs lead down to a cave which holds the places of prayer of Abraham and Elijah and David and Solomon. I am shocked to find them in a mosque, for I had always thought of these Bible characters as belonging exclusively to Christians and Jews, though, to be perfectly honest, I never considered the Jews' claims seriously.

"But no," says Nassib Bulos, "the Moslems worship the same Biblical heroes as the Christians and Jews. The Moslem even believes Jesus is a great prophet and have a deep reverence for Him. They just think Mohammed is greater, that's all."

Mohammed's place of prayer is also in the cave, and above it, in the Rock, is a recess which was formed, so the story goes, by the stone receding so that Mohammed wouldn't bump his head when getting up from his knees.

There is much more to see, of course—two hairs from the Prophet's head, and a lance and banners; but the hour is late, thank goodness, and we must hurry to make the crossing back to Israeli Jerusalem. I am bone tired and mentally dazed. It is too much to begin a day with the Stations of the Cross and end it in Mohammed's prayer closet.

19. "I am a stranger here"

OUR SOCIAL LIFE had a brief spurt. One evening we invited Ruth and Moshe Dayan, and Ella Japhet of the Israeli Foreign Office, and Mike Comay (a former South African and

don of Cambridge) who also works in the Israeli Foreign
Office, which, incidentally, is made up of the very smartest
people, to have dinner with us.

After dinner we went dancing at The Eden, and to everyone's surprise, including Mrs. Japhet's, it was discovered that
Mr. Comay was as beautiful a dancer as Fred Astaire. (Of
course this could have been because he was "there" and Fred
Astaire was in Hollywood.) For hours he maneuvered gracefully about that tiny floor and out in the entrance hall and
in and around tables and chairs, and when the place closed
at the first stroke of midnight, according to the rules, he
mopped his wet brow and unburdened himself to the roommate: "You know, we Jews need to play more. We in Israel
take life much too seriously. We are too tense, too high-strung;
we don't have the gift like you Americans to relax and enjoy
ourselves."

"You seem to have done all right tonight," said the roommate, smiling.

He grinned boyishly and would have blushed, I am sure,
if the blood had not already been pounding in his full cheeks.

I took to heart his desire to relax and spent considerable time
weeks later when I was some distance from Jerusalem fashion-
ing a telegram: "Come, come, come, Comay," but at the last
minute I didn't send it for fear that by then he had Israel
again on his shoulders and would think me flip.

Then one evening we went to a party at Government
House. Now, Government House is no night spot. It is the
magnificent mansion built by the British during the mandate to house His Honor, the High Commissioner of Palestine,
but now, of course, there is no High Commissioner and it is
occupied by U.N. observers. Atop the highest hill around
Jerusalem, in neither Israeli nor Arab territory, but U.N., it
has a glorious view of practically the whole country.

To get to it at night from Israeli Jerusalem is a major operation. First, you have to get permission from the Jerusalem powers; then the lines must be crossed at specified hours, and midnight is the latest returning hour; and last, a bumpy, winding, rutty road, which sometimes exploded with mines, had to be negotiated.

Another evening, or rather late afternoon, we went to the American consulate over which our United States Consul, Bill Burdette, presided. It was on the Saturday before Easter and Bill was entertaining at a cocktail party for Ambassador and Mrs. McDonald and their daughter Barbara, who were spending the week end in Israeli Jerusalem. Mrs. McDonald and Barbara had come with the hope of attending the Easter services in Old Jerusalem, and Mr. McDonald had come along, evidently, just for the ride, for knowing himself *persona non grata* to the Arabs, he would make no effort to cross over into Arab Palestine.

Our consulate in Israeli Jerusalem is a modest building, sitting back from the street in a grove of trees. On the first floor are the offices and on the second a large living room with white plaster walls, a fireplace at the far end, and a half-dozen pieces of furniture. It is monastic in its simplicity.

The afternoon was slow getting under way. Mr. McDonald drinks nothing stronger than orange juice, and hasn't what I'd call a "party heart." He likes to lean against the mantel and talk seriously about Israel, and that, naturally, makes all his "hirelings" feel they should lean against the mantel, too, and talk seriously about Israel.

Fortunately for the party, the Ambassador felt I needed extracurricular coaching on certain matters and invited me into an adjoining room, and by the time we returned to the main "salon," the roommate had everyone singing "Lili Marlene" at the top of his voice. Even gentle Mrs. McDonald was in the circle and singing, though I won't go so far as to say at the top of her voice. After "Lili Marlene" there was "Marching through Georgia," which necessitated my leaving the room again, and then "You Take the High Road and I'll Take the Low Road," and "I'll See You Again," and all the other old favorites of the roommate.

The singing went on and on long after the departure of the Ambassador and Mrs. McDonald, and, alas, long after the dinner hour at the King David. When the roommate starts singing, he never tires; after all, he sings on only one note.

Finally, though, hunger prevailed and we thankfully accepted the invitation of Allan Fletcher, the code clerk of the Commission, and of one or two others to have supper at the bachelor quarters of the members of the U.S. consulate. Allan insisted he had spent the afternoon baking a big cake.

So, dismissing the cars, for the house the bachelors occupied was just a few blocks from the consulate and the night was brass-bright with moonlight, we marched, singing, through the streets. If it had been Christmas eve instead of Easter eve and we had been caroling instead of singing "It's a Long Way to Tipperary," it would have been better. But it wasn't our fault it was April instead of December.

While Allan Fletcher and a coworker cooked, the rest of us danced. Girls had come from Haifa, Tel Aviv, and other spots to spend Easter in Jerusalem, but still there weren't nearly enough to go around. At one time, the competition for even me grew warm. I was dancing with Bussy when the roommate, of all people, broke in on us, and Bussy turned upon him, his own boss, remember, not to mention my husband, and snarled: "You just wait; I'll get even with you for this!"

Toward midnight, Allan in a big, white apron and big,

wide smile appeared and announced, "Supper is served," and we trooped into the kitchen and helped ourselves out of the pan to the most delicious pork and beans, cooked in the Boston manner, and fat Vienna sausage out of cans from the United States, and a wonderful mixed green salad.

Leaving a good bit later to make our way on foot back to the King David, we were shocked to find an Israeli soldier waiting at the door. We shouldn't have been shocked, of course, for there was always one guard and frequently six somewhere around, but the party had lasted so long that we had simply forgotten about security.

The roommate was apologetic. "I had no idea you were still waiting," he said.

"It's perfectly O.K.," the guard answered, and, with his Sten gun on his back pointing almost straight up to the moon-washed sky, he started off down the middle of the road.

Sheep-like we fell in behind him. There were five of us and we were all dead tired, especially Millie Smith, one of the secretariat, and I, who had danced steadily, except for the supper break, for five hours. In fact, my feet felt as if they had been crushed with stone mallets, and here I was in three-inch heels and a few straps plodding down an unpaved road lumpy with small rocks.

For a long time we trudged in a dazed fashion behind the guard. Wouldn't he ever come to the King David? Why, the whole of Jerusalem had never seemed this big.

"He must be taking us the long way," Millie suggested.

"Is there a long way?" I asked, terrified.

"There always is, isn't there?"

This sounded irrefutable, and on we struggled in silence.

Then, suddenly, Millie gave a cry: "Look! Look! There is the King David over there to the right. We're going away from it as fast as we can."

We looked where she pointed, and, sure enough, looming against the pale horizon, was the tall outline of the King David, and we were headed in the opposite direction.

"Stop the guard!" I cried, like a woman being robbed. "Stop the guard!"

Joe Reeves whistled shrilly and, instantly, the guard wheeled and rushed back to us.

"Look," we said, "there is the King David back over there toward the right, and here you are leading us to the left." He looked. "That the King David?" he asked.

"Certainly, it's the King David. What do you think it is?" Slowly he shook his head. "I don't know," he answered quietly. "I am a stranger here. I was just transferred from Tel Aviv to Jerusalem this afternoon."

This, we unanimously voted, was the guard to end all guards, and the party to end all parties.

20. Easter in Old Jerusalem

CHURCH BELLS RINGING INSISTENTLY waked me Easter morning. With a swoop I jumped out of bed. My one thought was that we had overslept; the hotel had failed to wake us.

A few fortunate members of the Commission and other government representatives were supposed to cross into Old Jerusalem at six o'clock through the Jaffa Gate to celebrate the pontifical Mass in the Church of the Holy Sepulcher. The famous gate is in the section of the walls of the Old City facing Israeli Jerusalem and has been closed since the beginning of the Arab–Jewish troubles; but this morning the Arabs were opening it as a special courtesy to the foreign visitors.

My eyes rushed to my watch on the bedside table. I saw the hands at five after seven. . . . Oh, stars, how awful! How perfectly awful! We had missed the crossing. We had missed the pontificial Mass. I began to weep and to mourn. "Mark, we've missed the crossing. We've overslept. . . . Nobody waked us. . . ."

He turned slowly and peered at me out of heavy eyes. (We had gone to bed just a few hours before.) "Did you say we have missed the crossing?"

"Yes, nobody waked us." I began to pace up and down the floor. "We can't possibly make the Mass now."

"We can't make the Mass now?"

"No, we can't possibly make it."

"You're sure?"

"Yes. I'm sure."

"Thank God." And having so said, he turned over and instantly went back to sleep.

I couldn't stand it. To be so close to Old Jerusalem on Easter and then to miss it. What a tragedy! I walked to the window. I would at least look out at the creamy walls; the slender minarets slipping skyward like expensive, fancy-shaped bottles holding white wine; the domes, the spires, the wavering ridges of old roofs.

The sky was an ever so pale blue, as if drained out with the long night, but low on the horizon, behind the spires and steeples and the towers and the minarets, were small streaks of bedroom-slipper pink. It seemed early to me, early as new dawn, but then I'm no connoisseur of the dawn. . . . Still, how could it be after seven and look so definitely before six?

Excited, I ran back to the bedside table and grabbed up my watch. It had been turned around. Instead of five minutes after seven, it had been seven minutes to five!

I pounced upon the poor, dear roommate, and as I pounced,

Rosa, the maid, arrived with rolls and coffee. Quickly we ate, bathed, dressed, and dashed down the stairs and out to the sidewalk in front of the King David. Other members of the American delegation were there, but no Israeli guards to show us the way. We knew we first had to cross the Israeli lines at some point in the valley and then climb a narrow path up the hill to the gate, but where was that point?

Suddenly there was a roar of engines from a nearby corner and a short parade of jeeps and government cars with tossing flags flashed into view and out again.

"Hell, were we supposed to have been on that corner?" the roommate asked.

Nobody knew.

"Hell, do you suppose they have left us?"

We supposed they had. We had better jump into our car and try to overtake them. We jumped, stepped on the gas, and tore down the avenue. At the corner we had to slow up to let two women go by. They were Mrs. McDonald and Barbara.

"Where do you think you're going?" called the roommate.

"We were supposed to meet Bill Burdette here on this corner at ten minutes of six, but we're late and we are afraid he has left us."

"He couldn't!" we chorused. "He wouldn't!"

Who ever heard of a consul leaving the wife and daughter of his ambassador?

We streaked on, trying to overtake the official cars, but we couldn't find them. Now it was five minutes of six. We had just as well give up, but at that second we saw the car of the French minister returning from the rendezvous. We yelled at him to lead us to the spot. He nodded, swoshed about, and in another minute was gesturing to us to get out of the car and walk down a short, dead-end street, piled with debris.

Crumbled stones, slabs of plaster, rolls of barbed wire, and iron pipe were scattered everywhere. I detoured to miss a small mountain of stucco and the roommate barked: "Be careful! Stoop, this place is full of mines!"

The end of the street was blocked with blown-up buildings. We could find no outlet anywhere. We were doomed, that was all, to miss the crossing and the mass. We turned to climb back up the hill and met two Israeli soldiers. So far as we could see, they had simply popped up out of the debris.

"Oh," we cried, relieved. "Where is the place to cross?"

"It is now too late," the senior soldier snapped.

"What do you mean too late?" asked the roommate, looking at his wrist watch. "It is now one minute after six."

"Yes, but the crossing was at six." With his hand, he slapped an open piece of paper on which our names were written. "It says here, black on white, the crossing is at six."

"But one minute after. . . ." The roommate choked. This was too much.

Slowly we turned and retraced our steps up the littered street.

"Maybe we can make the Mandelbaum crossing," Bob said suddenly.

Then we remembered for the first time that just a few had been given permission to cross at Jaffa; the majority were going through at Mandelbaum. We began looking frantically for a car. Ours had left when it put us out and now there was none in sight. Maybe, at the King David. . . . We began to run in the direction of the King David. A United Nations jeep, without sides or top and painted white, came by. We waved it down.

At the corner near the King David, Mrs. McDonald and

Barbara were still waiting. We hoisted them in. The jeep was now packed to overflowing. I was sitting on an elevated seat on the side, the roommate was clinging to the wind-shield. This was not the proper manner, I felt sure, to go to a pontifical Mass on Easter morning, but. . . .

We slowed down at the King David only long enough to see that there was no car at the curb; then dashed on to Mandelbaum. The barriers had not yet lifted. Cars, jeeps, trucks, and station wagons were backed up a quarter of a mile, waiting for the signal to move. The Israeli soldiers were ready at their road block, but something was holding up the Arabs. A young Jew climbed up on the concrete pillar from which the blockade was suspended and, with his hand above his eyes, peered across the space of no man's land.

The roommate, Mrs. McDonald, Barbara, and I were nervous about the crossing. Our names were on the list to cross at Jaffa Gate, and here we were at Mandelbaum. It was most irregular. Perhaps, after all our struggles, we would not be allowed to pass over.

The sky on its eastern slope ripened, like the lush flesh of a summer cantaloupe, to a yellow-pink. Two fat sparrows hopped lightly about in a loose tangle of barbed wire.

An Arab Legionnaire appeared atop his road block, his red and white *kaffiyeh* gay against the sky, and signaled that his side was ready.

We had no trouble with the Israeli guards, but when we reached the Arab lines, the situation grew tense. Miss Haliby immediately recognized, of course, Mrs. McDonald, and her loathing of the wife of that outspoken champion of the Jews was plain to see in her face, in her whole short, rod-stiff body.

She studied Mrs. McDonald's pass for many painful minutes; then asked her to sign a small slip of paper—a brand-new innovation.

"That, Mrs. McDonald," she said in low, cold tones, "gives you permission to come into Arab Palestine." The word "Arab" shook the air like the growl of an enraged dog.

Her eyes then swung about to the roommate. "Good morning, Mr. Ethridge. I looked for you and Mrs. Ethridge at Jaffa Gate."

"We couldn't find the Israeli crossing and were a minute late."

"Why, how absurd! We held the Jaffa Gate open for you for a half an hour. That is why we were late here."

"I apologize."

"It's perfectly all right." Her tone was pleasant, but not friendly as on other mornings. She didn't like the company we were keeping and she wanted us to know it.

Casually she nodded to the other occupants and ordered the driver to move on.

"Whew!" whewed the roommate, wiping his perspiring face. "Whew!"

That was a mild word for him, but he was too undone to speak more forcefully. He despises all scenes, except home scenes.

Without more ado, thank goodness, we arrived at the Church of the Holy Sepulcher, walking, of course, the last mile through the narrow, cobblestone alleys. The church covers several acres of ground, having had chapels, apses (I have no idea what apses are, but they must be parts of churches), aisles, balconies, lofts, and what-have-you added down through the centuries and nothing, absolutely nothing, taken away. It is now ribbed with scaffolding preparatory to major repairs, and has been for years, but the various sects who worship there can't agree on whose job it is. Not, as you might expect, that anybody wants to get out of doing it. Not at all. They are all mad to do it and so far refuse to let any one of them have the great honor.

You see, the Church of the Holy Sepulcher is built over the tomb where Jesus is supposed to have been buried and from which he arose on the third day, and it is used for worship by four different Christian sects: the Roman or Latin Catholics, the Greek Orthodox, the Armenians, and the Copts, who are Egyptian in origin.

They vie with one another over the number of lamps each can hang in certain places, the number of candles each can light, the square inches of space each can occupy, the number of minutes each can hold services. The jealousy among them is so intense that if one sect's service runs over its allotted time, bedlam breaks loose.

To ensure peace, if possible, there is a custodian, or keeper of the keys. He doesn't belong to any of the four sects; he is a Moslem. The position has been hereditary in a Jerusalem Arab family for generations.

The Easter Mass was held in one of the two main sections of this huge structure—a domed, circular building erected over the tomb. It was packed when we arrived; but because of the roommate's mission, he and I were shown to seats in the front row of a small section set aside for this service. The tall, young, swarthy-faced governor of Arab Jerusalem, Abdullah Tel, wearing his Arab Legion uniform, and Monsieur Boisanger, chairman of the French delegation, sat beside us.

The Mass had already begun; this didn't seem too bad, as it was scheduled to last for four hours and the church was cold as a deep-freeze. As we took our seats, the papal legate, standing in front of his gold, thronelike chair, was taking off his sumptuous, cerise satin robe, and putting on layer after layer of other robes, tying them like maternity dresses with strings about his waist, and ending up with a glorious brocade encrusted with gold. During the robing, he wore on his wispy white hair a purple skullcap, but this was soon topped with a steeple-shaped arrangement, which is called, as you no doubt know, a miter. It was set with precious jewels as big as pecan nuts.

What followed I didn't understand, not being familiar with the service, but even if I had known it I couldn't have heard it after the second hour. It was then that pandemonium, more raucous than Mr. Big's ninth birthday party, took over. Competing choruses sang in the lofts, competing priests chanted in balconies, competing bells rang in belfries.

At first I thought all of it must be a part of the Latin service, and though I secretly felt it was being overdone a bit, I sat fairly still; but when my ears began to throb I shouted to M. Boisanger, "Is there another service going on in here or am I imagining things?"

At which he shouted back, "Copts."

Unaccustomed to religious Copts, it was on the tip of my tongue to yell, "and robbers," but I caught myself just in time.

The papal legate advanced to the altar for the most sacred moments of the Mass. It was an improvised altar in front of the Chapel of the Holy Sepulcher, which is a complete building, roof and all, inside the rotunda of the Church of the Holy Sepulcher. Small and beautiful in detail, it sits directly beneath the big dome and holds in an intimate fashion the tomb of Christ. Before the entrance are candelabra as tall as the roof of the chapel and lovely swinging lamps of many rich colors.

As the papal legate was at the climax of the Mass, holding the golden chalice in his hand, the rotunda rolled with the thunder of thudding sticks and into the church marched *kiwass,* those people, you know, who go before dignitaries to announce their coming and to clear their way. They carried huge, silver-knobbed staves and they pounded them in unison upon the stone floor of the rotunda, making the most deafening noises.

Behind them marched robed monks. Maybe Greek Orthodox, maybe Armenians, maybe Copts. I didn't know and I couldn't yell loudly enough for M. Boisanger to hear me. They started around the rotunda, in the opposite direction, thank goodness, from where we sat, but one monk stepped out of line and came to the very edge of the Latin altar to light with a pole as long as a bamboo fishing rod the candles in the candelabra before the chapel entrance. I found myself watching him raptly as he struggled to hold the lighted tip of the swaying pole to the distant wicks.

The last part of the Latin Mass was a procession around the rotunda. We were given candles at least five feet long and we marched slowly three times around, stopping ever so often to hold services which, again, I did not understand. And all the while the bells clanged more and more madly as if they would bring down the walls of the church as the trumpets did those of Jericho. And the wax dripped down the front of the roommate's blue suit and down my pinkish-beige number; but it couldn't hurt them seriously—they were too old. We really were underdressed for the occasion. Our American consul, Bill Burdette, wore white tie and tails, and the Belgian and French consuls were dressed in their finest uniforms of blue and gold, with swords swinging at their sides.

As we marched, black-robed monks dismantled the altar swiftly, like sceneshifters, and whisked it out of sight. But even so the Mass didn't finish within the time limit, and on the last swing around the rotunda the Copts came out of their small chapel and began a service directly in our path. For some nervous seconds we were stymied; but one by one we slipped through them.

"That's the way people get slugged here," commented the roommate out of the side of his mouth. "Let your Mass run over and wham! a brother slugs you." And then he added in his most serious mood: "It's outrageous, isn't it, when it is done in the name of so gentle a person as Jesus?"

I could only nod before the procession swung into a chapel adjacent to the rotunda, and then from the chapel toward another sanctum. Though I had no idea where the procession was headed I intended to stay with it to the end; but at the door I was halted by my old friend, Brother Francis. "I'm sorry," said he, "but no skoits allowed inside."

Grinning delightedly, the roommate moved on, and I made my way outside to the welcoming warmth of the sun and of Frazer and Bob and Joe. Frazer was taking pictures of the people going in and out of the church. There was no Easter finery, but plenty of color in the robes of the monks, in the headcloths of the Arab soldiers, in the mammoth headdresses of the nuns.

When the roommate appeared he was still in the papal legate's procession, but it was pretty informal by now. The papal legate had disrobed and everybody was chatting with everybody else. Loudly we yoo-hooed to the roommate to let him know where we were, but he refused even to glance at us. A rather dazed look on his face, he marched doggedly by and turned up a narrow alley.

"We'd better stop him," said Bob solemnly. "In this re-ligious fervor that grips him, he's likely to walk to David's tomb."

Quickly, we followed him.

21. Fooling around with Arab eggs

EASTER LUNCH in a garden, green with grass and showered
with flowers, made me homesick for a moment. Except for
the Arab food, which was exotic, it was so much like a spring
lunch in Kentucky.

There was the same informality about it, the same vague-
ness of the hostess about the number she had invited, the
same lounging about in a wide assortment of chairs, the same
tinkling of glasses, and the same type of happy, friendly, enthusiastic talk about a great variety of subjects. The only
thing, the Arab hostess and Arab guests spoke more England-
English than we in the Gateway City to the South.

This lunch on Easter was my first one with that fabulous
woman, Katie Antonius. Katie is the widow of the Arab patriot, George Antonius, who wrote the book, *The Arab
Awakening*. She is an arresting-looking woman with smut-
black hair, gray eyes, and fair skin. The first time I saw
her she was wearing, twisted about her hair and falling over
her shoulders, a flimsy veil the color of her eyes; but today
she was bareheaded, as were all of her Arab women guests.

She talks excitedly, as if the house is burning down over
her head, and frequently violently, vituperatively, viciously.
She knows the Palestinian cause both with her heart and with
her mind, but she gets so emotional explaining it that her
tongue ties her in knots.

She was born, I believe, in Egypt. Her father, Dr. Faris
Nimr Pasha, was a Lebanese Arab, and her mother was

French, but her father moved to Egypt in 1883 and has lived there ever since. Today he is one of the best-known journalists in the Arab world. He is constantly urging Katie to join him in Cairo and live in luxurious comfort, but she adores Jerusalem and refuses to leave. She feels she must do for the Palestinian Arabs, so far as her capabilities go, what George Antonius would have done if he had lived.

Before the War, she had a beautiful home and, according to her friends, one of the very fine gardens of the Middle East, but she is now living in a small, yellow, stucco cottage, half-hidden by vines, on one of the main roads of Old Jerusalem. Sitting in its garden we could see a corner of the roof of her former home, high on the side of a hill near the Hebrew University and Hadassah Hospital.

"It was so lovely," Katie says wistfully, pointing it out to me. "But now . . ." she shrugs her expressive shoulders. "You can't imagine what it is like. Not a window left, the ceilings sagging, the plaster cracked. Why, you know, I haven't seen myself from head to toe in over a year. The Jews took every mirror."

Before the British withdrew from Jerusalem and the War was on at full tilt, they allowed Katie two Arab guards to protect her and her house; but they should have sent two guards to protect the guards. According to the stories circulating in Palestine, Katie carried on a feud with them continuously. She was either lashing them with her tongue to blow up the trucks of the Jews on their way to the Hebrew University or berating them for taking pot shots at Jews from her trampled flower beds.

The story is typical of her. She is a bunch of contradictions. Crowded about by beggars, she explodes: "I hate the poor. Why should they live?" And the next second she opens her pocketbook and hands them five pounds.

One day she threatens to flee to Cairo. She is discouraged, brokenhearted. The home and school which she runs for forty Arab orphan boys is hopeless. The boys are dull, they have no ambition, they will never be leaders. The following day she is giving them a party, they are tearing through her house and garden, and she is adoring them. They are the only hope of the Arab world.

She loves to give parties, and in the old days she entertained practically every person of note who came to Jerusalem. Not for political reasons, her friends say, but purely for social ones. "I'm going to have a very few people in for dinner," she whispers to a companion in the best, keep-this-under-your-hat manner. "You must come." The friend, of course, goes and finds a hundred other people.

At this Easter lunch, people kept coming: the mayor of Arab Jerusalem, who is different from the military governor; Mousa Husseini and his wife, with whom I spent such pleasant hours in Jericho; Sally Kassab, a young Arab-English girl with a fluent tongue, quick sense of humor, and an appealing face; John Pruen, the British consul; Frazer; Bill Burdette, who has managed amazingly to cross into New Jerusalem, change his tails for a business suit, and return to Old Jerusalem on the twelve o'clock crossing; Wells Stabler, our one and only diplomatic representative to Transjordan, with headquarters in Amman, the capital, and his slim, tall mother, who is visiting him and looking just as the mother of a diplomat should; and a goodly number of other people, mostly Arabs, who, in my inimitable way, I never did get straight. But the roommate was not among them. Four hours of church—and it cold—had collapsed him.

Now that the bells had stopped ringing it was a heavenly day—quiet as deep country, except for one minute when a

quick explosion shattered the peace. "Somebody has hit another mine," Sally Kassab said casually.

During the hour before lunch proper, hors d'oeuvres were
served. They were of all kinds, and all strange and exceedingly good. Nothing like the little dishes of salted peanuts
and potato chips and olives which I whip out of the pantry.
My favorite was *homus,* a thick paste made out of those little round, yellow chick-peas, mashed and mixed with *teheny,*
the Arab name for the second stage, or dregs, of sesame. My
second favorite, and here I promise to stop, was *sansbousick,*
a crescent-shaped pastry stuffed with highly seasoned ground
meat and fried in oil. I must have eaten, conservatively speaking, a dozen of these.

Naturally, I had a hard time getting to the lunch table
groaning (the lunch table groaning, though it could as well
have been I) beneath a eucalyptus tree.

Because it was Easter and the word fish, in Greek, spells
Jesus Christ, the Son of God (I don't understand it, either,
but John Pruen very soberly told me so, or something similar) the table was centered with a large baked fish, elaborately decorated, and surrounded by dyed eggs. Everybody
being boys at heart, as the saying is, grabbed an egg and began challenging everybody else to a tapping contest. Frazer
and I were especially eager. We had just learned, after Mass,
a new trick. Walking about the streets of Old Jerusalem,
where people were calling out "Happy Easter" on all sides, we
had seen small boys testing the strength of the shells of their
eggs with their teeth. Immediately we had bought three for
twenty-five cents and tried them on our teeth. The eggs all
broke and we had a fine time eating them, but not before we
learned which ends were most firmly packed and thus less
likely to break.

Now I began tapping eggs to teeth and tossing challenges

about. The only trouble was that the Arab guests knew this trick, too; evidently have known it for centuries, and I got smashed on the first round.

I was lucky at that, the roommate said, when I reported the matter to him at his sickbed. "Did you stop to think you could have knocked out your teeth as easy as not?" he asked. "You go fooling around with those Arab eggs and see what happens to your teeth. Don't forget they are not as young as they once were."

But they did all right at lunch. They went right through crisp, fried eggplant spread with leban (sour milk); and broad beans cooked in their pods with *seameh* (another oil, derived I am sure, from sesame), and wonderful rice, every grain separate and chock-full of nuts and raisins; and *kaftas* (flattened meat balls), packed with minced parsley and onions and fried, without a doubt, in oil; and a salad called *baadounsia* which is chopped parsley dressed with that second stage of sesame—*teheny*; and, for dessert, *kanafeh*.

Now this *kanafeh* is something very specially Arab. I saw it again and again in the suks, but never tasted any that melted in the mouth like Katie's. For the roommate's sweet-tooth's sake I tried to learn how to make it, but I must say Katie's directions were rather vague.

"Take an enormous piepan," said she, "and sprinkle the bottom with a layer of shredded wheat, then a layer of cheese, then another layer of shredded wheat and so on until you get to the top, and then sprinkle the top with roasted pine and pistachio nuts; and, finally, pour over the whole thing a lot of melted sugar and put in the oven and bake. Simple, see?"

"Oh, sure," said I, and took another helping.

22. They can have it—I don't want it

"ALL ABOARD," yelled Miss Haliby.

The members of the P.C.C. and a few camp followers such as I hoisted ourselves into the U.N. C-47 plane, perched in the runway of Jerusalem's airport. We were going to fly over the Negeb, that debatable piece of land in southern Palestine about which the Israelis sing in ecstasy and the Arabs weep. It is twelve million acres of desert, according to reports, but both sides long for it with all their hearts.

The U.N. partition lines left a considerable part of it in Arab Palestine, but during the War the Israelis occupied a portion of this Arab part and after the War they took over the city of Akaba at the extreme southeastern tip. The Arabs, of course, protested violently at this loss, and have been insisting ever since that it be returned to them.

Though the P.C.C. refused to confide in me, I gathered that they nourished the hope of persuading Israel to swap the Negeb land they had occupied for the Gaza strip, which was in the hands of the Egyptian Arabs, but being so far removed from Egypt, doing them little good.

But no matter what they hoped, they felt it was necessary to see for themselves this contested area, and the only practical way to see it was by plane.

The hour was early when we took off. (We were always taking off early. The entire time we were in Israel and Palestine we were starting out when all decent people should be asleep.) That morning, though, the Arab Legion was up before us. They have a large camp on the airport grounds, no doubt for security reasons, and they were briskly marching up and down the runway, their boots gleaming, their khaki pants sharply pressed, and their checkered *kaffiyehs* fresh as new-laundered spreads.

But some Legionnaires were hanging out the laundry—all shirts and pants. If they wore underwear and pajamas they didn't wash them, at least not in the week of the eighteenth of April. With the wet clothes in their hands, they waved at us as we climbed by.

"See the Mediterranean, see the Dead Sea," cries the roommate as soon as we are in the air.

And sure enough, we can see from one side of Palestine —or, rather, what was Palestine before the partition—to the other; from the Mediterranean on the west to the Dead Sea and the River Jordan on the east.

"It's a helluva little country," says the roommate, "to cause so much trouble." He shakes his head, as if trying to throw off the headaches it has given him.

We are flying over Arab country toward Hebron. The perfectly spaced terracing spirals from the narrow rounded summits of the mountains to their widespread bases. I feel I can reach down and mash them into a roll as firm and neat as movie film.

Hebron is a city of about 25,000 population "solidly Moslem," so *The Palestine Guide* says. It was the home of Abraham and there is a very large mosque there called, of all things (here my Christian bias is showing) the Mosque of Abraham. Practically everybody in the Bible is buried here: Abraham, and his wife Sara; Isaac, and his wife Rebecca; Jacob, and his wife Leah; and Joseph, to name just a few. The roommate visited their tombs before I arrived, which was all right with me, for I never have cared especially for tombs. From the air they didn't show and Hebron looked like any other Arab city—low blocks of creamy walls and creamy, flat roofs.

Below Hebron, the terracing ends and the swells of gray rock spread out over the land like the rough, humped, outside surface of giant oyster shells. Here and there in the crevices, the Bedouin Arabs have pitched their oblong tents, not as big from the air as dominoes.

"See those tiny, black specks?" Frazer asks me. "They're goats."

Shortly, word goes about the plane that we have lost Beersheba. I go up into the nose and sit in the copilot's seat to help find it, but as you can imagine I am no help.

"I think we had better go to Gaza," the pilot suggests, "and pick up that road leading out of Gaza to Beersheba."

We find Gaza easily. It is on the Mediterranean and is surrounded by thousands and thousands of camel's-hair tents, sheltering Palestinian refugees. To the south, along the shore, is the much-talked-of Gaza strip; to the north, Israel.

"Give me the Weems plotter," says the pilot to the copilot standing a few feet behind him. Something resembling a ruler is handed over and the pilot moves it above the map spread on his lap. "I think we will take 135 out of here," he says.

The plane is swung about and in just a few minutes we are over Beersheba. It is not surprising that we lost it. Though it has been the tribal center of this whole area for hundreds of generations, it has a population of only 6,500 Arabs. I see a finger of a minaret above a mosque and many low, flat houses, calcimined both cream and blue; but most colorful of all, the rounded tips of trees here and there between the walls.

Frazer has come up into the nose of the plane to take pictures and has eased me out of the copilot's seat. I half-sit and half-kneel on a cushion on the floor. Peering down at Beer-sheba he asks soberly: "How long do you suppose it can stay an Arab town with Jewish land all about it?"

No one answers.

Just below Beersheba we pass a new Jewish settlement. It looks centuries different from an Arab town. No old walls, sagging flat roofs, faded colors, slim minarets.

"The Jews have been rushing to put settlements in here," Frazer explains, "so they can have a better claim to it at the peace table."

"But in God's name, why do they want it?" exclaims the pilot. "I can't see killing people over it."

I personally agree with the pilot, but the night before I had been reading Dr. Weizmann's *Trial and Error* and had marked the passages in which he had told how he had fought —and why—for the Negeb and the Gulf of Akaba during those days before November 29th, 1947, when the U.N. General Assembly was struggling to draw the lines for the Jewish and Arab areas. He wrote:

"There were many tense moments preceding the final decision on Nov. 29, and these had to do not only with the probable votes of the delegates. There was, for instance, the actual territorial division. When this was discussed some of the American delegates felt that the Jews were getting too large a slice of Palestine, and that the Arabs might legitimately raise objections. It was proposed to cut out from the proposed Jewish State a considerable part of the Negev, taking Akaba [the gulf] away from us. Ever since the time of the Balfour Declaration I had attached great value to Akaba and the region about it. I had circumnavigated the gulf of Akaba as far back as 1918, when I went to see the Emir Feisal, and I had a notion of the character of the country. At present it looks a forbidding desert, and the scene of desolation masks the importance of the region. But with a little imagination it becomes quite clear that Akaba is the gate to the Indian Ocean, and constitutes a much shorter route from Palestine to the Far East than via Port Said and the Suez Canal.

"I was somewhat alarmed when I learned, in the second week of November, that the American delegation, in its desire to find a compromise which would be more acceptable to the Arabs, advocated the excision of the southern part of the Negev, including Akaba. After consultation with members of the Jewish Agency Executive, I decided to go to Washington to see President Truman and to put the whole case before him.

"On the morning of Wednesday, November 19, I was received by the President with the utmost cordiality. I spoke first of the Negev as a whole, which I believe is destined to become an important part of the Jewish State. The northern part, running from Gaza to Asluj or Beersheba, is beautiful country. It needs water, of course, which can either be brought from the North, as projected in the Lowdermilk scheme, or provided locally by desalting the brackish water which is found in abundance in these parts. . . .

"I then spoke of Akaba. I pleaded that if there was to be a division of the Negev, it ought to be vertical and not horizontal; this would be eminently fair, giving both sides part of the fertile soil and part of the desert. But for us it was imperative that in this division Akaba should go to the Jewish State . . . As part of the Jewish State it will very quickly become an object of development, and would make a real contribution to trade and commerce by opening up a new route. One can foresee the day when a canal will be cut from some part of the eastern Mediterranean coast to Akaba. . . . This would become a parallel highway to the Suez Canal, and could shorten the route from Europe to India by a day or more.

". . . I was extremely happy to find that the President

read the map very quickly and very clearly. He promised me that he would communicate at once with the American delegation at Lake Success.

"At about three o'clock in the afternoon of the same day, Ambassador Herschel Johnson, head of the American delegation, called in Mr. Shertok [now Sharret] of the Jewish Agency in order to advise him of the decision on the Negev, which by all indications excluded Akaba from the Jewish State. Shortly after Mr. Shertok entered, but before the subject was broached, the American delegates were called to the telephone. At the other end of the wire was the President of the United States, telling them that he considered the proposal to keep Akaba within the Jewish State a reasonable one, and that they should go forward with it. When Mr. Johnson and General Hilldring emerged from the telephone booth after a half-hour conversation, they returned to Mr. Shertok, who was waiting for them, tense with anxiety. All they had for him was the casual remark: 'Oh, Mr. Shertok, we really haven't anything important to tell you.' Obviously the President had been as good as his word, and a few short hours after I had seen him had given the necessary instructions to the American delegation."

So the southern part now below us was Israeli land—and almost desert. Only the basins of the wadis, which fill briefly with water during the spring rains, are swatched with fragile green. In the distance we see Egypt and more desert. Great white dunes, streaked with brownish sand, ironically set me to thinking of mounds of vanilla ice cream spread with caramel sauce.

"Look, there are a couple of trees," exclaims the pilot.

Now the hills become flat-topped and black, as if burnt to a crisp by the sizzling heat.

Peering at them with unhappy eyes, the pilot and I begin to talk about land in Georgia. He is from Florida, but he has an uncle who is a farmer near Leesburg, Georgia, and he wishes the Arabs and Jews could see that land.

"My uncle planted five hundred dollars' worth of watermelon seed last year," he tells me.

This seems such an astounding amount of watermelon seed, I feel I must pass the news on. "His uncle planted five hundred dollars' worth of watermelon seed last year," I shout to Frazer.

"What for?" Frazer shouts back.

But the pilot is not offended. Pleasantly he goes on: "He also planted three thousand acres of peanuts. I tell you, that Georgia land, you can't beat it."

Thinking of the black south Georgia land, we shake our heads over the barren, bleached, cracked-open country beneath us.

"We are seeing a continuation of the Desert of Sinai," the roommate explains on a brief visit into the nose.

Near the Gulf of Akaba, the ridges and gullies and gulches get as dark red as clotted blood.

"I wouldn't give this land to my worst enemy," declares the roommate.

"I think from the looks of it there must be iron under it," I suggest.

"God knows there must be something under it, there is certainly nothing on top of it. It's a helluva place for people to get excited about."

The Gulf of Akaba shines with the blue intensity of a sheet of tin in the noonday sun. A ship, no bigger to our faraway eyes than a bathtub model, sits perfectly still upon the metallic looking surface.

"British destroyer," suggests Frazer, and then adds, "The Gulf of Akaba, you know, joins the Red Sea."

I trust he is addressing the pilot, for as far as I'm con-

cerned this is spot news. I really must have stayed out of the
classroom all the years in which geography was taught. But
I'm learning.

The town of Akaba sun-bathes in a sheltered cove at the
northeast corner of the Gulf. The plane swoops very low and
Frazer pokes his camera out of the side window in the nose to
get a picture.

We turn slowly and head north up a wide, rocky valley,
known as the Wadi el Araba. Empty of water, it stretches to
the Dead Sea, the purple-red mountains rising layer upon
layer on both sides of it. The land has no resemblance to
ground; it could be a huge relief map fashioned of plum-dyed
plaster of Paris. Our Grand Canyon is something like it, but
not so wild, not so desolate. This valley is not touched except
by the shifting shadows of an uneasy sky.

In the distance is the Dead Sea and I am reminded again
that there is no outlet at this southern end. I keep forgetting
that. It seems so queer to have so large a body of water, fed
by the Jordan and by innumerable springs, and have it go
nowhere—except up in evaporation.

We don't go over the Dead Sea, but just before reaching
it cut west toward Jerusalem. Staring straight down once more
at the garnet-colored earth I become a fly on a ballroom chan-
delier. The hills eroded so systematically from their narrow
tops to their spreading bases are really hooped skirts of stiffest
taffeta corded at regular intervals from waist to floor. I listen
for music, but there is only the steady rhythm of the plane.

Nearing Jerusalem, the ruggedness softens a little and the
Arabs have taken advantage of this and broken up the land
with lines of rocks into millions of small squares.

And now we are over the sun-tanned walls and minarets
and towers and steeples—and now we are coming down over
the landing strip of the airfield.

"Come on down!" the pilot begs the plane. "Come on down!" Then, turning to me, he shouts in mock excitement: "Come on, do something. Don't just sit there."

Though I know he is teasing, the airstrip *is* short and for a breathless moment I am sure we will pass over it before the wheels touch.

But, ah, there is the roller-coaster bump. We are down. We have seen the Negeb. But if the members of the P.C.C. understand any better what to do about it, they don't mention it. We tumble out in steeped silence.

23. *You name them; Israel has them*

ONE OF THE THINGS I wanted to see most in Israel was the landing of a boatload of immigrants at Haifa. I had originally wanted to go to Israel on such a boat from Marseilles, and catch, if possible, from the expressions of their faces and the words of their mouths the true meaning of this country to people who felt that at last they were coming home, but the State Department, when I asked permission, discouraged it. Knowing the sensitiveness of the Israelis and Arabs to every act of any citizen of the United States, but particularly to one married to the United States representative of the P.C.C., the Department felt it wasn't very smart. I could do it, but. . . . You know what position that leaves a woman in.

So, after weeks in Israel I still wanted to see the homecoming of an immigrants' ship. It wouldn't be difficult, Ruth Dayan assured me. One came in practically every day; all I had to do was get myself to Haifa. And one day that, too, was easy. The roommate and Frazer were going to Tiberias to have a conference with Mr. Ben-Gurion; I could catch a ride with them as far as Haifa.

The ship for that day, though, had already docked when I reached the Absorption Office of the Jewish Agency, which handles all incoming settlers, and, as my luck would have it, no more were expected for two or three days. But if I hurried to the docks I might see most of the day's arrivals before they left for the Receiving Center. I hurried, accompanied by an efficient young woman from the Absorption Office.

Driving to the docks, the young woman stressed, as she well might, the gigantic job of her office. Around 30,000 immigrants had been coming into Israel every month. Were the United States, on a population basis, to equal this Israeli effort, we would take in 55,000,000 immigrants a year. In 1948, Israel absorbed 126,979 immigrants, and during the first three months of 1949, 80,000. At the time of my visit in late April, 1949, there were indications of a slight let-up, and the officials were saying frankly that they were "scraping the bottom of the barrel." They had removed all the D.P.'s from the camps of Europe except 40,000 (by July this figure, according to a news story in the Louisville *Courier Journal,* had been reduced to 28,000). There had never been more than 250,000 Jews in the D.P. camps—Hitler had seen to that. As you remember, six million had been killed. Now the job of transferring the survivors was practically finished; the ones remaining were bedridden with tuberculosis and other diseases, or too old to be moved.

"We must look to the United States for the majority of our immigrants in the future," the member of the Absorption Office said.

Most of the immigrants who had landed this day had come from North Africa and Turkey, and a few had come from Europe. None was from the United States.

They were milling about in front of a huge shed on the water's edge, waiting to be taken in open trucks to the Receiving Center. Their ship, the *Theodor Herzl,* rocked ever so slightly at its pier, the blue and white flag of Israel with the Star of David fluttering at the mast. The ship looked small; how a thousand human beings could have crowded on it puzzled me.

"Today for a change there were only eight hundred," the Absorption spokesman said, "and considering the conditions under which they had been living, they were very comfortable."

These conditions were manifest in the possessions they clutched in their hands: a little girl hugged to her body a naked, one-legged doll; an old woman grasped a red umbrella; another a box of matzoth; another held a dishpan and a cord shopping bag crammed with clothes and a half-dozen lemons; a man, dapper in a beret, balanced on his shoulder a roll of bright-colored rugs and pink blankets; and practically everybody lugged a large tin can for milk or tea or some sort of drink, a chamber pot, and a dilapidated pasteboard suitcase that would not close, but was tied together with strings, ribbons, ropes, straps, and rags.

Baby carriages were all over the place. In one a baby lay, his straw-thin legs in the air, a nipple in his mouth. Only one woman wore a hat, a frowzy brown felt; but there were two elderly sisters, short, wrinkled and gray-haired, wearing bright green scarves over their heads and raincoats, though it was not raining. They were Polish, and from a D.P. camp.

A truck backed up to the warehouse entrance and a man shouted: "Everybody able to go on this truck, get on." There was a mass movement toward the truck.

"People with baby carriages first," cried the man.

In a twinkling, the truck was packed, everybody standing,

of course, wedged against his neighbor. An undersized Orthodox Jew was pressed against the side, his black beard, side
curls, and black felt hat just topping the rail. Next to him,
a man was eating an orange, puffing the seeds indifferently
into the crowd below. "Ma-ma," wailed a blond-haired baby.
"Ma-ma."

The truck starts to move. There are excited cries. A stout
woman waves her arms wildly, screaming something in an
unknown tongue—at least unknown to me. A man shoves
through the throng left behind, a much-stained baby mattress above his head. Hands reach out to pull him and his
awkward load up into the last square foot of space. The
woman beams, and the truck moves off.

In a few minutes there will be another truck, and another,
and another, until all eight hundred are carried off. I'd like
to watch each of them fill up; but there is so much else to see.
My escort and I walk around to the side of the warehouse on
the water front. There sits a structure about the size and
shape of a bus. It is divided in two—one half for women, the
other for men.

Each immigrant, as he steps off the boat, enters this structure, to be disinfected with DDT. Next he goes into the
warehouse, where government officials stamp his visa. Next,
officials of the Jewish Agency give him a green booklet con-
taining papers that entitle him to enter a receiving camp and
have food and lodging free for approximately three months,
though the time limit can be indefinitely extended. It depends
on whether at the end of three months there is a place for
him to live and a job for him to fill. Finding a place to live
has been more difficult than finding a job. On leaving the receiving camp, he is given seven pounds (approximately $23)
if he is under forty-five and twelve pounds if he is older.

The shed is practically deserted as we wander through it.

Only one man and woman from the ship are left and they, evidently, do not belong to the regular stream of immigrants. They are people of property. They have it with them, a full line of goods to open a store. It is spread on a table for the scrutiny of the customs officials: quilts, sheets, tablecloths, shirts, towels, dishcloths, dresses. . . .

"You see, they are not allowed to bring money out of whatever country they come from, so they have put their money in goods," the Absorption Office member explains to me. "There is no duty, of course, for personal belongings, but when people bring in things to sell they must pay duty."

In front of the warehouse, the trucks are still being loaded. Up they go: a little girl in a bright blue bonnet and blue coat; a young boy with a pack on his back; a woman in a sheepskin coat, hugging a basket as high as her chin; an old crone from North Africa, her gray hair plaited and zigzagged across the back of her head, and in her arms a thermos bottle and a bright red-and-green shawl; a group of boys in their teens, extremely dark complected, talking excitedly in a language that sounds faintly familiar.

"Can they be speaking Arabic?" I ask my escort.

She grins ruefully. "Yes. They are Jews from North Africa and they speak Arabic, but it is a bit different from Palestinian Arabic."

"That must be hard to take," I suggest.

"Oh, they will learn Hebrew soon enough."

We follow a truck to the Reception Center, which is on the outskirts of Haifa. It is the only one in Israel, and has just recently been opened. Before, immigrants went straight to one of the twenty-four receiving camps; but, with the increased influx of immigrants, an intermediary stop to weed out the ill and the other misfits became necessary.

Huge yellow barracks, used by the British during the mandate, house the Center. It is circled by a wire fence and Israeli soldiers guard the gate. "Jewish Agency," my companion murmurs to the guards and we are waved through.

We draw up at the office of the director of the Center and I meet Mr. Weisberger, a very businesslike individual. He suggests that I sit down with two other visitors and have a "briefing."

"This is purely a transient camp," he begins. "We get in a thousand immigrants a day and we turn out a thousand."

"You can't!" I exclaim.

"We do." He looks at me sternly and I know I shouldn't interrupt again, but I hear myself saying: "So every night you're empty?"

"Not at all. We have a backlog of almost four thousand and of that number over a thousand are children. There is a very high birth rate in Oriental families and we are getting a lot of Orientals now. They have six, seven, eight, and sometimes eleven children.

"Language is a problem. This is a regular Tower of Babel. I speak eight languages, but they are not enough. People come from all countries in the world; you name them, we have them."

"Do you have many from the States?" It seemed impossible for me to keep quiet.

"Very few . . . very few, and they are visitors."

"What do you do with all the luggage, all the baby carriages?" I'm at it again.

"That's a problem I haven't solved yet."

But there are many problems Mr. Weisberger has solved. The Center is mainly a medical channel for new arrivals. The medical personnel numbers thirty-six doctors and twenty-four assistants and nurses. First, they sort out those with diseases dangerous to the country. They found two with leprosy; one

was from Shanghai, the other from Turkey. They sent them
to the leper colony at Jerusalem.

Then there are the venereally infected. They hold these
in the hospital at the Center, or if that is overflowing, they
send them away to a hospital. The number of arrivals with
tuberculosis is steadily rising, and the general health of those
arriving lately from North Africa, Turkey, and even some
Balkan states has been increasingly poor.

Then everybody, the healthy and the sick, must have blood
tests and vaccinations; the Israeli government has found it
can't, with any safety, recognize the certificates of other countries. When all these tests have been made, the healthy are
issued health-insurance stamps, which are vital in Israeli, for
no one can get a job without them. And incidentally, though
I don't believe "incidentally" is the word in this case, no one
can get a job without joining Histadruth, the General Fed-
eration of Jewish Labor.

Also, at the Center, there is an army recruiting station.
Every person of military age, man or woman, must enlist, be
catalogued "fit" or "unfit," and given his grade before leaving
the Center.

The briefing session over, we start out to see the Center.
An old man is walking down the road in pantaloons, a blanket draped about his shoulders, and sandals on his feet, and
a woman sways by with the peculiar grace of the Arab, balancing a pottery jug on her head.

"We see all types," comments Mr. Weisberger, "and we
will for the next forty years."

We visit clinics for the examination of eyes, nose, and
throat; for tuberculosis; for skin diseases; for innoculations for
typhoid and smallpox; we see the isolation wards; the hospital rooms for the transient sick; the baby welfare station; the

rooms where delicate children are kept under observation; the children's kitchen; the showers. . . .

"The hot-water showers run all day," Mr. Weisberger says proudly.

At one of the outdoor laundries, women are chatting and laughing gaily over their washing, like the light-hearted members of a sewing circle. I am intrigued; I never suspected scrubbing clothes was such fun.

Near by, a red-cheeked boy of four or five is having himself a time, pulling up yellow daisies.

A continuous parade of men and women go by, carrying pieces of old straw matting, bedding, hats, cloth, pots, tubs, shoes, baby chairs, pitchers. . . .

Mr. Weisberger, eyeing them, shakes his head forlornly. "They bring what they have, even if it is just a piece of bedding; but we give everybody a mattress, two blankets, a sheet, and a knife, fork, and spoon."

We move to the kitchen and dining halls. Washtubs of oranges soaking in water stand outside the doors. There are two dining rooms which hold eight hundred each, but even so, two, and frequently, three sittings are necessary. The people stand in long queues and are served cafeteria fashion. The kitchen bulges with Jack-the-Giant-Killer cauldrons, filled with soup, rice, and cauliflower; but the midday meal will also include cheese, matzoth (since it is the Passover), and oranges.

"Feeding is a problem," Mr. Weisberger confides. "The people have such widely differing tastes; the Bulgarian Jews want milk and cheese; Turkish Jews want fish; and so it goes *ad infinitum*. All the food is kosher, and it costs an average of a dollar a day per person."

From the Reception Center, the newcomers move to the receiving camps or immigrants' homes, which are huge blocks of buildings constructed to care for thousands. During my visit there were forty thousand housed there, waiting for permanent places to live.

"It is absolutely overpowering," Mr. Weisberger declares, and I couldn't agree with him more.

What will Israel do with all these immigrants and the thousands of others who are being urged to come? The housing problem should be greatly eased by the forty-eight Arab cities, towns, and villages which have been taken over and now stand practically empty. Though some of the houses have been destroyed and others will have to come down, many can be used, and those that come down can be replaced by prefabricated houses. The government has already ordered prefabricated houses from Belgium, Italy, France, and the United States. But what will all these people do for a living? Will there be widespread unemployment? There was already some unemployment in the late spring of 1949 and there were unemployment riots in Tel Aviv in July.

For years the Jews have been claiming that Palestine has an economic absorptive capacity of two million. Now the Israelis have the opportunity to prove that assertion. They now have seven-tenths of Palestine, including every foot of the coast, except the Gaza strip; practically all of the rich plains and valleys; and all the cities of any appreciable size, except Jerusalem, the final disposition of which is still in doubt as this is being written.

The year 1947 is a long way back now, especially to the Israelis who have experienced partition, statehood, the War, the truces, and the armistices, and who now have at least three times as much land as they owned before partition and at least two hundred thousand more people. It is, however, the last year of any reliable statistics and, though they don't cast too much light on the employment problems of today, they do indicate the channels into which labor must flow.

In 1947, the Jewish Agency estimated that the citrus industry could absorb 5,300 additional workers. In the 1945–46 season, 8,000,000 cases of oranges were shipped from Jewish-owned groves and the estimate for 1946–47 was 12,000,000 cases. That season 13,000 workers were employed, but only 4,500 were Jews; the remainder were Arabs.

The output of mixed farming was doubled during World War II, the report stated, and production was still growing. The number of persons fully employed in Jewish mixed farming was estimated at 22,500; but with the normal increase that was anticipated (the report, naturally, did not foresee partition and the War), 5,700 additional workers could be absorbed in farming.

"An investigation in the collective settlements," the report reads, "showed that these are prepared to absorb 10,000 newcomers of working age (5,000 of whom will be employed on mixed farming) in addition to at least the same number of juveniles and children. About a thousand families can also be settled in private tenure villages, which constitute roughly a third of Jewish mixed farming."

Then 8,100 new workers could be absorbed in industry, the Jewish Agency estimated. They would be distributed as follows:

Foodstuffs, Drinks, and Tobacco	1,200
Textiles and Clothing	3,200
Metal-working and Machinery	800
Wood-working	500
Tanning and Leather	200
Chemicals and Pharmaceuticals	200
Electrical Appliances	200
Building Materials	1,000
Diamonds	800
Total	8,100

Building and public works could use 9,400 additional workers, and the number of people to care for immigrant children
could be increased by 1,400.

All these figures added up to 29,900 new workers in the
basic occupations; but there were still the "services and other
occupations": catering trades, distribution and transport, commerce, and the liberal professions. The Jewish Agency estimated these could take up 12,000.

Then there were the dependents of these workers. According to the Palestine Government (during the mandate),
the proportion of dependents among Jewish immigrants in
the years of 1940 to 1945 was 38.5 per cent. Assuming the
proportion to remain unchanged, the dependents of these
new workers were calculated at 26,200. Last were the juveniles and children without parents, whose number was set
at 25,000.

Adding all the figures together, the Jewish Agency argued
that in 1947 Palestine could absorb 93,100 immigrants. Now,
93,000 is a far cry from the 126,979 that came in 1948, and
the 300,000 who were due to come during 1949, if the rate of
30,000 a month continued. But then Israel is a far cry from
the strife-ridden Palestine of 1947. Personally, I wouldn't put
anything past her.

24. Haifa's Liberation from the Arabs

"GET READY for gunshots at seven o'clock tonight," said a
young woman from the Public Relations Office in Haifa.

Naturally I did not know how one got oneself ready for
gunshots unless one had a bullet-proof vest handy.

"You mean," I asked hesitatingly, "run to shelter?"

"No, there will be no need for shelter tonight." She was silent. She saw she had me worried, and she was enjoying it. "No?" I persisted.

"No. We are celebrating tonight Haifa's deliverance from the Arabs. It happened just a year ago tonight. There will be firing of guns, blowing of sirens, and a torchlight procession."

"How many Arabs was Haifa delivered from?"

She looked blank; I had put the question awkwardly. "I mean, how many Arabs were living in Haifa before this deliverance?"

"I'm not sure," she answered.

(Later, I learned from our State Department that Haifa had approximately 72,000 Arabs just before the termination of the mandate [though the Arabs claim that several months before they had 80,000] and approximately 75,000 Jews.)

The young woman and I were driving through the downtown area of Haifa to visit a Hostel for Pioneer Women, and there was a great deal to keep both my eyes and mind occupied. Before the exodus of the Arabs, Haifa was, and I imagine still is, the third largest city in Palestine. The business section curves about the lovely Bay of Acre, but the residential sections climb steeply up the green slopes of Mt. Carmel. Handsome office buildings and banks and stores in modernistic design line the wide avenue of Kingsway, and more construction is afoot. The old Arab quarters are being blown up; debris spreads for blocks, as if bombs had been dropped. Here a new and wide boulevard from Tel Aviv will intersect at right angles with an equally new and wide boulevard from Hadar Hacarmel, the fine residential section on the first "terrace" of Mt. Carmel.

The Hostel for Pioneer Women is a narrow, three-storied building near the ocean front. Groups of one hundred and sixty girls, picked on their arrival in Israel by the Jewish

Agency, live here for a few months while they learn dress-
making or mattress making or cooking or pressing or book
binding or weaving or spinning. These are girls who do not
wish to join a *kibbutz*; they want to stay in towns and cities.
But, since they know no trade, off they are packed to the hostel to learn one.

This hostel in Haifa is one of four in Israel; there is another one in Haifa, one in Jerusalem, and one in Tel Aviv.
The Tel Aviv hostel, in addition to the trades taught in Haifa,
carries on dollmaking, the girls making the heads, bodies,
and clothes. The four hostels teach trades to a total of two
to three thousand girls a year.

During their apprenticeship, the girls also must learn Hebrew. Classes in Hebrew are held every afternoon from five
o'clock until eight.

The hostels are sponsored by a United States organization,
the Women's League for Palestine, and are headed in Israel
by Fania Malnik, an inspiring, dramatic, huge woman, who
sweeps aside, as if they were old shoes, obstacles that would
paralyze others in their tracks.

She was telling me of her plans for building a new hostel
in Nathania which would cost a quarter of a million dollars.
Was she worried? Heavens, no. She was confident the money
would come from the League when the members understood
the need.

"As yet, they don't know the cost," she says, throwing out
her hands. "I'm afraid to write them. But ven they come—
you know, members of the board—I vill tell them." She tosses
back her huge head and laughs elatedly. "Here I can make
them see; here I have moral support.

"They write me sometime, 'You're swallowing money.'
You see, it takes a hundred and thirty thousand dollars to
run the four houses. Dis means vithout building money. So

I say, 'Vat can I do? Maybe, I can save here; maybe, I can make economies there.' Then they say, 'No, don't cut any-vere,' for they know every penny is used for a very impor-tant task."

Miss Malnik was a native of Lithuania, but she came to Palestine twenty years ago. An ardent Zionist, she came alone to make her contribution to the building of a Jewish Home-land. She has, as she expresses it, a "double doctorate"—Doctor of National Economy and Doctor of Philosophy.

When I comment that she must be very smart, she shrugs. "No, I'm not so smart. I had time to study. I finished high school in Lithuania in 1921—that's twenty-eight years ago. My God, that tells how old I am!"

Her hearty laugh booms out. Her chin rolls into other chins; her small, gray eyes sharpen with amusement. I am fascinated. She is not good-looking—there is her Amazonian size and three large moles on her cheeks—but she is dynamic, terrific, hypnotic.

While talking to me, she sits erect behind a large flat-topped desk in her office. Several times she is interrupted by girls who come in to ask for information. All but one speak Hebrew, and when that girl goes out Miss Malnik turns to me and exclaims: "All the time ve are fighting vith them to speak Hebrew. It is very, very important that they learn Hebrew; ve cannot be a nation of polyglots. In the hostels ve have girls from twenty-eight countries vith twenty-eight different languages. Vat can ve do?" Again that great shrug.

"Girls come into my office and they ask me am I speaking this language and this language and this language? And I say I am speaking first of all Hebrew. After a veek they are com-ing back into the office and saying Hebrew. It cannot be othervise."

Though Miss Malnik fights for the Hebrew language, she speaks Russian, Yiddish, German, French, Polish, Bulgarian, Czech, and English.

"What, no Turkish?" I ask flippantly.

She spreads her hand on her full breast (they look as one) and sighs deeply. "No," she says. "No Turkish." Then her loud, jolly chuckles join mine.

When our laughter subsides, she tells me that there are at the moment a lot of girls in the hostel from Holland, France, England, and the United States; they are social workers who have come to Israel to do social work, and they are taking a three-month course in Hebrew, studying it from eight to ten hours a day.

It is my turn to sigh. "Everyone in Israel works too hard," I mourn.

"Vork!" She throws out her arms. "It is not enough. I feel I must do more; I must redouble my efforts. To have girls here from twenty-eight countries, from the ages of seventeen and a half to thirty-six and to uniform them into one!" Her outflung hands testify to the bigness of the task. "And, too, they must have social life."

A brilliant smile breaks over her face. "Ah, one is marrying here shortly. I'm very lucky. I can take in another girl." She chortles. "I like girls to marry; but I cannot go to all the veddings. Impossible! On this special day, twenty-two veddings. Can imagine? Today, as you must already hear, is a very special day."

I nod. I know she is speaking of Haifa's liberation from the Arabs.

"A year ago today I vould not have invited you for a cup of tea. The battle began at twelve o'clock at night and this was a terrible spot. Here we vere on the border of the Arab section, and the shots vere pouring down from the heights. It vas awful.

"I vas here present vith one hundred and sixty girls—all new girls—all new arrivals. Ve had two girls from concentration camps in Germany, from Maidanek, that most dreadful camp. They vere buried alive. In the moment the Germans buried the dead, they vent into the graves vith the dead. Ven the Germans left, they crawled out." She makes crawling movements over the top of her desk with her big, fleshy hands. "Not as human beings are going on two feet, but like animals they are.

"Naturally, I vorry about these girls. Bullets are flying here through all the vindowpanes. A Jewish officer comes and orders me to move the girls, but ve cannot leave. Vere can we go? So I say I von't go.

"The girls are mobilized. Each girl who knows how to hold an arm, a gun, they vant. I ask, 'Who is going?' Every one held up hand." She flings both her hands above her head to illustrate.

"I stay here vith the sick. Not everyone strong enough to fight. I go by myself to third floor, vere they sleep, and ask them is anyone afraid. I say it is not ashamed to be afraid. And nobody asked me can they be moved from third floor to first floor. I vas surprised." She puts her finger to her mouth and looks at me keenly with her small bright eyes. "They asked me, 'Vat can happen to us after Europe?' I tell you, I don't know vere they took all the sureness.

"The shooting vent on for hours. It vas terrible to hear. I vent on roof to see vat was going on. It vas bright moonlight and the streets leading to the port vere full of Arabs. They vere flying in a paroxysm of fear. I vill never forget it. It made a sad impression on me. Their shops vere not

closed; their dishes vere not taken off the table. Panic com-
pelled them."

Excitedly she lights a cigarette and puffs upon it. I wait
quietly for her to go on.

"I came off the roof, but I did not sleep. Nobody slept. Ve
made all night sandviches for the boys and girls who fight.
At four o'clock in the morning there vas such a quietness. I
don't know vat has happened. But I'm not a fighter; how
could I know vat has happened?

"Then the girls who fight came and said, 'Haifa is free!'
Every girl came back—one vith a gun, one vith a rifle, one
vith a gun. . . . Ve made hot vater. Everybody had a
shower! The Jewish boys came too, and say, 'Can I stay here?'
They brought some vounded. Ve put beds in corridors. Ve
prepared food. Now I can't imagine how ve managed it all.
It vas something special."

That I can well believe.

Still under Fania Malnik's spell I go back to the Zion Hotel,
perched on the lower slopes of Mt. Carmel, to meet the roommate. He returns depressed and unhappy, and undresses and
crawls into bed for a short nap. I am much too keyed up to
sleep. It is already dusk and the celebration of Haifa's freedom will soon begin. I sit by the window, going over my notes.

The telephone rings. It is General Riley. He, too, is in
Haifa, either coming from or going to his tents on the Syrian–
Israeli border. He is making no appreciable progress in the
armistice talks, and feels the need of company and a drink.
Will the roommate and I join him in his room before dinner?
We will be delighted, I say, but I, perhaps, will be late for
I must first see the torchlight procession.

At seven o'clock I climb to the flat roof of the hotel and
catch my breath at the beauty of the view. A mile, perhaps,
below, are the curving harbor and the downtown streets

aglow with lights. Eight ships are silhouetted against the black-
ness of the harbor. One is the *Theodor Herzl* and all its port-
holes are coins of shining gold.

My eyes follow the circling shore toward the north—and
Acre. In a fountain of indirect lighting stand the spacious,
spick-and-span white walls of the Electric Power Company,
and beyond it, against the translucent early evening sky, the
stacks and tanks of the Haifa Oil Works and Refineries, idle
these days and weeks and months because the Arab boycott
has stopped all oil from coming into Israel through the pipe
lines.

Slowly my eyes return to the heart of the city. Near by,
just one block away from the hotel, steady white fans of light
concentrate on a shaft which has been erected in memory of
the eighteen Jews that were killed in the Haifa battle. It is to
be unveiled as the climax of the evening's ceremony.

A block to my right a band is playing. People are thronging
the streets, moving steadily toward the monument. Flags are
flying from every post, store front, house roof.

My eyes swing to Mt. Carmel. Like a huge cloud, sum-
mer-thick with burning stars, it spreads against the still,
faintly light horizon. As I watch, bonfires, flaring with long
gold and cerise banners, spring up close to the sky's dome.

Guns on the heights begin to boom, and a corvette in the
harbor lets go with two rounds; but soon, very soon, all firing
ceases. The Israelis are much too careful of their ammunition to blow it up in a celebration. There are other and less
expensive ways to make a noise. Sirens screech, the deep
horns of the ships bark, bands play, people cheer. And now
and then, near the shore, a Roman candle lazily tosses up
bright, Christmasy balls to shatter against the ceiling of night
into trillions of shimmering pieces.

I am standing rather starry-eyed, I like to think, though no doubt dazed is the more truthful word, when Mr. Blevin, head of the Haifa Public Relations Office, appears beside me. He has tracked me down, or rather up, to the roof and wants me to go across the street to an office in the Municipal Building where the view is better.

Gladly I accept (there is really nothing difficult about me). In the hotel lobby I am introduced to Sir Simon and Lady Marks, and together we proceed to the Municipal Building. It is a beautiful building and occupies the entire block in front of the Zion Hotel. Inside, we climb flight upon flight of wide marble steps (the elevator has stopped running for the evening) until we reach the desired office. There is a terrace that opens off the office and so Sir Simon and Lady Marks and I go out there and hang over the balustrade. Yes, the view is better, but Haifa would be lovely from any point.

"I don't think there is a city in the world more beautiful than Haifa," says Lady Marks. "Not Cannes, Venice, Naples. . . ."

She's out of my depth, but I agree it is very beautiful.

"In Palestine he who doesn't believe in miracles is not a realist," comments Sir Simon, quoting the same person practically everyone else quotes, though I still haven't caught the name.

"Look, the parade!" Subdued cries of excitement run about the terrace.

Near the water front, between buildings, we catch glimpses of marching men, suffused with the red reflection of burning torches. Like a bright ribbon running in and out of eyelet embroidery, they appear and disappear. They are moving along Kingsway, parallel to the shore, but soon will swing right, up the ankle of Mt. Carmel, and then right again until they reach the monument to the dead. It is a long route,

Mr. Blevin tells me, and will take considerable time to cover. I had better come in out of the cold and wait in the office.

I agree it is cold, and my teeth are chattering, but I am afraid I will miss something if I go in. Already the unveiling ceremonies have begun. I can see the people, spread as black as water around the base of the shaft, and I can hear a man speaking. He is worked up; his voice rises from one crescendo to another, but, alas, I can understand only one word, "Haganah," and though he shouts it again and again, it is not enough to hold my attention.

I decide to go back to the hotel and join the roommate and General Riley and any others the General may have gathered together. I am already unforgivably late.

The General's room has a balcony and I dart off and on it, looking for the parade. Finally it comes, right by the corner of the hotel, an almost solid mass, four men wide and heaven knows how many deep, with torches flapping an angry red in the cold wind.

"Where are they headed?" asks an American who joins me on the balcony. I don't know him well, but I have seen him several times since coming to the Middle East.

"To the monument in commemoration of the eighteen Jews who lost their lives in the Battle of Haifa," I tell him.

He takes a long drink from the glass in his hand; then asks in a voice as cold as the night: "Where is the monument to the 43,000 Arabs who lost their homes in that battle?"

Of course, I have no answer; but I come in from the balcony. Suddenly, the parade has lost its magic.

25. No story for a tea party

MY BODY returned to Israeli Jerusalem the day after the celebration, but my mind stayed on in Haifa. The story that Fania Malnik told me of the Battle of Haifa haunted me. I felt I should find a Haifa Arab and get his side. But where to find an Arab who had been there and could give an eyewitness account? In Lebanon, maybe, or Transjordan, or Syria.

I put the idea away from me as impractical. I had too many other things to do. I was invited that very afternoon to a tea party in Ramallah and then that evening there was a dinner, and the next day a visit to King Abdullah.

The tea party was being given by an Arab woman with the lovely name of Matiel Mogannam. She had been born in Muktara, a small village in Lebanon, but when quite young had moved with her parents to the United States and there she had met, loved, and married a Palestinian Arab, who was just graduated in law from the University of Rochester. For several years after their marriage they continued to live in the United States, Mr. Mogannam having a successful law practice in both Rochester and Brooklyn; but in 1920 they grew homesick and went to Jerusalem.

Back in her Arab world, Mrs. Mogannam began to take an active part in the problems of that world and to arouse other women to those problems. She was one of the organizers and secretary of the first Arab Women's Congress, which met in Jerusalem in 1929; and her book, *The Arab Woman and the Palestine Problem* was published in 1937.

She was having a tea for the roommate and me, but at the last minute the roommate couldn't go (I secretly suspected the idea of tea had something to do with it) and I had to beg a ride with Colonel Shelby. He came down from Government House to pick me up, and I could see he was troubled. His florid face beneath the shiny cap of red hair did not wear its usual genial smile; nor did his bright blue eyes twinkle in their customary fashion.

"Bad news?" I prodded him.

"Rather."

"What?"

He grinned at me. "Didn't your mama ever tell you what happened to little girls with too much curiosity?"

"No, my mama didn't believe in telling her daughter the facts of life. Now, go on, tell me."

"Oh, well, you'll hear it sooner or later. As I was leaving Government House we received a report from an official U.N. observer that the Israelis have killed thirteen Arabs, fourteen camels, and seventeen donkeys just south of Hebron."

"No!"

"Yes." His voice was clipped. "It seems the Arabs were working in their fields and unknowingly got over the Israeli lines—you know the lines are very indefinite anyhow—and without even calling to them, the Israelis shot them down."

I was distressed. It not only seemed such a waste of life, but such a stupid thing for the Israelis to do. No doubt, some hotheads, some terrorists. . . .

After this any subject of conversation seemed unimportant. In silence we made the three-o'clock crossing, curved around the outskirts of Old Jerusalem, and climbed rather steadily into the hills to the north. The hills are rugged but nice. Every inch of them is terraced from the curving feet in the valleys to the rounded crowns near the sky. Olive groves, vineyards, orchards of figs and green almonds ascend the steps, shoulder to shoulder.

Ramallah is an Arab town of approximately 5,000 permanent inhabitants, but now it is overrun with refugees. Even Mrs. Mogannam is a refugee from the Israeli side of Jerusalem. Fortunately, she is a woman of means and has been able to rent an exceedingly comfortable, cream stucco house on the edge of town. The walls are bright with charming water colors of Palestinian scenes, painted by her daughter.

Several distinguished Arab officials were gathered in the large living room waiting, of course, for the roommate; and here I, a woman of no position, showed up without him. Acutely conscious of their disappointment, I crept about the room, head and eyes cast down, shaking hands.

To cheer them, Mrs. Mogannam ushered us into the dining room where the table was spread with more whole pies, cakes, cookies, and cream puffs than ever decorated a bakery window. "Oh's" and "ah's" filled the air. These weren't only sweets to eat, but sweets to admire. Especially the cream puffs; they were made in the shape of swans. I must have one to take home to the roommate. Certainly, cried Mrs. Mogannam, and by all means a lemon pie, too.

With my plate heaped high I sank down on a sofa by an exceedingly nice-looking man who didn't seem to be too disappointed about the roommate. His name was Achmed Khalil, and he was the military governor of the Ramallah area. Later, I learned he had been graduated from Cambridge (England, of course) in 1939 and was a lawyer as well as a soldier.

"And, Mrs. Ethridge, what have you been doing with yourself in Palestine while your husband has been working?" he asked pleasantly.

I suspected it would destroy his illusions of an American

woman if I answered, "Working, too." So I said I had just returned from Haifa where I saw the "deliverance" celebration.

He made a terrible face, simply terrible. I thought immediately he should be on television and, if possible, in the "squeaking-door" program.

"And did you enjoy it?" he asked.

I shrugged. (This business of being on the Jewish side of Palestine one day and on the Arab side the next was giving me a split personality. And, especially, when my sympathies seesawed so constantly. No matter how enthusiastic I waxed over the accomplishments of the Israelis, let someone mention the Arab refugees and I did a flip-flop.)

"You know Haifa?" I asked.

"Do I know Haifa?" His voice was high with outrage. "I was born in a village a few kilometers from Haifa, my father was born there, my grandfather was born there, and you ask me do I know Haifa."

"Were you there during the fighting?"

"I was the liaison officer for the Arabs with the British."

Naturally, he was the man I had been wanting to see all day. Even in the Middle East, it is a small world.

He put aside his cup and plate, lit a pipe, and began at the beginning of the partition, on November 29th, 1947. "When the United Nations voted to partition Palestine, the Arabs in Haifa had a three-day strike to show their disgust," he related. "Few incidents took place during the strike, but the people knew this was the start of a major struggle. To save Haifa from destruction, the Jews offer to make it an open city and we accept; but every time they offer and every time we accept, the Jews break it and claim it is the Stern gang or Irgun over whom they have no control.

"One morning the Stern and Irgun gangs threw a big

bomb at the entrance of the oil refineries where the Arab laborers work. They were in line that morning to get their pay and when the bomb was thrown many of them were blown to bits. The Arabs then took their shovels and attacked the Jews. Fifty were killed." He said it quietly, but his face was contorted again into a ghastly grimace.

"In the months following the strike, conditions grew steadily worse. At the beginning, there were eighty thousand Arabs in Haifa and they lived in the low, flat part of the city, but the situation became so intolerable that about half of them moved away. You see, the Jews were shooting down at them all the time and they couldn't shoot back. They were unarmed. The British were still here—this was early in 1948, you know—and they were very busy searching the Arab houses and the Arab shops for arms. If some shots were fired from Arab houses, the British would come and blow down the houses. Business, of course, was very dull; every Arab's life was in danger, so many Arabs left."

Mrs. Mogannam passed a plate of cake. Governor Khalil and I shook our heads, murmuring hurriedly, "No, thank you." The Governor shifted his position a bit on the sofa, crossed his legs, and continued, "At the beginning of April, General Stockwell said that unless shooting stops he is going to withdraw all British forces from Arab areas in Haifa. We told him (I was liaison officer at the time), 'You have told us the British would not leave Haifa until August 1st.' He said, 'Yes, we are staying until August 1st, but there must be an end to the shooting. We are responsible for the safety of the people.'

"But the shooting never stopped, especially from the Jews. I can remember many a day we had seventy casualties, and when I used to go to visit the hospital the doctors said they never stopped operating for thirty and forty hours." He puffed on his pipe for several seconds. "I remember, too, about this hospital; it had a mixed staff of Jews and Arabs, but the Jews withdrew and the Arabs had to deal singlehanded with all these casualties."

His dark face was heavy with gloom. People stood about the room and eyed us curiously. We were queer guests for a tea party, both so serious, so unhappy.

"On April 20th, General Stockwell called me and said, 'I am withdrawing my forces from the Arab quarters.' He withdrew them and the Jews attacked. And the Jews were helped by the British; don't let anybody tell you differently. They were helped by British tanks from Mt. Carmel."

"I simply can't believe it," I said; but he ignored me. He was again furious, his face screwed up in rage and misery. "So, all the Arab population ran from their quarters to the port. And at the port, as they were running for their lives, the British stopped them and searched them for arms. I was there and saw them with my own eyes.

"The port grew tight with people. They packed and jammed every square foot. They were like animals, they were so terrified; but they were safe for the moment. The port was still in the hands of the British, and the Jews did not attack them there.

"During the night of the 21st, they left in droves. They took small fishermen's boats—Haifa was well known for its fishing industry—they took small launches, small ferries. Anything to get them across the bay to Acre. A navigating company at Haifa sent boats, Sidon and Tyre sent boats, and a rich Lebanese sent Hitler's yacht from Beirut. There were scores and scores of boats. What a sight! What a sad sight!"

He was quiet for a few puffs; then said bitterly: "Many were drowned; no one knows how many. It was a very rough sea." He made sorrowful noises with his tongue against his teeth. "It was a very rough sea from April 20th to the 28th. Many small boats capsized and the people were lost."

I was much more depressed now than when I had come to the party. Though I was sure Governor Khalil was finished, I felt too sodden to move, and it was just as well, for after tapping his teeth with the stem of his pipe for some time, he started again: "After April 23rd, everything is quiet in Haifa. There are a few Arabs still left. The mayor of Haifa was a very nice Jew named Levy. He was the first Jew ever to be mayor of Haifa; before him the mayors had always been Arabs. He made an appeal to the few Arabs who were still there to stay, but they were afraid. The British authorities helped them to leave; they sent them in British tanks to the border.

"My sister stayed until the last day. She came out May 1st. She and the others who were left went around in the Arab quarters gathering up the dead and taking them to the cemeteries. They buried seventy. As I said, no one knows how many died at sea."

He made another face. "There were three Arab villages near Haifa—Tirah, Tantura, and Kafr-lam. Kafr-lam, that's my village." He gave me a quick smile. "When the British pulled out, the Jews took over those villages, put the Arabs in trucks, and drove them outside of Jewish territory."

This time he was through, and I was glad. It was no story for a tea party, but I had asked for it.

26. "Hat-ty" talk

His Royal Highness, Abdullah, the king of Transjordan, was having the roommate and me to lunch in his little palace at Amman. This was more of an honor to his guests, 'twas said, than entertaining in the big palace, but I, who don't often get into palaces, would have preferred "the works."

Amman is about a two-hour ride from Jerusalem, traveling east and slightly north. On the ride, the roommate said, we would have company, Dr. Husseini, who wanted to explain some Arab problems which he felt the Commission should understand better.

"Fine," said I, having discovered on the trip to Jericho that Dr. Husseini is a pleasant traveling companion.

But when we reached the Israel–Palestine lines, Miss Haliby announced: "Mousa Bey is planning to ride with you, Mr. Ethridge. He will be waiting for you at the American Colony."

"Yes," said the roommate in his best State Department manner. "I am looking forward to talking with him."

Huh, thought I, two people are going to try to clarify the roommate's mind.

At the American Colony, out walked Dr. Husseini, his large, handsome head wreathed in smiles. He took the last comfortable seat, and Bob Yount turned on the engine.

"Wait," I cried. "We haven't got Mousa Bey."

"What do you mean we haven't got Mousa Bey." The roommate's voice was slightly irritated.

"Well, have we?" I demanded belligerently.

233

"We have. Dr. Husseini, of course, is Mousa Bey."

"Oh, is Mousa Bey a pseudonym for secret government work or something?"

"Hell, no. I don't know where you've been all these weeks, or all your life for that matter. 'Bey' is a title, like 'mister.' That's all—just mister. When you're speaking of the military governor of Arab Jerusalem, for instance, you say Abdullah Bey el-Tel."

"I don't."

"Well, you should."

"I don't say Mark Bey Ethridge."

He turned his back upon me. He and Dr. Husseini or Mousa Bey had more important things to talk about.

The road to Amman drops to Jericho, then across the salt flats to the River Jordan, and then over the Jordan on the handsome Allenby Bridge. The Palestine–Transjordan border is now on the banks of the Jordan, but soon, everyone seems to agree, Palestine, or rather what's left of it, will have to be joined to Transjordan. The Palestinian Arabs don't care for this idea one bit, for their standard of living, level of education, and social concepts are far superior to that of the Transjordan Arabs. The Arabs are not a homogeneous group. The Lebanese and Palestinian Arabs are head and shoulders above the Arabs of North Africa and the desert countries of the Middle East. But what can the Palestinian Arabs do? The narrow strip of hills and valleys and desert still called Palestine cannot possibly exist as a viable state. Already King Abdullah handles Palestine's negotiations with Israel, and many other Palestine matters. (On January 1st, while these lines were being proofread, King Abdullah did annex what little remained of Palestine, except the Gaza strip, which remained in Egypt's hands.)

Crossing the border was simply a matter of waving of

hands and nodding of heads; but the climb into the hills was not so easy. The armored cars of the Iraqi army were still moving out of the Tulkarem triangle and they stretched for miles along the highway. I had no idea the Iraqis had such a fighting force; in truth, I had no idea the Iraqis had any force at all; but they had crawled all day through Jericho when I had been there, and here they were still moving back to their own country. Unfamiliar as I am with military matters and so judging solely from the looks of things, I would have thought these Iraqis, if they had really fought, could have mopped up Israel. I know I would have run like a rabbit if I had seen them coming. Just seeing them going sent shivers along my spine.

When I can stop worrying about the car maneuvering past the military traffic, I enjoy the scenery. It is surprisingly lovely after the eroded hills and salt flats around Jericho. We are following a heavenly stream, the Wadi Nimrim, which kicks up wide green hems to show its lacy ruffles. So much water skipping so heedlessly to the Jordan starts us scheming. Why not a small TVA? If just this one stream could be dammed during its spring spree, think of the arid land it might irrigate.

But it's too bad to be so practical, for the stream now is a thing of joy and beauty. Oleanders grow wild along its banks, the leaves a rich green, the blossoms a sunset pink, and the whole intimate valley is deep in grass.

We pass through several small villages where flowering apricots fan across cream walls and clumps of pomegranates cluster in sheltered corners.

Shortly the valley is pinched together with hills. (I knew all along it couldn't last.) We start climbing and vineyards climb with us. At an altitude of 2,608 feet we reach the city of Es Salt. Its flat-roofed houses are pyramided haphazardly up the steep valley walls. With a population of over twenty thousand, it is the second largest city in Transjordan. The majority of the people are Moslems, but there is a goodly sprinkling of Greek Orthodox, Roman Catholics, and Armenians.

Just before we enter the city we cut sharply to the right and continue to climb toward Amman. At one high point, the hills open and in the distance we see a flat stretch of land under cultivation. Though I'm never sure about north, south, east, or west, I suspect it is part of that strip of tableland, two hundred miles long and twenty-five miles wide, that supports five-eighths of Transjordan's population. In 1945, before the influx of Palestinian Arab refugees, Transjordan's population was estimated at only four hundred thousand, and it was divided into three groups: the settled inhabitants, numbering approximately two hundred and fifty thousand; the seminomads, living in tents, but cultivating the soil; and the nomads, who move with their flocks as the seasons turn, searching for grass.

On reaching Amman we go to an exceedingly comfortable downtown club, reminding me faintly of the Pendennis in Louisville—except the Amman club allows women to come in the front door, whereas the Pendennis shunts them to a side entrance—and meet Wells Stabler and his mother. Thus reinforced, we drive to the little palace which is nothing more than a simple cottage tucked behind trees and shrubbery.

The King greets us practically at the front door. He is Dewey-sized, but the elaborate white turban atop his head adds a foot to his stature. His swarthy face is genial; his small brown eyes, friendly and alert; and his dark mustache and beard are neatly trimmed into a circular frame for his full lips. Over his small body is draped one of those kimono-like wraps of natural-colored camel's hair, bound with gold braid.

Abdullah is a descendant of the House of Bani Hashim, the noblest of all Arab families, for it traces its male line back to Mohammed's daughter, Fatima. He is one of the three sons of the Middle East hero, King Husain ibn Ali, who first stirred the Arab nations to revolt against the Turks and is the co-author of those famous Husain–McMahon letters.

After World War I, Transjordan, like Palestine, was put under a British mandate with the same High Commissioner ruling over both countries, but in April, 1923, the British government authorized the High Commissioner, Sir Herbert Samuel, to announce Transjordan's independence from the mandate. This did not raise her, though, to absolute statehood; that was achieved only early in 1946, and even then there were special treaty arrangements under which England was to provide money for the upkeep of the Arab Legion and British officers to train it. With the creation of the new state, Abdullah, who had held the title of emir, was crowned King.

When Mrs. Stabler is introduced to King Abdullah, she curtsies beautifully, almost to the floor, but I, without practice, am afraid to try it and settle for a clasp of the hand. We are ushered into an ordinary sized living room with bunk-like seats built around the walls and heaped with cushions and pillows. The men, just as if they were in the States, sit on one side of the room; Mrs. Stabler and I in a far corner.

In addition to the King and us, there is one of the King's sons, Emir Naief, who has recently been made a colonel in the Arab Legion to head a newly created Hashimite Regiment. He is the son of the King's number-two wife and is married to a Turkish princess, the granddaughter of the last Sultan of Turkey. He, too, is small and dark complected, but lacks, on first meeting, the warmth of his father. Also there is a delightful interpreter and a slim, rather beautiful young man who has no official position, as I understand it, but is just a favorite of Abdullah's.

We wait for the King to speak. This I find most difficult, but both the roommate and Mrs. Stabler impressed me before coming in with the propriety of it. The King eyes Mrs. Stabler, who is wearing a bright red velvet hat, interestingly draped and trimmed with a feather, and he says in Arabic that he likes it; it reminds him of the hats of Dowager Queen Mary of England. Well, he might consider this a compliment, but I can see from the look on Mrs. Stabler's handsome face that she doesn't care for the idea at all. In fact, she answers that she would have never thought of it, but adds in her most diplomatic manner that she is deeply grateful to His Majesty for making such a charming remark.

His Majesty then talks about the weather. It is rotten, we all agree, and most "unusual." It is raining again, and it is late April.

Mrs. Stabler says, "It is so very kind of Your Majesty to have us for lunch. We are deeply honored."

His Majesty waves his small, delicately fingered hand through the air and declares it is his pleasure. He has had several visitors this week. Just the day before, Sir Herbert Samuel, who is now visiting in Israel, had called upon him to plead on behalf of the Israelis for the potash lands on the west banks of the Dead Sea. He and Sir Samuel have been dear friends since Sir Samuel was the first High Commissioner of Palestine, the King says, and they have been through many tight places together.

As the King talks he holds the roommate's hand and plays with his fingers. It is not surprising; Arab men are frequently affectionate and demonstrative, but I can see that the roommate doesn't know how to take it. Like a nervous girl, he sits on the edge of the bench in a ready-to-spring position.

At lunch I get off to a bad start. The first course is so strange and delicious I take two helpings and by the fourth course I'm out. Gorgeous trays heaped with gorgeous foods go by and I can only shake my head.

The King eyes me ruefully with his soft brown eyes. He has planned this lunch with care: the table appointments are exquisite; the china and silver, handsome; and the food the very best. And I sit there, shaking my head—and chatting. And chatting, of all things, about women. Suddenly, he stops me, and how!

"Tell me the names of your great women in the United States," he says.

The only name that comes into my mind is Mrs. Roosevelt, but her name I know is poison to the Arabs. But still I must mention her.

"In the United States we think Mrs. Roosevelt is a great woman. Of course, she makes mistakes. . . ." I look pleadingly at the roommate.

"We don't have many great women in public life," the roommate rushes in, "but there are quite a number who are famous in literature and journalism and. . . ."

Mercifully, His Majesty interrupts: "The women of the United States are famous because they've given famous men to the world. They are good mothers; they produce strong stock. (Suddenly I feel as if I should be in a pasture.) Look at your men: Franklin Roosevelt, Wendell Willkie, Eisenhower, Marshall. Arab women are no good. They bring weaklings into the world."

I am aghast. This is no way for a King to talk about his female subjects—even if they can't vote. But what to say? Nothing that I can think of. Absolutely nothing.

Leaving the dining room, the King sweeps his hand toward the rug and asks Mrs. Stabler and me how we like it.

"Oh, Your Majesty, it is perfectly beautiful!" cries Mrs. Stabler. "It is simply gorgeous; in fact, I never saw a more gorgeous rug."

"Yes, it is gorgeous," I echo.

The King claps his hands and a huge black man, robed in white, dashes into the room and flings two rugs, similar to the one on the floor, but much smaller, at our feet. One is for Mrs. Stabler and one for me.

"You'll have to take it home on your shoulder," the roommate mutters to me.

The fact that he, too, has a shoulder never crosses his mind.

Shortly Mrs. Stabler and I withdraw; it has been arranged for us to have an audience with the Queen. As we go out, the King is gently stroking the roommate's back.

King Abdullah has three wives. Under Moslem law he is allowed four, but he keeps one place open just in case. . . . Only the first wife has the title of Queen; the other two are princesses. But even the Queen is not called by her title. She is Om Telah (the mother of Telah, the crown prince). And the second wife is Om Naief (the mother of Naief).

The third wife is Princess Nahdh, but she is generally referred to as the Black Queen, for her skin is black and shiny as tar. She is young, slender, and moves with grace. She was a serving maid to the Queen when the King first spied her. He built her a fine palace, which I saw only from the outside, and imported decorators from Jerusalem to furnish it.

The first Queen lives in no such elegance. Far from it! She occupies what I'd call a second-floor flat in a walk-up. The front room is depressing, with mammoth chairs of shiny light wood and a big stove.

The Queen enters unattended and, smiling warmly, comes toward us. Mrs. Stabler again does her beautiful curtsy and I my inadequate handshake.

"It is so very kind of Your Highness to receive us," Mrs. Stabler says. "We are deeply honored, indeed fortunate."

She stops. The Queen isn't getting it. She looks at us blankly, helplessly. It is apparent that English is an unknown tongue to her.

"Oh, what shall we do?" cries Mrs. Stabler.

Neither the Queen nor I know.

The three of us stand about, staring at one another in the silliest fashion. Finally, it is too much for the Queen; she lets go a flood of Arabic.

Mrs. Stabler and I throw up our hands. "Oh, Your Highness," Mrs. Stabler shrieks softly, "we don't understand a word. Not a word. What are we going to do?"

As nobody still knows the answer to that one, we decide simultaneously to sit down and think it over. We sit and we look at one another and we shrug our shoulders and grin sheepishly.

The Queen is short and stout and her ankles are badly swollen with arthritis or varicose veins. She wears heavy, low shoes; a shapeless brown skirt; a bright green sweater, open down the front and hooked at the waist; and on her head a huge turban of a thin, soft material.

Mrs. Stabler is fascinated by the turban and she begins making gestures toward it and rolling her eyes toward heaven in awestruck admiration.

The Queen seems to understand. She smiles brilliantly and lets go with another flood of Arabic. Evidently she thinks that we have learned Arabic while sitting there.

"Oh dear, dear Your Majesty!" Mrs. Stabler wails. "We don't understand a word. Not a word. We couldn't be more stupid, Your Majesty! It is such a pity. We are just two stupid Americans. You will have to forgive us."

Evidently Mrs. Stabler thinks that Her Majesty has learned English while sitting there.

But no. Nobody has learned anything. The Queen shrugs, we shrug, and then we all giggle. It couldn't be sillier.

Mrs. Stabler returns to her admiration of the Queen's turban. There are tiny crocheted dangles hanging from it, striking the Queen's cheeks. Mrs. Stabler trips across the room and with enthusiastic impulsiveness puts out her hand to touch them. The Queen's enormous black eyes, painted about with kohl oil, beam with pleasure.

Mrs. Stabler returns to her chair and subsides.

It is my turn to do something, but my mind is a blank.

At long last, the Queen sits up very straight. Eyeing us sharply she slowly enunciates: "Tel-e-phone!"

Well, if she'd said we had come into money we couldn't have been more pleased. "Tel-e-phone!" both Mrs. Stabler and I carol. "Tel-e-phone! Tel-e-phone! Tel-e-phone!"

Finally, we wind down, and again we sit in silence, contemplating. Now and then we shrug, but our shoulders are beginning to get sore.

"Tel-e-phone," the Queen says again, and this time she leans over and picks up a tel-e-phone from the low shelf of a table beside her and speaks into it.

"I think she's calling for an interpreter," Mrs. Stabler whispers to me. "Yes, I'm pretty sure that is what she's doing."

The Queen replaces the tel-e-phone and smiles at us brightly.

More silence. Contemplation. Living death.

Mrs. Stabler, with her highly cultivated social consciousness, can't take it. She claws about in her bag and comes up with the picture of her grandchild. Again, she trips over to the Queen. "My grandchild," she exclaims, offering her the picture. "Ma petite fille."

She spreads her hand out level with her knees; then she clasps her hands over her bosom. "My own, dear grandchild, Your Majesty. A little love."

Her Majesty studies the picture closely with her big eyes, and then points with one finger at Mrs. Stabler.

"Oh, no, no, not mine, Your Majesty. My grandchild. My child's child."

Mrs. Stabler moves back to her chair and sinks into something resembling a deep swoon.

And so she remains until a young woman bursts into the room. She is the interpreter for whom the Queen telephoned. The Queen had tried to reach her earlier, she explains, but she had been out. The second call caught her just as she came into the house. She is distressed that we have had such a difficult hour.

"It is perfectly all right," declares Mrs. Stabler, coming instantly out of the swoon. "We've had a lovely time with Her Majesty. I've been telling her how much I admire her turban. I think it is beautiful, simply beautiful."

When the young woman interprets this, the Queen gets up and goes out of the room and returns a few minutes later with a large, amazingly soft piece of white cloth. Holding it out to Mrs. Stabler, she makes a speech.

"Her Majesty is so happy, Mrs. Stabler, that you like her turban," the interpreter says, "that she is giving you a piece of cloth just like the piece out of which hers is made. When you go back to the States, she hopes you will have one made to suit you."

Of course, I want to yell, "I like it, too," but it is too late.

Until we back ourselves out the door and down the steps, Mrs. Stabler is saying: "Tell Her Majesty how deeply grateful I am. Tell Her Majesty I can't wait to wear it in Washington; I know I will be a sensation. Tell Her Majesty . . ."

Yes, I know I'm bitter. And it *is* terribly little of me. After all, King Abdullah didn't say my hat looked like Queen Mary's.

27. *"And supper being ended"*

RELIGIOUS SERVICES take up a large slice of life in Jerusalem. No sooner is the observance of the Passover and the Easter of the Latin Catholics finished than the Easter services of the Greek Orthodox, Syrians, Copts, and Abyssinians begin. It is exceedingly easy to do nothing except go to church for ten full days. At one point I thought I was going to have to start taking box lunches.

On a day called Maundy Thursday I rose before dawn and with several other members of the delegation made my way across the lines into Old Jerusalem to attend the Greek ceremony of the washing of the feet. It was scheduled to begin at eight o'clock in the courtyard of the Church of the Holy Sepulcher, but I was urged to be there no later than seven-thirty.

As I was shoving my way through the crowd near the church I was rescued by a short, rotund, elderly gentleman, by the name of George J. Said and the title of Secretary to the Greek Orthodox Patriarchate, who whisked me through a door and up a flight of stairs to a small balcony overhanging the courtyard. The only other occupant of the balcony was Colonel Abdullah Tel, who welcomed me with a smile as kind and gentle as a child's.

Directly in front of us in the courtyard stood an oblong platform painted grass green, with an iron rail around it and an iron arch at each end, decorated with old carriage lamps and tiny, bright blue wooden angels. Six chairs lined each side of the platform and one stood at the far end.

The courtyard, the windows, the arches, the eaves, the belfry, and the patches of roof of the church and its many additions bulged with people. Policemen moved everywhere, their silver-spiked helmets showing prominently in the crowd.

The gong in the Holy Sepulcher began to bang in a queer, spine-tingling rhythm, and out of the main door of the church marched the *kiwass*. In unison, they slammed their silver staves upon the cobblestones. Behind them came twelve priests in red and gold brocade, representing the twelve disciples, and behind them, walking alone, a most resplendent figure in a ruby-red velvet cape encrusted with gold, and on his head, a gold bejeweled crown.

"The Archbishop of Philadelphia," whispered Mr. Said.

"From the United States?" I whispered back.

"No, from Transjordan."

The archbishop is substituting for the Greek Patriarch, who, according to Mr. Said, "has been ailing in his residence for one year now." He represents Christ.

The priests and the archbishop take their seats upon the platform and a "gospeler," hidden from sight—at least from my sight—begins to read in Greek the accounts of the Last Supper from the Gospels and a choir begins to sing very beautifully in response to the reading.

Mr. Said reminds me of the words in the Gospel of St. John:

"And supper being ended, the devil having now put into the heart of Judas Iscariot, Simon's son, to betray him;

Jesus knowing that the Father had given all things into his hands, and that he was come from God, and went to God;

He riseth from supper, and laid aside his garments; and took a towel, and girded himself;

After that he poureth water into a bason, and began to wash the disciples' feet, and to wipe them with the towel wherewith he was girded."

Slowly the archbishop stands and is disrobed. His crown is put to one side, his chain and cross of precious stones and his cope of red velvet and encrusted gold are removed. Beneath, is a simple robe of pale lavender. He ties a towel about his generous waist and puts another across his shoulder. Now he is ready, except for rearranging his long white beard. Daintily, he pats it into place upon his bosom.

Taking a gold ewer and basin, he stoops before the first disciple on his right. Off comes one shoe and one sock—a navy blue—and the archbishop pours water on the foot and wipes it with the towel. The disciple leans forward to work his sock back on and his rich black beard sweeps the planking.

The archbishop continues around the imaginary table. The crowd watches in awed silence. Next to me, Abdullah Tel leans against the balcony rail and follows every move with his soft brown eyes. For him, too, it is a new sight. He, a Moslem, is here officially in the role of governor of Arab Jerusalem.

"Last time this year," he murmurs to me, "I was too busy fighting to attend church services."

When the last foot has been washed, the archbishop and the disciples march with deliberate tread into the Church of the Holy Sepulcher and, loudly, the gong in the belfry begins to bang and leisurely the people begin to descend from the eaves and the windows and the roofs to take up the tasks of the day. The sun has not yet reached into the courtyard; the morning is still very young.

Abdullah Tel and I have wine and sweet cakes with Mr. Said and some dignitaries of the church and then part for a few hours. There will be another washing of the feet and more services, but between them, the governor will entertain at lunch for a few visitors.

The main dish at lunch is a glorious Arab concoction of rice, pine nuts, almonds, and barbecued lamb called *mansaf*. All morning the lambs were on spits being turned over coals and basted with herb-steeped juices; but before our arrival they were torn into hunks and mixed with the rice and nuts.

As we enter the dining room, this mixture is heaped in a flat dish as big around as a full-sized wagon wheel and sitting alone upon a round table not much larger. Abdullah Tel waves his guests toward it, and says with his shy smile that it is to be eaten with the hands in the Arab fashion; but, he adds, there are plates and knives and forks and seats placed for those who prefer them.

The roommate, who has very refined tastes, and Mrs. Stabler, and a few others choose to be served, but Wells, Abdullah Tel, Nassib Bulos, and one or two other Arabs and I crowd about the wagon-wheel platter and dig in. I take to it naturally; my mother must have had an uphill fight to teach me to use a knife and fork. I work the *mansaf* into a round ball, as I see the Arabs do, and pop it, with a slight flip of the wrist, into my mouth.

"Look at me!" I call to the roommate. "Look at me!"

"Why should I?" he calls back. "You're no treat. I've seen you eat watermelon, remember?"

Several Arabs want me to add a sort of clabber to my portion of *mansaf*. They have already poured it upon theirs and declare it adds a delicious flavor. I pour on about half a pint, but the experiment for me is not successful. Before I can get the balls into my mouth, the juice runs down my arm and drips off my elbow.

When I've cleared a triangular space as large as between two spokes of said wagon wheel, I back away and join the

roommate at his table. I didn't think I could eat another
mouthful, but his green vegetables look so tempting I decide
to try some of them.

The roommate is embarrassed. He shakes his head and explains to his near neighbors: "She's the living proof of the
failure of the Rockefeller endowment for the eradication of
tapeworm. The poor old man spent millions to rid the South
of tapeworm. And now look at her!"

Directly from the luncheon table, everyone except the
roommate rushes to the next washing of feet. He insists he
has seen foot-washings in Mississippi, and besides there is
the work of the Commission; but I know he has never seen
any washing of feet as the Armenians do it. This service is
held inside the Church of St. James, which is so exception-
ally beautiful it is a pleasure to sit inside it. Hundreds of
silver lamps with glass bowls of ruby red, Hebron blue, amber, green, and rose hang on thin silver chains from the
vaulted ceiling.

"See the eggs on the chains?" asks Katie Antonius, who is
sitting beside me in a small section reserved for visitors.

I hadn't noticed them; I had been too busy admiring the
bowls of the lamps, but now I see that each silver chain is
strung with a gaily painted white china egg.

"When the lamps used to be full of oil, mice ran down
the chains to drink it," Katie explains, "and the idea of stringing eggs on the chains to block them was hit upon. Though
oil is no longer used, the custom continues. They are delightful, don't you think?"

Indeed, yes.

And the walls of the church are delightful and beautiful,
too. Lovely old, old tiles cover the walls to a height of six feet,
and above them are large oil paintings. The church is named
for James, the brother of John and the son of Zebedee. It is

built on the spot where Herod is supposed to have cut off James's head with a sword. The burial place of his head, which gives me the creeps to think about, is off the north aisle.

The church also houses three stones which I should think the Jews would eye with envy. They are stones said to be taken from Mt. Sinai, Mt. Tabor, and the River Jordan at the spot where the Israelites crossed on their way out of Egypt. Pilgrims are allowed to kiss them, but I was too busy watching the preparations for the foot-washing to avail myself of the privilege.

A church dignitary comes by gloriously dressed in black lace over garnet-colored taffeta, and another in a stiff, royal-purple damask faced in watermelon pink. Though I know it is not Christian of me, I want them both terribly (the robes, not the dignitaries). All the monks wear high, peaked, wa-tered-silk hats that look as if the material were draped over Spanish combs.

Candelabra, as large and many-branched as medium-sized trees, are lit on each side of the nave. Choirboys in cream damask embroidered in gold, carrying silver candlesticks with lighted tapers, appear and begin to chant.

Blue satin curtains, elaborately hand painted and hand em-broidered, part and pull back. We see a performance as care-fully staged as any Broadway show, and with props much more gorgeous. The Patriarch kneels at one side of the stage with a basin that has a raised platform in the shape of a foot in the middle of it, the disciples come, one by one, and the Patriarch laves their feet with a few drops of water, wipes them with brightly colored, individual towels, and anoints them with oil. The incense lamps swing constantly and the choirboys sing in high, sweet voices.

Coming out of the candle-lit interior into the bright sunshine of Jerusalem I try to jerk myself back into the stark doings of the twentieth century, but it is difficult, especially in the Old City. It must be similar to the city Jesus knew— the worn cobblestones; the dim, narrow alleys, partly roofed over; the low, whitish walls with doors opening into one-room shops no bigger than cows' stalls; the rancid smells; the tinkling noises; the ragged people.

Without warning, the leather bow pops off my shoe. Nassib Bulos steers me into a cobbler's shop. The cobbler sits cross-legged on the floor, amidst mountain ranges of shoes, sewing with a half-foot-long needle a new sole on an old slip-per. Hides hang on the walls, pieces of leather are scattered about like rugs, bunches of sandals dangle from the door, cobwebs cupboard the corners.

I sink upon a low, three-legged stool and remove my bowless number. The cobbler brings tiny cups of black coffee and then nonchalantly threads a new needle with black thread and nonchalantly sews the bow in place. He could be of Jesus' time. And suddenly I entertain the happy notion that maybe he will wash my foot before he hands me back my shoe.

28. "The equal sisters of men"

THE ARAB WOMEN whom I met socially in the Lebanon and Palestine had culture and great charm, but as a Westerner I was curious about the majority with whom I had no contact. I had not seen a harem or even heard of one, and the only man I had met who admitted to more than one wife was King Abdullah. I asked many people about Arab women, but I learned more from Matiel Mogannam than from anyone else.

She, remember, was the secretary of the executive committee of the Arab women's movement and wrote a book called *The Arab Woman and the Palestine Problem.*

One morning I drove back to Ramallah to spend a whole day talking with her—she talking, I listening—and at the end of it she gave me an autographed copy of her book. From our conversation and that book, I learned many new facts—at least, new to me.

For one thing, I knew so little about Mohammed and she knew so much. Instead of Mohammed's being responsible for the backward state of the Moslem woman, he, according to Mrs. Mogannam, elevated her to "the Queen of her home." He regulated the laws of marriage, which had never been binding by written law or rule before, and he insisted that "all believers are equal."

Mohammed's ideas about women were revolutionary for his time and were due largely, in Mrs. Mogannam's opinion, to his exceptional wives. The time, remember, was the early part of the seventh century, and the wives were Khadijah bint Khwailed and, after her death, Aisha. Khadijah had been twice a widow and was fifteen years Mohammed's senior when she first saw him and made up her mind to marry him. (As you will see, there was nothing backward about her.) Up to this point, Mohammed was a most ordinary mortal doing all sorts of odd jobs: sometimes he was a shepherd, and sometimes he acted as an arrow-bearer in the tribal Arab wars, and once he piloted a caravan of merchandise to Damascus.

It was when he piloted the caravan that Khadijah saw him. She was rich and in trade and the merchandise belonged to her. She watched his departure with eyes, no doubt, already soft with love and when he returned she was waiting for him. She sent her old nurse, Nafisa, to see him and find out whether he "has any desire to get married."

The nurse hurried through the streets of Mecca to Mohammed's house and after a few passing-the-time-of-day remarks, asked him bluntly: "What prevents you from marriage?"

"Lack of the necessary means to meet the needs of a family," Mohammed answered.

"But if you were to have a woman with money, beauty, and standing?" Nafisa persisted.

"Who will that be?"

"Khadijah bint Khwailed."

"Will that be possible?" Mohammed's voice was full of doubt.

"Certainly," Nafisa answered. "If you will accept the proposition, I will take it upon myself to convince her."

This was pretty canny of Nafisa, considering Khadijah had suggested the idea in the first place.

Mohammed didn't answer, and Nafisa correctly interpreted his silence as acceptance and rushed home and told her mistress.

When they were married, Mohammed was twenty-five years old and Khadijah forty, but it worked out beautifully. Khadijah had sufficient wealth to relieve Mohammed of the irksome business of making a living, but, more important, she believed he was the long-looked-for prophet. She came by this belief before she married him through a vision, so it is said, or a dream. One night she saw a star as big as the sun shine all about in the neighborhood and into her house, and, excited, she rushed next morning to her cousin, Waraqa Ibn Nofel, a famous astronomer, and recounted the experience. Unhesitatingly he said the light signified the coming of the last of all the prophets and its brilliance in her own house meant that she was to marry him.

Though her faith wavered now and then, as I'm sure any

woman's would under the circumstances, she encouraged Mohammed and gave him the leisure and peace of mind to devote himself to meditation. He retreated to a cave in the Hiraa Mountain, not far from Mecca, for long, solitary vigils.

When he received the first revelation and the first Sura of the Koran was inspired, he was greatly troubled. What did it mean? What should he do? He confided his perplexities to Khadijah. She was everything a sympathetic wife should be. He was the prophet, she was sure, but to be doubly sure she hurried with him to Waraqa Ibn Nofel, who had interpreted her star dream. Waraqa Ibn Nofel was optimistic. He believed that the same angel who had appeared before Moses had now come to Mohammed and that he undoubtedly had been chosen as the prophet of his people.

Khadijah became the first of his many, many converts. She immediately accepted Mohammed's faith in only one God, to be called, as you know, Allah; previously the Arab tribes had worshipped innumerable gods.

After Khadijah's death, Mohammed married Aisha, who loved and revered him and sat at his feet more like a pupil than a wife. No doubt he, being human as well as a prophet, basked in this adoration and thought fine thoughts of all the female sex. Anyway, he announced: "Women are but the equal sisters of men," and through his teachings undoubtedly elevated the status of women in his part of the world. Instead of encouraging polygamy, as I for one had always thought, he discouraged it. The conditions laid down for marrying more than one wife are so strict and difficult that it is practically impossible for a true believer to meet them. He spoke as follows in the Women's Sura:

"O mankind be careful of your duty to your Lord who created you from a single soul and from it created its mate, and from them twain had spread abroad a multitude of men and women. Be careful of your duty to Allah, in whom ye claim your rights to one another, and towards the wombs that bore you, and if ye fear that you will not deal fairly with the orphans, marry of the woman who seem good to you two or three or four, and if ye fear that you cannot do justice to so many then only one. Thus it is more likely that you will not do injustice."

Then, evidently after more thought, he added this advice:

"Ye will not be able to deal justly between your wives, however much ye wish to do so, therefore marry only one."

To Mrs. Mogannam and other Moslems that seems a fairly clear order against polygamy; but there is that loophole for the man who feels he is another Solomon.

But marriage in Islam is not a sacrament in the same sense as we understand it in the Christian world; it is a matter of agreement. "It is a contract between both parties concluded either directly or through agents," Mrs. Mogannam explains. "The wife offers marital privileges, while the husband offers the *mahr* or dowry. The consent of both the bride and the bridegroom is essential. Each must convey his willingness to marry the other in person or through a *wakil* (agent) duly authorized by him before a marriage officer called *mazoun,* or else before a *qadi* (judge). The function of the marriage officer is not, however, to join the bride and bridegroom . . . but to witness the marriage contract."

The fact that the groom, instead of the bride, furnishes the dowry interested me considerably. Also, the fact that it is divided into two portions: prompt and deferred. The bride receives the "prompt" portion at the time of the marriage, but the "deferred" is not payable until the marriage is ended, either by divorce or death. As this deferred amount is usually fairly steep, it makes a man at least stop and think before putting aside his mate.

Divorce is permissible in the Moslem faith, but Mohammed called it the "most detestable of all permitted things" and commanded: "Marry but divorce not, as divorce shakes the throne of God."

Even better than Mohammed's command to my way of thinking is the advice of Allah (God) to disgruntled husbands. (Wives, evidently, aren't supposed to be disgruntled.) Allah said: "Be patient at what failures you may see in your wife; do not give up hope in improving her and in the restoration of good understanding between you. You may obtain through her after your extreme hate to her, ample reward."

When I have the time I plan to embroider this on a sampler and hang it at the foot of the roommate's bed.

But if worse comes to worst between a husband and wife, a divorce is obtainable in what Mrs. Mogannam terms, "three main degrees. In the first degree the wife continues to live in her husband's home until completion of a period called *Iddah*. During this period the husband can resume conjugal relations with his wife.

"The second degree is *Talaq Ba'in,* and in this degree the same conditions prevail, but if for any reason they fail to make a reconciliation between them a divorce is declared for the third time and enters its third or final degree."

After divorce women have the right to remarry. Allah doesn't mention men's right; no doubt he didn't consider that necessary; but he does say to the men: "And when ye have divorced women and they reach their term, place not difficulty in the way of their marrying their husbands if it is agreed between them in kindness."

Moslem women, from custom, veil their faces and keep themselves in seclusion, Mrs. Mogannam said, and not from law or the word of Allah. The fashion came to the Moslem communities from Persia, where it was in vogue from early times; but Mohammed did give impetus to it. He introduced the custom into his own family to get more privacy. Mrs. Mogannam explains in her book:

"Many people used to assemble at the Prophet's house every day in order to listen to his teachings and parables. Omar, a leading companion of the Prophet, advised him not to allow people to enter his house, but the Prophet himself, a democrat by nature, refused to act upon this advice. At last a revelation came to the Prophet that his wives should be veiled and that no one should be allowed to enter his house except on special occasions.

"The believers followed the example of their Prophet . . . and in time the custom of veiling was established and spread."

Now the custom of the veil and seclusion are slowly passing. Rarely did I see women veiled in the cities and big town, but frequently in the villages and fields. And though, no doubt, the veil is bad psychologically, it certainly adds glamor and color to the Arab scene.

29. "Like a nest"

THE ARABS call the town of Ramallah "little New York" because so many of its inhabitants have been at one time or another to the United States to make their fortune. Whether they made it or not I don't know, but they picked up the English language and many American customs.

Walking with Mrs. Mogannam along the hilly, narrow streets I heard many recognizable phrases and saw more people than usual in Western clothes; but the background was

still Middle East. The clear, warm sun on the rough walls of
faded beige; the small, smelly courts with vines clinging to
sagging balconies; the steep inclines of cobbled streets; the
small, one-story suks spilling cheap wares onto the sidewalks;
the slender, balcony-encircled minarets; the donkeys, sheep,
goats; and over all, the cloudless sky as blue as a young girl's
sash.

Mrs. Mogannam was showing me the town. There were
two institutions she felt I must visit. One was a small center
where a dozen or more old women wove table mats, cloths,
runners, and other pieces from yarn bought in India and
Egypt. The idea is to create work for a few of the hundreds
of refugees who are now idle in Ramallah and to sell the output to soft-hearted visitors who are coaxed in to see it. I'm
not mentioning names, but my old Kentucky home is going
to blossom out any day now with a sand-colored set of mats
enlivened with a green-and-yellow border.

The other institution was the radio station, which had
been in the now Israeli-held section of Jerusalem but had
been moved on the eve of capture to Ramallah. It was and
still is the largest radio station in the Middle East. Before the
War it was a 21,000-watt station; now it is 11,000.

Mrs. Mogannam and I had to motor a few miles to the
outskirts of Ramallah to reach it, and then had practically to
sign our lives away to get inside. It is housed in one of the old
British barracks and is surrounded by a heavy wire fence at
least ten feet tall. Arab soldiers guard the gates.

The Arab director, Azmi Nashashibi, is taking no chances
on being surprised by enemy forces or being bombed by sabo-
teurs. His escape with enough equipment to carry on was
much too narrow for him ever to breathe easily again.

"We had a huge, up-to-date building in Jerusalem," he
told me as soon as we were introduced. "We had eleven stu-

dios; everything very modern. Now look at us. . . ." He
flung his hands out in that familiar gesture of helplessness.
"We just had time to tear the microphones from the walls
and leave."

Fortunately for Mr. Nashashibi, the station's sending tower
was on a hill near Ramallah and the former British barracks
close by had sufficient empty space for his equipment, but
there was no electricity. That had been cut off from the Arab
side by the Israelis during the War. But Mr. Nashashibi was
not to be defeated. He flew to Cairo and bought engines to
generate his own electricity. He wasn't able to get as many
generators as he wanted and his power is greatly curtailed,
but the station can still be heard as far away as Athens,
Bagdad, and throughout the whole of Palestine, Israel, Transjordan, Lebanon, Syria, and Turkey.

He showed me around the small apartment in which he
and his staff work. The newsroom is in the former kitchen,
a tiny, dingy, absurdly equipped spot for the gathering, cutting, and editing of programs; but the inconveniences haven't
curtailed the output. They use three services: the United
Press, Associated Press, and Reuters; and they broadcast five
news programs daily. The bulletins at seven o'clock in the
morning are in English; the others in Arabic.

At lunchtime we were back at Mrs. Mogannam's home, sitting in the sun on a low, rock wall that kept the yard from
plunging into the valley below us. Near by, an almond tree
was heavy with nuts and now and then I would reach up
and pluck one and munch upon it like a squirrel. I didn't
like the taste; the greenish hulls and meat were bitter; but it
seemed so novel to be picking almonds off a tree and eating
them that I kept at it.

The air was as clear as a freshly wiped mirror, and everywhere I looked across the valley I could see hills moving with mincing steps up the blue façade of the sky.

"Oh, the rocks and the labor that must have gone into those immeasurable miles of terraces," I said with a deep sigh. "It makes me weary just to see them."

Mrs. Mogannam smiled. "The building of terraces in this part of Palestine is, as you say in America, 'a natural.' First, you rid the land of rocks to plant it, and, second, you take the rocks and make the walls."

"We wouldn't have the patience in the United States," I answered. "If we build a rock wall around a field, we carry on like mad. We would never build them around and around mountains like rickrack around children's skirts."

"In Palestine we have patience; we have had it for fourteen hundred years; but I don't know how much longer we will have it."

On the hillside, which must have been many miles away, but looked close in the brilliant light, I could see an Arab woman gliding toward her house with a pitcher on her head.

"It is beautiful here," I said.

"Yes," Mrs. Mogannam admitted, but there was no enthusiasm in her voice. Then she added: "You should have seen my home in Tabieh (an Arab section in the new part of Jerusalem), but you would have had to come before 1948. I was the first one to be put out of Tabieh. In January of '48 I got a telephone call from a Jew who had been a friend of my late husband's. He said, 'The Jews are going to blow your house up. You had better get out immediately.' I called the British police; this was, you see, still during the British mandate, and told them about the message. They said no one could help me and I had better get out quickly.

"It was raining very hard, but the children and I got out. We didn't know what else to do. But the next morning we decided that the man who called us had been a fool and we went back. That night at eight o'clock we were shot at. One bullet went right over my son's head. You can imagine the panic I went through. We hurriedly packed a few things and drove to Jericho. Later we came here."

She began crying. I felt unhappy and inadequate. I reached up and picked another almond off the tree and bit into it.

"Our house was like a nest," she said, still crying. "My husband and I had bought everything in it with sentiment. Through the years we had collected many beautiful things." She wiped the tears from her cheeks with an already wet handkerchief. "You being a woman know how it is."

Yes, I did know, but that didn't help.

She began to cry harder. "To lose all the things you love. . . . to . . ." She blew her nose, wiped her eyes and looked at me with a forced smile. "I'm sorry, but our house was one of the best in Jerusalem and now it is occupied by Jews." The same tones of bitterness that I had heard in the voices of so many Arabs colored hers.

The young daughter appeared with a tray of cocktails, a rare sight in this Arab world, followed by Mr. Nashashibi, who had been invited to lunch during our visit at the radio station, and by another gentleman who had been encountered during our stroll about the town and had been told "to come along about one o'clock" if he could get away from his duties. His name sounded like Major Anwar Khatih and he was, I understood, commander of the military contingent of the Arab Legion that had first marched into Jerusalem.

They joined Mrs. Mogannam and me on the rock wall and we talked of many things: the original area of the Dead Sea, which Mr. Nashashibi was sure had been much greater than at present because of the wide deposits of salt; the industriousness of the Arab farmer; the present condition of the Israelis.

As if asking about a little-known race on some distant shore, Mrs. Mogannam asked: "Is life normal among the Jews in Jerusalem?"

"Yes," I answered. "It seems so."

"Do they have enough food?"

"Yes, but judging from the menus of the King David there is terrific monotony. Almost every meal we have canned peas and carrots."

Screeches from both Mrs. Mogannam and daughter rent the air, but not, as I first thought, because of the monotony of peas and carrots endured by the Israelis. The Mogannams were having canned peas and carrots for lunch.

For once, though, I didn't mind. The main dish was rice, and because the roommate likes rice better than any other one article of food and warned me when were married that unless I had rice every Sunday for dinner he would divorce me, I spent a considerable portion of the meal mumbling: "Take one cup of macaroni and fry it in oil until it is slightly brown; add two cups of rice, soaked in warm water for half an hour, and fry it with the macaroni for two minutes, stirring vigorously. Pour four cups of boiling water on rice and macaroni and cover, using strong fire for the first ten minutes until there is little water on rice and then low heat until cooked. Fry pine nuts; cut meat into pieces and fry. Mix meat and nuts and place in a cake pan and put cooked rice on top and serve with sour milk."

But, alas, I forgot to mumble what kind of meat and how much. And where does one get pine nuts in Kentucky?

30. Exceedingly uncomfortable moments

PRACTICALLY all afternoon and evening, the roommate packed and unpacked his clothes and papers. The Commission was leaving Israel for Lausanne, to continue its negotiations for peace. The roommate was unhappy over leaving the Middle East. He had argued valiantly that the Commission and the Arabs and Jews should be able to find some near-by spot to sit down together and come to peaceful terms. He had suggested Government House, but there was no decent road leading to it from the Arab side and, of course, the Arabs could not and would not travel over Israeli land to reach it. He had suggested the Greek Isle of Rhodes where Dr. Bunche had held the armistice talks, but the Arabs would not hear of that either; they referred to it as the Isle of Shame, for in their eyes the armistice terms were unjust and forced down their throats. He suggested—well, in the course of days he suggested almost every spot in that part of the world: Constantinople, Athens, Beirut. Beirut is in Arab Lebanon and thus "untouchable" for the Israelis, but couldn't a ship be anchored ten miles offshore for the Israeli delegates? (This last in desperation.)

At times, hearing of these arguments, I felt that the place for the talks was looming larger than the purpose of them. If the Commission and Arabs and Israelis couldn't even get together on a spot to talk, how could they ever get together on terms?

Finally, it had to be western Europe. M. Boisanger of

the French delegation and Mr. Yalcin of the Turkish delegation had leaned toward that idea all the time. Well, how about some place in Italy—Milan, Florence, Naples? No, the Israelis turned thumbs down on Italy. Their application for membership in the United Nations was coming up shortly before the Security Council and they didn't want the name of Israel associated in any shape or form with Italy, whose application for membership had been turned down. The psychology of the thing, you know. Well, how about Geneva? No, said the Arabs, Geneva was under the domination of the Jews. Well, then, Lausanne? Everyone held his breath. Amazingly, there were no objections. Lausanne is a big city on the shores of Lake Geneva. The Arabs would stay up on the heights in the Lausanne Palace; the Israelis down on the edge of the water at the Beau Rivage.

I was not going with the roommate and the Commission. I had a hunch that peace between the Arabs and the Israelis was a long way off. (As I am revising this in January, 1950, it is still a long way off. Nothing was accomplished at Lausanne.) I wanted to stay on in the Middle East. I felt I could learn more that way.

The roommate's packing and unpacking was due to a ruling handed down by George Barnes of the United Nations that no one could take over sixty pounds of luggage. The United Nations plane that was flying the Commission to Geneva was small and could not safely carry more. It had made a trip the week before with the vanguard of the secretariat and had been so overloaded it almost failed to get off the ground. The pilot refused to endanger the lives of his passengers and himself that way again.

A scale was placed in the middle of the marble lobby of the magnificent King David and all day members of the Commission were struggling down the stairs with luggage, weighing it, and struggling up again to take out or put in a few more items. Only Bussy was having no trouble. To get enough money to leave Jerusalem with his bills paid up he had sold all his suits except two. (Weeks later I heard he had thrown the rich *grandes dames* and Beau Brummells of the swank Beau Rivage and, too, the American members of the Commission into a heart seizure by appearing in the dining room one noon in a sweat shirt and a shrunken pair of khaki pants. In an absent-minded moment he had sent both suits to the cleaner at the same time.)

When the roommate was packed we went for tea to Ruth and Moshe Dayan's. I took soap as a farewell gift. I knew they had soap, I was quick to say, but realizing how scarce and expensive it is in Israel, I thought they might like it.

A dozen or so friends were gathered to tell us good-by, and we parted from them reluctantly; but the one person, next to Ruth, to whom we wanted to say good-by most, Moshe Dayan, spent all the time we were there talking on the telephone to his opposite number in Old Jerusalem, Abdullah Tel, about the release of several hundred Arab prisoners scheduled for the next afternoon.

The Commission got off at dawn with a surprising lack of commotion, only Bussy (it seems it is always only Bussy) left his passport on the table in the middle of his room at the King David and had to fly without it. I had visions of him spending the night in the plane at Rome and languishing for days at the airport in Geneva.

Around noon I moved over to the Arab side of Jerusalem. I was warned there would be no King David comforts; there would be no heat, no lights, and little water, but I wanted to experience the life in Old Jerusalem without any of these conveniences. Of course, the cold weather was past, so I'd never know what the Arabs endured during the bitter winter.

Dr. and Mrs. O. R. Sellers invited me to stay at the American School for Oriental Research, which is serving temporarily as a shelter for several Arab refugees, including Sally Kassab and Nassib Bulos, from Israeli Jerusalem.

When I arrived, Mrs. Sellers was on a trip to the ruins of Petra, and Dr. Sellers showed me to my room and to a community bathroom where water ran usually three days a week. On other days servants brought up tins about the size of milk cans, with wooden handles; these were used as long as they lasted for flushing the toilet, cleaning teeth, and bathing.

"I don't suppose you need a bath now?" Dr. Sellers asked in tones which said plainly: "You'd better not need a bath now."

"No, thank you, but, maybe, tonight before I go out. . . ."

He looked unhappy, but said nothing.

Now I was in a rush to be off to the yard of a public school right next door to the American school. When I had passed its gate I had seen a large group of people pressing against it and caught a glimpse inside the yard of many tattered old men. The Israeli government was returning the Arab prisoners whom Moshe Dayan and Abdullah Tel had been discussing over the telephone the afternoon before.

At the gate there were mostly countrywomen, their long, voluminous skirts stirring the dust and their veils hiding all their features except their dark, troubled eyes. They cried out to go inside, but the cold-faced, khaki-clad guards held them back.

The magic of the English language or, maybe, my face which no doubt had grown familiar to guards these weeks, got me through. The flat, sandy yard was crawling with scrawny, emaciated, withered men, mostly in pieced-together rags and soiled white turbans.

Two of them slowly spread out prayer rugs, knelt and

straightened up, their faces turned, no doubt, toward Mecca.
The soles of their bare feet were road maps of fine lines; their
murmuring lips, withered and blue. A dozen or more sat upon
their drawn-up legs stuffing themselves with dates from pack-
ages of rations they had just received; another dozen, before
their prayers, were washing their faces and their feet at a
trough of running water.

A little boy in a blue and white wrapper squirmed through
the waiting women and guards and leaped upon an octogenarian. He kissed his hands, cheeks, mouth as tears ran
down the fissures of the old man's face.

Close by me a young man with bronzed skin, set off by the
folds of his bright yellow headcloth, discovers his father, en-
veloped in one of those huge camel's-hair robes that so many
Arabs wear, and he takes him into his arms and kisses his
face over and over, cooing soft, soothing words. There is no
such restraint as in the United States when sons greet fathers,
and fathers greet sons. After a little time, I hear them thank-
ing their God. They murmur together, "Allah . . . Allah
. . . Allah."

Now and then an ancient goes toward the gate and peers
into the crowd. Questions bombard him. Has he seen this
husband? This father? This grandfather? The women cry,
holding out their bony arms.

A slim lad of six or seven is allowed through the gate. He
runs swiftly here and there, looking anxiously up into each
face, calling out a name. Finally, he sees the one he seeks, a
doddering creature in a robe of blue and white mattress tick-
ing. The reunion is wildly demonstrative.

Abdullah Tel appears in the schoolhouse door. His dark
young face is sober as he stares out at these derelicts of war.
Slowly he moves among them, shaking their hands, patting
their shoulders.

"These old men didn't fight," he says with bitterness when I join him. "They really aren't prisoners of war; they were just too old to flee when their villages were taken, so they were rounded up and carted off."

Today three hundred and sixty-four are being returned, which increases the number who "have come across," as Abdullah Tel expresses it, to approximately two thousand. There are about four hundred more to come. As the Arab authorities check out each prisoner, they give him a blanket, a towel, and a bag of rations that includes flour, margarine, and a package of dates.

One ancient stumbles out the school door and, after a step or two, falls flat upon the ground. He is too weak to walk, but no one seems particularly shocked. They simply look at him lying there and despondently shake their heads. The one young prisoner in the group attracts much more attention. He is a boy of eight, with small, slanting eyes and matted black hair, and he has been a prisoner for six months.

As I go out of the gate to return to the American school, many of the women are still waiting. Perhaps their old ones will come with the last four hundred—or, perhaps, they will not come at all. The pain in their dark eyes above the veils testifies to the strain of waiting.

Now that night has come, I definitely must have a bath. After mingling with the prisoners, I feel not only dirty but itchy. But before I can achieve the bath I must, of course, have light. This is more of a problem than it should be simply because I can't remember there is no electric current and I go up and down the walls—that is, my hands do—trying to locate the switch, and when I do locate it and no light comes I'm amazed and hurt.

This means I must find the matches and light something. I feel along the mantel, the table, the top of the bureau. But no matches—would that I were a smoker and carried my matches with me! I feel my way into the hall. The face of a very pretty Arab woman, Mrs. Habbab, looms on the stairs in the yellow glow of a lamp. She is making her way from the first floor to the third, and very smartly she is carrying her light with her. She offers to help me find my matches. They were on the table all the time.

The lamp lit, I sigh with relief. It seems such a silly, small thing to be without light; but I don't believe there is anything more crippling. I skip around the room getting out clean clothes and then I skip across the hall to the bathroom. Inside the bathroom, with door locked, I begin going up and down the walls for the switch. This seems fairly reminiscent of some recent experience, but then almost everything does, don't you think? Unable to find the switch, I fan the air. There is, no doubt, a cord dangling from the ceiling. I fan and fan, as if I'm taking exercises for my upper arms. When I'm convinced there is no cord, I return to the walls. Ah-h-h, at last I have it. I snap it up—and again, of course, there is no light. When will I learn? I go back to my room, get my lamp, return with it to the bathroom and place it on top of the flushing contraption of the toilet.

I will not forget it again, I vow, but by the time I've heated one of the pails of water on a tiny oil stove, hoisted it to the rim of the tub, practically rupturing myself, and dumped it in, where it is completely lost in the shadows, and got in after it, or rather under it, and washed myself, I am too exhausted from the complications of a Palestine Jerusalem bath to give it a thought. Clutching a towel about me, I creep back across the hall to my room, shut the door and begin to go up and down the walls. . . .

Yes, I couldn't agree with you more, I'm not right bright.

But when one has been conditioned as long as I have been to electricity, it takes time to become unconditioned.

That evening, like all evenings except the moonlit ones, the streets of Old Jerusalem are as black as an unwired barn before dawn. I walk through them with Miss Haliby on the way to the burial service at the Greek Orthodox church and I cannot see my feet, much less where I am putting them.

Miss Haliby usually carries a flashlight, but tonight hers is broken and she has not been able to borrow one. Like an animal with night eyes, she moves over the cobblestones, going up and down the narrow steps and turning corners surefootedly.

"How do you know where you're going?" I whisper to her.

"I know it by heart, not by sight," she answers. "Many a night during the battle of Jerusalem, I ran continuously back and forth through these streets."

Completely unnerved, I cling to her arm. She is wearing her big, white sheepskin coat, for the night is cold and damp, and I get a little reassurance from the bulkiness of it, but not enough. I am absolutely certain somebody or something will hear the shuffle of our feet and jump upon us. The idea of two lone women walking this black-crepe night along narrow, twisting, alien alleys—at least alien to me—strikes me as foolhardy, shocking, stupid.

"Aren't you frightened?" I murmur.

"No," she answers calmly. "I've never been frightened in my life."

A moment later a man brushes against me and I am scared out of my wits. But he hit me by mistake. He didn't see or hear me in the dark, nor I him. Afterward, listening intently, I make out the lapping noise of his bare feet on the rounded cobblestones.

To quiet my nerves, perhaps, Miss Haliby begins to talk.

She has been that day to look over the Tulkarem triangle area which King Abdullah has ceded to the Israelis in the Israel–Transjordan armistice, and she is heartsick and bitter.

"The area includes 250,000 dunums [about 85,000 acres] of the very best land we had," she says. "To Palestine, which now has so little good land, it was worth its weight in diamonds. Not gold, but diamonds. I could cry like a schoolgirl."

"I know," I answer sympathetically. "But why did King Abdullah agree to it?"

"He was high-pressured into it. . . . Look out, here's a step. . . . The Jews wanted it—they, of course, want all the good land—and they refused to sign an armistice until they got it. And Dr. Bunche's one idea was to get an armistice. King Abdullah did cable Mr. Truman for help, but none came."

I don't know what to say to this, but after a moment or two I hesitantly suggest: "I don't suppose Dr. Bunche or Mr. Truman realized what that land meant to Palestine."

"You are exactly right," she agrees. "To them they are just lines on a map."

Encouraged, I say: "We don't mean to be unfair. I'm sure of that. In the United States we simply don't understand the circumstances."

"Of course, the United States doesn't understand." Her voice is furious and I realize I've said the wrong thing. "The United States is so naïve she will believe anything she's told. But since she doesn't understand, why doesn't she keep her nose out of other people's business?"

I have no answer and we move on in unhappy silence through the dark.

Life in Arab Jerusalem, I have learned in just one day and night, can have exceedingly uncomfortable moments.

31. My kingdom for an asbestos suit

THE MIRACLE OF THE HOLY FIRE on the Saturday before the Greek Easter is a terrifying experience. I prayed the whole time for an asbestos suit and a coat of mail.

No doubt it is terrifying every year; but this year of 1949, with the Arabs' hatred for the Jews burning more fiercely than the Holy Fire, it was particularly frightening. I would have crawled under my chair if there had been room when the Arab youths riding wildly on the shoulders of other Arab youths began, in the most un-Christian fashion, to shout:

> "Oh ye Jews
> Your feast is a feast of apes
> Our feast is a feast of Christ
> Christ is come to us
> And with His blood has redeemed us
> Joyful are we on this day
> Sad and sorry are the Jews."

The Miracle of the Holy Fire takes place in the tomb of Christ, which is in the middle of the rotunda of the Church of the Holy Sepulcher and stands like a solitary Eskimo igloo on the wide spread of floor beneath the soaring, arched sky of the dome. On two sides of it are small windows through which the flames rush. The fire is supposed to be symbolic, but the Greek Orthodox, Armenians, and Copts act if it really comes from heaven and practically go crazy with excitement.

For hours before the fire appears, the open area around the tomb is jammed with pushing, shoving, swaying, squirming, panting people. They hold bundles of white candles tied with ribbons, and they fight to get close to the two little windows to light their candles from the Holy Fire. Soldiers and police, grasping the ends of long poles, form barricades to hold them back.

Happily, I'm not on the main floor; I would have been crushed long ago. I am in one of the many boxes that circle the rotunda and which are reserved for officials, prominent laymen, and visitors. The only drawback is that the boxes are now obstructed by scaffolding for repairs to the dome, and I either have to crawl under one and peer out like a turtle or straddle one, like no lady. But I'm not complaining. It is the box of Abdullah Tel and he is sharing it with Katie Antonius, Sally Kassab, and me.

Katie, Sally, and I arrive before Abdullah Tel and distribute ourselves among the scaffolding. "The church is like a maimed old man," Katie mourns. "It was once so beautiful, but now look at it, falling to pieces and propped up with sticks. I could weep."

But she should have saved her tears for herself and me, for when Abdullah Tel arrives he eyes Katie and me in the front row with a troubled frown and then, turning to Sally, behind us in the rafters, whispers: "Shall I sit down between the two old ones?"

If I hadn't been already in a state of nervous collapse, that remark would have put me there.

On the heels of Abdullah Tel's arrival, an organization of Arab youths charges into the church like football teams upon the playing field. Yelling, they drive through the crowd to the far side of the rotunda and there three stalwarts with riders on their shoulders begin galloping as fast as horses

back and forth through the mob. The riders wave sword-slim
sticks and shout in a frenzied rhythm to the people:

"Oh ye Jews
Your feast is a feast of apes. . . ."

The crowd swoops up the chant. The riders rock to and
fro. Hands clap in time. The sword-thin sticks flay the air.
One rider falls from his steed; the speed at the turns is too
swift.

Kiwass clump in, followed by Patriarchs with retinues of
priests and monks and choirboys, carrying many banners.
The police with their poles make two lines facing each other
and press the people back. Slowly, but steadily, they shove.
. . . An old woman, clutching her candles, slips beneath
the poles.

"Ah, a Russian pilgrim," sighs Katie. "She wants to be the
first to catch the fire."

A soldier tussles with her.

The Patriarchs and their retinues march around the rotunda. The people go wild. They fight to join the parade.
They climb over one another's shoulders and heads. It is the
nearest thing to a Democratic national convention I have
ever seen, except a Republican national convention.

Then it happens! Flames blow out through the windows
and instantly fires flare here, there, everywhere. The whole
place is in flames.

"We will be burned alive," is my one, unholy thought.

Suddenly the Greek Patriarch is swished by us like a black
veil in a hurricane. His candles are lit and he and his followers are literally running like the wind to the Greek altar.

In the belfry the church bells are clanging, and in the
gallery the Armenians are pounding their eerie wooden gongs
with strips of metal. Pandemonium! Madness! Chaos!

I shrink as small as possible behind a timber, only one eye exposed around it. I would never do as a runner to carry the Holy Fire to Moscow.

32. "And mourn sore like doves"

SIGHT-SEEING is not my strong suit. What is, I haven't discovered, but definitely it is not looking just for looking's sake. Still, on that Saturday after the Miracle of the Holy Fire, I did considerable wandering about Old Jerusalem with Katie and Sally and John Pruen and, with their eyes to help mine, I sight-saw fourfold.

We started out by having lunch, which is the best way I know to start sight-seeing. Katie had located a little restaurant run by a Greek in the heart of the Old City, and had ordered lunch for four or more (Katie never knew how many she had invited for any meal), but she added to the menu on the way. Spying a stack of those beret-looking loaves of Arab bread before a baker's shop, she purchased one and, without wrapping it, folded it casually beneath her arm.

"This bread is so good," she said, "and there might not be any like it at the restaurant."

There wasn't and it turned out to be a very lucky purchase. Katie put it in the middle of the table and the four of us tore at it to eat with a bowl of *homus* (those yellow chick-peas mixed with dregs of sesame oil) until not a crumb was left. After that came many strange dishes, concocted by an imaginative Greek with Arab materials, and when we finished I was so full of yellow beans, white beans, meat, herbs, peppers, onions, and sesame oil I could scarcely climb up one side of a cobblestone.

But before the afternoon was over I climbed more than a million. We began near Jaffa Gate and passed the lovely yellow walls and towers of that ancient fortress, known as the Citadel, dating back to the era of Herod the Great; and the Church of St. James; and the Armenian Garden and Monastery; and through sun-printed courtyards until we came to the old wall near Zion Gate. Beyond it was the Church of the Dormition and, near by on a gentle hillside, several cemeteries. In one of them George Antonius was buried, and Katie was almost frantic to see his grave. Sally had just told her that she had heard the Jews had plundered the cemeteries when they captured this area and she wanted to see if it were true. But she could see nothing. The only people who could see into the cemeteries were the Arab Legion sentries striding along the top of the old wall.

Frustrated, she started back along the route we had come. She was in a great hurry and walked ahead of us, leading us behind some walls into a parklike area where several dozen soldiers were idling. Approaching two, who were sitting cross-legged upon the ground and nibbling on blades of grass, she spoke to them in Arabic, but when one of them answered her in Arabic, she translated his answer for me.

"I asked permission for us to go up on the walls, but he says he is not a guard but a prisoner, and I asked him why a prisoner, and he says because he cut the throat of Shertok." Her laughter bubbles out at this piece of fabrication and the prisoner, watching her with his sharp, black eyes, beams at the success of his joke.

An officer detached himself from a near-by group and asked if he could do something for us. Katie put her request and he looked exceedingly grave. No civilians were allowed on the old walls now. On the other side were the Jews and who could say when they might decide to open fire. Still

Katie argued in her earnest, persuasive way, and finally, as we knew she would, wore him down.

Narrow steps lead to the top of the old walls and a path has been levelled among the rocks through the long, long centuries. The walls are terrifically thick; a wagon could be driven along the top and in the happy years before the War, the people of Old Jerusalem had moonlight picnics on them.

We made the ascent near Jaffa Gate and hiked along the rocky expanse directly opposite New Jerusalem, but a valley full of rubbish and a lazy slope with houses badly smashed lay between. We had no time, though, until the return journey to stop and look, for Katie was in a fever to get to the section of the wall that overlooked the cemeteries. She went around the sentry boxes upon the wall as if they weren't there; with eyes that didn't see she brushed by great clumps of wild flowers in the rocks' crevices; and she stumbled over boulders that jutted into the narrow path with feet that didn't feel.

And in an amazingly brief time she was leaning over the crenelated ledge that rises above the great wall on its outside edge, peering intently into the distance where the cemeteries lay. It was difficult to tell much; there were trees and walls and buildings in the way, but Sally's rumor seemed groundless, for the cemeteries appeared in perfect order.

Sally and John and I hung back. This was the first time in over a year Katie had seen George Antonius's grave even from this distance, and it seemed no time to intrude upon her. So frightfully much had happened in that year; so frightfully much to break the heart of an Arab patriot. Maybe—and this, of course, was a very big maybe that I plucked out of the blue—maybe Katie was grateful that the man who wrote with such hope *The Arab Awakening* didn't live to see the Arab collapse.

Katie turned away from the ledge and looked at us with bitter eyes. Her face was white; her unpainted lips tightly set. Without saying a word, she began to walk quickly back along the wall.

"Would you like to see a Jew?" a sentry asked as we passed him.

"Oh, yes, yes!" Both Katie and Sally spoke at once and with wild enthusiasm.

I thought they were going to see a dead Jew and was sickened at the idea; it never occurred to me they could be so excited over seeing a live one; but it was a live one that the sentry pointed out. He was walking along St. George Avenue in the Israeli part of Jerusalem, and looked about the size of a doll.

When Katie located him, she exploded: "Oh God, he's too far away to spit on!"

She and Sally and the sentry continued to search the street for others. If they had been looking at specimens of life on Mars they couldn't have been wrought up to a higher pitch.

"There are two playing tennis," Sally cried. "Look . . . look, there to the right of that red-roofed building."

Then they began to pick out the homes that had belonged to friends of theirs and to conjecture about the Jews who were living in them now. They seemed to have had friends living all over the place.

And ah, the King David! They began to reminisce about the good times they had had there. Sally, I believe, had been on the way there to meet John for lunch when the Jews blew the right wing to bits. And her mother . . . well, I'm not sure. Sally and Katie talked at once and so rapidly it was impossible to follow them.

But in time they ran down and we climbed from

the walls and continued on our tour. In a street of suks stacked with small objects of art Katie glimpsed a piece of Jerusalem pottery and we sauntered in to ask the price. Immediately, the proprietor rushed up chairs, then dashed out to get cups of coffee.

"A little amber in your coffee, madam?" he inquired upon his return.

"A little amber?" I repeated stupidly. "I thought amber was something you wore around your neck."

He tossed back his dark head and chuckled. "Ah, madam, a lit-tle amber is very good in the coffee."

"Yes," Katie encouraged. "I like it very much for a change."

So, we had a "spot" of amber dropped into the coffee and then sat among the jumble of antiquities and the cobwebs and the dust and slowly sipped it down. I loved the taste of it —a very subtle, mysterious flavor. No doubt Oriental. (Everything strange I call Oriental.)

Katie didn't buy the pottery, but I bought an old brass ink-well, centuries old—the kind that soldiers stuck in their belts.

On and on we trudged through the narrow streets, no wider in some places than hallways, until we came to the famous Wailing Wall. It is here that the Orthodox Jews used to gather on Fridays to wail for the departed glories of the Temple of Solomon and of Israel. Few Zionists ever came; they had little patience with this custom of the Orthodox and, besides, they were much too busy rebuilding the new Israel; but now all Israel is wailing for the Wall's return.

The Arabs are outraged at their wailing, especially sharp-tongued Katie. "What have the Jews got to wail about?" she demanded of me. "They've got everything. We Palestinians are the ones who need the wall now. We should begin this moment to wail—and wail—and wail."

Her gray eyes flashed with fury. No unreconstructed rebel of the old South ever despised the enemy more.

Sally abetted her. She took a small fur shawl from about her shoulders, tied it around her head to resemble the fur-brimmed hat of an Orthodox Pole, twisted her hair into two tight curls along her cheeks, and approached the wall.

It was too much for Katie. Her wrath gave way and she laughed until the tears ran down her cheeks.

I was thankful no Orthodox Jews were about. They would have been outraged at the sacrilegiousness of Sally's act. Riots between the Arabs and Jews have started at the Wailing Wall over less offensive incidents.

The Wailing Wall looks just as it does on picture post cards, so it came as no surprise to me. It is about fifty yards long and sixty feet high, made of gigantic blocks which have turned as yellow-brown as parched grass, and there are tufts of wild flowers hanging from the wide cracks. The Jews claim it is a fragment of Solomon's Temple which neither Titus nor Hadrian succeeded in destroying. To them it is holy ground.

And the Moslems? Yes, you've guessed it, it is holy to them, too. As the walls that enclose the sacred Temple area, where the Mosque of Omar and Mosque el-Aksa are located, follow the same foundation lines as those of Solomon's Temple, this fragment is part of those walls.

Ah, yes, it is truly a wailing matter. Standing that Saturday afternoon at its feet, gazing at it almost in a hypnotic daze, I understand why the Jews wail, why Katie and Sally and the other Arabs wail. I feel like wailing myself and suddenly the words of Isaiah, which I should have read, of course, in the Bible, but read instead in H. V. Morton's *In the Steps of the Master,* popped into my mind:

"We grope for the wall like the blind, and we grope as if we had no eyes: we stumble at noonday as in the night; we are in desolate places as dead men. We roar all like bears, and mourn sore like doves."

This mood would never do. Almost simultaneously we pulled back our shoulders, tilted up our heads and started walking toward the American school. It was already dusk, and the weathered yellow of the Wailing Wall was deep in shadow. We had been sight-seeing for five hours—and on foot.

33. "He is not here, but is risen"

I THOUGHT after I had seen the Miracle of the Holy Fire I had seen everything in the religious line, but the most amazing was still to come. It is an Abyssinian rite known as "Searching for the Body of Christ," and takes place, of all places, on the roof of St. Helena's Chapel, one of the many chapels of the Church of the Holy Sepulcher. Fortunately, the roof is flat, except for the dome that mushrooms up in the middle of it, or else the searchers in their frenzy would plunge hundreds of feet to the stone pavements below.

The roof is not the choice of the Abyssinians; they once had a place of worship inside the Church of the Holy Sepulcher; but through the centuries they have been pushed, poor dears, up and out through the roof.

The search for the Body is at night, which, as you can imagine, makes everything weird as magic. A long tent with the end flaps rolled up is pitched on one side of the roof and two rows of record-black monks and choirboys, dressed to the height of their wildest dreams in brilliant red vestments and gold crowns splashed with jewels and tipped with spikes, sit facing one another.

The bishop enters, attended, of course, by more monks, and occupies a chair at the head of the two rows. His gold crown is so heavy with emeralds and rubies (honestly) and other precious stones as large as quarters that it shoves his small head deep into his shoulders and causes his body to huddle one-sidedly into the chair.

Two monks begin slapping at peculiarly shaped silver-rimmed drums between their knees, and several others start shaking *sistra* (small instruments with jangling rods across them), and soon the hazy, candle-lit air of the tent seems to sway like a hula dancer's skirt.

A chanting springs up between several monks that is absolutely toneless, but sad and plaintive like small children's singing. Surely, I keep thinking, somebody will stop them, but nobody does and they go on—and on—and on. They are mourning, a neighbor whispers to me, the death of Christ. At long last, they stop and sit down, but the slow, uneven slapping of the drums and the shivering of the sistra continue.

Now the bishop takes over. His head weighted down, his eyes protruding above his sunken-in cheeks, he reads in a hollow, eerie voice. It is a language I have never heard before, but am told it is Geez, the literary language of Ethiopia, and the bishop is reading the story of the crucifixion of Christ. With the incense from the swinging censers creeping about him as thick as fog he reads through those verses that tell of Mary Magdalene and the other women returning to the sepulcher very early in the morning of the first day of the week "and found not the body of the Lord Jesus."

"And it came to pass, as they were much perplexed thereabout, behold, two men stood by them in shining garments:

"And as they were afraid, and bowed down their faces to the earth, they said unto them, Why seek ye the living among the dead?

"He is not here, but is risen. . . ."

At this point tom-toms begin to throb, or, maybe, they had been throbbing all along and I had been unconscious of them, but now they become insistent, hammering faster, faster, faster. . . . A parade forms. Everyone gets into it, even I. We are each given a long lighted candle and go out of the tent to search for the body of Christ.

Ahead, the monks with the drums continue to stroke them. They are frightening the lions and other wild beasts out of the way. Evidently we aren't supposed to be on a roof at all, but in an African jungle a thousand or more miles away. Also ahead, a huge red and gold umbrella, hung with bright ornaments and long fringe, twirls and bobs above the bishop in time to the beating of the drums and tom-toms.

The sky is as close as a cathedral's ceiling and it is a wet, shiny blue, for the moon is full to running over. Like a big snow mound, the dome hunches above the flat roof and casts a black-derby shadow.

Four times we parade around the dome, the drums and tom-toms pulsing and a woman raising her high, thin voice in mournful keening.

This is out of this world, I keep saying to myself. But, alas and alack, it is not. Even though a refugee on a roof, between heaven and earth, it is one more religious rite that ties Jerusalem in knots and confounds the commission that tries to untie them.

After the fourth turn, we return to the tent. Whether we have found the body of Christ I'm not sure. Maybe some monk, darting off to some near-by roof, had found it while I was moon gazing.

At the close of the service, I ease up to the bishop. "Did
we find the body of Christ?" I ask him.

His little black eyes sparkle in his thin, mulatto face. "No,"
he answers. "We left that for you Americans to do—you're so
smart."

He didn't sound sarcastic; but I wondered. . . .

34. In a bed big enough for four

I FELT so indebted to the Arab friends I had made in Old
Jerusalem that I wanted to have a party for them—a party
with electric lights and a victrola run by electricity and drinks
with ice in them made in an electric refrigerator. Though
they had suffered many more deprivations than doing without electricity, this seemed a thorn in the flesh that I might
remove for one brief evening.

I conferred with Colonel Shelby who lived, as I've said, at
Government House, the only near-by place outside of Israeli
Jerusalem with electricity. Yes, he said, I could have a party
there on Saturday night if I could possibly get there from
Arab Jerusalem. The only usable road to Government House
was from the Israeli side, and, of course, we couldn't travel
that. The road on the Arab side was unpaved, rocky, washed-
out, and no better than a goat path. He knew cars couldn't
make it, but there was a thin chance that jeeps might.

Betting on the jeeps, I invited Katie Antonius, Dr. and
Mrs. Husseini, Sally Kassab, Mr. and Mrs. Habbab, Nassib
Bulos, who were all Arabs, and John Pruen and Dr. and Mrs.
Sellers.

As the hour approached I was much more excited than my
guests. I was dressing happily in my room when there was an

authoritative knock on the door and I peeped out to discover, in a pale yellow pool streaming from a flashlight, a Belgian major, wearing the blue band of the U.N. on his arm, and Miss Haliby in her sheepskin coat. The party was off for this evening, they informed me. For security reasons, the Arab authorities and the U.N. major had decided I shouldn't try to reach Government House at night.

"You mean it's dangerous?" I persisted.

Simultaneously they shrugged their shoulders. "One never knows in these times," Miss Haliby said.

But I could have the party, the major said, on Sunday afternoon if I promised to return to Jerusalem before dark. I promised.

When we set out in two jeeps the next afternoon we were pleased we hadn't gone the night before, for the weather was so very beautiful. The sky was polished a gold blue by the steady strokes of the sun and the air was as clean and cool as a dinner knife.

There were too many of us for the jeeps, the U.N. drivers said, and so dear Dr. and Mrs. Sellers insisted on staying behind; but they had no sooner turned their backs upon us than one of the drivers spied a pretty Swiss miss entering the American school and urged her to join us. It was the sum total of ages, I decided, that was worrying the young driver and not the number of bodies, though they did spill perilously over the sides.

We headed down the Valley of Kedron between the hills on which Jerusalem spreads and the Mount of Olives. We passed the quiet Garden of Gethsemane with its gnarled old olive trees soaking in the spring sun and, near by, the Moslem and Jewish cemeteries facing each other on the valley's gentle slopes. There are thousands of tombs of both faiths, for the Moslems and Jews believe that the Last Judgment will be held here. The Moslems claim that on the Day of Judgment "the souls of men will be forced to walk a single horsehair" that will stretch from the top of the Mount of Olives across the valley to an arcade in the courtyard of the Mosque of the Rock, and that Jesus will sit at one end and Mohammed at the other, weighing the risen souls in scales set up for the momentous occasion.

We turned off the main highway and dipped deeper into the valley. The road was two faint lines over rock and sand and at one point the driver of the jeep in which I was riding missed it entirely and went careening off into the blue. Convinced after some distance that he was lost, he called to an Arab peasant, working in his field of artichokes, for directions.

We caught up with the other jeep at the brink of a dry wadi. Everybody except the driver was piling out so he wouldn't be thrown out. Down the jeep dived into the rocky bed, then over and, plunging like a horse, up the other side. The Sunday afternoon quiet was shattered with our cheers.

Next, it was our jeep's turn. We too got out and walked, and discovered it was much pleasanter walking than riding; but we had to ride if we were ever to get to Government House before it was time to turn around and come back.

The wadi passed, we began recklessly to switch up the steep sides of the mountain. Frequently the head jeep hung directly above us, almost within touching distance. Nearing the top we spotted a figure with field glasses standing on the roof of Government House, watching our ascent. Though he was too far away to make out the red of his hair or the high coloring of his blond face, we decided it had to be Colonel Shelby.

The jeeps didn't quite make the top. At an Arab outpost we left them and walked through a grove of small pines, with wild lupines and poppies pushing up through the brown needles, until we came to the formal garden of Government House. With no British High Commissioner there any longer to oversee it, the garden is high in grass, but the roses continue to throw a starry span of yellow blossoms over the walls and arches of gray stone, and the iris and Shasta daisies continue to skip unconcernedly from border to border.

A tea table heaped with sandwiches, cakes, and tea, a victrola heaped with records which the Colonel himself had lugged all over the Middle East, and chandeliers heaped with lights got the party off to a good start, but I didn't realize how good until it was time for the downward trek to Jerusalem, if we were to make it before night, and nobody wanted to go.

"Why not spend the night," the Colonel suggested graciously, "and go back by the light of another day?"

"Can we?" everyone shrieked at once. "Can we?"

"Certainly," answered the Colonel. "There might not be enough beds for everybody, but there are couches and rugs and . . . oh, we'll manage somehow."

But then the Habbabs remembered they must go back to look after their young child (the Arab baby sitter, no doubt, refusing to stay on Sunday night) and so one jeepload went back and the other remained behind. I, being the hostess, had, of course, to remain.

The long supper table in the big state dining room was closely set that night to accommodate the Colonel, the male members of his U.N. staff, and the unexpected guests, and the food was stretched a wee bit thin, but no one minded, and after supper we smashed old packing boxes and built a fire in the mammoth fireplace in the drawing room and there we sat, when we weren't dancing, until far into the evening, listening mostly to the semitragic experiences of the U.N. photographer, Mr. Wagg. With his tiny goatee wagging and his small eyes apple-seed bright, he told tale after tale, ending each one with the remark: "Things are bad all over."

And at times they were, especially at one point, when the Colonel took Nassib Bulos and me to his office to see the last armistice map between the Arabs and Israel. With a stricken face, Nassib studied it for a few moments, then slumped into a chair and buried his head in his hands. Since partition, Israel through fighting, infiltration, and armistice terms had gained 40 per cent more land than the original U.N. lines had allotted her. The map on page 289 shows this graphically.

One by one those who had beds drifted off to them; the others curled up on sofas. I had the Colonel's pajamas and the Colonel's bed, the huge, kinglike affair of the former British High Commissioner. It could have easily held four, but I slept in it alone until I was waked around four o'clock by the young U.N. radio operator who wanted, of all things, my telephone number.

In the most matter-of-fact manner he crouched by the side of the bed, paper and pencil in hand. He was trying to contact by short wave, he said, a "ham" operator in Kentucky who would get the offspring on the telephone and hook them up to speak to me. As you can imagine, I wouldn't have understood it if I had been awake, but with my mind dulled with only two hours' sleep, it made no sense at all. Nevertheless, it had been so long since anyone asked for my telephone number that I gave it freely.

I needn't get up yet, said the young operator, but just hold myself in readiness. There was a chance he might not get through to an amateur operator near Louisville, but if he did, he would send for me instantly.

In spite of the operator's advice, I decided to get myself into something besides the Colonel's pajamas. I might get tripped running over Government House in pajamas that were four feet too long for me, counting both legs. So I dressed and lay halfway down upon the bed, my head and back propped against the pillows and headboard. I was much too excited to go to sleep; I'd just rest until the operator sent for me.

The next thing I knew the room was full of daylight and the Colonel. He was grinning down at me, crouched so uncomfortably against the pillows and headboard.

"If I had known you weren't going to make better use of my bed than that I'd never have given it to you," he said, raising his long arms above his head and yawning.

"I'm sorry."

"You're sorry?"

The tone of his voice startled me. "You did have a bed, didn't you?"

"Oh, sure," he answered carelessly, and walked toward the enormous windows that extended from ceiling to floor to draw up the blinds. The sun was not up, yet, but the sky was aglow, waiting for it.

"Where?" I persisted.

He shrugged. "Oh, I slept on the operating table in the clinic."

It was a heavy-lidded group that gathered a few minutes later on the terrace above the garden to have black coffee. Across the slopes of the mountain, and across the valley, and up the slopes of Jerusalem's hills we could see the rich yellow walls of the Old City; the graceful, creamy curves of the minarets; the domes of the mosques; the tawny, square towers of the Citadel, the flat roofs, the umbrella-steeples. . . .

"O Jerusalem, Jerusalem . . ." It was Jesus, I was sure, who yearned over it in words that began like that. "O Jeru-

salem, Jerusalem that killest the prophets, and stonest them
which are sent unto thee . . ." I couldn't get any farther.

We sat on the walls of the terrace gazing at it in silence.
It was so lovely in the glass-clear morning light, with the
curving sky above it and behind it a smiling morning blue.

But we must be moving; there was work to be done down
in the city. Silently we began trudging across the garden,
through the piny woods, to the jeep a quarter of a mile away.

The collar of Nassib Bulos's shirt was open and he looked
tired enough to die. The evening before he had danced for
hours with that smooth, rather slinky grace that many Arabs
seem to possess, but now he scarcely lifted his feet from the
ground. Turning to the driver of the jeep, who was French,
he asked rather dourly: "Why did you come in this morning
and ask me if I would have tea and then never appear with
it?"

"Just to speak something," the driver answered simply.

This delighted us and the day brightened. A few minutes
later, jolting in the jeep down the precipitous slopes we began to sing. Though we were a United Nations mixture—
one Swiss, one Frenchman, two Arabs, one Englishman, and
one American—we had no trouble finding songs we all knew.
As we waved at the Arabs working in the fields and at the
children rushing like puppies to the side of the road to see
us go by, we sang:

"It won't be a stylish marriage,
We can't afford a carriage . . ."

I thought it a fine way to begin a Monday morning.

35. "Where is the just?"

LEAVING JERUSALEM was painful, but I wanted to see more of the Middle East, and I had the offer of a ride to Damascus with the U.N. photographer, Mr. Wagg, and the U.N. reporter, Hamilton B. Fisher. They were making an official documentary movie of Israel and Palestine, which they hoped would be shown in movie houses all over the United States, but up to this writing (January, 1950), I haven't seen a flicker of it. Not that I actually expected to; Mr. Wagg, I felt, was taking too many drab pictures of the Arab refugees in the desolate areas of the Dead Sea to turn out a movie acceptable to the theater managers or the American public. The whole business is packed away, no doubt, in the U.N. files at Lake Success at Flushing Meadows.

And when I think how we struggled to make it! That is the editorial we, of course, for all I did while Mr. Wagg took the pictures and Mr. Fisher made mental notes was to listen to refugees talk under a lashing sun that sent the temperature up to 120 degrees. But not in the shade; there is no shade around the six camps of ragged camel's-hair tents, holding 73,253 refugees, in the Dead Sea area, approximately 1,000 feet below sea level.

This heat is terrifically hard on the refugees of Camp Anja, our second stop that morning, for most of them had lived in those lovely shady towns of Ramleh and Lydda at the tip end of the rich Plain of Sharon, which I had seen on my very first day in Israel.

Though I didn't want to hear any more stories of Palestinian refugees and even refused to get out of the station wagon at the first camp where Mr. Wagg took pictures, the heat at Camp Anja forced me into the open air and immediately I was surrounded by a circle of at least twenty ragged men. They wept and shouted and flung their arms into the air.

"We are the Palestinians," an intelligent-looking young man declared. His eyes were sharp, and his teeth very white beneath a neatly trimmed black mustache. He wore a blue and white shirt open at the neck and it was clean in spite of the heat, the dust, and the scarcity of water. "And we want to go back to Palestine. We tasted the life. We did not fight the Jews—our village was taken during the truce; but if we are not allowed to go back we are going to fight the Jews for 100 years. It will be like the war of the Crusades and there will be no peace in Palestine for 100 years—no peace."

He looked at me intently and his black eyes were somber with purpose. "My dear, we are not going to another country. We do not care if we are given the whole world, we will not go out of Palestine. Are you going to move from America?"

I shook my head unhappily.

"Where is the just?" he asked. "If there is a just we are going to stay in Palestine. That is not my idea alone; it is the idea of the public." He swept his hand about to include the crowd around me.

"We are people," he said. "We are educated. We want you to treat us like you treat the Jews. I do not speak for myself; I speak for everyone. We cannot stay here. We are not trained for the weather. We live like animals. Where are we to go? Is it a mercy?"

An old man in his late sixties, with a dirty white rag

wrapped around his red tarboosh, let go a flood of Arabic; but the young man did not interpret all of it. He summarized: "He remembers me to remember you that we must go back to Palestine, but I have told him I have spoke everything."

I had to smile, though I was sure the tightly packed group would see nothing to smile about. Then quickly I asked the young man did he have land back in his village.

"I was employed as a branch manager for a chain of stores," he answered, "but now I have nothing to do. Nothing. My father had land."

"Is your father here?"

"Sure. All my family here."

A voice in the rear of the circle shouted out a few words in Arabic and I looked inquiringly at the branch manager.

"He says he wants to give you a present from the local products here."

I feel like bursting into tears. From many experiences I know how generous and hospitable the Arabs are; but this offer is too much. I begin to shake my head.

There are some more words in Arabic and the dark, serious faces close to mine break into laughter.

"You know what it is he wants to give you?" asks the young man.

"No."

"A scorpion, for that's the best local product we have. Here in this place too much insects, snakes, mosquitoes, flies, scorpions." Then the young man adds importantly: "That's what they call 'slowly death.' And they're right. It is slowly death."

Others insist on having their say. The interruptions grow louder and angrier. One cries out that he had farms, oranges, vines, olive trees, fig trees—"everything." He had about 500 dunums (about 165 acres) "and was very rich." He claps his hands, then spreads them out in a wide gesture to show that he owned the world or at least a great part of it.

"I was attacked by the Jews during the truce," he shouts. "By airplanes, guns. Most of our villages were taken during the truce. If we can't go back to our lands peacefully, we will go back and be killed." He slashes his hand across his throat and closes his eyes in an imaginary, dramatic death.

Another Arab drums his chest with two fingers and then swings them toward me, spouting a gusher of words. Others spout, too. The interpreter listens, but does not translate. Several gesture at him excitedly to remind him of his task.

"They are saying the same thing over and over," he says to me with a sad smile. "They say they will never forget their country in a hundred years."

A drooping auburn mustache, accompanied shockingly by black eyelashes and long, thick, bushy black brows pushes close to my ear. He, too, was a landowner; he had had 300 dunums in oranges, watermelons, potatoes.

"Not only does he work the land," interprets the branch manager, "but he brings in many others to work."

The auburn-mustached landowner shoves forward an old man in rags with a tarboosh atop his head.

"This is one of the men who worked for him," the interpreter explains.

The old man stands docilely before me, his forehead deeply wrinkled, his eyes mournful; but, happily, his small white mustache is jaunty.

I am pleased to see him, I say to the interpreter, for he is the only man I've met in the camp who didn't own several hundred acres of land before the War.

The interpreter does not find the remark amusing.

"Practically all these people were landowners," he declares hotly, "and are now ready to fulfill the General Assembly's resolution of December eleventh."

He is referring to Paragraph 11 of the General Assembly's resolution that states:

"[The Assembly] resolves that the refugees wishing to return to their homes and live at peace with their neighbors should be permitted to do so at the earliest practicable date, and that compensation should be paid for property of those choosing not to return and for loss or damage to the property which under principles of international law or in equity should be made good by Governments or authorities responsible. . . ."

It sounds clear and simple, but that's a snare and a delusion. The General Assembly's resolution runs absolutely counter to Israel's determination not to have them back. So what? Israel, no doubt, will have her way and these people will have to be settled in alien desert countries at a cost of millions of dollars. (Between two and three hundred million is the figure I heard mentioned most frequently.) But with their resettlement the problem doesn't end. Just so long as these Arabs remain dissatisfied with their fate they will form an irredentist core in the heart of the Middle East and a constant threat to world peace.

Thinking these disturbing thoughts, I rejoin my companions in the station wagon. Mr. Wagg is mopping his bald head and lamenting, "Things are bad all over." Nevertheless, he believes he has got some very fine shots and retires to a darkroom which he has rigged up in the back of the station wagon. It is a tent-sized black-satin bag, with a zipper for absolute privacy.

While Mr. Wagg works in the darkroom, Mr. Fisher and I career across the River Jordan into Transjordan, and up the valleys and hills to Amman. It is far past our lunchtime and, though we are timid about mentioning it after seeing the emaciated bodies of the refugees, we are starved.

We stop at the Amman club, and ironically have one of the tastiest meals of my life. It is the regular luncheon of the day. It begins with a plate of appetizers: sliced tomatoes, hearts of lettuce, potato salad, stuffed eggs, and olives. Next, the most luscious broiled partridges, and a vegetable something like a squash, stuffed with rice and meat; and for dessert, cream puffs, fruit, and, of course, black coffee.

At a table next to us, sitting over coffee, are several of our Jerusalem friends, to whom we had bid tearful farewells seven hours previously. Among them are George Barnes of the U.N. and Nassib Bulos, who has gathered from a rocky ledge, inaccessible, to hear him tell it, to anyone else, an armful of magnificent wild Moab iris, which he thoughtfully presents to me. They are a velvety blue-black.

"Before the War I used to grow these in my garden in Jerusalem," he says wistfully. "I had a nice place in the new part of Jerusalem and a very beautiful garden. I had all kinds of iris: black ones, speckled ones, yellow ones, white ones. . . ."

I don't want to appear unsympathetic, but, smiling, I say: "I have heard all the refugee stories I can take for one day."

"You haven't heard anything yet," he answers, and there is no answering smile in his eyes. "Your American consul, Bill Burdette, informed me this morning that the United States no longer recognizes a Palestine passport. How do you like that? We Palestinians are now people without a country; we no longer have any legal status in the world."

I say nothing—I know nothing to say; but as he and George and the others head back toward Arab Jerusalem I stand on the sidewalk in front of the Amman club, waving at them forlornly and feeling sorry for them and the whole messed-up universe.

And I stand there, surprisingly, late into the afternoon. The members of my own party had hurried away from lunch to locate U.N. tins of gas and oil, assuring me they would be back in two or three minutes; but the two or three minutes extend to thirty, to forty, to fifty, to sixty. . . . I begin to feel most uneasy. In their zeal to make movies, they have forgotten me, I am sure. I know artists; well—I think I know artists.

People pass and repass me, staring at me boldly. Children hang about and several come close and touch the Moab iris wonderingly. I give them away one by one until I have only three left.

When I've grown positive I have been deserted, Mr. Wagg, at the wheel of the station wagon, whirls up. There has been an accident, he says. A gasoline can which had been sitting in the hot sun blew up in the face of our driver, burning his eyes. He is now in the hospital.

Returning to the hospital, we find he has recovered sufficiently to travel, but he should not use his eyes for a day or two. Mr. Wagg will have to abandon the darkroom and drive.

At a good speed we head for Damascus and very soon are just a tiny moving speck in a flat, empty, pastel-colored world. I have never before seen such emptiness, such bareness on such a vast scale; it spreads out vacantly in all directions until low, naked hills on the skyline halt it. Not even a Bedouin tent breaks the bareness of it.

If this is the desert, I like it. I like the openness of it and the lovely late afternoon light on the stretches of sand and on the far-away bony hills.

"Man has room for man here," says Mr. Wagg. "And woman, too, of course. I am speaking in the broad sense."

The sun is still in the sky, but it contains itself completely in a primrose-yellow ball. Not one single strand of it slips outside the circle; the whole Western horizon is as bland a blue as a sky can possibly be.

We pass a bus, its top piled high with chairs with hand-woven bottoms; we see a shepherd, looming as large as a giant, watching his sheep, though what the sheep are finding to eat is a mystery; we see a stork. . . .

"He hasn't been working very hard judging from the looks of this country," Mr. Wagg comments.

The late light that is an old ladies' lavender slowly fades. A wavering line of camels cross the spats-gray sky where there are no hills to seal it to the flat earth, and far away a few scattered campfires glow as lonely as early evening stars.

We ride on—and on. Where can Damascus be? Surely we have driven long enough to reach it. Yet we haven't even come to the Transjordan–Syrian border. Something is definitely wrong. Somewhere on that wide "prairie" we have made the wrong turn.

Suddenly Mr. Fisher notices the sky to our right has a pinkish cast. "Do you suppose those are the lights of Damascus?" he asks.

"Most likely they're the northern lights," replies Mr. Wagg, wearily. "We've come far enough to be approaching the arctic circle."

At long last we come to a village and stop a man in uniform to ask for directions. Unfortunately, his English is limited and the conversation goes like this:

"Damascus?" calls Mr. Wagg.

"Damascus," calls back the soldier.

"The way?" calls Mr. Wagg.

"The way," calls back the soldier.

"Yes, yes, the way to Damascus?" Mr. Wagg is getting excited.

"You go there?" asks the soldier.

"Yes, we go there."

"I go with you as far as border, yes?"

"Yes."

Deliberately the soldier gets into the station wagon, but before he has time to give any directions Mr. Wagg says: "Hurry up now, boy, get on the ball. Where is Damascus?"

"Do not be troubled," he answers soothingly, sounding like the Scriptures. "I will tell you. I am with you."

And in time he does and it is unpleasant news because a good many miles back we had missed a road that cut off sharply from the one we were traveling.

Retracing our steps we talk to the soldier. He has been in the Syrian army for eleven years; that is what he signed up for, but now his time is almost out. "I have one month, twenty-four days, then I be free," he says.

"Were you in the Arab-Israeli war?" I ask.

"Yes, but no war now. This moment, friendly with Jews, but not friendly always. Jews have done Arabs wrong and now Jews and Arabs can't live together. Either all Jews dead or all Arabs dead."

This is too pessimistic a view to pursue, so we are silent until the soldier abruptly announces that we will not be able to cross the border this night. No cars are allowed to move after six o'clock. He is a border guard and he knows.

"Things are bad all over," Mr. Wagg mourns and I have visions of the four of us spending the night in the station wagon. It is already dark as carbon paper and fairly chilly.

When we reach the border, it does appear hopeless. Cars and trucks are strung out for about a quarter of a mile on each side of the barricade. Still it will do no harm to try to cross, Mr. Fisher argues, and goes with our papers into a small, lamp-lighted shack by the side of the road. He is gone for ages. Finally, I decide to look for him. I poke my head in the door and see him standing dejectedly before an angry official; but before I can say anything he turns and scowls at me and I creep back to the station wagon.

A good while later when he appears, he is still upset and growls at me: "You are the cause of all this delay. And what's more, we're lucky not to be in jail. When that bird in there opened your passport he found a pound note in it and he thought we were trying to bribe him. My God, was he hurt! He said all Americans looked down upon Arabs; he said the Americans would have never taken Palestine away from them and given it to the Jews if they had respected them as they should; he said they considered all Arabs good-for-nothing wastrels, wanderers, crooks. My God, was he hurt!"

I am hurt, too, to think how careless I had been to let a pound note float about in my bag until it lodged in the passport.

But it all ends well. The official forgives us; we are passed across the border, and I get back the pound note.

The rest of the trip is uneventful. At least for Mr. Fisher, the driver and me. We sleep soundly until poor, weary Mr. Wagg, muttering, "Things are bad all over," wakes us in the heart of Damascus.

36. Damascus days are Arabian Nights

FOR FOUR CROWDED DAYS I stayed in Damascus with Mathilde and James Keeley, whom I had met in 1947 in Greece where Mr. Keeley was our counselor of embassy. But now he is minister to Syria, though why not ambassador is one of those puzzles that only our State Department has the key to—if there is a key. Little Israel, for instance, with an area of just a few thousand square miles—maybe two, maybe three (I have it in square kilometers: 21,000 square kilometers at the last count, but who can do that into square miles? Definitely not I.)—and a population of about a million, rates an ambassador, while Syria with an area of 54,300 square miles and a population of over 3,600,000 and Lebanon with 3,600 square miles and a population of over 1,160,000 rate only ministers. Not that I've got anything against ministers, you understand; they couldn't be nicer if all of them are like Mr. Keeley and Mr. Pinkerton. I was just wondering.

But I really had little time for wondering in Damascus; I was much too busy wandering. Damascus is the oldest city in the world that is still in existence, authorities say, and in the suks and downtown areas it looks it, if not older; but out in the residential sections and suburbs it has a modern, big-boom air.

It is built in an oasis in the desert, and everywhere there are streams of water gurgling, and fountains bubbling, and small pools mirroring the sun, and flower gardens blooming, but still there is the feeling of the nearness of the desert, which is at its very gates.

And while I was there, the desert came inside on high winds. The air was thick as if with fog, but instead of being a misty white, it was a tobacco-leaf brown. The wide porches of the Keeleys' house and the outdoor furniture grew an inch deep in sand and even the floors and tables inside the closed-tight house grew gritty.

I drove out into the desert with the Keeleys' chauffeur to see the storm better; but I could see very little, for the world was smoked out with the blowing sand and the sky was low and an angry tawny color. A few solitary shepherds continued to guard their sheep on the fringes of the oasis, but the members of the Armistice Commission fled their tents on the Syrian–Israel border; we saw the car of General Riley race past us, headed for the Orient Palace Hotel in Damascus.

Sometimes these sandstorms continue for six days; but fortunately for my wanderings this one lasted for only two. On the first clear day I went up into some barren beige hills on the west side of Damascus and looked at the city with its mats of green, its rows of trees, its domes and innumerable minarets—three hundred and sixty-five of them, one for each day of the year—and beyond it the sand, stretching unbroken for six hundred miles to fabulous Bagdad.

And then I came down and toured about the city, more curious about the waterways that course through the streets than the mosques and markets and public buildings and houses. All the water comes from the Barada River which rises from a few small springs in the Anti-Lebanon Mountains. It is not a big river, but the water is parceled into seven streams that flow on different levels and these spread out into houses, courtyards, gardens, fountains, watering troughs, and what-have-you. With my meager engineering mind I don't understand it at all; but I do know it is an amazingly complex feat, and dates thousands of years back.

This ancient irrigation project not only makes the desert into an enchanting spot of sycamores, poplars, pomegranates, and flowering gardens, but an amazingly productive center. In summer, so Robin Fedden says in his book, *Syria,* "trees groan if ever they have groaned. The orchards seem weighted down beyond endurance and the olives at the time of the great heats are pressed out into tons of lukewarm oil." But apricots are Damascus's most famous crop. This crop alone amounts annually to about 145,000 tons.

The apricots weren't ripe, I'm sorry to say, when I was there, but the proprietor of a candy shop beckoned me in off the street one morning to try a crystallized one and it was delicious. He beckoned me again the next morning, but I felt I had imposed on his hospitality sufficiently, so reluctantly I refused.

I was doing the bazaars and other downtown sights with Mr. Keeley's *kiwass,* a handsome Arab by the name of Babjad. (I had long ago worn out dear Mathilde Keeley, and as for Mr. Keeley, he, of course, was about his country's business.) Babjad was politeness and kindness itself, and a well of information.

We began with the Great Mosque. At the fountains and troughs in the wide flagstone courtyard, many men were washing their hands and arms with the motions of surgeons before operations, and also washing their legs and feet.

Eyeing a meticulous washer, Babjad explained, "He make everything to be clean before praying in Mosque. It is the custom. His nose, his teeth, between his fingers, his feet."

White pigeons fly about the heads of the people washing, and peck at pieces of grain between the flagstones.

"The pigeons are sacred here," Babjad continues. "We have an example in Arabic (a saying, he means), 'If you want to do well in your life you must do two things: give food for the pigeons and water for the flowers.' You understand?"

The Mosque is a mammoth building of faded mosaics, hundreds of lamps on gold chains, and acres of thick, deeply colored Persian rugs. There are, of course, no benches. If the Moslems sit at all in a mosque, they sit upon their crossed legs. Usually they are on their knees, prostrating themselves to the floor.

"Why is the Mosque so big?" I ask Babjad.

"Four or five thousand people pray together. On Friday, one cannot find a place to walk. The president of the government come here one Friday; another Friday, come to another mosque to let all people be in friendship with him. He go up (he points to a sort of pulpit by one of the large columns) and make a speech and give his advice."

The Mosque was once a Christian church dedicated to St. John the Baptist, and there is still a tomb in the center of a large open space with iron grillework around it, holding, so 'tis said, his head. A priest of the Greek Orthodox faith stands before the grille, and at one corner sits a very old, blind man teaching the Koran to a small boy with head shaved close. The old man's eyes are red rimmed and his heavily veined hands tremble as they count the conversation beads, but his mind is alert to the words of the scripture. When the small boy mispronounces a word he taps him on his knuckles and corrects him.

Coming back into the sun-filled court, with the sound of water splashing into basins, Babjad shows me an unusually tall and beautiful minaret circled with five balconies.

"That is called the Jesus minaret because the Moslems are sure that the prophet Jesus is still living in the sky," Babjad says, "and some day he will come back by that minaret. When he comes back to the ground he will be called Mahdi because *mahdi* in Arabic means the wrong made straight. He will make all the world in security."

We go out into the narrow streets of the bazaars that crawl about the Great Mosque and I see, as I did in Beirut and Arab Jerusalem, the street of gold, and of shoes, and of candy, and of silver, and of brass, and of rugs, and of leather goods, except here there are more of them.

In the street of the gold suks, two women completely sheathed in black, only their eyes bare above their veils, sit in a small booth while a man holds a nugget of gold above a small blue flame. He is evidently making one of them a ring, but whether it be for a finger or ear or nose, I know not.

There appears to be as much gold here as in the jewelry shops of Fifth Avenue. Babjad says there are many wealthy people, as well as a great many poverty-stricken ones, in Damascus, and the wealthy ones deck themselves in jewelry.

We turn our backs upon the crowded, dusty suks, step through a narrow door, and are in a court where lemon and orange trees are both in bloom and in fruit and where narrow pools, starred with lilies, stretch in the sun. It is the courtyard of the House of Asad Pasha and around it are balconies opening into three hundred rooms, many of the walls and ceilings exquisitely decorated with murals, mother-of-pearl, old tiles in faded red and blue.

It is so beautiful I dawdle for hours through it, but Babjad is patient. "All time ladies come and come," he says with pride. "They don't have anything like it in their countries."

We step back through the narrow door in the thick wall and are in teeming bazaars again. Camels loaded with rugs, donkeys carrying baskets of olives on both bony sides, women in bright orange robes, striped in black. . . .

Another door, and we are in another court—this time the court of an ancient, abandoned inn, now used as a warehouse. Graceful Moorish arches and dainty balconies opening onto bedrooms surround it on three sides and in the middle there is an old fountain, velvety with moss. The rich merchants of the camel caravans coming across the desert used to make this their lodging place, and the camels and Arab ponies quenched their thirst in the fountain.

We walk and walk; the whole city to me is Arabian Nightish. The bright glass in the shoes; the bolts of hand-woven gold and silver brocade; the tables and chairs inlaid with mother-of-pearl; the trays of jade, coral, turquoise; the pink and chartreuse and purple and yellow sandals; the large-lipped pitchers of silver and copper; the candies. . . .

One pushcart peddler is doing a big business with rock candy, and Babjad informs me that it is considered excellent for the breast and kindly offers to buy me some; but having no breast trouble, I decline.

A midget mosque in the heart of the suks, with a tiny bright blue minaret—so tiny indeed that the balcony does not entwine it, but juts out over the narrow street like a stage prop for Juliet—starts Babjad off on the Moslem religion and its uncertain provision for four wives, which he is not enthusiastic about. "A man should be foolish if he married four wives and lived with them," he argues. "There would always be trouble. At times I find one is too much. Christ! how can a man live with four?"

He shakes his head in bewilderment for a few moments, but then brightens. "But I will show you a man who has four wives. When he feels one of his wives is sick and going to die he engages another and brings her straightaway to his house. This man has twenty-seven boys and the boys have boys and now he doesn't know which are his boys and which his boys' boys."

He hurries me through narrow alleys and points out a patriarch of a man sitting in the doorway of his suk, cutting on a piece of leather. His long beard is as white as the turban about his tarboosh.

"He works very hard," Babjad whispers, "and walks like the young people without a stick."

Having seen this curiosity, Babjad decides we have seen everything, and we return to the car, which had been parked in a street wide enough to accommodate it, and drive back to the legation. We pass many open carriages with whole families piled in them and pulled by pairs of sleek horses, and we see other carriages lined up in front of the Ministry of Justice like the carriages by the side of the Plaza in New York, but these have bright-colored dusters in the holders made for whips. The coffee shops have capacity crowds drinking coffee, and in the grassy squares and on the banks of the streams are gaily dressed people having picnics.

After Israel and Palestine, the scenes have a musical-comedy quality, and yet I know underneath Syria is seething with unrest like all the other Arab countries. The very morning of this sight-seeing day, the United States recognized General Husni Zayim as the new head of Syria, he having taken over the government some weeks before in a *coup d'état* and thrown the president and the president's secretary, my old friend of the Balkan tour, Sam Inglizi, into jail. But would Zayim last? (Though I didn't know it that afternoon, of course, the answer was no. Several months later there was another *coup d'état,* and his government was overthrown and he was shot.)

37. A period for me. But a big question mark for Israel

DAMASCUS SPELLED the end of my Middle East travels. There I caught a plane and said good-by to Syria, Palestine, Israel, the Lebanon. . . . I was not happy about it. I felt I left in the middle of everything; I put down the problem with the ends still unknit. But how long would I have had to stay around to see it all wrapped up, tied, and addressed to a peaceful future?

Certainly, I haven't the answer. I have learned a great deal; indeed, I have learned much too much for my peace of mind. There have been times when I wished I hadn't gone at all, that I hadn't exposed myself to the painful facts of Palestine. I feel as if a chair had been pulled from under me, as it used to be in that children's game, "Going to Jerusalem." My life will never move as complacently, as securely, as happily as it did before this journey. But, in spite of the facts, I haven't the answer.

I wish I did because peace, of course, is terribly important to both the Arabs and the Israelis, but especially to the Israelis. If Israel is to become an economically sound, stable state, which she is a long way from now, she needs many years of peace with her Arab neighbors.

She needs peace particularly to get the Arab boycott lifted. She needs to buy from the Arabs; she needs their fresh, green foods, their meat, and, of course, their oil. I read in the newspapers recently that she was going to bring crude oil from Venezuela, halfway around the world, to open the oil refineries at Haifa.

But, even more important, Israel needs the Arabs as customers. To become the commercial center of the Middle East, which is certainly necessary if she is to survive by the labor of her own hands, she must sell the bulk of her production to the Arab states. Now she is having to ship her manufactured goods across the seas and offer them in highly competitive markets, where she can be undersold.

This is too bad, for Israel needs money—lots of money. Her expenses are terrific. Just to mention two: the immigrants and the army. She is urging immigrants to come; indeed, she is carrying on extensive propaganda in the United States, the Balkans, China, Yemen—well, wherever there are Jews—to get them to emigrate to Israel. She wants to fill up the vacant land and have plenty of man power in case the Palestinians ever decide to try to take their country back.

The army, of course, is a gigantic expense. It is a vast army in proportion to her size and income. In terms of the population of the United States, it would be equal to an army of 18,000,000 men. We've never tried to support such an army, even in war. The largest figure our United States Armed Services ever reached was 11,000,000, I believe, at the height of World War II.

Altogether Israel's budget, as estimated in the recent report of the United Nations Economic Survey Mission for the Middle East, chairmaned by Gordon Clapp of T.V.A., was $322 million. The report broke it down like this:

(a) Ordinary budget $112,000,000
(b) Security budget (about one-half
of $112 million—a guess).............. 56,000,000
(c) Development budget 154,000,000
                                        _____
    Total $322,000,000

"Of this total of $322 million," states the report, "not more than one-third is covered by ordinary receipts at their present rate. It may be that the above $56 million for the security budget is too high. But Israel's financial budget would remain precarious even if the figure were greatly reduced."

But the real crux of Israel's economic position lies in its balance of international payments, and this balance is definitely unhealthy because such a large portion of her imports are financed by grants and donations which are likely to fall off drastically in the future.

In 1949 Israel's imports amounted to $220,920,000. Of this sum, approximately seventy-five per cent was spent for food, fuel, industrial raw materials, and other consumer goods. The remaining twenty-five per cent went for capital goods, such as industrial and agricultural equipment, building materials, and the like.

Israel paid for only twenty-five per cent of these imports last year from her own resources, according to the report; the other seventy-five per cent came from such uncertain quarters as donations and loans. Her own resources were from her exports —citrus, fruit juices, and diamonds, and from tourists. The "unrequited" receipts were from the Export–Import Bank, which has granted Israel a loan of $100 million; from national institutions and funds, such as the United Jewish Appeal; personal assets of immigrants; transfer of capital and similar items; and from the release of British frozen sterling (this last item, my personal income expert explains, is in repayment of money which England borrowed from Jewish–Palestine interests during World War II).

The commission's report breaks down these receipts in this fashion:

Exports ....$ 28,840,000
Tourists 21,280,000
Donations, etc., in kind........ 56,000,000
National institutions and funds.. 75,600,000
Release of sterling balances..... 22,400,000
Export–Import Bank loan 16,800,000

Total $220,920,000

So, from these six sources she paid for her imports in 1949. But what about 1950? There is small chance of lessening these import requirements. In fact, the Survey Mission foresees a considerable increase in 1950 and 1951 to provide for additional immigrants. It costs $2,500 to absorb one immigrant into the national economy, according to the Israeli government estimate. This figure covers housing, capital equipment to provide employment, food, and government services. Even if Israel sharply curtails immigration and takes in only 150,000 new settlers in 1950, she will need to increase her imports by $28 million.

But what about after 1950? The long future? How can she continue to import goods, seventy-five per cent of which are consumer goods, and for which she can pay only twenty-five per cent from her own earned revenues? The conclusion of the Mission is pessimistic indeed. They say: "Although the Israeli authorities express confidence that new commercial investment may be counted upon to narrow the gap to manageable proportions, foreign investors are unlikely to venture any substantial placements in Israel as long as Israeli wage costs remain so exorbitantly high in terms of dollars and sterling."

There seems no escape from the conclusion that Israel must rely upon outside donations and loans, which is nerve-racking, to say the least. Any sharp curtailment of these outside revenues will bring on a terrific financial crisis and a painful drop in the standard of living of the Israeli people.

Bluntly, the future of Israel is a very large question mark. The pioneer Jews and the Zionist leaders have made heart-breaking sacrifices to bring to life the Jewish Homeland; but whether the present leaders are wise enough to lead this infant into sturdy, healthy growth, only time will tell.